Clare

and

her Sisters

Clare

and

her Sisters

Lovers of the Poor Christ

Madeline Pecora Nugent, SFO

Library of Congress Cataloging-in-Publication Data

Nugent, Madeline Pecora.
  Clare and her sisters : lovers of the poor Christ / Madeline Pecora
Nugent.
       p. cm.
Includes bibliographical references.
  ISBN 0-8198-1561-6 (pbk.)
  1. Clare, of Assisi, Saint, 1194-1253—Fiction. 2. Monasticism and
religious orders for women—Fiction. 3. Christian women
saints—Fiction. 4. Assisi (Italy)—Fiction. 5. Women—Italy—Fiction.
6. Poor Clares—Fiction. I. Title.
  PS3564.U348 C58 2003

                          2002153411

Cover art: Affresco di Tiberio di Assisi 1506. Bas. S. Maria degli Angeli / FSP,
Italy

Printed and published in the U.S.A. by Pauline Books & Media, 50 Saint
Pauls Avenue, Boston, MA 02130-3491.

www.pauline.org

Pauline Books & Media is the publishing house of the Daughters of St. Paul,
an international congregation of women religious serving the Church with
the communications media.

1 2 3 4 5 6 7 8 9   11 10 09 08 07 06 05 04 03

Dedication

To the sisters of the Monastery of Saint Clare in Langhorne, Pennsylvania, and to Sister Mary Francis Hone, OSC. Without the generosity, prayers, time, and patience of these wonderful daughters of Saint Clare, this book could never have been written.

Contents

PART ONE

To Set Out on the Path of the Lord

PART TWO

~•~

The Lord Gave the Light of His Grace

PART THREE

~•~

On Bended Knee to the Father

Part Four

~⁂~

To Dwell in the Church of San Damiano

Part Five

~⁂~

The Abundant Kindness of God

Part Eight

❧

What Is Painful and Bitter

Part Nine

❧

To Progress in Serving God More Perfectly

PART TEN

Visited by Divine Consolation

PART ELEVEN

The Father of Mercies

Part Twelve

To Return to the Lord an Increase of his Talents

Part Thirteen

The Increase and Final Perseverance

PART FOURTEEN

In the Name of the Lord!

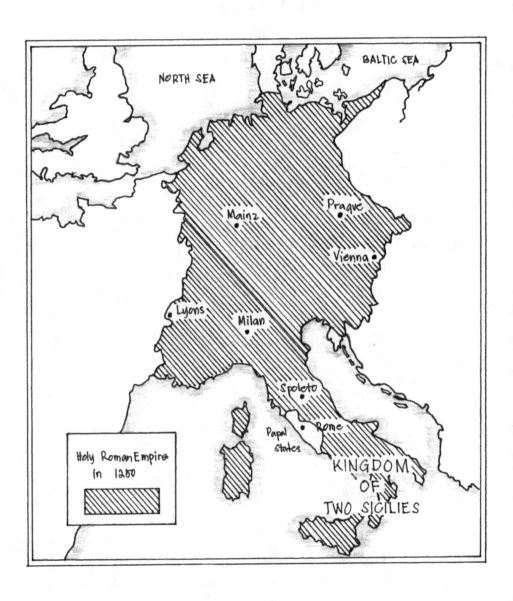

NORTH SEA

BALTIC SEA

• Prague

• Mainz

• Vienna

• Lyons

• Milan

• Spoleto

Papal
States

• Rome

KINGDOM
OF
TWO SICILIES

Holy Roman Empire
in 1250

Clare's Family Tree

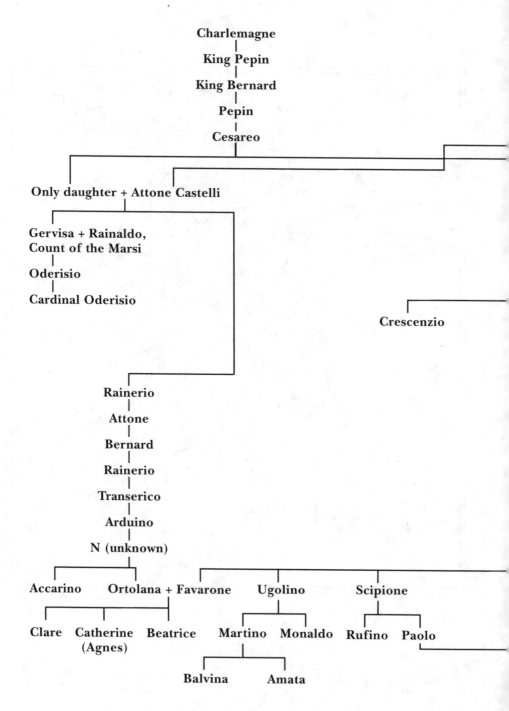

Charlemagne

King Pepin

King Bernard

Pepin

Cesareo

Only daughter + Attone Castelli

Gervisa + Rainaldo,
Count of the Marsi

Oderisio

Cardinal Oderisio

Crescenzio

Rainerio

Attone

Bernard

Rainerio

Transerico

Arduino

N (unknown)

Accarino   Ortolana + Favarone   Ugolino   Scipione

Clare   Catherine   Beatrice   Martino   Monaldo   Rufino   Paolo
          (Agnes)

Balvina   Amata

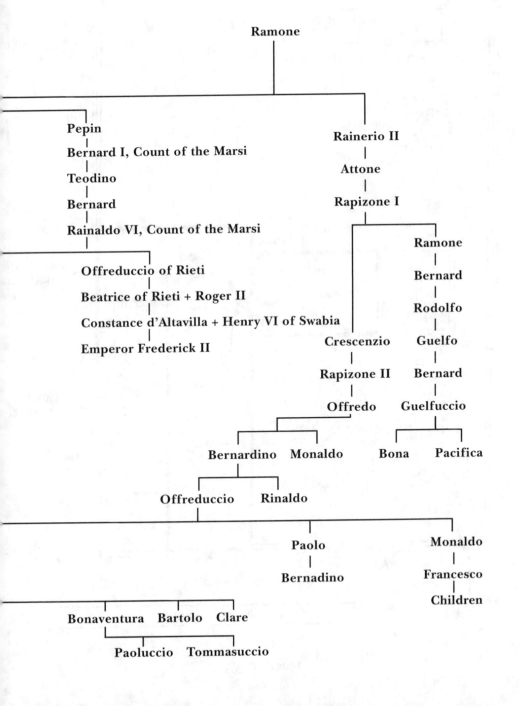

SAN DAMIANO AT TIME OF SAINT CLARE

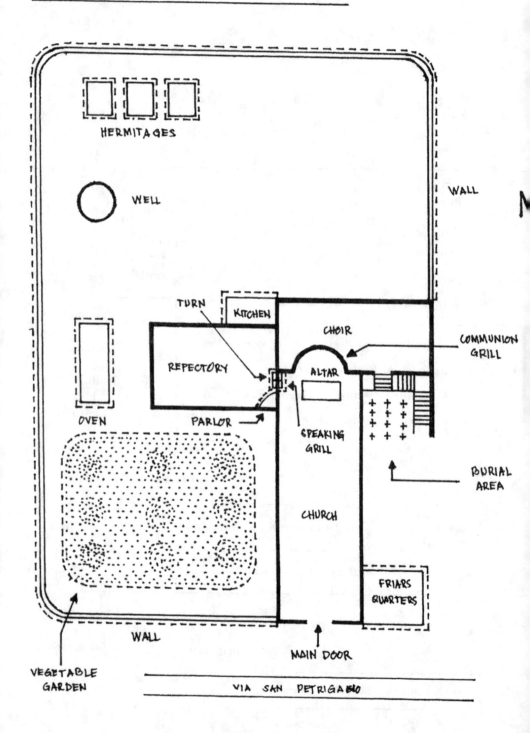

HERMITAGES

WELL

WALL

TURN

KITCHEN

CHOIR

COMMUNION GRILL

REPECTORY

ALTAR

SPEAKING GRILL

OVEN

PARLOR

BURIAL AREA

CHURCH

FRIARS QUARTERS

WALL

VEGETABLE GARDEN

MAIN DOOR

VIA SAN PETRIGANO

FIRST FLOOR

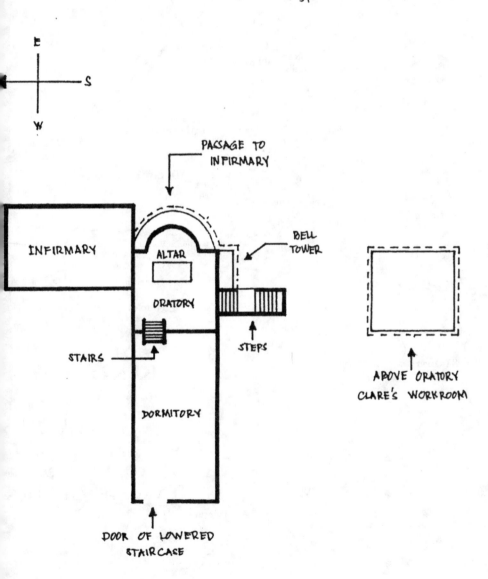

KEY:

——————— Verified locations of structures known to be in existence at the time of Saint Clare.

- - - - - - - Hypothetical locations

E
S
W

PASSAGE TO INFIRMARY

INFIRMARY

ALTAR

ORATORY

BELL TOWER

STAIRS

STEPS

DORMITORY

ABOVE ORATORY
CLARE'S WORKROOM

DOOR OF LOWERED STAIRCASE

SECOND FLOOR

THIRD FLOOR

To Lyons

Italy at the Time
of Saint Clare

◄ Trento

Milan ►
Vercelli ►
Turin ►
◄ Piacenza
Verona ► ◄ Padua ► ◄ Venice

◄ Ferrara

THE ROMAGNA
Genoa ►
◄ Bologna
Faenza ►
◄ Ravenna

THE MARCHES

Lucca ►
Florence ▼
Pisa ►
◄ La Verna
Arezzo ►
Siena ►
Gubbio ►
Ancona ►
MARCH OF ANCONA

Cortona ►
Perugia ►
◄ Fabriano
◄ Norcera
Deruta ►
◄ Assisi
Spello ►
◄ Foligno
DUCHY OF SPOLETO
Todi ►
◄ Spoleto
Terni ►
◄ Greccio
Viterbo ►
◄ Rieti
◄ Sabina

CORSICA

Civitavecchia ►
PATRIMONY OF SAINT PETER
◄ Rome
Ostia
◄ Lucina (section at Rome)
◄ Velletri
Sant' Angelo ►
Lucera ▼
APULIA

SARDINIA
Benevento
◄ Naples
Salerno

KINGDOM

OF THE

CALABRIA

N

TWO SICILIES

Palermo ►
SICILY

Acknowledgments

Among the many people who helped make this book possible, the following deserve special thanks:

Father Regis J. Armstrong, OFM Cap., answered detailed questions about Clare and permitted me to quote Clare from her writings as translated in his book *Clare of Assisi: Early Documents*. Mother Mary Francis, PCC, likewise granted permission for me to use her translation from the booklet "Dance for Exultation: Letters of Saint Clare to Saint Agnes of Prague." Some words of Clare in this book are taken, and sometimes adapted, from these translations.

On a trip to Assisi, the following people were most helpful. Brother Jacopo Pozzerle took me on a tour of San Damiano, and Brother Gabriel Aceto, OFM, showed me around Santa Maria degli Angeli and the Portiuncula. Brother Joseph Woods, OFM Conv., spent much time discussing Francis and Clare with me. Father George Masler, OFM Conv., gave me a tour of the Basilica of Saint Francis. The sisters and work staff at the Suore Americana convent at which I stayed were most helpful and made my stay most enjoyable. They also gave me information on fall crops and farm work in Assisi (used in the chapter on Lord Ugolino). Brother Daniel Geary, OFM Conv., visited San Damiano to discuss the results of recent excavations with the friars there. Sister Chiara Anastacia, OSC, spent two hours with me in Assisi and also answered many questions via mail.

Father William Lynn, SJ, of the Pontifical College Josephinum, answered my questions regarding reception of the Eucharist and how the Mass was offered at the time of Saint Clare.

Sister Giacinta Zambonati and the community at the Monastery of Vallegloria in Spello kindly researched Abbess Sister Balbina and sent information about her.

Dr. Lubomir Gleiman told me how to say "Peace and blessings" in Czech for the chapters on Sister Aneska.

Father Marino Bigaroni answered my questions regarding an indulgence supposedly given to the oratory at San Damiano.

Dr. Robert Carrellas discussed some of the illnesses of the sisters at San Damiano and told me other symptoms they may have had along with the ones described in the histories.

Maria Dolores Zannoni, a professional translator, translated three letters into Italian, taking nothing but my gratitude. Antonietta Calori translated another letter into Italian.

How can I ever sufficiently thank all the sisters at the Monastery of Saint Clare, Langhorne, Pennsylvania, for allowing me to spend a week with them so that I could experience the lifestyle of the followers of Saint Clare? The time spent with these delightful daughters of Clare meant a great deal to this book and to me personally.

Sister Mary Frances Hone, osc, lent me many of her materials on Saint Clare and was an invaluable resource. She spent hours speaking to me, checking details, and reviewing the manuscript. For her I have the deepest gratitude. She is indeed the hidden author of this book, because without her it would never have been written.

Sister Ingrid Peterson, osf, Sister Ramona Miller, osf, Jean François Godet-Calogeras, Father Cyprian Lawrence, and Father Conrad Harkins, ofm, shared many insights into Francis and Clare and their times, researching historical details for me. Sister Ramona and Father Conrad gave me information about the layout of San Damiano, and Father Conrad also photocopied information for me and translated portions of the bulls *Etsi omnium* and *Quo elongati*. Sister Ingrid also suggested giving the monastery cat an Italian name and updated me on the latest findings regarding Clare. Historian David Flood read the manuscript and provided tremendous help in checking its historical accuracy.

Father Claude Jarmak, ofm Conv., Father Julian Stead, OSB, Rita Maltoni, Fausto Devecchi, and Dr. Ascanio Dipippo gave me on-the-spot translations of works and letters pertaining to Saint Clare. Father Claude also photocopied information for me regarding medieval liturgy. Father Julian discussed theological points, obtained various reference materials, and translated two letters.

I thank the librarians who assisted me, especially the staff at Salve Regina University, Theresa Shaffer and others at Saint Bonaventure University, and Beverly Wilson at Saint Hyacinth Seminary, Granby, Massachusetts.

Noel Riggs of the Franciscan Institute provided valuable information.

The Franciscan Friars of the Immaculate (New Bedford, Massachusetts), the Monastery of Saint Clare (Andover, Massachusetts), and Brother Gabriel at the Franciscan Retreat House (Andover, Massachusetts) assisted me with various Franciscan publications.

Mary Lee Nolan shared her insights into medieval pilgrimages.

The historians at the Slater Mill explained the operation of early mills and referred me to written materials on such mills. This was useful in describing the mill owned by the Girardone family.

Linda A. Hughes, the admissions coordinator of Remuda Ranch Center for Anorexia and Bulemia, provided me with materials on anorexia and discussed how Clare's excessive fasting could have damaged her health.

Several members of the Franciscans of the Primitive Observance and Franciscans Friars of the Immaculate, especially Father David Engo, FPO, and Brother Bonaventure, FFI, researched the thirteen wounds of Christ and came up with the final list mentioned in this book. Father John of the Trinity, TOCarm., told me how the Portiuncula indulgence might be obtained today.

In writing the chapter on Lady Filippa, I needed guidance in choosing flora and fauna that actually existed in Assisi at that time. Chris Nerone of the University of Rhode Island assisted me in choosing nightshade as a poisonous, berry-growing vine of the region. Mark Schenck, proprietor of the Butterfly Zoo, Middletown, Rhode Island, identified a caterpillar and swallow-tail butterfly that lived in Umbria.

Father John Broderick and Father Thomas Carnavale answered a variety of questions regarding Catholic customs, Mass rubrics, altar vessels, and so on.

Heather Minto spent a most delightful afternoon showing me flax and the medieval spinning process using a drop spindle. She also shared how thread is woven on a medieval loom.

In trying to determine how Clare did her needlework, I contacted many people, especially Norma Smayda, Susan Hay, Genevieve Hartigan, Barbara Gifford, and Leslie Tomaino. Lee Depot gave me good insights into handwork at the time of Clare. Alda Kaye, curator of the University of Rhode Island's Historic Textile Collection, researched and photocopied information on drawn embroidery at the time of Clare. Joan Hitchcock explained the stitches in this article to me.

I thank especially those others who read the manuscript in whole or in part—Sister Ingrid Petersen, OSF; Mother Mary Francis, PCC; historian Jon François Godet-Calogeras; history professor John Quinn; the Poor Clare community at Langhorne, Pennsyvania; the Capuchin Sisters of Nazareth in Tunkhannock, Pennsylvania; and my husband Jim, who graciously encourages my writing and who picked up many library books for me. Jim also researched the dates for Easter in the early 1230s and typed Clare's family tree as shown in this book. Sister Eileen Heugh, OSF, proofread the manuscript for correct punctuation and grammar.

John Quinn checked the birth date of Pope Gregory IX, found a map of the Holy Roman Empire in 1250, and made the valuable observation that the title of this book should reflect its dual emphasis on Clare and her sisters.

Finally, I thank my friends; members of my Franciscan fraternity, other fraternities, and the Brothers and Sisters of Penance; my relatives (especially my mother and my husband); many priests and religious; and many others I do not even know who prayed for this project and for those involved in it. Their prayers meant everything, for God is the One Who is ultimately behind this book. Anything good herein is due solely to His boundless and undeserved grace. Therefore, it is to God and to Saint Clare, who shared herself with me through this work, that I owe the greatest gratitude.

Introduction

Many people believe that Saint Clare of Assisi decided to follow Christ because she heard Saint Francis preach. He enclosed her in a convent where she lived a relatively uneventful life for forty years.

That is not the real Clare of Assisi.

This book attempts to present the real Clare from childhood to death, the many people she loved and influenced, and the complex, frightening, radical, disheartening, and joyful encounters of her life.

Clare began something new and radical. During her time, convents were comfortable places for pious noblewomen who continued to have servants and property. Clare had a different vision. She created a monastery that would neither own property nor make money and in which all classes of women lived as sisters, serving each other.

Many excellent, scholarly works have been written about Clare. Many of them were used in writing this book, which adheres to the primary sources (the first biography of Clare, her writings, and the testimonies of eyewitnesses) and to the life of Clare and the first Poor Clares, as many Poor Clares today understand them. However, *Clare and Her Sisters: Lovers of the Poor Christ* goes beyond scholarly works to allow the reader to experience Clare and her sisters in a personal way. Thus, while sticking to historical facts, this work adds imagination, keeping the fiction as factual as possible. Chapter notes at the book's end distinguish the factual from the fictional in this life of Saint Clare. They also note differences of scholarly opinion regarding certain parts of Clare's history.

God was Clare's first love. She challenges us to follow "the footprints of the poor and humble Jesus Christ," so that we may "taste the hidden sweetness that God Himself has reserved from the beginning for those who love Him" (Clare's Third Letter to Agnes of Prague). May this book teach us to do so.

Information for the Reader

The following information will be helpful in understanding this story.

PENANCE

Penance means a conversion from sin to God. When people "begin to do penance," they begin their conversion. Saint Clare and Saint Francis began their conversion as penitents and always viewed themselves as such.

During the early 1200s, a great penitential movement swept Europe. The Church recognized the penitential life as a legitimate vocation for the laity, a vocation encouraged by the friars and sisters. Penitents followed rules that were written for them. This book contains some examples of the penitential practices they followed. Today some of these seem strange and masochistic, but they were common at that time. With the permission of a spiritual director or religious superior, penitents undertook these practices as a means of prayer, sacrifice, self-discipline, and identification with the poor and suffering Christ. The practices fostered surrender to God and its accompanying joy.

Fasting on bread and water is popular today. In medieval times, bread was made from whole grain; thus, with water, it could sustain health. Those who fast on bread and water today need to use the same whole grain breads.

Those who wish to undertake other types of penance should consult a spiritual director for guidance, as did Clare and Francis.

The Brothers and Sisters of Penance is a Catholic association of the faithful whose members have the Church's permission to live a penitential life under a spiritual director and in their own homes. Their Rule is an updated version of the one lived at the time of Clare. For information, contact either the communication center of the association: RI Communication Center, 520 Oliphant Lane, Middletown RI, USA, 02842-4600 (phone: 401-849-5421) or MN Communication Center, 20939 Quadrant Avenue N., Scandia, MN, 55073 (phone: 651-433-2753). Or consult http://www.bspenance.org or e-mail bspenance@hotmail.com or bspenance@yahoo.com.

CLARE'S ILLNESS

Clare was so determined to be completely detached from the world and from sin that she undertook many bodily penances, including such rigorous fasting that her health was affected. Those who eat very little for a long time often lose bone mass and can sustain heart damage, electrolyte abnormalities in the blood, kidney problems, intestinal ulcers, and loss of muscle and other body proteins. Clare's persistent illness had many of these symptoms.

TONSURE

Hair was an object of beauty in the Middle Ages. Tonsure, which involved cutting the hair in unattractive ways, was a sign that a person had abandoned a sinful life and was consecrated to God. A male religious kept his hair short and had a bald patch shaved in the center of his scalp. He went bareheaded except in inclement weather, when he might wear a cap or a hood. A female religious had her hair cut up to her ears, kept her hair short, and covered her "baldness" with a veil.

CLARE'S HABIT

The earliest paintings of Clare show her dressed in a floor-length gray tunic that covers her feet, a hooded gray mantle (cape) that reaches to the floor in the back, a knotted rope cinched around her waist, and a black veil lined with white. Later artists depict Clare with a white wimple that covers her neck and throat. Clare and her sisters did not wear the wimple, which became popular after Clare's death.

RECLUSES

Also called anchorites, recluses were considered extremely holy penitents. During Clare's lifetime, nearly every city in Umbria supported recluses who were enclosed voluntarily in a small cell or cells, usually adjoining a church. A window in each cell looked into the church so that the recluses could participate at Mass. Recluses followed detailed rules of life, lived on alms, and spent most of their time in prayer—although they often gave spiritual counsel to visitors through a small, curtained window. The recluse was allowed a cat and a vegetable garden, tended by a servant. He or she could also stroll in a small, enclosed yard that might adjoin the cell. Some pious people lived reclusive, hermit-like lives at home.

THE EUCHARIST

Clare and Francis both had a great devotion to the Eucharist because they recognized Christ in it. The consecrated Host was retained in pyxes, precious boxes, small cupboards, miniature towers, or dove-shaped receptacles, then placed in a niche in the church wall or suspended. In the Church of San Damiano, the Eucharist was kept in a suspended dove and, in the sisters' private oratory, in a small box in a wall niche to the left of the altar. The location of the Eucharist in other churches mentioned in this book is purely hypothetical.

NUNS AND SISTERS, FRIARS AND MONKS

A "nun" was a consecrated woman living in a convent, while a "monk" was a consecrated man living in a monastery. Most monks and nuns came from the upper classes of society. Convents and monasteries owned property, had servants, and were often rich.

Francis and Clare wanted their followers to come from all social classes and to live as family members in poor, simple communities. Francis called his followers "brothers" ("friars"), who were to pray, preach the Gospel, and work. Clare called her followers "sisters." They were to pray, work, and minister spiritually to others.

SAN DAMIANO

This book uses the word "monastery" for San Damiano to distinguish it from the rich "convents" of the time.

Archeologists agree about some of the layout of San Damiano and speculate about the rest. I have read various theories and archeological studies and have pondered early Clare rules to determine a probable layout for the San Damiano complex. Not every scholar will agree with my conclusion. Moreover, the way San Damiano appeared in Clare's lifetime is not how it looks today.

Francis gave the sisters a Form of Life that Clare records as a single sentence. Was this Francis's entire Form of Life for the sisters? How did the sisters live? Scholars disagree on the answers to these questions. I believe that Clare envisioned a life of reclusion lived in community and poverty.

In 1215, Clare had to choose a papally approved Rule of Life and chose the Benedictine Rule. With this came a stricter enclosure than she may have been following. By 1219, she was given a Rule by Cardinal Hugolino. At that time, the speaking grill, Communion grill, choir, parlor, turn (if there was one), and so on would have been introduced if they were not already in place.

I have studied the strictness of Clare's enclosure and have undertaken much prayer, reading, and counsel with Poor Clares and Clare historians to determine how Clare and her sisters most likely lived. Not all the people and sources I consulted agree with my conclusions.

THE PRIVILEGE OF POVERTY

Historically, Clare is said to have received the "privilege of poverty" at various times and from various popes. Currently a difference of opinion exists among Clare scholars regarding whether this privilege was received and, if so, in what form and when. This book follows the traditional sources, but not all scholars will agree with its treatment of the "privilege of poverty."

TITLES FOR FRANCIS

At some point, Francis was ordained a deacon, but he never became a priest. The friars and sisters called Francis "Father

Francis" because he was their spiritual father. Others called him "Brother Francis."

TITLES FOR CLARE'S SISTERS

Primary sources and documents list several titles for Clare's sisters, including the Poor Ladies, the Enclosed Sisters, the Lesser Sisters, and the Ladies of Saint Mary of Saint Damian at Assisi. Papal documents called the sisters the Damianites of the Order of Saint Damian. Citizens of Assisi seemed to know the women by this term.

Recluses around Assisi were called "Christianas" (Cristiana in Italian) or "Christian women" by the townspeople. As stated in the chapter "A New Fioretti" in Marion Habig's *Omnibus*, Francis always called Clare "Christiana" (Cristiana). I have used Christiana as Francis's name for Clare, to distinguish Clare from other sisters at San Damiano who were actually named Cristiana.

In *Omnibus* Habig states that Francis always called Clare's sisters "ladies" and Celano uses that term in his biographies. Francis, it seems, wanted his friars to use this term to preserve a respectful distance between the sexes.

Clare called the women "sisters," thus making them equal family members. In formal correspondence, she used the terms "enclosed Ladies," "Poor Ladies," and the "Order of the Poor Sisters."

CLARE'S WORDS

In this book, Clare speaks some of her own words. They are adapted or taken directly from the four letters to Agnes of Prague; the fifth to Ermentrude (some historians dispute Clare's authorship of the letter); her Form of Life, Testament, and Blessing; and from words attributed to her in the process for her canonization and in her first biography, *The Legend of Saint Clare*. Titles for the major sections of this book are phrases from Clare's Testament.

CANONICAL HOURS

Time in the Middle Ages was referred to by the canonical hours whose approximate times are as follows:

Matins (Vigils)—First prayer of the night. Clare and her sisters said Matins sometime around midnight.

Lauds—Prayer said at dawn.

Prime—6 A.M.

Terce—9 A.M.

Sext—Noon.

None—3 P.M.

Vespers—Prayer said between 3 and 6 P.M.

Compline—Last prayer of the day, said before retiring for the night.

CAPITALIZATION

In this text, all pronouns referring to God the Father, Son, and Holy Spirit are in capital letters. This is not always the case in translations of Clare's writings.

VOCABULARY

Unless otherwise noted, the names of personalities in this story are spelled as Father Regis Armstrong, OFM Cap., spelled them in his book *Clare of Assisi: Early Documents*. Other historians sometimes use other spellings.

Because some Italian names lose their cultural richness when translated, a glossary follows:

Biscotti: Italian biscuits.

Consortium: a group of lords who, by mutual consent, share property and power in a certain area.

Convento: the house where friars live.

Domina: a title of respect given to ladies and noble-women.

Grazie: thank you. *Mille grazie:* many thanks.

Mi figliolo: my little son.

Monte: a mountain.

Piazza: a wide, open space where several streets come together.

Podesta: the elected head of the commune, who had a council to advise him.

Poggio: a hill. Umbria, the district around Assisi, is a series of hills. Many castles of Umbria were built on these hills.

Porta: a gate of the city.

Rivo: a river.

Signore: a title of respect given to lords and noblemen.

Via and strada: a street or road.

People are named in relation to their ancestors. Favarone di Offreduccio means Favarone, son of Offreduccio. Bona de Guelfuccio means Bona, daughter of Guelfuccio. Hugolino dei Conti dei Segni means Hugolino, son of Conti who was the son of Segni. The presence of the word "di" or "de" or "dei" in a name means "child of."

Sometimes history did not record the name of a real character. At other times I created a character to illustrate a certain point. In these instances, I assigned these people Italian names that indicate one of their qualities. The created names in this book are:

Bellezza (the beauty), Mattiolo's mother

Brontolone (the grouch), the grumpy, old beggar

Cappellano (chaplain), San Damiano's chaplain

Forte (the strong one), Lucia's father

Gatta (female cat), San Damiano's cat

Pia (the pious woman), the pious, demon-possessed woman from Pisa

Scherno (the scoffer), Pia's brother

Scuro (the dark one), Mattiolo's father

The word "del" means "of." Therefore, the Piazza del San Rufino is the Piazza of the Cathedral of San Rufino.

Expressive terms such as "Wow!" translate into the Italian "Splendito!" or "Accidenti!" "Good day" is "Buongiorno." "Good evening" is "Buonasera." "Good night" is "Buonanotte."

"Pace e bene" is Italian for the Latin greeting "Pax et bonum," which means "Peace and all good." This was the greeting that Saint Francis used.

PART ONE

To Set Out on the Path of the Lord

$$\sim 1 \sim$$

Lady Ortolana di Favarone

Bedroom, Offreduccio House, Assisi, Italy (LATE JANUARY, 1200) ~
In her dreams, Lady Ortolana di Favarone smelled smoke. Despite
the haze that engulfed her and her galloping chestnut palfrey,
Ortolana could see herself clearly, her long, slender legs gripping
her mount, sidesaddle, her firm, narrow nose, small chin, wisps of
blond hair around her prim cap. A plodding line of ox-drawn
carts, piled with goods and servants, magically kept pace with
Ortolana's rushing steed.

She was racing toward the flame-engulfed, towering, red rock
castle of Sasso Rosso, home of friends Lord Leonardo di Gislerio
and his family. Flames turned everything red and orange as Ortolana
dismounted and pulled loaves from her saddlebags while servants
grabbed blankets, pottery, weapons from the carts. Suddenly,
Ortolana's servants mutated into a mob of Assisi merchants and artisans. Shouting, they flung the goods at the castle, laughing as each
item burst into flame against the walls.

Merchants from the marketplace, the Mercato, were throwing
grappling hooks over the walls, climbing through flames, pulling
down the house. In a billow of black smoke, Sasso Rosso crumpled
like a child's tower of blocks.

The mob disappeared. Terror stricken, covered with ash,
Ortolana was standing in smoldering rubble with Lord Leonardo,
his lady, children, and servants. Dainty, five-year-old Lady Filippa was
clutching a charred doll with which she and Ortolana's daughters
often played. As Ortolana attempted to wipe it clean, the doll
crumbled to soot.

The Gislerios disappeared. Now the smoking rubble was that of
Ortolana's house and in it, as dumb eyed as oxen, stood Ortolana,
her husband Lord Favarone, and their children—six-and-a-half-
year-old Lady Clare, almost three-year-old Lady Catherine, and tod-
dler Lady Beatrice. Instantly, pudgy, tow-headed Clare, wearing a
scarlet dress, was alone in the prayer chapel, its fire-riddled wall

tapestries wafting smoke into a clear sky as the chapel burst into flame. A bright spark floated upward from where Clare had been. As Ortolana reached for the glowing cinder, it vanished against the sun.

Ortolana shrieked and awoke.

She was in her dark bedroom.

Through the cracks in her tightly shuttered windows came shouts and the dancing light of flames. The dream must be real.

For centuries, nobles, lords, and knights, like her own family and the family into which she had married, had ruled Assisi. Now the common people challenged that order. Barely two years ago, they had forged a new city government, a commune. Far more merchants, artisans, and farmers than nobles made up the commune. These lower classes had attacked and burned Sasso Rosso and several other castles and had chosen as governor their own consul in place of the emperor's appointed official.

Now the mob must intend to burn this immense Offreduccio house.

When his father Count Offreduccio di Bernardino died, Lady Ortolana's husband Favarone had inherited this house and much of the count's huge estate. Daily, after early morning Mass in the prayer chapel, Favarone either visited his vast properties or hunted game. A quiet, stocky, raven-haired man given to squinting, Favarone could become an enraged bull if anyone threatened his household, but tonight he was away in Cannara.

Throwing back the feather coverlet and woolen blankets, Ortolana bolted out of bed, feeling for her gownlike chemise. Swiftly, she clad her body, not bothering to lace her sleeves or back. Unable to find her mantle, she ran into the torchlit hallway without it, bolting toward the main door that led into this second floor of the house. Young Ioanni di Ventura, his dark beard still fuzz, was supposed to be guarding that door. Ioanni was capable. Courageous. Alert. With deadly accuracy, he could aim his watchman's huge crossbow. Why had he not awakened her?

Ortolana pounded at the front door. "Ioanni! Ioanni!"

"Yes, my lady," came the puzzled reply.

"What's happening out there?"

"Domina Savia escaped again, my lady. Her family is here in the piazza, trying to take her home."

Ortolana unbolted the door from the inside and cracked it open. A blizzard of driving snow swept across the Piazza del San Rufino. In front of the locked doors of the Cathedral del San Rufino milled a noisy cluster of servants and lords, torches in their hands. Above the noise came a piercing, heartrending wail. "Let me alone! You're trying to keep me away from my babies!" From the Offreduccio stable on the right, beggars, whom Favarone allowed to sleep in the stalls, were shouting, "Shut up! Go home!"

Domina Savia. When her children and husband had died from plague, the noblewoman had become crazed. Despite guards assigned to protect her, she sometimes managed to escape her household and wander pitifully through the city, crying for her dead children.

Ortolana closed the door and leaned against it, her knees weak. She was the Countess of Sterpeto, scion of the fearless Fiumi family, sister of bold Count Accarino, descendent of brave lords and knights going back to Emperor Charlemagne. Possessing great energy and faith, she had made pilgrimages to Rome, Monte Gargano, and the Holy Land, her life endangered by harsh terrain, plague, and bandits. But, because of tonight's dream, the courage that surged in Ortolana's bloodline failed her.

Ortolana sometimes had vivid dreams, each containing some truth. Although Lord Favarone had forbid her to ride to Sasso Rosso herself, he had agreed to sending provisions. Servants had described the rubble, so she must have dreamed it accurately. Yet in her dream, this house had been torched and Clare had burned to a cinder.

Terrified, Ortolana hurried through cold halls to the unheated bedrooms. The door to the children's bedroom was open. Oil lamps in the room were lit.

Lady Bona and Lady Pacifica, the Guelfuccio sisters who served the Offreduccios, stood as Ortolana entered. In the stark light, the women, wrapped in dark fur mantles, looked exceptionally pale.

Two little bodies, one plump and one thin, each wrapped in a heavy, hooded cape, plunged into Ortolana's gown. Four little arms grabbed her legs. Lady Clare and Lady Catherine.

Catherine was sobbing, her thin ribs heaving. "Mama, they're gonna bun our house like they bunned Lady Filippa's."

"We'll fight them off," Clare declared, stamping her foot.

"No, mi bambinas." Ortolana stooped and stroked the children's heads. She had to be strong. "No one is burning anything. No one is fighting anything. Domina Savia got away again. That's all."

"Oh, my God, grazie!" Pacifica dropped to her knees, her full mouth wide with a joyful smile.

Bona planted her fists firmly on her hips, her elbows jutting out from her big body like two wings. "I wouldn't put it past the mob to burn this place."

Catherine sobbed louder. "They're gonna bun us!"

"No one is burning anything," Ortolana said sharply to her lady-in-waiting. She glanced at the shutters. There was nothing beyond them but blackness. The night was still.

Ortolana put her finger to her lips. "Caterina, shh. Listen."

The only sound was Catherine's panting.

"They've gone home," Ortolana said gently. "Back to sleep." She kissed the girls, then looked up at Lady Bona. "Lady Beatrice didn't awaken?"

"One-year-olds sleep through anything," Bona said.

"Then good night," Ortolana said. "I'll put the girls back to bed."

Bona and Pacifica returned to their bedroom, which adjoined the children's room. These sisters, Ortolana's distant relatives, had served Ortolana ever since her marriage. Big boned, outspoken, and gregarious, Bona generally accompanied Ortolana about town and knew everyone's business. Timid Pacifica, a brunette whose roman nose indicated her noble background, deserved her name—woman of peace. Pacifica lived as a penitential recluse, leaving the house only to pray, attend Mass, and accompany Ortolana on pilgrimage. She spoke little and kept her eyes downcast in the presence of men so that she recognized no man in the Offreduccio household.

Ortolana slipped off the girls' capes, then tucked Catherine and Clare into their shared bed. She wrapped her chilled body in a feather-stuffed quilt from a chest at the foot of the bed, then sat on the bed and stroked her daughters' foreheads.

Sandy-haired Catherine, worn out from sobbing, fell into swift, peaceful sleep.

Under the layers of warm blankets, Clare was lying still, her eyes closed.

"Mama, if they burn our house, I'm going to fight." The child's thin lower lip was firmly set.

"Shh, Chiara. Go to sleep."

"I'm going to fight with Papa and Lord Monaldo, Lord Ugolino, Lord Scipione, Lord Paolo." All her uncles. "And Lord Martino, Lord Giorgio di Ugone, Lord Angelo di Tancredi." Her cousins.

"Shh. Go to sleep, Bambina." If Ortolana could sing, she would sing her daughter to sleep.

Clare was quiet, her eyes closed. But her little body was tense. Ortolana stroked and stroked the child's forehead and patted the snug nightcap that covered Clare's ash-blond curls.

If they burn our house.... Our house. The first-floor granary, storage rooms, kitchen. The second-floor bedrooms, ladies' sewing room, the great hall with its single hearth. The third-floor servants' quarters and family chapel.

If they burn our house.... The flames will rise above the Piazza del San Rufino, threatening the adjacent Cathedral del San Rufino. Water in the nearby fountain would be useless against the blaze. Flames might leap across the piazza, destroy the stable, the canons' residence, the Guelfuccio home.

If they burn our house.... Our servants will be homeless. Watch-man. Almoner. Maids. Cook. Stablehands. Steward. Squires. Kitchen workers. Butler.

If they burn our house.... We will have to move. Familiar beggars will have to beg coins, food, and clothing elsewhere.

If they burn our house.... What will happen to Lady Clare?

Like smoke, fear billowed up within Ortolana, the same fear that had swelled within her while she was pregnant with Clare. As Ortolana stroked Clare's cheek, the memory of her first pregnancy returned. She had feared that her unborn child would die, so she had prayed unceasingly for the baby to live.

One day Ortolana had been given a sign. The day had begun ordinarily enough. Prayer. Mass. Morning work. Prayer. Midday meal. Siesta. Then four ladies had assembled in Ortolana's sewing room to stitch, chat, encourage, and counsel each other.

Young, delicate-featured Lady Alguisa, wife of Lord Giorgio di Ugone, dreamy-eyed, romantic mother of Lord Paolo and Lady Emilia, anxious to have another girl and to name her Ginevra after the queen of Camelot.

Domineering Lady Bona, whose desire to marry had been thwarted since so many knights had died in war.

Sweet and gentle Lady Pacifica, content in her secret, single life of penance.

And Ortolana.

After a few hours, the women had walked to the Cathedral del San Rufino for their daily prayers. The women's families had made the cathedral possible. Over sixty years earlier, Giorgio di Ugone's family had given property for the church's expansion. Fifteen years later, the consortium in which Count Offreduccio and Lord Guelfuccio were members did the same.

Above the altar hung a huge crucifix, Christ in glory suspended upon it, His gentle eyes smiling on those who came to worship. Ignoring the shouts and banging of workmen enlarging the cathedral, Ortolana knelt, her eyes fixed on the Lord's face, shadowy in the semi-darkness. On this hot, sultry day, Ortolana, big with child, was weary. Closing her eyes, she had let her silent heart speak.

YOU WILL BEAR A CHILD WHO SHALL BE A LIGHT FOR ALL THE WORLD.

From where had come the words, spoken in a masculine voice? Had only she heard them? Bona, Pacifica, and Alguisa were kneeling silently, their heads bowed.

To Ortolana, that promise became a rare jewel. She had repeated it to herself during labor and then each time plague touched Umbria or Clare fell ill.

This child whose face she was stroking had been conceived in ardent love. Ortolana had stitched her baptismal gown, breastfed, bathed, and dressed her. She was teaching Clare to sew, write, read Latin, pray. Servants would not rear Ortolana's children.

Clare. The name meant "Brilliance."

YOU WILL BEAR A CHILD WHO SHALL BE A LIGHT FOR ALL THE WORLD.

In Ortolana's dream, Clare had disappeared in fire.

Please, God, Ortolana prayed. *Whatever the dream meant, don't let it mean that.*

~ 2 ~

Lord Favarone di Offreduccio

Piazza della Minerva, Assisi (LATE JANUARY, 1200) ~ Round-faced Lord Favarone di Offreduccio and his brothers Lord Paolo and Lord Scipione eased their horses through the crowded Piazza della Minerva. Under his jaunty blue cap, Favarone's curly black hair plastered his forehead, while his fur cloak billowed about his blocky body.

Three days ago, the men had left Assisi on a wearisome journey down the Strada del'Arce to inspect Offreduccio lands near the leper colony by San Gregorio's and in the vicinity of Castelnuovo. Then they proceeded to Cannara where a peasant was accused of stealing and butchering a neighbor's hog, a crime almost excusable during this unrelenting famine. The brothers had stayed two nights in the bailiff's house while deciding in favor of the lord.

Yesterday morning a snowstorm had swept down from the north, detaining the men until the snow ended and a warm wind, preceded by soft rain, blew in. Today the men had spurred their steeds along the muddy roads, eager to conclude a meeting with Lord Monaldo and return home.

"My lords!"

Favarone squinted toward the left, but, in his nearsightedness, he could only recognize the blurry, colorfully dressed figure when young Francis Bernardone was but a few yards off.

"My lords, tell your ladies that the damasks from France have arrived." Francis gestured toward blurred tables covered with indistinct cloth that his father Pietro Bernardone had edged into the street.

The men nodded as they continued inching their way through the crowd, which suddenly parted around Francis as a bony, bent simpleton whipped off his cloak and cast it at Francis's feet. In a high-pitched voice, the senile elder cried, "He is worthy of every reverence, because he will accomplish great things in the future and for them will be magnificently honored by all the world."

The brothers nudged their horses through the laughing shoppers and shortly arrived at the less crowded Via San Rufino, where they could ride three abreast.

"Did you ever see anything like that?" Large Paolo's voice and body dwarfed his steed.

"The old man has been treating Francis like that for months." Turning toward his brothers, Scipione's ruddy face looked redder than usual.

"Dangerous when people treat merchants like kings," Paolo said.

"Does God distinguish merchants from kings?" Scipione questioned.

"You think like your friend Lord Tancredi di Ugone," Paolo said.

Tancredi di Ugone was Assisi's much respected city consul. Last year, at the merchants' request, the stately lord had ordered that a gate be broken through the city wall near his house in the rich Parlascio section to provide a better route to the March via the Norcera and Gualdo roads. In a historical first, the names of merchants and lord together—and a cross of Christ—were etched into the great stone, pilfered from a Roman ruin, which was set over the gate's arch.

The men reined their muddy horses in front of Lord Monaldo's house. Two squires appeared and took the reins. They would feed and clean the animals.

"So what's the meeting about?" Favarone asked as the men clambered upstairs to the second floor.

"Only Monaldo knows," Paolo shrugged.

Resembling twin giants, Monaldo and Ugolino were waiting in the great hall. A blazing fire warmed the room, so Favarone and the others threw their fur cloaks across the far end of one of the long oaken tables. Sitting at another table, they watched Monaldo bolt the door.

Ugolino turned to Favarone. "Guilty?" he asked, his black eyebrows bobbing.

"He stole the pig," Favarone said. "We fined him."

"Pig business done." Ugolino slapped the table with his large, powerful hands and turned to Monaldo. "So, brother. Why this meeting?"

Broad-shouldered Monaldo eased to the bench next to Favarone.

"I've taken up citizenship in Perugia."

"Come on," Paolo groaned, rubbing his huge hand through his thinning hair. "We want to get home. Stop making jokes."

"I'm not joking."

"What!"

"No!"

"Impossible!"

"Perugia!"

"Assisi's enemy!"

"Without consulting us?"

"Better to be a citizen in hell."

"Quiet!" Monaldo boomed.

The brothers fell silent.

"I became a citizen in Perugia and so will you."

"You can't make our decisions," Scipione decreed, his ruddy face ruddier with anger.

"You will become citizens in Perugia or you will burn with Assisi."

"No one is burning Assisi," Ugolino noted.

"Look!" Monaldo pushed away from the bench and flung open the shutters of the window behind him. "Out there."

To Favarone the distant scene was blurred, yet his brothers could clearly see on Monte Subasio the skeletal ruins of the fortress Rocca Maggiore.

"The emperor's men ruled Assisi for centuries from the Rocca. Then, two years ago, Duke Conrad goes to Narni to meet with the Pope, and the people of Assisi—*Assisi*—destroy the Rocca, ignoring Lord Pope's envoys and the emperor's men who tell them to desist."

"Duke Conrad was vicious," Favarone said.

Monaldo stared at his younger brother. "He was the emperor's able captain."

"His did nothing to stop his men from raping and torturing," Favarone shot back.

"War is not nice, Favarone."

"Old Fly-in-the-Brain governed Assisi, Foligno, Spoleto, Norcera, and Rieti brutally and ineffectively. Where was the war then?"

"Don't be stupid, Favarone" Monaldo said. "We are discussing Assisi, not the Duke. Have you forgotten how the people destroyed the castles and towers? Sasso Rosso. Montemoro. Poggio dei figli di Morico. San Savino. Davino. Poggio San Damiano. Poggio di Bucaione. What next? Our castles?"

Monaldo looked from one brother to the next.

"Merchants, artisans, and farmers destroy castles because we ask for our due. Isn't it fair to charge tolls on roads that we build, repair, and patrol? Isn't it right to tax people who keep from starving because they live on our lands?"

"The people want fair treatment." Scipione pushed to his feet, towering over his seated brothers. "Then they will not bother us."

"The people are a mob," Monaldo said. "Merchants and artisans aspiring to be knights, wearing noble clothes, carrying swords. With money they buy titles, status, and respect."

"Scipione, you saw how the merchant was treated," Paolo reminded. "Francis Bernardone's outfits rival ours. His father buys him all he needs to be a knight like us, yet he attacked knights' castles with the mob."

"Even angels are in hierarchy," Monaldo said. "Since Jerusalem fell into pagan hands thirteen years ago, people have challenged society's structure."

"Are we gods with rights over other men?" Scipione asked.

"Does it matter?" Monaldo asked. "Commoners outnumber us. We are not safe in Assisi."

"But Perugia?" Ugolino questioned. "Perugia has been Assisi's enemy for centuries,"

"Assisi is now the enemy," Monaldo argued. "Lord Girardo di Gislerio of Sasso Rosso has become a Perugian citizen. So has his brother Lord Fortebraccio and his nephew Lord Oddo. The rest of the family will follow."

By becoming citizens of Perugia (loyal to the Pope), the Gislerios, who had property in Assisi (loyal to the emperor), had acted cunningly. Assisi collected taxes on property within its boundaries, but kept only taxes paid by Assisi citizens. Assisi would never give Gislerio taxes to Perugia, so Perugia would declare war. If Perugia won, the Gislerios would recover their lands. If Assisi won, the Gislerios would switch their allegiance to Assisi and still recover their lands. The Offreduccios, as Perugian citizens, would do the same thing.

"Since we've been good to the people, they may not bother us," Scipione said.

"You have sons," Favarone declared. "Lord Rufino and Lord Paolo are almost knights. I have daughters. How safe would women be in war?"

The men were silent.

"Caterina has had night terrors ever since the castles were destroyed." Favarone looked at the men around him. "What can I do but leave Assisi?"

"Once the people find out that Monaldo has joined Perugia, none of us will be safe. We should leave within the week," Ugolino said.

Thus the decision was made.

The week was filled with packing, preparations, and archers at the windows in case their secret leaving leaked out. How stupid Favarone had been fifteen years earlier when a strange prophet had wandered through the streets, singsonging "Pace e bene! Peace and all good." Then young Favarone had wanted war. Now, war wearied and frightened him.

Unlike Ortolana, who prayed before deciding, Favarone acted first and prayed later. Tonight he would stop to ask God to bring his family safely to an enemy city.

A single candle on the simple altar lit the third-floor prayer chapel. In its ghostly glow knelt a small figure, her chemise almost translucent. Lady Clare. She turned toward Favarone as his slippered feet brushed the wooden floor.

"Papa, why can't we stay and fight?"

Favarone knelt and enfolded Clare's plump body in his arms. The small stones on which she, like a little monk, counted her prayers tumbled out of her lap and clattered against the floor.

"Chiarita, some battles are fought, others avoided. This one we avoid. We will fight others."

Sitting back on his heels, Favarone drew Clare to his chest. Her thick blond hair, pushed up into a snood, felt like a soft pillow on his breast. With his large hands, he rubbed her pudgy, icy fingers to warm them.

"Why can't we take the beggars with us?"

Favarone sighed at this Offreduccio persistence. For a week, she had been asking this question. "Chiarissima, we cannot take the beggars to Perugia."

"Who will feed them, Papa?"

"Let the merchants feed them." The bitterness in his voice surprised him.

"Some merchants never give the beggars anything."

"Francis Bernardone is generous."

"Will he feed the beggars?"

"If they go there."

The child's hands felt warmer. Favarone stretched his overblouse over them.

"I'll tell the beggars to beg from Francis."

Favarone began to rub Clare's tiny, almost frozen bare feet. "You tell them, Chiarita."

"Is Lady Ginevra going to Perugia?"

"I don't know. If Lord Giorgio leaves Assisi."

"Will they burn her house? Or ours?"

The child's toes were warming under Favarone's rubbing. "I don't know, Chiarita."

"Does God care about us, Papa?"

"God cares about everyone."

"But does He care about *us?*"

"Of course He cares about us." *I think.*

"Then why are these things happening?"

Favarone tucked the child's warmed feet close to her body and pulled her chemise over them. Then he wrapped his arms tighter around her. How cold she was in this unheated room! "Why do bad things happen, Chiarissima? Only God knows."

"Does God ever tell anybody why they happen, Papa?"

"Maybe. But He has never told me."

Two weeks later, in Perugia, word came that merchants and commoners had torched the Offreduccio house. Not long after, Perugia and Assisi were at war.

❧ 3 ❧

Lady Benvenuta di Peroscia

Children's Play Room, Benvenuta's House, Perugia, Italy (EARLY AUTUMN, 1205) ∼ Hefty, eleven-year-old Lady Benvenuta di Peroscia sat on a large pillow in front of her puppet stage and picked at the tangled strings of a Mary Magdalene marionette. Benvenuta, Lady Filippa, Lady Ginevra, Lady Clare, and Lady Balvina had been practicing a puppet show on the resurrection of Christ when Benvenuta had dropped the Magdalene. The puppet show was better, Benvenuta thought, than any performed by the canons of the Basilica of San Pietro.

Benvenuta's short, awkward fingers were so clumsy!

"Ladies," came a soft voice.

Benvenuta hadn't heard Mother enter because Mother always walked silently in her softly slippered feet. "Lady Ortolana wants to go to the marketplace to buy some vases from Deruta. All your mothers are coming and Catherine, Beatrice, Pacifica, and Bona, too. Do you ladies want to come?"

"Are you going to buy sweets?" Balvina asked. Fat as a puppy, Balvina was two years older than Benvenuta.

"Not today," Mother said.

Balvina shrugged. "Then I don't want to come."

Benvenuta looked at Clare, Filippa, and Ginevra. They shook their heads. "We don't want to come either," Benvenuta said. "We're trying to practice this puppet show for Lady Catherine and Lady Beatrice."

"Fine," Mother said. "We'll see you later." She closed the door gently behind her.

Benvenuta admired Deruta ceramics splashed with dancing maidens, delicate ferns, and beautiful, shimmering flowers. Perhaps Deruta pottery was not sold in Assisi, so the ladies wanted to purchase some before returning home.

"Now we can make the cords," Clare said. At twelve, Clare was the tallest of the girls and, with her blond curls, oval face, and high cheekbones, maybe the loveliest.

Benvenuta shoved the Magdalene into Filippa's hands. "You untangle her." Running to the window, Benvenuta stood on tiptoe to watch the women.

"They're gone!"

"And the Magdalene is untangled." Dainty Filippa's melodious voice resembled a sweetly ringing bell.

Benvenuta hung the puppet on a peg behind the puppet stage.

Square-faced Ginevra straightened the puppet, then announced, "Now we can go to the stable."

So they did, with no one to stop them. At Clare's request, the young, obese groom cut five lengths of rope, his onion-shaped nose bobbing as he sliced. He asked no questions, and soon the girls raced breathlessly back to the playroom, ropes in hand.

"Do you think the groom will tell anyone?" Benvenuta huffed.

"Why should he?" Balvina puffed.

"Penance isn't as good when everyone knows about it," Ginevra noted.

"Let's never tell anyone," Filippa suggested.

The girls agreed.

"Let's start tying," Clare suggested. "Thirteen knots, one for each of Christ's wounds."

The girls recited the wounds as they tied the knots. Christ sweating blood in the garden of Gethsemane. Soldiers binding Him with rope. High priest slapping Christ. Scourging at the pillar. Crowning with thorns. Soldiers striking Jesus with a reed. Christ's shoulder wound from carrying the cross. Nails in His hands and feet. Gall that burned his parched tongue. Lance in His side.

Balvina extended her finished cord. "If we wear these, we'll be penitents."

"Wearing a cord doesn't make you holy." Clare's deep voice was direct. "The cord must remind us to love God, to obey Him, to help others. Then maybe we will become holy."

"Let's put on our cords right now," Filippa suggested. So each girl did, hiking up her billowing gown and chemise and cinching the cord tightly around her waist, next to her skin. Each girl smoothed out her skirt, then looked at the others. The gowns hid the itchy cords perfectly.

"Aren't penitents supposed to offer their sufferings to God?" Benvenuta asked. "Let's pray."

As Benvenuta led the way to the chapel, she felt older, wiser, and holier. Penitents had seemed heroic and mysterious until she had met Lady Pacifica who laughed, sang, and liked candied oranges, but who secretly wore a hairshirt, prayed, fasted, and shared her food with the poor. Two weeks ago, Lady Ortolana had the girls read a Latin commentary on the thirteen wounds of Christ. Pacifica, who was listening while she embroidered, casually commented that penitents sometimes secretly wore rough rope cords with thirteen knots to remind them of the wounds of Christ. Each girl had immediately thought of making such a cord, and, during playtime, they had agreed to do so. Today was the first time they had been alone to make them.

The girls knelt in the chapel to dedicate their penance to Christ. The cord was itching madly, but Benvenuta would not scratch. She had chosen this itching penance. *She would not scratch.*

Benvenuta raised her eyes to the tapestry behind the altar. On it, Christ was holding a lamb while a second lamb stood alongside, gazing at Him in adoration. *God, I love You,* Benvenuta began to pray. *Let these itches be little prayers of love.*

She tried to think of something else, but Christ and the lambs were distracting her. She imagined Lady Clare and Lady Balvina as those lambs. Christ was taking them back to their flock in Assisi. Tomorrow the Offreduccios were going home.

When the Offreduccios had left Assisi, Clare's family had moved in with Benvenuta's. Balvina's father, Lord Martino, the son of Lady Clare's uncle Lord Ugolino, had lodged two streets over. For the past five years, Clare and Balvina were part of Benvenuta's life.

Filippa and Ginevra were like Benvenuta's sisters, too, but Filippa's family might stay in Perugia forever. Her father, the dark-faced, lanky Lord Leonardo di Gislerio, hated Assisi for destroying Sasso Rosso, for killing his son Lord Oddo and his brother Lord Girardo, and for mutilating and dismembering the enemy dead. On nights when Filippa would awake with nightmares of destruction, Leonardo would rush into her bedroom, enfold her thin little body in his arms, and rock her while cursing Assisi. He mistrusted the recent peace treaty and said he would never return.

Although Ginevra's father Lord Giorgio di Ugone had moved his family to Perugia because he feared that the mob might attack his vast, rich household, which bordered the Offreduccios', Lord Giorgio didn't hate Assisi. Ginevra thought he might return.

The cord was itching. Benvenuta would not scratch. But she could not think about the thirteen wounds. She could only think of Clare and Balvina. Balvina was kneeling on her heels, her head bent low. Clare was lying on the floor, weeping silently. They always prayed that way.

She would never see Clare or Balvina again. Tears squeezed out of Benvenuta's eyes and trickled down her cheeks.

Was suffering in the heart worse than suffering in the flesh?

How many goodbyes did Jesus say? Goodbye to God the Father when He came to earth. Goodbye to Bethlehem when He went to Egypt. Goodbye to Egypt when He went to Nazareth. Goodbye to Joseph when Joseph died. Goodbye to Mary when He left home to preach. Goodbye to John the Baptist. Goodbye to disciples who deserted Him and to relatives who did not understand Him. Goodbye to those He cured. Goodbye to Lazarus, Martha, and Mary. Goodbye to Judas. Goodbye to His Mother and to His apostle John at the cross. Goodbye to those in the afterworld who saw Him after he died. Goodbye to everyone when He ascended into heaven. Thirteen goodbyes. Like thirteen knots on the cord. Like thirteen wounds of Christ.

Saying goodbye was like a wound.

But goodbyes didn't have to be forever. Wouldn't Clare and Balvina always be part of Benvenuta's life? Weren't all the girls one in Christ?

Benvenuta rubbed the irritating cord. The girls had pledged to wear their cords always. The ropes bound them to God and to each other. Bound them together like sisters. Forever.

❦ 4 ❧

Lady Pica

Bernardone House, Assisi (EARLY AUTUMN, 1205) ∽ At the hour of Sext, stoop-shouldered Lady Pica locked the doors to her husband Pietro Bernardone's basement cloth shop and wearily climbed the stairs to the family's living quarters. After the midday meal and rest, Assisi shops would reopen. Too tired to work at standing erect, she entered the dining room hunched but relaxed.

As usual, Francis was littering the table with bread. Before Pietro had left on this buying trip to France, he had tried to stop Francis from giving the beggars so much food. "Give them trenchers only," he had ordered. Trenchers were the discarded sliced loaves on which the wealthy took their meals. Now Francis was serving food on many sliced loaves, creating many trenchers.

Quick, sturdy footsteps sounded on the stairs, then Pica's lithe, dark-haired son Angelo bounded into the room. "Lord Tancredi di Ugone wants fine silk for thirty banners," he whooped. "Perhaps the other city consuls will want new banners also. Won't Father be delighted?"

Angelo bent to lightly kiss Pica, then playfully slapped her back. "Straighten up, Mother. You look like an old woman." Then he sat at the table and picked up a loaf in each hand. "So, Francis, you are still crazy."

"Angelo, you mustn't say that," Pica scolded.

"Mother, he is only joking," Francis said.

Pica wasn't so sure.

"No need to put all this bread out tomorrow," Angelo said, slicing one of the loaves in two and putting it on his platter. "Tomorrow you can send all the San Rufino beggars back to San Rufino. The Offreduccios returned last night." Angelo scooped some eel onto his trencher. "You must go to see them, Mother."

"Angelo, we have not said a blessing," Pica reminded.

Angelo bowed his head. Pica and Francis settled into their seats. Together the three recited the Our Father.

"Amen."

Angelo smacked his lips. "The Offreduccio lords have absolved the commune of any responsibility to rebuild their homes." He set aside his slightly soiled trencher and put a fresh one on his platter. "Lord Aguramonte di Giovanni di Matteo, Lord Andrea dell'Isola, and several others have done the same thing." Angelo laughed. "The lords say that Assisi has already compensated them for their damages." Angelo looked from Pica to Francis, then broke into a detestable, know-it-all grin. "They have never been compensated. But the lords wish to return so badly that they will say anything. Five years ago, they left Assisi fast enough. Now they scramble to return."

All because of Philip of Swabia.

Would war never end? First the commoners had rebelled. Now they ruled Assisi through their elected consuls. The war with Perugia had been bloody. In 1203, Perugia declared that it would make peace if Assisi repaid damages to the lords who had left. Lord Leonardo di Gislerio and Lord Monaldo di Offreduccio each claimed 30 libbre in damages. Where was Assisi to get that amount of money?

Assisi wrote its own "peace paper," levying heavy penalties against the deserting lords. The commune would confiscate their goods and appropriately punish any turncoats who returned to Assisi.

Philip of Swabia changed the stalemate. Since Emperor Henry VI died in 1198, Philip and Otto of Brunswick had been vying for the empire. They challenged each other and the Pope, who claimed several cities for the Church. Last year, Philip sent his forces into this part of the empire to reconquer papally occupied cities. Perugia remained loyal to the papacy, but Assisi swore allegiance to Philip. Philip recognized the city's commune government led by the common people and the guilds as long as their elected consuls pledged allegiance to Philip. Philip threatened to revoke privileges of lords who opposed this arrangement.

Philip was strong. Surely he would conquer the Church-controlled cities, because God seemed to have abandoned the corrupt Church. Many priests kept mistresses. Some were drunkards. Others were more concerned with acquiring money, land, and honor than with God. The majority knew nothing about preaching.

Papally controlled Perugia had evaluated the situation and had issued a peace treaty on August 31. As before, the treaty ordered Assisi to compensate the nobles for damages and to rebuild their homes, but the nobles claimed that Assisi had already compensated them and did not have to rebuild their homes, leaving Assisi no reason to punish returning lords.

When a lord returned to Assisi, Pica, under orders from Pietro, was to forget that her sons had helped destroy the lords' homes. She was to welcome the lords back, bring a few sweet cakes and remind the ladies that Pietro's shop supplied the best cloth to remake ruined wall hangings, bed coverings, banners, and pillows.

So, after a midday rest, Pica planned to go to the Offreduccios. Angelo would manage the shop. What Francis would do, Pica did not know. Sometimes he worked with Angelo. Other times he disappeared, sometimes returning home only when dawn pinked the sky. He said he was praying through the night in abandoned churches.

What had happened to Francis? As Pica lay on her bed during the siesta, she reviewed his life, trying to make sense of it.

Francis had always wanted to become a knight. In the war with Perugia, Pietro had equipped him with the best armor. Francis had been confident in Assisi's eventual victory until November three years ago when the cities had clashed at Collestrada. What brutality had Francis witnessed on that knoll that marked the border between the two cities? The Perugians, who mutilated, dismembered, and disemboweled the dead, had captured twenty-one-year-old Francis, imprisoning him in a dirty, dank cell with the nobles.

During that year of bitter, harsh confinement, Francis's songs, jokes, and humor had buoyed the spirits of the other prisoners and had soothed their peevish quarrels. Then, prostrate with a savage illness, Francis had been transferred to a cell with the sick and was finally returned, almost dead, to Pietro, who had negotiated for his release.

For weeks, Francis fought sickness, delirium, madness, and death. Pica had lived at his sweat-sopped bedside, begging heaven for his life and his sanity. Life had been granted, but sanity?

By mid-spring, a stronger Francis took to walking, first in Assisi and then outside. A restless uncertainty gripped her son; where he went, Pica did not know. When he began to work in the shop, he did so without his characteristic flair. Sometimes illness would recur, sending him to bed and Pica to her knees.

Francis's vigor returned when he heard that the noble, victorious knight, Sir Gautier de Brienne, was coming to Apulia. Francis begged Pietro to let him leave Umbria to join Gautier's forces. In high spirits, astride the finest steed, dressed in the most sumptuous clothes, the costliest armor, and singing a troubadour song, Francis set out. Shortly he returned, having given his finery to a poor knight. Groaning, Pietro outfitted Francis again, as extravagantly as before.

On the day of his second departure, Francis was exuberant. "I have had a dream," he told his family, "of an enchanted castle filled with the finest armor and weapons and a silent, smiling, beautifully dressed bride. A voice said, 'All this is for you and for your knights.' I am going to become a great knight. God has spoken to me."

Days later Francis was back in Assisi. This time he did not wish to leave.

"The illness returned when I reached Spoleto," he told Pica. Sick, he had taken to bed without feeling better. A few nights later, he dreamed again.

The voice had returned. "Who do you think can best reward you, the master or the servant?"

"The master," Francis had replied.

"Then why do you leave the master for the servant, the rich lord for the poor man?"

"Lord, what do You wish me to do?" Francis had asked.

"Return to your own place," the voice said, "and you will be told what to do. The vision must be interpreted in a spiritual sense."

So Francis had obeyed, cheerfully waiting for God to act. He even attended a party of the Tripudianti, that group of actors and dancers of which he had long been a member. As usual, they elected him head of the troupe, giving him the baton and the privilege of paying for their outlandish meal.

After the meal, singing his way through the streets with his friends, a surge of ecstasy had stopped Francis in his tracks. Sweetness washed over him, and he seemed to see again the silent, smiling lady in the castle, her face gentle, pale, tender, beautiful. But instead of a rich gown she now wore rags and went barefoot.

Francis's friends found him transfixed in the street.

"You are love-struck," they had teased.

"Indeed, I have found my bride, and she is the noblest, richest, most beautiful bride who ever lived on this earth," he had said.

Who was the woman? Was she a woman at all? The voice had told Francis to interpret the dreams in a spiritual sense.

Something bigger than Pica, Francis, or Assisi was happening to Francis. God knew what it was. Pica was only glad that burly, strong Pietro was frequently gone, because he would never understand Francis's behavior.

Pica prayed that God would care for her son, recalling that upon Francis's birth a pilgrim had prophesied, "Today two children have been born in this city. This one will be among the best of men and the other among the worst." Oh, God, let it be so!

With such thoughts, the rest time passed quickly. Soon Pica was crossing the Piazza del San Rufino and walking toward the severely damaged Offreduccio house. Forcing herself to stand erect, she made her way up the half-collapsed stairs and found Lady Ortolana attempting to bring some order to the charred master bedroom.

The women hugged a bit self-consciously. Pica shared the sweet cakes and invited Ortolana to peruse Pietro's fabrics to redecorate the house. Ortolana sent Lady Bona and Lady Clare, now a tall young maiden with an oval face and a husky build, to buy inexpensive cloth to cover the walls.

After Pica had visited other homes, persuading other ladies to purchase Pietro's goods, she returned to the shop. As she entered, Francis, his eyes shining, grabbed her hands and pressed them to his face.

"Mother! You remember my dream about the castle and the beautiful lady? And then the lady came again, barefoot and in rags?"

Pica nodded.

"The Lady Clare came today to purchase cloth. Mother, she looked like the lady of my dreams! What do you think it means?"

"I don't know," Pica said, stunned. "Perhaps God will tell you."

༄ 5 ༄

Lady Balvina di Martino

Offreduccio House, Assisi (Late January, 1206) ∾ Fourteen-year-old Lady Balvina was leaning over a small table in one of the women's rooms in the Offreduccio house. She had angled her bulky body to keep her shadow from falling across the parchment on which Lady Clare was writing. The letter was going to Lady Benvenuta and Lady Filippa in Perugia. Balvina was supposed to be thinking of news to share. So were Clare's sisters Catherine and Beatrice, who were seated on pillows on the rush-covered floor.

Brrr! Despite the tightly closed shutters on the narrow windows, the room was cold. Heat radiating from fireplaces in the great hall and the kitchen was minimal here. Balvina pulled her fur-lined mantle tighter about her and tugged her cap over her ears.

"Did you tell them how Lady Amata looks all over and how she holds onto your finger?" Balvina asked.

"I'll tell them."

Balvina's big-eyed, tiny-fingered sister Amata had been born at the family's castle Correggiano, but Balvina's mother had come to the Cathedral del San Rufino to be churched, blessed after giving birth. The family was staying with their Offreduccio relatives to celebrate.

What was that clatter? As Balvina looked toward the doorway, into the room burst Lady Ginevra, her solid, square face red with exertion, her mantle cockeyed.

"Come on! Now! Or we'll miss it!" Ginevra panted.

"Miss what?" Balvina asked.

"Francis Bernardone is on trial at Bishop Guido's. For stealing. Now, come on!"

"How do you know?" Balvina asked.

"Because my big old brother Lord Paolo was talking with the other knights and they told him. He and Lady Emilia are at the bishop's palace already. Now *come on.*" Ginevra tore out of the room.

23

The girls followed, bounding through the hall and clattering down the stairs.

"Ioanni," Ginevra called to the house watchman, "we're going to the bishop's. Tell Lady Ortolana." And the girls were racing across the piazza and down the steep, winding streets to the bishop's court, the Vescovado, their luxuriant mantles billowing behind them.

In the January air, the piazza in front of the bishop's palace was misty with human breath. Even the balconies were packed. All of Assisi seemed present.

"I can't see," complained seven-year-old Beatrice.

"Excuse us," Ginevra said, elbowing through the crowd, making way for the girls who pushed forward to the extreme left of the bishop's stairs. A few snowflakes drifted down. The girls tugged their mantle hoods over their hats.

"Oh, there's Francis," Ginevra said, pointing to their far right.

There in a tight circle stood the Bernardone family. Smiling Francis. Scowling Pietro. Worried-looking Pica. Self-assured Angelo.

"Don't Francis look happy?" a man behind the girls sniggered.

"Crazy you mean," a woman's high, thin voice responded. "That green cloak and tunic he's wearing are beggar garb."

"I seen him wearing worse than that, going about the streets half dazed."

"People say he's praying." The voices behind came quick and sharp.

"I seen kids sling stones at him. He bows to them like they was little princes."

"Went on a pilgrimage to Rome."

"Been tending the lepers at San Lazzaro d'Arce. Gotta be crazy to do that."

"I seen Pietro try to beat some sense into Francis. Didn't work."

"Pietro even imprisoned him in his house. No use."

"Lady Pica let him out."

"Shhh." A great hush swept the crowd as Bishop Guido, wearing his immense mitre and wrapped in a blue velvet mantle, emerged from the doorway of his house. With great dignity, he maneuvered his huge body to sit in the bishop's chair placed at the top of the stairs. Around him swarmed the canons of the bishop's church, Santa Maria Maggiore, the acolytes, assessor, vicar, notary, and knights.

Snow was drifting lightly earthward. Balvina pulled her hood far over her head to keep the snow out of her face.

A bell rang.

"Shhh."

Silence.

"Pietro, what is the problem?" Bishop Guido's voice thundered across the piazza, a huge puff of steam coming from his mouth.

"Lord Bishop, my son is a thief." Richly dressed Pietro grabbed Francis by his thick, dark hair and dragged him to the stairs. "He took bolts of cloth from my shop and my horse, then sold them in Foligno and gave the money to the priest at San Damiano."

"Is this true, Francis?" Bishop Guido asked, his eyes widening in his rotund, beardless face.

"Yes, Lord Bishop."

Pietro shook Francis violently.

"Francis, does the priest have this money?" the bishop asked.

"No, Lord Bishop," Francis grunted. "He would not take it. It is here." Squirming under Pietro's grip, Francis patted the pouch attached to his belt.

"Good." Bishop Guido settled back in his chair. "So, what do you want, Pietro?"

"I want my money back." Pietro shook Francis again and lifted his massive hand as if to strike his son, then thought better of it and released his grip on Francis's hair. Francis rubbed the sore spot.

"Francis, why would you steal your father's goods and sell them without his permission, then give away the money that was rightly your father's?"

"Lord Bishop," Francis said, straightening up, "the crucifix at San Damiano spoke to me. 'Francis, rebuild My house which, as you can see, is falling into ruin.'" Francis's voice was exultant. "The money was to rebuild San Damiano."

"Who in God's name is San Damiano?" asked a raspy voice behind Balvina.

"Him and his brother San Cosmas was famous doctors. Don't you know nothing?"

"Where the hell is San Damiano?" the voice croaked.

"Down in the woods near the Via Cupo di San Petrignano. In the Balia di Genga. You go out the Porta San Giorgio."

"The road past them old Roman tombs and funeral monuments. Down the steep hill of San Feliciano."

"That old church? He gotta be crazy. Why'd God tell anyone to rebuild that dump?"

"Did God tell you to steal?" The bishop's voice boomed across the piazza.

"No, Lord Bishop." The answer came softly, contritely.

"Francis," the bishop continued, "a disobedient son may be banished from Assisi at his parents' request. No one may feed or help him in any way. Upon the request of two of your relatives, you could be imprisoned until your family chooses to release you."

Francis squared his shoulders. "Lord Bishop, those laws do not concern me. By the grace of God, I have become a servant of the Most High by living as a lay brother with Father Peter, the priest at San Damiano."

"Do you presume to tell me what I already know?"

"No, Lord Bishop, I was merely pointing out…"

"Francis," the bishop interrupted, "you have been brought before this episcopal court precisely because you have declared yourself to be a lay brother. Had you taken the money and horse under other circumstances, you would be subject to the penal laws."

"I know, Lord Bishop."

"Do you know, too, how wrong it is for a man dedicated to God to do what you have done with another man's goods?"

"I had not thought of it, Lord Bishop."

"Well, think now, Francis. You have greatly upset your father. Give him back his money. God will provide other means for the restoration of the church."

Quickly, Francis removed the pouch from his belt. "My Lord Bishop, I will gladly give back to my father all his gold." He handed the pouch to Pietro, who grabbed it forcefully. "In fact, I will happily give back to him everything that belongs to him." So saying, Francis bounded up the stairs past the bishop and into the bishop's residence, leaving shoe prints behind on the snow-dusted steps. An acolyte bounded after him.

"Wait," the bishop called to the acolyte. "Let him go."

Moments passed before Francis, holding his clothes and shoes, reappeared. But for a sleeveless hairshirt, he was totally naked, as destitute as the poorest beggar.

The crowd gasped.

The bishop bolted to his feet. "Francis, what are you doing?"

"I am giving to my father even the clothes he has given me," Francis called out in a clear, joyous voice. He ran down the stairs and handed his clothes to his father. "Up to now, I have called Pietro Bernardone my father, but from now on, I shall say, 'Our Father, Who art in heaven....'" Francis's voice trailed off as he gazed heavenward, snow whitening his black hair.

Quickly Bishop Guido descended the stairs, then deftly undid the golden clasps of his mantle and tenderly draped the cloak over Francis's shoulders. Wrapping the mantle around the young man's wiry body, the bishop guided Francis back up the stairs. Then he turned toward the crowd and called in a loud but tremulous voice, "This trial is concluded. Francis has declared publicly his desire to follow God and to relinquish all that his family could give him. Pietro, take what is yours and go."

Lifting his right hand, the bishop traced a silent sign of the cross over the piazza. In a giant, sweeping motion, the crowd crossed themselves. Then the bishop put his arm around Francis's shoulders and led him into the bishop's house. The acolytes, canons, knights, notary, assessor, and vicar silently followed. The door closed. The light snow fell.

The speechless crowd parted to let Pietro stalk through, followed by straight-backed Angelo and stoop-shouldered, weeping Pica. Then the spell of disbelief began to lift. Here and there whispering began, sniggering, jeers. Suddenly everyone seemed to be talking.

The girls began to stamp their feet to get warm when the door to the bishop's house reopened and finely dressed Bishop Guido, minus his mitre, appeared in the doorway. Beside him walked Francis, barefoot and clad in a long ragged farmer's tunic. Bishop Guido must have given the tunic to Francis—the bishop's farmland lay just outside the wall.

Francis fell to his knees. The bishop made the sign of the cross over him, then laid his big hands on Francis's head. After a few moments, the bishop raised Francis to his feet and hugged him, then kissed him on one cheek and the other. Francis bowed slightly, then skipped down the stairs, bowed to the girls, and called, "Pace e bene!" Dancing and singing, he wove through the laughing, jeering crowd, bowing to those on his left and right, prancing toward the

Piazza del Santa Maria Maggiore exactly as he had done when he led the Tripudianti.

Soon Francis was out of sight.

"Let's go home," coaxed Beatrice. "I'm cold."

The crowd had thinned enough for the girls to push their way through. They had made their way through the Piazza del Santa Maria Maggiore when Balvina realized something.

"Where's Lady Clare?"

"She was still standing in the Vescovado when we left," Ginevra said.

"What was she doing?"

"Looking at where Francis Bernardone had gone. Don't worry about her. She knows how to get home."

Balvina felt odd heading home without Clare. But Balvina was hungry, and it was time for the evening meal. The girls chattered about Francis, how he would survive, and whether or not he was crazy or holy to do what he had done.

On the stairs of the Offreduccio house, Balvina hesitated before following the other girls inside. She was starving, and she could smell roasted peppers, garlic, and savory sauce—dinner in the warm great hall. But what about Lady Clare?

Before she could decide whether to look for her, she spotted Clare, her mantle pulled tight around her, walking briskly into the piazza from the Via San Rufino. Her gaze was cast downward, as if she were deep in thought. Clare hurried past the Offreduccio house, tugged open the door of the Cathedral del San Rufino, and disappeared inside.

How could Clare pray when it was time to eat?

Impulsively Balvina scurried down the stairs and ran to the cathedral.

Inside, in front of the wall niche holding the ornate silver box that contained the Body of Christ, Clare, clad in her mustard-colored dress, was kneeling, her head almost to the floor.

Brrr. It was cold in here. Why had Clare taken off her mantle?

From the shadows, a hand poked at Balvina. Startled, she turned and caught the gaze of a grimy faced beggar. Having no alms to give, Balvina turned away, then gasped as she realized that the beggar was snuggled in Clare's mantle.

Christ's words flashed across Balvina's mind. I WAS NAKED AND YOU CLOTHED ME.

Something of grace was happening here. To disturb that would be wrong. Quietly, Balvina opened the cathedral door and backed out into the lightly falling snow.

PART TWO

The Lord Gave the
Light of his Grace

❧ 6 ❧

Lord Ranieri di Bernardo

Piazza del San Rufino, Assisi (May 1210) ❧ Beneath his shirt of
scarlet silk and his fine gray cape, Lord Ranieri di Bernardo's heart
was pounding. He plucked off his small cap with its upturned brim
and ran his fingers through his curly black hair. Again he checked
the four bulging saddlebags. Each was securely fastened. His angu-
lar, lightly bearded cheeks and strong forehead felt tense. Never
had he been this nervous. Fighting for love was worse than fighting
for life.

How intensely he loved his distant cousin Lady Clare! Polite.
Pleasant. Beautiful. Good. People said that she was a saint because
she fasted, prayed, and sent choice food to the lepers at San Lazzaro
d'Arce, where Francis Bernardone and his men tended the outcasts
and sometimes ate with them.

Ranieri's tension was spooking his dappled-gray mount, so he
slacked the reins. The knights accompanying him fell into line on
either side. Hooves beat an uneven staccato on the stone piazza del
San Rufino.

Lord Rufino di Scipione maneuvered his horse alongside
Ranieri's. The short knight's broad face was earnest. "Don't worry.
Lady Clare always used to tag behind you at family feasts. She
likes you."

"She has rejected so many other suitors," Ranieri said.

"She is not yet seventeen. She does not know who she wants,"
Lord Ugolino de Pietro Girardone commented. The knight's statuesque posture lent credence to his words.

"The others were not as wealthy as you," remarked Lord Martino
di Ugolino di Offreduccio, the creases on his forehead arching.

"Or as good-looking!" Rufino's gentle eyes sparkled.

"Good-looking is a matter of opinion," Ranieri said.

"But wealth is not," Martino pointed out. "Lord Rufino and I
know that our uncle Lord Favarone wants Lady Clare to marry well.
You are well-off indeed, my cousin."

"Lady Clare will obey her parents," declared Lord Ugolino de Pietro Girardone. Naturally Lord Ugolino would think of obedience. Years ago, he, wed barely six months, had sent his disobedient and willful wife Lady Guiduzia back to her parents. He had refused to see her since.

"My sister Lady Ginevra says, 'Talk to Lady Clare about God,'" Lord Paolo di Giorgio di Ugone offered, his dark eyes flashing.

"And about Brother Francis Bernardone," Rufino added. "He has often spoken to her about Christ. Lady Clare follows all that Francis does."

The Offreduccio stable doors creaked open. At last! Here came the women. Lord Paolo's sister, Lady Emilia, girlish-looking with a splash of freckles across her nose. Lord Bernardo da Suppo's doe-eyed daughter Lady Cristiana, who was living as Clare's companion. Clare's constant escort, the imposing Lady Bona. Lord Martino's daughter, the incredibly plump Lady Balvina. Clare.

The women were seated sidesaddle, their colorful gowns draped across their legs, covering even their feet, their dainty caps perched on their heads. Although the older Bona's hair was caught up at her neckline in a pouch of thick net, the younger women had let their long hair cascade across their shoulders to their breasts and beyond. In her saffron gown and deep blue mantle, fastened with a golden brooch, blond-haired Clare rivaled the sun and sky in radiance.

Ranieri bowed to Clare and she, smiling daintily, bowed back. Ranieri spurred his horse into an easy walk. Clare urged her walnut-colored palfrey to keep pace with Ranieri's. The others stayed behind, out of earshot, for Ranieri had planned this excursion to court Clare.

"God has answered my prayers for a perfect outing, Lady Clare."

"God be praised for this beauty." Clare's voice was musical, lilting, almost a song.

I praise Him especially for you, Ranieri thought. *You are more beautiful than anything else in God's creation.*

Ranieri led the way to the Porta San Giorgio, then down the wide, gravel-lined path that soon led into the Via Cupo di San Petrignano. The horses walked lazily down the steep hill of San Feliciano. Ranieri's conversation was light. What were they even discussing?

Clare was so beautiful, her complexion flawless, her body well-rounded in all the right places. If only they were wed. Then, alone in this quiet forest, he would remove Clare's cap and run his fingers through her long, golden curls, pushing them away from her spacious forehead. He would stroke her soft, flushed cheeks and kiss her full, pink lips, and love her. How badly he wanted to make her his wife.

Ranieri caught himself. He could see, farther down the steep incline, the pinkish white stone of San Damiano. How many times had he rehearsed what he was about to say?

"Lady Clare, just ahead is San Damiano, the church that Brother Francis first repaired." Ranieri always passed San Damiano on his way to the Strada Francesca, the road that led to France. "Would you care to go in to offer a prayer?"

Clare broke into a grin. "Most happily."

Ah, things were going as planned. The riding party reined their horses in front of the chapel. Ranieri dismounted, then helped Clare from her saddle. Taking her by the hand, he led her into the dimly lit church.

Who was leading whom? Clare was walking ahead of him, directly to the front of the church, where steps led up to a raised altar. Other steps led down to the dark crypt below it. Clare fell to her knees directly in front of the altar. Ranieri knelt beside her, with the other lords and ladies clustered about them on the rose-colored pavement.

Behind the altar was a huge crucifix of the glorified Jesus. On a red, gold, and black background, Jesus' thin arms were stretched over the faithful. His eyes were wide open, His face serene. A golden halo protruded from the background so that Jesus' face tipped forward. The crucifix was teeming with angels and human figures. At its top, a miniature risen Jesus stepped into glory.

Lord, let her consent to marry me.

Ranieri's gaze strayed to Clare. She was kneeling sturdily, a few tears snagged on her long lashes, her eyes fixed on a wooden dove suspended above the altar that held the Body of Christ.

He should not stare at her beauty, so he closed his eyes and bowed his head. In his imagination he could still see her shapely, kneeling form.

When Ranieri finally heard Clare shift and stand, his knees were stiff. He led the way out of the chapel and helped her mount, then swung into the saddle and returned to the road.

"I was down this way when Brother Francis was up on that outer wall, and he called out in very poorly spoken French, 'Come and help me build the monastery of San Damiano because ladies will someday live here, and they will give glory to God by their holy life.' I sent him some stones and some of my workmen to help him."

"One stone for one blessing. Two stones for two blessings." Clare was quoting Francis's promise to carry each donated stone on his shoulders down the steep incline to the church.

The horses plodded as the road became more swampy. Through the thick trees to the left, the Rivo Torto was twisting its lazy way through the low-lying forest. Eventually the Via Cupo di San Petrignano veered away from the river and became less swampy.

"There is San Pietro della Spina, which Brother Francis also rebuilt. Would you like to go in?"

"Of course. My lord, how kind of you to take me here."

After praying at the small chapel, built for the countryside folk, the group headed west on the Via Antica before turning north on the Strada della Porziuncola. Immediately ahead, in a small clearing in the twisted, wild oak forest, stood a small, pinkish gray stone building, the Porziuncola church named Saint Mary of the Angels, another church built for the inhabitants of the country.

"The people say angels often visit this church," Ranieri said.

Clare smiled agreeably.

Francis, who allowed the friars to own nothing, yearly paid a hamper of fish to rent the Porziuncola, even though the owners, the Benedictine monks on Monte Subasio, wanted to give it to him free.

A glimmer of movement around the shaky reed huts surrounding the church caught Ranieri's attention. A gray tunic. Another. Another. Good. The friars were here. Last year the men had gone to Rome to see the Pope, who had approved their way of life. Ranieri knew these men, their once trim, flowing locks shorn, their beards untidy, and their scalps shaved in the center in clerical tonsure. For Clare's sake, he would overcome his unease in their presence.

A friar came striding toward the group. His scraggly gray beard bobbed as he called out, "Lord Ranieri! Lord Rufino! My lords and ladies! Pace e bene!"

The friar was Peter Catani, the former lawyer who had once won a lawsuit for Ranieri's father.

Peter grasped Ranieri's palm. Turning toward the church, he called out, "Brother Angelo, look who is here!"

A tall, vigorous man in a ragged gray tunic turned from the church toward the group. "The Lord be praised!" With his head held high and his spine straight, the former knight Angelo di Tancredi sprinted toward the group. Last year after Lord Pope had approved Francis's Form of Life, Francis or another friar had preached every Sunday in the Cathedral del San Rufino. Right before Christmas, wealthy, gentle Lord Angelo had left managing his serfs to join Francis.

Angelo was beaming with exuberance. "So, my relatives, you are no longer angry with me for coming here?"

Ranieri was no longer angry, just puzzled. Here was his relative who now worked the fields alongside his former serfs and who would take only stale bread for his labor. For Clare's sake, Ranieri would accept Angelo even if he could not understand him.

Leaping from his horse, Ranieri enthusiastically threw his arms around his cousin and kissed him on both cheeks. The other knights followed, sweeping Angelo up in a great surge of hugging, back patting, and exclaiming.

"Pace e bene!" Two other friars approached the group. Ranieri instantly recognized that black hair peppered with gray. Bernardo di Quintavalle! All of Assisi once consulted Bernardo in civil matters. When he sold his goods, gave away all his money in the Piazza del San Giorgio, and joined Francis as his first follower, the citizens of Assisi had been incredulous.

As Bernardo grasped Ranieri's shoulders in a tight hug, the younger, beardless friar called exultantly, "Lord Rufino!"

"Brother Giles!"

Giles and Rufino embraced heartily.

"So, are you going to stay with us this time?" Giles asked, his innocent face aglow.

A hearty laugh bubbled out of Rufino's expansive mouth. "You always ask that! Have you forgotten partying with Brother Francis? Partying is fun, but this life is boring."

The four friars burst into laughter.

"If only you knew," Giles grinned. "The world is boring. Not God."

"Pace e bene!" The cheer came from the church roof. A tiny gray figure was inching along the roof line. Francis.

Ranieri took Clare's hand. "Come."

As the couple approached, Francis looked down and pursed his lips. "My lord, I thank you for the roof tiles." Francis tapped the tiles directly in front of him. "We have placed them next to the ones Lady Clare bought for us." He pointed to his right, then leaped to the ground. "Come, see the chapel, rebuilt in part with donations sent from both of you and from many other good people of Assisi."

"Gladly, Brother," Ranieri said.

When Clare had finished praying in the chapel, Ranieri led her back to the horses and undid the four fat pouches on his saddle. They were plump with fresh bread, which he handed to the friars before bidding them farewell.

Ranieri led the way along the Strada della Porziuncola, toward Assisi. The sun was low in the sky, the shadows long.

Nervousness again swelled Ranieri's chest. *Get over your fear, Ranieri.* "My lady." The words were sticking in his throat. He forced himself to go on. "I was most delighted when your father granted me permission to court you. I would be honored to wed you."

At last! It was out.

"My lord," Lady Clare carefully began in her deep, firm voice, "any woman would be honored to wed you. But I cannot."

Ranieri groaned. He had feared this answer. His pounding heart rivaled the plopping of the horses' hooves.

"My lady, both your parents wish to see you magnificently wed. I have lands. Jewels. Servants. Houses." Ranieri's voice was trembling. "Gladly would I fight any battle to give you all you wish. You will be highly honored. I know that you are devoted to God, generous in alms and prayer. My money and power will be yours to use as you wish for our Lord Jesus Christ."

Clare gazed at Ranieri, her blue eyes full of sympathy, her voice tender. "My dear Lord Ranieri, Jesus said that it is easier for a camel to pass through the eye of a needle than for a rich person to enter the kingdom of heaven. I love worldly things too much. I must leave earthly things and seek heavenly ones."

Ranieri reached for Clare's hand. The touch of her soft skin sent a thrill through his heart. "My lady, can one not seek the kingdom and still live in the world?"

"Of course. But not me. The world tugs at me, my lord. It is a great struggle."

"As my wife, you could serve God as you wish." The horses were walking so closely together that Ranieri could have leaned over and kissed Clare, had he been so bold.

"My dear lord, my heart is with another Lord."

Ranieri was quiet. He did not know what to say.

"Lord Ranieri, is that not another church up ahead?"

"The monastery of San Nicolo dell Orto."

"May we go in? I should like to offer a prayer for you."

"As you wish, Lady Clare."

Clare spurred her horse and it trotted ahead, breaking pace with Ranieri's mount.

The party stopped at the small chapel and entered the dim coolness. Before the altar with its bold wooden crucifix, Clare knelt. Taking Ranieri's hand in hers, she bowed her head and prayed silently, her lips slightly moving, her eyes closed. Finally she opened her tear-filled eyes and looked directly at Ranieri. "Oh, gentle Lord Ranieri, let us always pray for each other."

"I will pray for you, Lady Clare." Ranieri's voice was barely audible. *And I will court you until you say yes to me. I love you so much, my lady.* Ranieri lifted his eyes toward the crucifix over the altar. *I cannot let you go, even to Him.*

⟶ 7 ⟵

Lady Bona di Guelfuccio

Offreduccio House, Assisi (LATE AUTUMN, 1210) ⟶ In the sewing room of the Offreduccio house, the ladies were chatting as they stitched. Ortolana. Pacifica. Clare. Cristiana. Catherine. Beatrice. Alguisa. Emilia. Ginevra. Bona.

Bona wasn't paying close attention to the conversation, so intent was she on the bodice of the olive-colored gown in her lap. Her specially designed, intricate pattern must be perfectly stitched. Shoving annoying strands of prematurely graying hair under her small cap, Bona carefully took another stitch.

"My ladies."

The butler's deep voice startled Bona, who jerked, almost bungling the stitch.

"Lady Clare is asked to come to the great hall at the request of Lord Rufino di Scipione."

Bona gasped. Lord Rufino? Here? After what he had done!

Almost too quickly, Clare hurried out of the room. Apprehensive, Bona put down the gown and hurried after her. Bona always accompanied Clare.

A few weeks ago, Bona had returned to Assisi after a pilgrimage to the shrine of Saint James in Compostela. Clare had urged her to make the penitential journey to gain the special indulgences given to pilgrims during this jubilee year, four hundred years since the discovery of Saint James' body in that far western corner of Spain. What graces Bona had received! She had touched the apostle's staff. Marveled at the church's elaborate sculptures. Prayed before the gold-adorned altar. Begged Saint James to deepen her faith. With the Compostela pilgrim's traditional scallop shell fastened to her bread pouch, she had returned, full of peace and joy.

Then she had heard what Lord Rufino had done, and her joy had died.

As Bona entered the great hall behind Clare, she caught sight of two youthful, barefoot friars in coarse, penitential tunics, awkwardly waiting. Rufino. And another young man.

The friars were bowing. Clare was curtsying. With disdain, Bona curtsied, too.

Then Clare threw her arms around short, fine-featured Rufino, who pressed his face against Clare's shoulder and began to sob. After several minutes, his weeping subsided.

"It is good to see you." Clare's voice was quivering, her arms tight around her cousin.

"And you." Rufino's words were husky.

Slowly the two broke their embrace and gazed at each other. "You are beautiful, Brother," Clare observed.

"To you. Not to the other Offreduccios. They loathe what I have done."

"They do not understand that you have chosen to serve the noblest Lord." Taking his hand, Clare led Rufino to the benches around the massive table. "Sit and introduce your brother. Share what life with Brother Francis is like."

Bewildered, Bona sat next to Clare and tried to sort her thoughts. This—this beggar—was a lord. Lord Rufino. Gentle. Courtly. Refined.

"This is Brother Barbaro." Rufino introduced his grinning, wiry, baby-faced companion. "An Assisi man whose hot temper helped bring me to Francis." Rufino smiled at the women's startled expressions. "About a year ago, I was riding to Limigiano to visit the Scipione castle. In the piazza I saw Brother Barbaro and another friar arguing!"

"Francis preaches peace," Bona objected.

"True," said Rufino, "so why were the friars about to swing at each other? Suddenly Brother Barbaro drops to the ground and stuffs donkey's dung into his mouth."

"Ugh!" Clare and Bona grunted.

"The argument was my fault," Barbaro said. "It was right that my mouth bear the penalty and the shame."

"My ladies," Rufino said, nodding at the women, "I was amazed. Who were these friars? So I went to Rivo Torto where Francis and his friars were living in an abandoned stable."

How sickening! Bona thought.

"When a peasant moved his donkey into the stable, the brothers moved to the Porziuncola."

"During this past summer, he visited so often," Barbaro smiled, "that we called him 'our rich friar.'"

Rufino's voice began to tremble. "There is so much love with Father Francis. If an Offreduccio offends an Offreduccio, there is yelling and arguing. But if one brother offends another, the offender prostrates himself on the ground. He asks the one whom he offended to put his foot on his mouth."

"Have you done this?" Bona asked.

"Since joining three months ago, I have offended three times."

"Did you think that you had offended me," Clare asked, "that you have not visited?"

"I saw my father's face and my uncles' when I preached in San Rufino in my breeches. They were offended."

"Disgraced is the word," Bona retorted.

Barbaro lay his hand on Rufino's shoulder. "Father Francis had ordered my brother to preach, but he is shy and not good with words. So he begged Father Francis to excuse him."

"I was disobedient," Rufino said quietly. "Prideful, afraid of appearing a fool. How could I obey God if I could not obey Father Francis? Therefore Father Francis ordered me to preach in my breeches."

Bona remembered the jeering congregation who had thought that Rufino had gone mad with penance.

Rufino found Clare's eyes. "Only your father, my lady, seemed compassionate. I think he would have thrown his cloak over me had Father Francis not come in." For Francis, also clad only in breeches, had entered the church and had begun to preach about penance, poverty, and humiliation for the Kingdom of God. As Francis clothed himself and Rufino in tunics, the jeers turned to weeping.

"How are you serving God this way?" The words burst from Bona before she could stop them. "You and Lord Angelo di Trancredi could buy bread for every beggar in Assisi, yet you have become beggars. Why?"

"Who can understand?" Barbaro asked. "For some of us, poverty is God's way."

"Lady Clare," Rufino said softly, "Father Francis would like to speak to you privately about matters of the spirit, about penance."

Clare leaped to her feet. "Brother Rufino, I have been praying for months for this."

"Tomorrow at the hour of Terce at the Porziuncola?"

"Yes!"

"No!" Bona blurted. Clare gave the friars goods and money for Masses and candles. What more did Francis want? "Your parents will not permit it."

"We will not tell them," Clare said.

"We have to tell them."

"No, we don't. I am of age to do as I wish." Clare's voice was firm.

Bona groaned. As a lady-in-waiting, she was to obey her mistress. Rufino stood. "Tomorrow, then."

"Now you must meet the other ladies." Clare's voice was eager as she started out the doorway. "About this meeting, we will say only that we visited."

Awkwardly, Bona and the friars silently waited until the other women burst into the room, chattering, questioning, giggling, hugging Brother Rufino.

Finally Rufino raised his hands. "My dear relatives, we must beg yet today."

"You have already begged," Ortolana remarked. "Wait here." She strode out of the room, returning with four servants carrying figs, bread, and meat.

"For the friars," Ortolana said.

Grinning, Barbaro and Rufino dropped the food into huge, deep pouches sewn into the sides and chests of their tunics and even into their hoods.

The women curtsied to the lumpy men. The friars bowed.

"Come again. Soon," Ortolana said, grasping each of their hands.

"We will. Grazie, all."

❧ 8 ❧

Brother Philip di Lungo

Porziuncola, Assisi (LATE AUTUMN, 1210) ∿ Raven-haired Brother Philip di Lungo heard bells before he heard clumping hooves. Putting down the wooden bowl into which he had been picking parsley to garnish tonight's meal, he hurried toward the Strada della Porziuncola and met Lady Clare and Lady Bona in the clearing.

The tall, slender friar, barely twenty, bowed graciously to the women dressed in matching green. Helping the women from their lavishly outfitted palfreys, he then tethered the animals, offered the women a seat on rude benches at the foot of a gigantic oak, and went to fetch Francis.

Two years ago, Philip, a native of Costa di San Savino, had left his sheep to another shepherd and had joined Francis who, just now, was praying beside his straw bed in one of the narrow, poorly constructed huts that encircled the Porziuncola.

"Lady Clare is here," Philip said softly.

Breaking into a grin, Francis bounded past Philip as Philip held aside the drape that served as a door.

"Pace e bene!" Francis called to the women. Francis straddled an empty bench as Philip sat on another bench across from him. Francis allowed no friar to speak alone to a woman. The presence of a companion preserved virtue and reputation.

So this was Lady Clare who, so Brother Rufino claimed, was pious. In his worldly life in Mandria within the commune of Assisi, Philip had never heard of Lady Clare. But he had heard of the Offreduccios, a family of twenty or so who held the greatest power and wealth in the commune.

"So, Lady Clare," Francis said, smiling, "I hear that you are a holy woman."

The lady's face reddened. "Perhaps you can help that come true."

Francis grinned. "Have you ever thought of leaving the world?"

"Frequently."

43

Philip caught his breath. Perhaps Francis was right in thinking this woman might share his vision.

Francis cocked his head. "Why haven't you?"

"Because I don't want what the anchorages and convents have. I want what you have. Or don't have. I want to give myself to Jesus in His poverty. Can you help me?"

"Perhaps." Francis propped his elbow on his knee and leaned his chin into his fist. "We observe the commands and counsels of our Lord Jesus Christ. We deny ourselves and place our bodies under the yoke of service and holy obedience. Can you embrace this?"

"I am not afraid of poverty, hard work, or difficulty, Brother. Nor do I care about public opinion."

Francis arched his eyebrows. "It is more than that. We must not be wise and prudent according to the flesh; rather, we must be simple, humble, and pure. We must hold ourselves in contempt and scorn, since through our own fault all of us are miserable and contemptible."

Clare was nodding solemnly. "I know how spiritually poor and needy I am, in absolute need of heavenly nourishment. Can you help me exchange the goods of earth for those of heaven and to live as you do?"

Philip's heart skipped a beat. This was exactly what Father Francis had hoped to propose to Lady Clare.

Francis furrowed his brow. "Would you meet weekly with me to discuss it?"

Clare's face lit up. "Yes."

"Surely you are not thinking of joining the friars?" Bona burst out.

Clare rolled her eyes. "That would be indecent."

"Nor would we permit such a thing," Francis noted.

"Then what will you do?" Bona asked.

"Brother Francis will have to tell me, because I do not know."

Lady Bona leapt to her feet. "You cannot come here again. If the Offreduccio knights knew you were here, talking like this, they might kill you."

Francis whistled. "Really?"

"Quite possibly," Bona said.

"They will not know," Clare declared. "We will continue to meet secretly."

"Your parents would disapprove," Bona objected.

"My parents have taught," Clare said, "that, ultimately, one must obey the Father of our Lord Jesus Christ."

~ 9 ~

Lady Beatrice di Favarone

Piazza del San Rufino, Assisi (JANUARY 1212) ~ Lady Beatrice, thirteen-year-old daughter of Lord Favarone di Offreduccio, and her older sister Lady Catherine had made ten snow figures beside the steps of the Offreduccio house. Now they were finishing a chambermaid.

Wouldn't Father and her uncles be surprised when they arrived home!

From the snow-covered Via del San Rufino came the muffled plod-plod of horses' hooves. Oh, no. The hunting party was home! The snow servants were not finished.

At the steps, Lord Monaldo leaped from his chestnut steed. "Out of the way! Get back!" he barked at the girls. In his dark furs, striding into the clump of fast-moving, grunting uncles milling around Father's horse, Monaldo looked larger than usual.

Lord Scipione was at Beatrice's side, his long, perfectly shaped fingers dark with blood and grime, probably from disemboweling a boar or stag. Fresh meat for dinner tonight!

"Move back, ladies," Scipione said softly. "Your father's been gored."

Catherine screamed

"Father!" Beatrice cried.

She tried to run after him, but Lord Scipione was blocking her way. "Let him in the house. He needs a doctor."

Her sturdy uncles were carrying her father up the stairs. The belly of his blue tunic was stained red. A huge red blotch smeared his fox-fur cape. Often Father came home splattered with animal blood. But these blots were huge, solid patches.

"You may go now," Scipione said.

Beatrice threw a swift glance at the snow people. A drop of fresh blood had bored its way into the chambermaid's skull.

The girls raced upstairs dotted with red.

Everything was out of kilter. The hall, dark, long. Mother and Father's bedroom crowded. Lords, blood flecking their clothes.

45

Servants. Confusion. Shrieking. Cursing. Father lying on his back, in bed. Clare kneeling at Father's side, holding one of his bloody hands. Mother crouched on the other side, her small, fine chin trembling, her gentle hands carefully rolling Father's clothing away from his wound.

Beatrice threw herself down beside Clare while Catherine fell to her knees next to Mother.

Father's life was seeping out of his belly in a widening red circle. The room shifted, expanded outwards. Beatrice clutched at her consciousness. *Oh, God, don't let me faint!*

"Everybody stay back but the family! Get back!"

The doctor's harshness startled Beatrice, cleared her head.

The doctor was hurrying, cutting away the bloody tunic. The room was flying away from her.

I will not faint.

Beatrice felt a firm hand squeeze her shoulder. "Take deep breaths, Lady Beatrice." The voice was Clare's.

One deep breath. Two deep breaths. Three. *I will not faint.* She could hear scissors cutting, could smell blood.

I will not faint.

A bandage of undyed cloth covered Father's belly, a pinprick of red in its center. Father's eyes were closed. Under his cockeyed cap, his gray-flecked black hair was plastered against his pale forehead.

Beatrice stroked back Father's hair. Father felt cool.

Father, speak to me. Are you dead?

If only she could think of a story, a poem. He used to tell her stories when she was sick.

The doctor was speaking to Mother. "Boar...four hundred pounds...very long tusks...wounds very deep."

No! Father, wake up. You're not dying. Talk to me.

"Move back. Give him air."

Beatrice recognized Canon Crescenzio's commanding voice. Lords and servants backed from the bed, making room for the youthful altar server and the grim-faced canon in his violet stole.

The canon was blessing the house, the people. A drop of holy water landed on Beatrice's forehead. *Why don't You heal him, God?*

"Lord Favarone!" Why was Canon Crescenzio shouting at Father?

Father's whisper was barely audible. "Yes."

"Do you wish to confess?" The words were softer.

"Yes."

The canon turned to the group. "Everyone out. The lord wishes to confess."

The murmuring crowd pressed out of the room. Lord Paolo lifted Beatrice to her feet and guided her backwards, away from Father.

"Father!"

This was a bad dream. Beatrice would awaken, go outdoors, and complete the snow people with Catherine. Father would come home and praise their artistry. This confused, deadened crowd in the hall-way—this was not real.

"He is absolved." Canon Crescènzio appeared in the doorway.

The people filed in, encircling the bed. The canon was opening a little wooden box, removing the Body of Christ, placing it on Father's tongue. More prayers. Canon Crescenzio dipping his fin-ger into a vial of holy oil. Anointing Father's eyes. Ears. Nostrils. Mouth. Hands. Feet. "May the Lord forgive you by this holy anoint-ing whatever sins you have committed. Amen."

God, do not let him die.

Canon Crescenzio scanned the room. "The lord wants to speak to his lady, his daughters, his brothers."

Shivering, cold, Beatrice moved as though in a dream. She and Clare knelt on Father's right, Mother and Catherine on his left. The uncles clustered around.

Mother's tiny, slender hand clasped Father's large fist. "We're here, my lord."

Father's eyelids flickered open. "My lady," he whispered, turning slowly to Ortolana, "Forgive me my faults for I have always loved you." Slowly he lifted his right hand to her face, tenderly stroked her cheek. "Pray for me."

"Until the day I die, I will pray for you." Mother's voice was deeper than Beatrice had ever heard it.

"Bicetta." Father called Beatrice by his pet name for her. "And Caterina. Do good in your studies and your duties. Obey your mother and uncles." Father stroked a lock of Catherine's sand-col-ored hair that was tumbling across her cheek. Then his blood-black-ened fingers pushed Beatrice's auburn hair away from her face. "May you marry fine, loving lords. Pray for me, eh?"

Beatrice nodded. Words would not come.

"Chiarita." Father slowly reached toward Clare and flicked her blond curls away from her forehead. Clare took his hand and pressed it against her cheek.

Father's breaths came deeply. "Chiarita, you wish…to remain a virgin for Christ…. May God bless you….When you give your life to Jesus…pray for me."

Trembling, Clare pressed Father's hand to her lips and kissed it tenderly. "Grazie, Father. I will always pray for you. I love you."

Father nodded weakly. "Lord Monaldo…will be your father…. Treat him with respect…love…obedience."

Father coughed, caught his breath. "Monaldo," he whispered, "you are now lord…of this household. Promise…that you will care always…for my lady."

Monaldo knelt by Father's right side and placed his massive right hand over Father's heart.

"I promise."

"Promise…that you will not oppose…Chiarita."

"I promise."

"And that…you will support…Bicetta and Caterina…in whatever they wish to do."

"I promise."

Father coughed, caught his breath. The red blotch on the bandage was widening.

"All my brothers," Father gasped, "support my household…. Care for them…. Be generous to the poor…. Manage the estates well.

"All here," Father's voice rose in volume as he slowly looked about the room. "Forgive…my offenses. Continue…faithfully…. Pray for me."

Staccato-like assent came from around the room.

Father's gaze lifted upward. "Our Father…who art in heaven…holy is Your name." A spasm shook him. A gasp broke from his mouth. Then Father's eyes closed, his head fell back and turned slightly to the left.

Catherine screamed.

"Damn!" Monaldo cursed, his hand still over Father's heart.

Canon Crescenzio dropped to his knees. The others followed. "Come to his aid, O saints of God. Come forth to meet him, angels of the Lord, receiving his soul, presenting it to the Lord Most High."

PART THREE

On Bended Knee
to the Father

~ 10 ~

Bishop Guido

Sasso del Maloloco, Commune of Assisi (Early March, 1212) ~
Bishop Guido and his servant were guiding their mounts along a
winding, rocky path that led to a hodgepodge of grottoes in the
steep, mountainous area called Sasso del Maloloco. Francis and
his friars had made hermitages of the caves, calling them their
Carceri, their holy prison, where, periodically, they came to be
alone with God.

On this cool spring morning, the two men kept their horses to a
slow walk, pushing out of their way the branches that overhung the
path, puddled with melting snow and pocked with hoof prints. Who
had ridden this way earlier? They had to be part of the secret meeting that Francis asked Guido to attend.

Self-assured and confident, Guido owned and managed half of all
the commune's land. Often he browbeat into submission anyone who
disagreed with him. Once he used his fists to get his way. He coordi-
nated an entire retinue of servants, farmhands, canons, knights, and
policy makers. He had overcome a great many irate lords and powerful merchants. Yet he was soft where Francis was concerned.

Guido had liked Francis the merchant for regularly praising
Guido's choice of cloth. He had admired Francis the religious that
snowy day six years ago when Francis had given up everything for
God. Now he loved Francis like a son.

Unlike other self-styled reformers, Francis did nothing without
his bishop's permission. Yet he would not allow Guido to make life
easier for the friars. Francis insisted on being as poor as Christ and
trusting God. Therefore, he refused to take sides in Guido's political battles. He preached peace based on equality instead of peace
based on treaties, concessions, and pacts of protection. Guido had a
million concerns and obligations, it seemed. Francis had one—to
serve God in humility, poverty, and love. No wonder Guido often
envied the friars.

Ahead through tangled, bare, holm oak branches, Guido spied two tethered horses. He recognized the trappings. Offreduccio horses. Now what?

"Pace e bene, Lord Bishop."

Guido returned the greeting from diminutive, gray-haired Father Silvestro, whose quick sharp steps always reminded Guido of a hopping sparrow. The former canon of the Cathedral del San Rufino looked healthy and happy in his patched tunic. Silvestro tethered the bishop's horses, left the servant with them, and led Guido to a grotto in the cliff. Just outside the grotto, four figures stood chatting. Brother Francis. Brother Philip. Lady Clare. Lady Bona.

Smiling and greeting Guido, Francis led the way into the torchlit, smoky cave. Guido and Clare followed while Philip and Bona remained outside.

A distance into the grotto, a crude stool sat in the center of a straw pile. Knowing that it was for him, Guido straddled the stool and plopped his huge frame onto it, then drew his fur-lined green cloak around his arms and chest to keep warm. Like eager students, Francis and Clare sat on the straw, directly in front of him.

"Lord Bishop," Francis began, "Christiana..."

Francis's pet name startled Guido. An eighteen-year-old noblewoman familiarly called Christiana—Christian woman—by a man her social inferior? The term referred to women recluses who lived in and around Assisi, enclosed in tiny cells adjoined to churches and devoted to prayer and counsel.

"...begs your blessing to begin a public life of penance."

The Lady Clare a public penitent in a sackcloth tunic?

Guido slowly shook his head. "No, my lady. Women of your class embrace penance at home, as your mother has done. Or they enter convents for women of your class."

"Lord Bishop, the convents are too rich," Clare politely pointed out.

Guido felt the hair on his neck begin to rise. Many of the convents were under his control. "Noble virgins enter convents. Or they are penitents at home or in an anchorage or a community such as that at Panzo."

Clare shook her head. "I want poverty and my God, like Father Francis."

Guido turned to Francis. "Have you proposed this?"

"I have proposed it," Clare said.

Guido grunted. He leaned forward and looked Clare directly in the eye. "My lady, do you know what can happen if you wander about as the Lesser Brothers do? Lustful men do not honor a penitential habit."

"Christiana wishes to be enclosed in a convent," Francis said.

"A poor convent," Clare added.

"Impossible," Guido said. "There are no poor convents."

"We wish to create one," Francis offered. "At San Damiano."

The abandoned church belonged to Guido. "San Damiano is no place for a woman to live."

"Religious consecrated to God lived there once," Francis said. "Builders tell me that we can lower the church floor and build a dormitory above the church. We can construct a few other necessary buildings, all poor. Some of my friars will go and beg for the women and say Mass for them."

"What women?"

"The ones who will join Christiana."

"Who would that be?"

"God knows," Francis said.

Was this God's new revelation?

"You want me to give you San Damiano."

"I don't want to own it," Clare qualified. "Just use it."

Guido slapped his hands against his thighs and rose. He looked at Clare's idealistic young face. "My lady, your uncle Lord Monaldo is one of the commune's most powerful lords. He was your family's most angry member when Brother Rufino and Brother Angelo joined Brother Francis. How do you suppose he will react to your decision?"

"Before he died, Father made my uncle promise not to oppose my vocation."

"Lord Favarone would assume that you wish to enter one of the convents of Assisi."

"My father would not oppose me."

"Yes, he would. So will Lord Monaldo, no matter what he promised. Women are physically weak, silly, and feeble of mind. They cannot live as the Lesser Brothers do."

"Please, Lord Bishop," Clare pleaded, "do not oppose God's plan. Permit me to embrace poverty as Christ did."

Guido pounded a fist into his palm. How could he control this woman?

"My lady, you do not need my permission to embrace a public life of penance."

Clare's gaze was penetrating. "I would like your blessing. I do not wish to do anything against the Church."

"This is not against the Church," Guido said.

"Will you tonsure her, Lord Bishop?" Francis asked.

"No, I will not tonsure her. She may tonsure herself. Or you may do it, or your friars. If God is calling the lady into this, I cannot oppose it. But I will have nothing to do with it. If Lord Monaldo comes to me, as he did about Brother Angelo and Brother Rufino, I will send him to both of you. I accept no responsibility for this decision."

"Palm Sunday is the beginning of Holy Week, of Jesus' Passion," Francis said. "Christiana would like to begin her life of penance then."

Palm Sunday was two weeks hence.

"How is this to happen?"

"One of my friars and I will accompany Lady Clare to Saint Mary of the Angels. At night, when her family is asleep."

"How is the lady to leave the city? The gates will be guarded and locked."

"Your own palace adjoins the wall and your own watchmen guard your gate," Francis said.

Guido shook his fist at Francis. "So you want me to tell my guards to open my gate for Lady Clare! For certain Lord Monaldo will show up at my palace."

"I want you to tell the watchmen to open the gate for some friars."

Francis was amazing. "Lady Clare in friar's garb? You have not forgotten a detail, have you?"

Francis was grinning.

Guido tried to look severe.

"Where is the lady to stay after you receive her at Saint Mary of the Angels?"

"At the monastery of San Paolo della Abbadesse until San Damiano is ready. That is, if you will ask the nuns there to accept her temporarily—as a servant, Lord Bishop."

San Paolo, a monastery of nuns under Guido's control. And one that had the privilege of asylum. If Clare's family tried to take her from San Paolo, they would suffer automatic excommunication. They would be placed outside the Church and unable to receive its sacraments. San Paolo also commanded armed forces to defend anyone seeking sanctuary. Francis was smart to think of taking Clare to San Paolo.

"I have to think about this."

"Will you know by Palm Sunday?" Francis could be so persistent.

"Let me think." Guido paced the cave. *Lord, give me an idea.* And, just like that, an idea came. An idea that would buy him time.

"My lady, you will be in the Cathedral del San Rufino on Palm Sunday. Brother Francis, you must be there as well. When I distribute the olive branches, do not come up, my lady."

"Do not come up?" Clare asked, incredulous.

Of course, the suggestion was startling. All the women came up for olive branches.

"If I agree to these plans, I will bring a branch to you. That will be a sign that I have told my watchmen to let friars through my gate and that the nuns at San Paolo have agreed to accept you. But if I do not give you a branch, you will have to think of an alternate plan."

"Grazie, Lord Bishop," Francis said. "May we begin the renovations on San Damiano tomorrow?"

Guido grabbed Francis by the shoulders and shook him playfully. "I have not yet decided to give you San Damiano. Let the lady live at San Paolo first. Maybe she will want to stay."

"Lord Bishop," Clare protested, "San Paolo is rich."

Guido cleared his throat. "If I approve this plan, you will stay there out of obedience. If you do not like convent life under the Benedictine Rule, I will permit you to transfer to the community at Sant'Angelo in Panzo." The women there were a holy community of penitential recluses who supported themselves by selling cheese and wool from their flocks and farms. The women had no definite rule but were subject to Guido.

"Sant'Angelo is not poor," Francis offered.

"Poverty is not the only virtue, Brother." Guido tried to look stern as he stared down into the two young, disappointed faces. "Obedience is the most salutary form of penance, Lady Clare. If both San Paolo and Sant'Angelo are unsuitable, we will discuss San Damiano. That is, if I approve this plan, which," he emphasized, "I have not yet done."

Clare looked from Francis to Guido. "Lord Bishop, I will go anywhere as long as I may observe the holy poverty that I have promised to the Lord and to Father Francis."

~ 11 ~

Brother Francis Bernardone

Offreduccio House, Assisi (PALM SUNDAY NIGHT, MARCH 18, 1212) ~
In the darkness, Francis and Brother Leo sat with their backs against
a corner wall of the Offreduccio house. They had come here at dusk
when the city was falling asleep after a day of Mass, processions, and
feasting. They had tried to doze, waiting.

How Francis's heart had leaped when, at today's Palm Sunday
Mass, Bishop Guido had descended from the altar and given Clare
an olive branch! After Mass, Francis remained in the cathedral to
pray in gratitude and Clare had remained too, kneeling before the
altar with Lady Pacifica beside her, for Lady Bona was spending Holy
Week in Rome. How right that Clare's espousal to the poor Jesus
should take place this holy night on which Jesus had begun His suffering, culminating in his death and resurrection!

"Father Francis."

The light whisper woke him. Before him stood two women, their
faces well hidden by the hoods of their penitential habits.

"Brother Leo." Francis shook the shoulder of the square-headed
priest of Assisi. Leo awoke with a start and leaped to his feet.

In silence the four made their way across the torchlit Piazza del
San Rufino. They walked in the light so that watchmen could see
them. No one stopped them or called for them to halt.

Francis marveled at what was happening. This was the woman he
had seen in that long-ago vision, walking these same streets. The
daughter of a knight, barefoot and in rags. *Grazie, my Lord.*

They came to the bishop's palace. Guido's watchman nodded to
them. His guard unlocked the bishop's small, personal gate, letting
the foursome out of the city. On the other side of the wall Brothers
Bernardo and Peter waited, bearing torches.

Wordlessly, the group began the steep descent from the city to
the plain, moving toward the Strada Francesca. They would follow

the Strada Francesca northwest until it fed into the Strada della Porziuncola. They would follow that road south to the church of Saint Mary of the Angels.

The descent to the plain was steep and the ladies, like the friars, were barefoot. Giving no sign that their feet hurt, the women were keeping pace with the men. Down, down. They had reached the Strada della Porziuncola a while ago. The incline began to level off as they approached the plain. The torches of the friars cast light across the road and on the trees looming on either side. The group seemed to be hurrying through a black tunnel, illumined by the fire of God.

The party reached the little church of Saint Mary of the Angels. From the torchlit church across the dark clearing came the deep, melodious chanting of the friars.

The men led the women to a small hut. Lighting a candle from one of the torches, Francis dripped a bit of wax onto the single table in the hut, then stuck the candle into it. He nodded at the women, then left the hut, proceeding to the chapel with his men.

Moments later, Clare appeared in the chapel doorway, the light from the candle in her hand casting her in an angelic glow. Her face was radiant, her smile brighter than Francis had ever seen. She was dressed as magnificently as a bride, as Francis had directed, in the same deep scarlet gown, studded with sapphires, that she had worn to the Palm Sunday Mass. Jewels and ribbons wove through her long blond curls. Pacifica, in a simple, mustard-colored gown, accompanied her.

As rehearsed, Brothers Bernardo and Peter, each carrying candles, approached Lady Clare and led her to the candlelit altar of the russet-walled church. There, Clare knelt at the foot of the image of the gentle Virgin surrounded by angels, glorious in her blue mantle and corona of stars as she entered eternal glory. The friars began to chant the Office of Vigils. Clare raised her eyes to the little tower in which the Eucharistic Lord resided.

The chanting for Vigils ceased. In a deep, resonant voice, Brother Angelo began to read. "From the Gospel of John, chapter twelve, verses one to eleven." Everyone made the sign of the cross. "Then Mary took a pound of ointment of spikenard, very costly, and anointed the feet of Jesus and wiped his feet with her hair. The house was filled with the odor of the ointment...."

Joy surged through Francis's heart. Mary had given all to Christ, as Clare was about to do.

The second reading was from a commentary by Saint Augustine. "Which of you wishes to be a faithful soul? Join Mary in anointing the feet of Jesus with precious ointment...that is follow in the Lord's footsteps by living virtuously.... If you have surplus goods, give them to the poor, and you will have dried the Lord's feet with your hair...."

Clare had sold all her inheritance and given it to the poor. She was now willing to give up the only thing she had left. Herself.

As the cantor began to chant, Francis walked from the group, scissors in hand. He took Clare's stubby candle, dripped wax onto the altar, and placed the candle into it. In a smooth motion, Clare plucked the jewels and ribbons from her hair, dropping them to the floor. Then, with her face lifted to her Eucharistic Lord, she waited.

Peter and Bernardo came forward and stood, one on either side of her with Francis behind. Francis placed his hands on Clare's head and prayed silently. *Lord, thank You for this moment. Bless our sister Clare. May she be Yours forever.*

As Peter and Bernardo lifted the ash-blond locks, Francis began to cut, dropping great, soft clumps to the floor. When Clare's hair was cut above her ears, a sign of penitence and of consecration to God, Francis raised her to her feet, handing her the candle from the altar and two lengths of cloth—one black, one white. He glimpsed her expansive smile, the tears on her cheeks glistening like flecks of gold.

Carrying a candle, Brother Leo came forward and, wordlessly, led Clare, followed by a weeping Pacifica, out of the chapel. In the chapel, the friars knelt in silent prayer. Leo returned and joined them.

Moments later, Clare appeared again in the doorway, dressed in the rough, shabby tunic she had worn out of the city. The rim of a white veil peeked out from beneath a black veil, totally covering her cropped hair. White for virginity. Black for penance.

Clare knelt at the altar. Francis moved forward to speak.

"Let us look, this night, to the Good Shepherd who suffered the passion of the cross to save His sheep. The sheep of the Lord followed Him in tribulation and persecution, in insult and hunger, in infirmity and temptation, and they have received everlasting life from the Lord because of these things. Let us praise the Lord this night for Sister Clare's decision to truly be a lamb of His flock."

The friars began to chant their final prayers. As they ended, Clare rose and silently left the chapel. Pacifica, Francis, and Philip followed, each taking a torch from the outer wall braces of the Porziuncola. The quartet started down the road. The air was crisp and tingly cool. A pale frost sparkled on the rutted road and the dried leaves. They would reach San Paolo della Abbadesse before dawn.

❦ 12 ❦

Lord Monaldo di Offreduccio

Offreduccio House, Assisi (MONDAY OF HOLY WEEK, MARCH 19, 1212) ∼ As he approached the stairs to the Offreduccio house, Lord Monaldo sensed something amiss. When he had left his steed at the stable, the grooms had averted their eyes, as they had done when Lord Favarone had died.

Monaldo dashed upstairs, the wood thudding under his heavy boots. Dwarfing the well-muscled house watchman Ioanni di Ventura, Monaldo shot him a question. "Is something wrong?"

"Last night the Lady Clare left...secretly. Through the door of the dead."

The door of the dead! That obscure, barricaded door was opened only to carry a corpse feet first out of the house, to send a bride to her wedding, or to flee an enemy.

Monaldo threw open the door of the Offreduccio house and raced down the corridors until he came to the seldom-used hall of the dead. The hall led to a small, second-story door which had no steps to the street. To exit the door of the dead, one had to leap. Those who left by this door were, in a real or symbolic sense, dead to the family.

The door was ajar. The light streaming in teased him closer. He walked slowly, trying to absorb what he saw. The thick wooden beams that had barricaded the door from the inside had been moved aside. The door was pushed open against the rubble. Monaldo stepped over the mess and peered outdoors into the empty street.

"Damn!" Monaldo slammed the door shut. He rammed into place the ponderous iron bar that bolted the door, then heaved the wooden beams against the door, barricading it again. How could a young woman have the strength to unblock that door, leap down into the street, and disappear?

He flung himself through the halls to the women's sewing room and threw open the door. Lady Ortolana, Lady Beatrice, Lady Catherine, and Lady Cristiana, visiting daughter of Lord Bernardo da Suppo, were sitting there, their sewing idle in their laps. They turned to him, conversation dying on their lips, horror spreading across their faces.

"Who helped Lady Clare out?" he demanded.

No one had. Even the servants had been questioned. Clare had left behind a note saying she had taken Jesus as her spouse. About an hour ago, Brother Bernardo di Quintavalle had returned her clothing.

Lady Pacifica was also gone from the Guelfuccio house.

Monaldo sent for the other Offreduccio knights. Lord Ugolino and his son Lord Martino. Lord Paolo and his son Lord Bernardino. Lord Scipione and his son Lord Paolo. Lord Ranieri. Others. They would ride to the Porziuncola and bring her back.

Monaldo did not have to threaten Francis for information. "She is consecrated to God and has sanctuary at San Paolo delle Abbadesse in Bastia," Francis told him.

The knights galloped to Bastia. Monaldo tried to calm himself. If Lady Clare had gone to San Paolo, the situation was not so unthinkable. San Paolo was a powerful Benedictine monastery whose nuns, all members of the highest nobility, lived in wealth and influence. The opulent stronghold that stretched along the banks of the deep Chiagio River was the perfect place for an Offreduccio who insisted on marrying God.

The abbess, in her tasteful black habit, politely instructed the knights to wait in the little pink-and-beige stone church of San Paolo, but to tether their horses outside. The knights, who usually rode their steeds into church, complied.

The men were standing awkwardly in the white-plastered church when the abbess entered through a small door on the left. With her came a black-veiled, limping penitent clothed in the poor gray tunic of the Lesser Brothers, a rope knotted around her waist, her feet bare against the red stone floor.

Lady Clare.

Every bitter emotion that Monaldo ever felt toward this niece surfaced. Her childish insistence on taking beggars to Perugia. Her weird, extreme fasting that had thinned her plump and pleasant face. Her rejection of marriage that would have allied another powerful family with the Offreduccios. Her refusal to sell her own and part of her sister Beatrice's inheritance to the family, defrauding them of what was theirs and giving it to the poor. Now, dishonoring her family further by making herself a pauper.

Monaldo tried to calm himself. "We have come to take you home."

"You are ill," Lord Ugolino said kindly. "We will obtain the best doctor."

"I need no doctor," Clare said firmly. "I am not going home."

"Your mother is worried," Lord Paolo noted.

"Tell her that I am fine."

Monaldo stuffed down his impatience. "Lady Clare, your place is at home."

"You have always wished to become a nun," observed Lord Ranieri, one of Clare's rejected suitors. "Why not as befits your class? You appear a pauper."

"My dear lord, this dress befits a spouse of the poor Jesus," Clare tenderly replied. "And your wife is well?"

"Very well."

"You do not know what is best," Monaldo declared. "No noblewoman would do what you have done."

"We care about you," Ugolino said. "Perhaps your fasting or your father's death has affected your mind. Come with us and recover."

Just then a bell pealed, its rich tones reverberating through the chapel. The side door opened and the abbess appeared. "I hope that you had a lovely visit," she said sweetly. "The Lady Clare must come now for prayers."

Clare bowed to the knights. "Good-bye, my lords. Please tell my household that I am well." Limping slightly, she followed the abbess through the side doorway and closed the door.

Monaldo slammed his fist into a thick pillar. "Tomorrow we return."

The knights returned Tuesday, Wednesday, Thursday. Each day they argued with Clare. Each day she disappeared through the door with the abbess.

Then came Good Friday. Clare needed to be home for Easter. On Easter, noble maidens dressed in their finest clothes and stunned the young nobles at Mass. If she did not return home by Easter, she would be lost forever.

The altar was draped with a plain white cloth. Gone was the little tower, off to the side, that held the Eucharist. The red cross traced on the pedestal of the altar appeared to be painted with blood. The church was as still as death.

Again the abbess ushered Clare through the side doorway. "Please respect the solemnity of the day on which Jesus was crucified," she requested. "Keep your visit short and your voices down."

Down? How? For four days Clare had refused to listen to common sense. She was a stubborn and spoiled child. She needed to know what she had done.

Monaldo stared at his niece, standing so tall and unshakable next to the white-draped altar. "You have done a detestable thing," Monaldo hissed. "You have made yourself a slave of these nuns who are less well-bred than you. You are more repulsive than pig's dung. You have dragged the Offreduccio name through mud and cast it upon a manure heap."

The words were spilling out, intense with fury, disappointment, and shock. "You—the one your father spoiled, his little Chiarita. You have sullied his memory. This is no honor to God. This is defiant idiocy. You have made the Offreduccios the target of Assisi gossip, the point of the crudest jokes."

Clare began to tremble.

"You despicable and unruly child. Do you know how many people you have wounded? Even if you came home now, you could not fully undo the destruction. I am ashamed to call you my brother's daughter. You are unworthy of Lord Favarone."

Clare's face was blanched, tears streaming down her cheeks. Blinking, she turned briefly toward the crucifix behind her, then dropped to her knees. She took the altar cloth in her right hand and lifted her sorrowful face toward the knights.

Monaldo knew what she meant by touching the cloth. She was claiming the right of sanctuary. To touch her now would be to commit sacrilege, to incur excommunication.

Sacrilege and excommunication could be lifted. Would Bishop Guido hold Monaldo's taking of Clare against him? It was Monaldo's duty to uphold the family's reputation. If Clare would not be sensible, he would use force. If the knights who were pledged to defend this monastery tried to interfere, the Offreduccio knights would fight.

Monaldo leaped up the pink-and-white marble steps that led to the raised altar. Grabbing Clare's right arm, he yanked her to her feet, pulling the altar cloth awry.

In one swift motion, Clare raised her left hand and tore the veil from her head. Her eyes and Monaldo's met in a frigid stare.

Her head was practically naked.

Monaldo dropped her arm as if it were a snake. He recoiled from her, stepping backward from the altar, almost tripping down the steps, staring in horror at her intense, tear-streaked face.

Never had Monaldo looked upon a woman's naked head. A woman's flowing hair was her crown, her riches, her beauty, her modesty, her wealth.

Clare's right hand slipped from the altar cloth, now skewed crazily across the altar. She joined both hands in front of her chest and bowed her head.

Was this was the woman who had never tarried near windows lest she spark lustful thoughts in passersby? The woman whose sleeves had always modestly covered her wrists and whose train hid her feet? Only a woman consecrated to God would cut off her hair. The tonsure was a definitive act, placing Clare securely under the guardianship of the Church. Because Clare was tonsured, Church law forbade the knights to take her home. Nor would they wish to. A woman without hair was as worthless as a lame steed.

"You should be ashamed." Monaldo spat out the words as if they were flaming embers. "You have destroyed your beauty and your value to any man and to your family. You are no longer an Offreduccio or the daughter of Lord Favarone."

He turned to his wide-eyed knights. His voice was quavering with rage. "Let's go home. From now on the Lady Clare is dead to this household."

～ 13 ～

Lady Catherine di Favarone

Strada di San Martino, Assisi (APRIL 4, 1212) ～ Lady Catherine and Lady Bona left after Mass and headed out the Porta San Giorgio toward Panzo. They walked past fields of fresh grass, grazing sheep, and poor, scattered cottages. For the first time in sixteen days, fourteen-year-old Catherine felt hopeful. Until Clare left, Catherine had never spent a day without her. The past two weeks were a bad dream. Clare gone as if dead. Pacifica, too. Her uncles furious. When Lady Bona had arrived home from Rome, Catherine had asked her to accompany Catherine to Sant'Angelo d'Panzo, a women's community south of Assisi where, as all Assisi knew, Brother Francis had moved Clare.

Above the road, the women saw a foreboding cliff, the Sasso Cupo, the cliff of dark stone. They passed the crumbling ruin of the Church of San Martino. Below, the dry streambed of Rigo Secco twisted like a scar. The women arrived at the monastery, which clung to the side of Monte Subasio.

All was quiet. Bona and Catherine walked up to the first building and peeked in at long dining tables.

"Are you looking for someone?" A gray-robed woman in sandals and black veil had come up behind them.

"For Lady Clare and Lady Pacifica," Bona said. "We're their sisters."

The penitent burst into a smile. "I see resemblances. Come."

The woman led the way to a large garden struggling for growth beyond the buildings. Several women in gray tunics were hoeing or pulling weeds. One weeder, Lady Pacifica, was dressed in a prim cap and mustard-colored gown.

Within moments, Clare was embracing Catherine, and Pacifica, Bona.

The superior sent the women to the refectory until prayer time.

So much love to share! So many stories to tell! Clare and Pacifica told of scrubbing floors, planting vegetables, making cheese. Bona told of her pilgrimage. Catherine told how the Offreduccio women spoke of Clare, although Lord Monaldo had forbidden it.

The stories and the laughing went on until prayer time, which was followed by a light meal of eggs, spring greens, and cool water. The superior allowed the women to continue to visit.

"What is it like to be married to Jesus?" Catherine asked. "I have always dreamed of marrying a lord. But now I sometimes think of marrying Jesus."

"I have prayed for this!" With her face glowing, Clare tried to explain her peace and joy. Love of Christ was like a sweet fragrance, a breath of air, a powerful embrace! "Do not be afraid. Run to Him joyfully, swiftly; abandon yourself totally to Him. Let nothing keep you from Jesus, who calls you into perfect love. He will give you the grace you need." Clare squeezed Catherine's hands warmly. "Father Francis will visit us tomorrow. Do you wish him to tonsure you?"

Catherine was not sure.

Late in the afternoon, Bona left, accompanied to the city gates by Pacifica and by two penitential women who returned to Panzo. Dusk came. Evening prayers. A light supper. Night prayer. Darkness. Silence.

Clare led Catherine to a small, tight hermitage, embraced her, and went off to her own hut. Lying on straw, Catherine drew two shabby blankets over herself. How could she sleep? Being tonsured tomorrow was thrilling, frightening. Did she want to be married to a lord or to the Lord?

Catherine was accustomed to plump mattresses and quilts, not straw and thin blankets. She was used to hoof beats, clamorous "Goodnights," and beggars arguing in the piazza, not to shuffling leaves, peeping frogs, and mournful, distant wolf howls. She always slept through the nightly ringing of the cathedral bells that called the canons to Matins, but tonight she was still awake when Sant'-Angelo's bell rang. She arose with the bell to pray Matins.

In the chapel, aglow with oil lamps, the women's chanted prayers graced the night with praise of God. Catherine could have this every night. She could have Jesus. Who else did she need?

When Matins ended, the women filed silently back to their hermitages. Whispering Christ's name, Catherine fell asleep.

Dawn came. More prayer, Lauds and Prime. Mass with the priest who lived at the hermitage. The end of silence. The women had a drink of water and went to work. Catherine and Clare were sent to weed the herb garden. The two sisters were chattering about Francis when Catherine heard the frenzied pounding of many boots.

Her heart froze.

"Lady Catherine. We have come to escort you home."

Lord Monaldo's huge frame seemed bigger than the garden.

As Catherine backed away from his looming shadow, she could barely speak. "I do not wish to leave my sister."

Monaldo moved toward her. Other knights emerged from the forest. Monaldo's son Lord Francesco. Lord Ugolino and his sons Lord Monaldo and Lord Martino. Lord Paolo and his son Lord Bernardino. Lord Scipione and his son Lord Paolo. Lord Giorgio di Ugone and his son Lord Paolo. Lord Ranieri. Twelve Offreduccio knights.

To the left there was a swift flash of blue wool and brown fur as a huge hand smashed into Catherine's cheek, knocking her to the ground. Instinctively she covered her face. Fists were pummeling her, feet kicking her. She shrieked, her face still covered. Someone grabbed her hair, banged her head against the soil. The pain in her scalp was unbearable. She was being dragged by her hair.

Cursing. Shouts. High-pitched, pleading women's voices.

Huge, thick arms were grabbing her, hoisting her. "Help me, dear sister!" she screamed. "Do not let them take me away from Jesus Christ like this."

She kicked and fought the knights as they dragged her through the brambles to the steep bank of the dry Rigo Secco. Above the cursing and shrieking, like a sweet, angelic song, Clare was pleading, "God, protect Lady Catherine! Keep her constant in her resolve! Protect her from these violent men!"

Something hard slammed into Catherine's chest with a terrific force. She caught her breath and everything went black.

She felt herself coming out of darkness the way one comes out of sleep. She could hear voices through her grogginess.

"I can't lift her."

"All together!"

"You! Farmers! Help us lift the lady."

Hands were grabbing her everywhere. She was groggy, throbbing with pain.

"There're twelve of us. Five peasants. Lift her!"

More pulling, grabbing.

Clare's voice again, strong. "God, give Lady Catherine your strength and perseverance! Protect her from these violent men!"

Lord Ugolino's voice. "She must have eaten lead to weigh this much."

Monaldo's demand. "Get up! Now. Or you die."

Catherine would die. *Oh, my Jesus, forgive me. Into Your hands I commend my spirit.*

"Arragh!" The shriek was unearthly, prolonged.

Men's voices. "What's the matter?"

Monaldo's anguished groan. "I can't...move...my arm. No! Don't touch it! The pain. You'll break it. I...can't...move it!"

"Go home." Clare's voice was commanding. "God wants my sister here. You cannot lift her. You cannot strike her. Go home."

Silence.

"Entrust Lady Catherine to my care and to God."

Muttering.

"Go home."

"Let's go." Monaldo's words were trembling. "No! *Don't touch my arm!*"

Shuffling. Boots moving away.

A gentle hand on her forehead, brushing her hair aside. Clare's soothing voice. "Dear sister, are you all right?"

Women's voices, all asking how badly she was injured.

Quite suddenly, Catherine felt strong and pain free. She pushed herself to a sitting position.

Beyond the clucking cluster of women, down the path away from Sant'Angelo, the knights retreated. Lord Monaldo's right arm was raised, bobbing along with him.

Catherine stood and brushed off her tattered gown. "I have to become a penitent. I can't wear this."

"Our relatives have halfway tonsured you," Clare said. She plucked a great clump of sandy brown hair from some brambles.

"You are more than half bald," Pacifica remarked.

"I must thank God for delivering me," Catherine said in awe.

"We shall all thank God," the superior announced.

In the chapel, the group fell to their knees, then, one by one, the women left to return to work.

Catherine felt a sturdy hand on her shoulder. Brother Francis and Brother Bernardo were standing beside her. *Oh, sweet God, now I shall become only Yours.* With her thumping heart, Catherine began to rise. Francis shook his head.

"My lady, do you wish to embrace the penitential life?"

"More than ever."

"Christiana, stand next to your sister."

Clare stood and placed her hand on Catherine's shoulder. Catherine knelt erect, her chin firm, her eyes closed. *Jesus, make me true to You, worthy of You, loyal. Make me Your spouse.*

Her hair was being lifted, cut. She tried to concentrate on her praying and on the cutting, so that she would forever remember this moment.

Hands pressed her skull. "Christ, the innocent Lamb of God," Francis was saying, "was beset by a pack of vicious men and killed for the world's sins. In memory of today's battle against vicious men who wished to tear you from Jesus and take your life, you shall henceforth be named after Agnus Dei, the Lamb of God. Lady Agnes."

Agnes. She had not expected a new name. But it seemed perfect. She liked it.

PART FOUR

To Dwell in the Church
of San Damiano

~ 14 ~

Lady Pacifica di Guelfuccio

Sant'Angelo d'Panzo, Panzo, Italy (MAY 1212) ~ Lady Pacifica threw herself to the rough wooden floor of her tiny hut and wept. Lady Clare and Lady Agnes had just left with Brother Francis to live as enclosed sisters at San Damiano, where they would have no servants, not even Pacifica.

She felt for the cross, two knotty sticks that she had bound together at right angles with a length of lace from one of her gowns. Pacifica clenched the cross tightly, squeezing her fingernails into her palms. Her mind swirled with thoughts of Clare and Catherine, now Agnes, whom she had known since birth. Her chest seemed about to split with sobbing.

You don't have to leave them. You can be a sister.

Pacifica gave a little gasp of surprise at this quiet, inner prompting. She had several times rejected the notion, but here it was again, like a mouse come out of hiding when the household sleeps.

She was already doing penance, but secretly. Was God now asking her to make her penitential life public? To be, in others' eyes, more than a pious lady who went to Mass, made pilgrimages, and prayed? To become a public penitent?

How could she ever do that?

Some people shunned, berated, and ridiculed penitents. Others extolled them. Penitents were to model holiness. Those who set a poor example gave scandal to the Church.

Pacifica shuddered, her hands still digging into her palms.

I am a sinner, a bad example of someone who follows You.

The Church had enough bad examples. In Assisi, some clergy were addicted to fornication, drunkenness, gambling, greed, or usury. Wealthy religious houses engaged in lawsuits. Grouchy, stingy, or harsh religious bickered among themselves. Some preached heresy or toyed with schism. No wonder most churches were nearly empty and many were abandoned. Assisians mocked religious even while claiming to practice their faith. Why would she become visibly religious in such an atmosphere?

Yes, Francis and his friars were converting many. Some priests and nuns were growing holier. They were great lights in the darkness, but Pacifica was not as good as they were. She was only a pinprick of light. What good was that?

It's enough light to see the cross.

The revelation startled her.

Lady Clare is starting something very different. You don't want me to join up with that, do You?

I have asked for surrender, not questions.

Lord, You said that prayer and fasting must be done secretly.

Religious garb does not reveal prayer or fasting. It reveals Me.

Pacifica knew what the internal voice meant. In contrast to the clergy and even to Bishop Guido—who dressed like nobility, concealing their tonsures with caps so as to appear as lords—penitents and friars wore poor, ash gray robes of lazzo, the homespun, woolen cloth of peasants. Their tonsures were evident. Garb became a sermon, proclaiming that Christ was important enough to follow radically.

Those who visibly displayed their religion were either praised or rebuked. What would her father, Lady Bona, or her other relatives say if Pacifica went public with her penance?

God, give me courage.

Courage to do God's will, not hers or someone else's. Only doing God's will would make her holy.

For twenty years, Pacifica had toyed with the idea of entering a convent. Something always held her back. Now she was faced with a decision. Assisi? Or San Damiano?

Surrender means total surrender.

Pacifica laid the cross on the floor. In the light coming through the cracks, she could see the cross clearly. She looked for the chink in the wall that was letting in light. Small as a pinprick, it helped light the darkness. That was about all her life as a sister would be.

Pacifica pressed her hand over the cross before rising. She pushed back the reed door and was flooded with light.

She would walk to San Damiano and ask Lady Clare to accept her as a sister.

～ 15 ～

Giovanna

San Damiano, Assisi (LATE FALL, 1212) ～ Giovanna was curled against the wall of the Church of San Damiano. The unbolting of doors awakened her. Tucking her mouse-colored braids beneath the hood of her shabby brown mantle, Giovanna stood and blessed herself with water from a large basin near the church door. Timidly she descended into the dark church, her sturdy bare toes tickling the cool floor. In the apse, a short, silver-haired friar bustled to prepare for Mass. Two noble couples, one old, one young, strode into the church and stood near the altar. Peasants, including Giovanna, a few servants, and farmers, stood in the back.

Giovanna was shepherdess for a Perugian lord whose daughter Lady Benvenuta had come two months ago, in late September, to this convent. Benvenuta's becoming a recluse pauper had baffled her household but encouraged Giovanna. Over a week ago, Giovanna had received permission from her lord's bailiff to come to Assisi while her father tended her sheep and his. She had promised to be back before the full moon.

She wanted to ask these pauper ladies if they would accept her as a pauper servant. Other convents had rejected her because she had never learned to cook the meats, sauces, and sweets that ladies liked—nor could she mend, launder, and scrub to a lady's satisfaction. Pauper ladies, however, might welcome a pauper servant.

Please, Lord. Giovanna sent her prayer toward a carved white dove pressed against the ceiling above the altar. Therein reposed the Eucharistic Lord. God, who whispered to Giovanna in nature, dwelt totally in that holy bread, the Lesser Brothers preached. How badly Giovanna wanted to be near Him!

Mass began, proceeded, ended. The noble couples approached a speaking grill in the apse and pulled a cord. On the other side of the wall, a bell chimed. The snap of a bolt. The sliding of a door. Unintelligible low voices.

After some time, the couples left the church while a waiting farmer approached the grill, rang the bell, spoke to someone. He chatted a bit, then left—on a rotating turn in the wall—a plump sack. The turn swiveled into the monastery revealing its curved outer side, then rotated outward again, the empty sack returned. The farmer took his sack and left.

Giovanna was alone. She had waited for this moment. She had dreaded it.

With her eyes glancing at the dove, Giovanna cautiously approached the black-curtained grill and pulled the bell cord. The sounds of a shutter unbolting, sliding, came from the other side of the grill.

"Pace e bene. May I help you?" The voice came through the black curtain.

Giovanna swallowed. "Would you be in need of a servant, my lady?"

"Just one moment. You must speak to Sister Clare."

The unseen shutter slid shut, was bolted.

Please, God.

The unbolting, sliding sound drew Giovanna's attention from the dove. The black curtain at the grill was being lifted. Giovanna was looking into the beautiful oval face of a black-veiled penitent. The woman was erect; her gaze direct, unwavering, and confident.

"Pace e bene. I am Sister Clare. And you, little one?"

"Giovanna of Perugia, my lady." Giovanna curtsied shakily.

Clare smiled and glanced at a taller penitent who stood near her. "Sister Benvenuta is from Perugia."

The sister was tall and sturdy, her deep, dark eyes set close to her nose. So like Giovanna's lord. "My father and I tend your father's sheep," Giovanna offered.

"Does my father mistreat you?" Lady Benvenuta asked, her dark eyes tender.

"Oh, no, my lady." Giovanna curtsied again. "I ask to be a servant here to be near my Lord Christ." She glanced at the dove.

"We have no servants here. All we sisters serve each other." Sister Clare's deep voice was gentle, her blue eyes kind. "Do you wish to become a sister, Giovanna?"

Anguish swept Giovanna. Only ladies could become nuns. "I have no dowry," she stammered.

"You yourself are your dowry. Will you give God yourself?"

Wonder rose in Giovanna's throat. "Is it possible, my lady?"

"Certainly. Do you know how old you are?"

Giovanna calculated quickly. She had begun to tend sheep when her flock's big, spotted ewe, now fifteen years old, had been born. "I am some years older than fifteen."

"Old enough. Giovanna, we sisters wish always to observe the Gospel of our Lord Jesus Christ by living in obedience, without anything of our own, and in chastity. We have promised reverence to our Lord Pope Innocent, to the Roman Church, and to our gracious Father Francis who brought us here. Do you believe all that the Catholic Church teaches? And all the sacraments? Do you use them?"

"Oh, yes!"

"Are you married?"

"No, my lady."

"Would you wish to marry our Lord Jesus and live with us, in prayer, penance, and service?"

"That must be like living in heaven!"

Clare laughed. "To us, it seems so. Not to others. We own nothing."

"I have only what I am wearing. Gladly will I discard it."

"Can you stay to see how we live?"

Giovanna had until the full moon. If she didn't return, she would send Papa a message. Someone else would shepherd her sheep. "I can stay!"

"Good. Now go out of the church and we'll lower the staircase into the monastery. Climb up, and we'll get to know each other."

Giovanna darted out so quickly that she forgot to curtsy.

~⊃ 16 ⊂~

Lady Ginevra di Giorgio di Ugone

Bedroom, House of Lord Giorgio di Ugone, Assisi (LATE SUM-
MER, 1214) ~ Twenty-year-old Lady Ginevra, daughter of Lord
Giorgio di Ugone, was lying in her silk covered bed, trying to sleep.
Neither the heat nor the humidity were keeping her awake. Her
thoughts were.

This morning, at Mother's insistence, she had sorted through
her gowns, discarding the ones she no longer wanted. Some she
had sent to the lepers at San Lazarro, but the better ones she had
taken to the Damianites, who would refashion them into priestly
vestments and altar trappings given free to the churches of the region. She had kept five gowns for herself, and even those she did
not like. Who was she trying to stun with her beauty? Every lord
whom Father was considering as her mate was boring. Ginevra
wrinkled her nose, thinking that in two months she might be sleeping next to one of them.

Ginevra shifted her broad shoulders and lay on her side. Her
freckle-faced sister Lady Emilia was happily married and mother to
a new baby. Her brother Lord Paolo seemed quite content to be a
husband. The problem with Ginevra was God.

Today at San Damino the crucifix that had spoken to Francis
had spoken to Ginevra. And a miracle had happened.

Bored with lords, tournaments, feasts, and silks, Ginevra had
walked with her servants and her lady-in-waiting to the convent.
What had Clare said there? "It's not where you go that's exciting. It's
who you're with. God is here. And He is not boring."

How could that be? Only the new sisters, Giovanna and Felicita,
left the convent at all, and they to beg. The others stayed on six acres
of sloping ground, behind high walls, curtained grills, and bolted
doors. Even Ginevra had to speak to Clare, her best friend, through
a black curtain. The big news at the convent was that the new cat,
fondly named Sister Gatta, had knocked over a candle, alighting

Sister Pacifica's blanket while she slept beneath it. Sister Balbina had smothered the flames with her own blanket, so the damage had been slight. That was the extent of excitement at San Damiano.

Like her namesake Queen Guinevere, Ginevra craved excitement. Sister Agnes's litany of people prayed for and lives changed at San Damiano may have excited Agnes, but not Ginevra.

But then there was that incident with the oil jar. Ginevra had seen the empty jar on the turn for old Brother Bentevenga to take to beg for oil. She had been speaking to Clare when he had limped into the parlor, chastising Clare for playing a joke on him and putting a full oil jar on the turn. Ginevra's servants, who had been waiting by the turn, swore that no one had filled the jar. However it was filled, Clare now had olive oil for the ill sisters without lame Brother Bentevenga begging for it. Brother had oil too, for himself and for the other three grumpy, elderly friars Francis had assigned to the monastery.

Ginevra pressed her hands against her soft mattress. Had the filled oil jar been a miracle?

Miracles happened. Here, in the Cathedral del San Rufino, the relics of Assisi's patron saint San Rufinus had recently been unearthed. Berta, a possessed child, had been dragged kicking and screaming to the crypt, where she was released from her demon. Domina Savia had climbed down into the crypt and had been cured of hysteria. Dropsy, fevers, scrofulas, fistulas—healed.

Then there was that voice from the crucifix. Ginevra had been kneeling, gazing up at it. *Why do I keep coming here?* she had asked. *What is there about this place?*

I AM ABOUT THIS PLACE, the voice had said.

What had Sister Agnes said? "In the silence and privacy of this place, we can speak to Him, know Him, serve Him."

From behind the curtained grill in the parlor, Clare had almost sung. "If only you could be the bride of the King of kings! You would run to Him without a thought of anyone else. You would find Him and cling to Him, and He would embrace you and take you into Himself." Clare's full, deep voice had trembled with passion. "All earthly joys pale at this. All other loves are as nothing. Then you embrace with all your heart the One who is more beautiful than any angel, more noble than any knight, more tender than any spouse. To think of Him brings all delight." The words had spilled from

Clare like a hymn. "To know His kindness is to know all love, to be with Him here is a taste of heaven."

What was love? Or who? Did love live at San Damiano?

I am about this place.

Over the next two months, Ginevra often visited San Damiano. There she found Love, and so she chose Him as her spouse. In His honor, she renamed herself Benedetta, "Woman Blessed by God."

How blessed Sister Benedetta felt to live where God was!

∾ 17 ∾

Brother Francis Bernardone

Church of San Damiano (DECEMBER 1215) ∾ Two friars—homely, scraggly bearded Francis Bernardone and tall, swarthy, black-haired Masseo di Marignano—were praying prostrate below the white dove in which rested the Eucharistic Body of their Lord. Before them loomed the huge golden crucifix that had called Francis to conversion. Francis's thin fingers pressed against the stone floor. Chilling dampness seeped through his worn, much-patched tunic.

My God, is there another way? As one of the fifteen hundred religious delegates to the Fourth Lateran Council last month, Francis had been unable to sway the council regarding the Poor Ladies. How was he to tell Christiana?

Francis respected Christiana. When he had considered retiring from preaching to live a contemplative life, he had consulted Christiana and Brother Silvestro, both of whom told him that God intended him to preach. So Francis had preached through the beautiful Romagna countryside north of here and through most of the Roman peninsula. Periodically he prayed at hermitages, yet he still managed to preach in France and Spain where, at the Cathedral of Saint James in Compostela, God had revealed that the Lesser Brothers would spread throughout the world. In Spain, Francis had contracted a persistent illness sometimes so severe that Bishop Guido often made him recover in the bishop's palace. Today, feeling stronger, he had come to San Damiano. God was silent. Francis pushed to his feet. Within moments, the dreaded meeting began, with Francis and Masseo seated on two rude wooden benches in the parlor and Christiana, Lady Pacifica, and Lady Agnes greeting him from behind the black-curtained grill.

After offering a prayer, Francis began. "I have come to tell you about the council, Christiana."

"Oh, Father, we've been praying for the council ever since Pope Innocent convened it." Christiana's voice was eager. "Were our prayers answered?"

"Some were." He would tell the good things first. "The faithful must now confess and receive the Body and Blood of Christ at least yearly, at Easter. But the council urged more frequent reception, even several times yearly."

"Praise God! We will receive the Body and Blood of our Lord on every solemnity!" Christiana said joyfully.

"The perpetual virginity of Mary is to be stated in the profession of faith."

"God be praised." The voice was Agnes's.

"So that priests will not be ignorant, schools to teach them about the faith will be established. No man may pay to become a priest. Nor can bishops accept money to fill a position. Sacraments must be freely given, with no donation required, although one may give money freely as an alms or thank offering. Nor may relics be sold. No money is to be demanded of anyone wishing to enter religious life. Those who wish entrance should be accepted if they are suitable, without a dowry."

The women were eagerly agreeing with the council's decisions. "Drunkenness and sexual license in the clergy will not be tolerated. Guidelines for the proper care of church buildings and tabernacles must be followed."

Francis paused. The ladies, he knew, would greet the next announcement less enthusiastically. "The Pope proclaimed a Fifth Crusade."

He heard a stifled groan. The ladies wanted the Holy Land to be in Christian hands, but they hated the violent wars against the infidels that would bring it about. The brutal Fourth Crusade had never reached the Holy Land. Instead, the crusaders had viciously pillaged Constantinople and violated its inhabitants. There followed the pitiable Children's Crusade, in which forty thousand unarmed French and German youngsters tried to walk to the Holy Land, believing that the innocent and pure of heart could retake it. All but a few had died of starvation, cold, disease, or drowning—or been captured as Muslim slaves. The survivors had returned home in shame.

"The Crusade will begin in 1219 with Egypt the first to be attacked." Behind the curtain came a thin gasp of horror. "During the next four years of preparation, there is to be a Truce of God."

"Four years of peace everywhere," Christiana breathed. "God be praised."

"No one is to trade with Egypt or with any infidel nation."

"Perhaps the Saracens will surrender the Holy Land without a fight," Pacifica suggested.

Francis doubted it. "Only if the Saracens became Christians."

Christianity reminded him of his gift. From one of his deep pockets, he pulled a small wooden cross in the shape of the capital letter T, the Tau, and poked it through the bottom of the grate.

"Lift the curtain, Christiana, and take this."

The curtain was lifted and the cross plucked from his fingers before the curtain was again lowered.

"The Pope said that this is the shape of the cross on which Christ died."

The women gave soft whistles of reverent wonder.

"Pope Innocent said that only those marked with the sign of the cross—the Tau—will obtain mercy." Francis was quoting the Pope almost word for word. "Those so marked fall into three groups. The crusaders. Those who combat heresy at home. And those who admit to being sinners, who mortify their flesh, and who conform their lives to that of the crucified Savior, as you ladies and we friars try to do."

Now to reveal his wondrous plan. "We will make the Tau the sign of the Lesser Brothers. And of the Poor Ladies, if you agree, Christiana."

"So perfect. So beautiful. How could we not agree?"

Francis smiled. "Brother Masseo made that Tau for San Damiano, and others for the Porziuncola and the Carceri."

"Grazie."

Francis pressed on. "The council condemned the heresies. Strongly. Some heretical groups practice strange penances. You can almost recognize a heresy by its penitential practices."

No word came from behind the curtain.

"Do you still sleep on vine branches, Christiana?" There, that was out.

"Yes, but no one else does."

"From now on you must sleep on a plank."

"I sleep well on the branches."

Francis shook his head. "It doesn't matter. Get rid of the vine branches. The Pope's visitator must not see a bed that resembles a heretic's."

"But, Father, I am very willful. Penance helps me to yield my will."

Francis broke into an irrepressible laugh. "The vine branches help you yield your will? Yet you are resisting me."

Agnes burst into a stifled chuckle. Christiana laughed lightly. "You are right. Out of obedience, I will sleep on a plank."

"And no stone for a pillow."

A moment of hesitation. "No stone, Father."

Francis heaved a little sigh of relief. "Good. Better to relinquish penances than lose a way of life."

Now a second hurdle. The Poor Ladies, like many enclosed religious orders, kept a perpetual Lenten fast, eating only one frugal meal daily. On Sundays, during Easter Week, and on the Nativity of our Lord, as well as on all non-Friday feasts of the apostles and of the Blessed Virgin, the ladies could take two meals as part of the general rejoicing. Other than during the greater Lent preceding Easter and the lesser Lent preceding the Nativity, each lady chose whether or not to fast on Thursdays, the day of the Lord's Ascension. Francis had given the ladies these rules for fasting.

Fasting was a bodily prayer that was meant to eliminate natural faults and master the will, making the soul more receptive to grace. As voluntary suffering united to Christ's voluntary self-sacrifice, fasting was a powerful means for the conversion of sinners. Both Francis and Christiana granted dispensations from fasting to the weak, ill, or young. But did Christiana herself fast imprudently?

Francis voiced his concern. "Before I left for Rome, the ladies had sent me a message that you are not eating enough, Christiana."

"I am eating what the other sisters eat. Bread. Water. Wine on Sundays if we have any."

"The ladies say you are too thin."

"I am fine."

"Lady Pacifica, is Christiana eating?" Francis asked.

"Some days." The voice was very small.

"Which days?"

"Sunday, Tuesday, Thursday, and Saturday."

"And the other days?"

"On the other days, she does not eat."

"Or drink, my lady?"

"Or drink, Father."

"I am fine," Christiana said. "I sew. I garden. I tend the sick sisters. Don't I, sisters?"

"Yes. Yes, you do, Sister Clare."

"How much food and drink does she take, Lady Agnes?"

"Very little, Father." Agnes's voice was very little.

"Even on Sundays, which are days of rejoicing?"

"Even on Sundays, Father."

"You ladies eat fruits and vegetables, don't you, Lady Pacifica?"

"When we have them, Father."

"And you, Christiana?"

"I need only bread and water, Father."

"Christiana," Francis's voice was firm, "the ladies fear that your fasting will make you ill. They often weep over how little you eat. You must begin to eat more on the days that you do eat. And eat something on the days that you are now eating nothing."

"Father Francis," Christiana said, "I have heard that you fast for forty days and eat nothing."

How had she heard about that? Francis took a deep breath. "I am healthy, Christiana."

"I have never gone without food for even four days, much less forty."

She knew that she had him cornered. "All right, Christiana. But eat enough to keep up your health."

"Enough to keep up my health, Father."

Francis shifted on his bench. That confrontation had ended in a draw. Now for the big battle, the one on which the future of the Poor Ladies depended.

"The council said that no new religious groups may be formed in the Church."

"Lord Pope Innocent has always been receptive to new religious groups," Christiana noted. "Did he not welcome back the Waldensians and Humiliati that some called heretical?"

"Lord Pope is receptive, yes. But not the council. Pope Innocent could not sway the abbots. The council has decreed that any new orders must take an already recognized Rule."

Christiana let out a little gasp of amazement. "It's good the Pope approved your Form of Life six years ago when you visited him."

"The approval is oral, not written. Lord Pope told the council that he had approved the Forma Vita. But the council will not accept it as a Rule because it was not composed by one of the Church Fathers."

"You can still live it, can't you?"

"Because Pope Innocent had approved it prior to the council, yes."

For a moment, Christiana said nothing. Then she spoke. "Lord Pope approved the Form of Life that you gave us, didn't he?"

"I showed it to him, Christiana."

"It's so simple, Father. And so beautiful. 'Because by divine inspiration you have made yourselves daughters and servants of the Most High King, the heavenly Father, and have espoused yourselves to the Holy Spirit,'" Christiana was reciting part of the Form of Life that Francis had written, "'choosing to live according to the perfection of the holy Gospel, I resolve and promise for myself and for my brothers to always have that same loving care and solicitude for you as I have for them.'" She paused. "The Pope must have approved that and the rest of it."

"He approved it," Francis said, "but he said that it is not specific enough."

"That is because we also follow the Form of Life you wrote for the Lesser Brothers. Did you tell him that?"

"I told him." *Lord, help me.* "The Pope said that our Form of Life deals with friars who travel about. It does not apply to cloistered ladies."

He heard a sharp rustle behind the curtain, as if Christiana had leaped to her feet. "But we do follow it."

"We had long discussions about it, Christiana. Lord Pope and the council were adamant. Ladies are not permitted to travel and preach, so they may not follow the friars' Form of Life."

"Bishop Guido has allowed us to follow it."

"Bishop Guido has never given you any official document that recognizes your community. Following this council, the Church will now recognize a community as authentic only if it follows an already approved Rule and is subject to the Pope."

"What must we do?" The question was almost too sharp.

"Choose a Rule that has been approved, that will give the Poor Ladies canonical status. Either the Augustinian Rule or the Benedictine or Cistercian one."

The silence behind the curtain was unnerving.

Lord, make her understand. "Christiana, the friars and I have been praying and praying about this. We know what you must do. You must accept the Benedictine title of abbess."

"Abbess? I cannot believe that you would say that."

"Christiana, listen..."

"God called me and my sisters into poverty and this way of life." Christiana's voice was shaky. "We wish to serve Christ and all others in poverty. I cannot believe that you want me to break that promise of poverty that I made to you, to the Lord Bishop, and to God. Do you want to turn this place into another San Paolo della Abbadessa?"

"No, Christiana. No. Never. Christiana, listen. The abbess has supreme authority in Benedictine convents. If you accept the title of abbess, you can run San Damiano as you please. You will answer to no one except the Holy See."

"I want to serve, in poverty, as I have been serving." Christiana's voice was still shaky. "I do not want people to serve me or to own anything."

Francis could feel her anguish. As gently as possible, he advised: "Then be a poor abbess who serves."

"A poor abbess who serves? That is a contradiction."

"Look at the cross that I gave you. God is the Lord of contradiction."

He could see nothing behind the curtain. Hear nothing.

"Christiana, please don't make me put you under obedience. To preserve the Form of Life for the Poor Ladies, you must do this."

Christiana groaned.

"Even Christ was obedient. To death."

"All right. My father used to say, 'One has to know which battles to fight and which to avoid.'" Christiana's words were feeble, wounded. "I want the Church to accept us Enclosed Sisters as an approved order. And if I must take this title, I will. But as abbess I will not accept possessions, money, or property." Her words were even, firm. "The Pope cannot make me accept them."

"If Lord Pope commands you to accept them, you must." The words were almost too painful to speak. "Just as I must accept them, if Lord Pope commands me."

"No. He will not make us accept property or possessions. He will not make us own this place or any other."

Francis did not want her to own this place or any other. "The Pope may argue that the friars live in huts. If someone turns us out of one place, we can build huts elsewhere. Women cannot do that. If you lose this place, you will have nowhere else to go."

"God will provide the place."

"You may have to convince the Pope of that."

"God will convince the Pope."

The woman's faith was unshakable. "I know what to do!" Christiana's voice was exultant. "I will write to Lord Pope and request from him the privilege of owning nothing."

The privilege of owning nothing! Monasteries and convents were always requesting privileges of owning many things. "You want to request the privilege of having no privileges?"

"He granted it to you, Father."

The answer caught him off guard. "The Lesser Brothers work..."

"We work. We make altar linens and vestments."

"You receive no money for them."

"You receive no money for your work."

"But," Francis pointed out, "we work in exchange for food. You give away your work in exchange for nothing."

"Not for nothing. In exchange for God's blessing."

"The Pope will say that you cannot eat God's blessing."

Christiana was silent.

"Christiana, we friars are not enclosed as you are. We can beg if we cannot find work, or if we work but are not given enough food."

"Your friars beg for us. I will send the friars at once to beg for parchment and ink. Then I will write to the Pope and tell him that you have made me abbess. I will then ask him to approve the privilege of poverty in writing so that no one can say that we have not received it."

Her confidence was contagious. "May God make you successful," Francis prayed. "May He convince Lord Pope to grant you the privilege of owning nothing."

PART FIVE

The Abundant
Kindness of God

❦ 18 ❧

Lucia

Via San Petrignano, Assisi (Late Winter, 1216) ∼ Lucia was very little and this hill was very steep. She and Papa had walked so many days from Rome that the cloths covering their feet were heavy with caked mud. They'd been sleeping in towns, cities, forests, caves. Under the dismal gray sky, Lucia's head was cold despite the cloths wrapped around it. All along this road, Papa had been asking ladies and lords for something to eat, but all of them had ridden by without stopping. Someplace up this hill, Papa said, lived Lady Clare, who would give Lucia some food. A penitent named Francis, who, in Rome, had given Papa his better tunic and taken Papa's worse one, had said so.

Had Francis seen Papa's face? Lucia had not seen it for months. Papa kept his face hidden in the shadow of his cloak's big hood. He said his face was no longer pretty.

Papa got sick after Mama had died trying to birth Lucia's baby brother, who had died too. Then Papa took Lucia away from the piazza that she had called home. They had wandered throughout Rome. Maybe they would still be in Rome had they not met Francis, who had told them about Lady Clare.

Lucia imagined Lady Clare to be a beautiful woman in a red silk gown sparkly with jewels. A little silk cap would sit like a nest on her head, and she would be aloof and grand as all ladies were.

"Bambina, we are here," Papa said gleefully. Lucia blinked. She had been fantasizing so intensely about the lady that she had not noticed that Papa and she had arrived at a church.

Papa scrambled down the stairs entering the church, then turned toward Lucia. "Jump, Bambina!"

Grinning, Lucia jumped into Papa's arms. He put her down before she could kiss him.

"No kisses, Bambina. Papa is sick."

Wasn't Papa ever going to get better?

Taking her tiny hand in his, Papa led Lucia to the altar where he picked her up and held her close to a rope hanging from the wall. "Pull that, Bambina. Hard."

Lucia pulled. On the other side of the wall, a bell chimed. An unbolting and banging so startled Lucia that she jerked in Papa's arms.

"Don't be afraid. It's only the good lady opening the window."

"Pace e bene."

The high, gentle voice came from behind a grate covered on the inside with a curtain.

"Brother Francis sent me to speak to Lady Clare."

"Wait a moment, please."

Something clunked into place behind the curtain.

"Was that your mother, Papa?"

"No, Bambina. My mother is dead."

"My Mama is dead, too."

"I know, Bambina. I miss her like you do."

The sliding noise came again. "Pace e bene. This is Sister Clare."

Why didn't the lady move the black curtain aside?

"My lady, I am a leper from Rome."

A leper? Lucia squirmed in Papa's arms and stared at him. Lepers were ugly and horrible. Nobody liked them. They made you sick. They had to live at the leper hospital. Papa was too good, kind, and handsome to be a leper. And he was not at the leper hospital.

"Brother Francis suggested that I ask you to take my child Lucia and care for her. She has no one else."

As the curtain slipped back from the grate, Lucia looked curiously at the woman behind it. Why, Lady Clare was a penitent woman in a black veil! They had come this far to see a penitent?

"What is your name?" The voice was soft.

"Forte. But I do not feel strong today."

"Are you sure about your leprosy, Signor Forte?"

Signor? People called a lord signor, not Papa.

"Yes, my lady. Look." Papa threw back his hood. Above his black beard, Papa's forehead and cheeks were red and blotchy. His fat eyebrows were gone.

"Ugh. Papa!" Lucia grunted.

Papa drew the hood back up over his head. "Ugh is right, Bambina. I am not a pretty sight for your young eyes." He turned to the window. "My lady, the leprosy has spread to my arms and legs. The tunic hides it. I can beg while keeping my hand and arm covered, but it is a miracle that no one has discovered I am ill. When someone does, I shall be forced into a leper hospital. And that is no place for a child." Papa reached up and patted Lucia's rag-bound head. "Who will want to care for a leper's child if I do not take her with me? What do I do with her? Let her in the streets to starve? Or have worse befall her?" Papa's voice trembled the way it had when Mama had died. "She is all I have. And she is a good girl, aren't you, Bambina?"

Lucia nodded.

"For the love of the good God, would you care for her? I have no one else to ask."

The lady's eyes were wet with tears. Was she thinking about Mama? "Of course we will take her, Signor."

"God be praised. Grazie. Grazie." Papa hugged Lucia fiercely.

"Now Lucia," Papa said. He always called her Lucia when he had something important to say. "Someday, probably very soon, I will have to go to the leper hospital. It is not a good place for you. You can live here with Lady Clare and all the ladies. They will be like Mama to you." Papa's voice began to shake. "Say good-bye to Papa now."

From behind the window grate came the plaintive mewing of a cat. There it was! Sleek, gray, rubbing against the gown of another penitent woman standing behind Lady Clare.

"They have a cat, Papa!" Lucia wanted to play with the cat. "Good-bye, Papa," she said.

"Remember, Lucia, that I love you."

"May I bless you, Signor?" Clare asked.

"No one," Papa stuttered, "except Brother Francis has ever blessed me."

"Come closer to the grill, Signor Forte, so I may touch you."

Shakily, Papa approached the grill. Clare placed her hands on Papa's shoulders and closed her eyes. Her lips moved but Lucia could hear only an unintelligible whisper. Then Clare made a strange motion above Papa's head. "In the name of the Father and of the Son and of the Holy Spirit," she said.

"Amen," Papa answered in his tiniest voice.

"Signor Forte," Clare said softly, "will you meet us at the front of the church? We will lower the staircase so Lucia can climb up to us."

Lucia was disappointed. "Can't I see the cat, Papa?"

"I will bring Sister Gatta with me." The lady smiled.

"Papa, come on!" Lucia tugged Papa's sleeve. "She is going to show me the cat."

"All right, Bambina." Taking Lucia by the hand, Papa started out of the church. They waited by the door. Then Lucia heard a clumping. On the floor above the church, a wooden door was opening. A big penitent woman was unfastening a chain that held a wooden staircase flush against the outside wall of the building. The chain slipped slowly through the woman's hands as she lowered the staircase to the ground, where it struck with a clump.

Standing in the doorway at the top of the staircase was Lady Clare with the sleek gray cat in her arms. "Would you follow Lucia up the staircase, please, so that she does not fall?"

Eagerly Lucia started to climb. Partway up, she halted. The ground was far below. There were holes between the steps.

"Papa!"

"I am here, Bambina." Papa pressed his chest against her back. "Go on."

"Come, Lucia. Come and see Sister Gatta," the lady called encouragingly.

Up she went. One step. Another. Papa pressed against her, protecting her. Finally she scampered into a big room with long, low wooden platforms pushed against the walls. Near the door in a little open compartment sat the big penitent woman who had lowered the staircase. The woman smiled broadly at Lucia, who smiled back. My, that lady had fat red cheeks.

"Signor Forte, here is some bread for your journey." The red-cheeked lady handed Papa, still on the ladder, a pouch.

Papa slipped the pouch's strap over his head. "Grazie."

"Did Father Francis tell you that his friars help care for the lepers at San Lazzaro d'Arce?" Lady Clare asked.

"Yes, my lady. Pray that I may be taken there if I am discovered. But I will do all I can not to be discovered. I have heard of those places." Papa's voice was harsh. "I would rather die than go there. Now, Bambina," Papa said, his voice softening, "give Papa a big hug."

Lucia bent down and flung her arms around Papa's head, her hands mashing his hood against his face.

"I love you, Bambina."

Kneeling before the staircase, Clare placed one of her hands on Papa's hand. The cat was quiet in her arms. "Go in Christ's peace. We will take good care of Lucia. You will always be in our prayers."

"Grazie." Papa's voice was hoarse and odd. "Bambina, let me see your little dark eyes one last time." Lucia wretched her gaze away from the cat and looked at Papa. "Good-bye, Bambina. Always remember that I love you."

"Can I play with the cat now?" Lucia asked.

"Yes," Papa said. His voice was very deep.

Clare turned to Lucia. "Sit down, Lucia, and I will put Sister Gatta into your arms."

Lucia sat.

Clare placed the cat into Lucia's lap. The cat nestled its head under Lucia's stained gray cloak and purred. Lucia scratched, patted, and stroked the animal. The whirring came louder and louder.

"Papa, she likes me," Lucia said.

Papa did not answer.

"Papa?" Lucia looked up, confused.

Clare and the other penitential woman were fastening the staircase against the outside wall. They closed the door and pushed a big log across it.

"Your father is very brave," Clare said. "He loves you very much."

She knelt in front of Lucia. "Sister Balbina," Clare nodded at the red-cheeked sister, "has brought clean cloths for your feet."

Lucia thrust her feet out in front of her, tumbling the cat out of her lap. Quickly Clare unwrapped the muddy cloths and gave them to Sister Balbina. Then Clare rubbed each of Lucia's feet vigorously, warming them just like Papa did, before she wrapped them in clean rags.

"Why don't you ladies wear rags?" Lucia asked, noticing Clare's bare feet.

"Because we don't wish to." Clare smiled as she took Lucia's hand and helped her to her feet. The lady's hand felt warm, like Mama's or Papa's. They began to walk through the long room.

"Are you going to beg for something to eat?"

"No. We can find something to eat in the kitchen."

"Is a kitchen a pouch?"

"It is a room."

"Do you live here?"

"Yes."

The ladies had a house to live in. Lucia had never been in a house. She pointed to the low wooden platforms against the walls. "What are those?"

"Beds."

"What do you do with them?"

"Sleep on them."

Sleep on them? And not on the ground? How strange!

"Lucia," Clare whispered softly at the top of some steps, "we will go down into the oratory now. God is there. He is greater than any lord. We show Him respect by being quiet in the oratory. We kiss the floor before Him because He is so much greater than we are and He loves us so much. The kiss says, 'I love You and honor You, my God. I give myself to You.'"

Clare walked down the stairs and kissed the floor. Lucia copied her. Then they walked down more steps and into another room that held long, high platforms with colorful clothes on them, such as lords and ladies wore. Some other penitents were in the room, too, doing something with the clothes. Clare called the penitents to her.

"Sisters, this is Lucia. She is staying with us. Lucia, these are your sisters. You will learn our names very quickly." Lucia looked from one smiling face to the next. These penitents seemed to be very nice. "We will make you a little tunic and mantle, just like ours, to keep you warm."

Then, still holding Lucia's hand, Clare led Lucia into a smaller, narrower room. "This is a kitchen, Lucia. Here we keep things that are used for cooking."

Imagine! A room for cooking. Sometimes beggars cooked over fires in the piazza. Cooked food was good—especially in winter, because cooked food was warm.

"Now as soon as we thank God for our food, you can eat."

Thank God? Lucia had never heard of such a thing.

"Kneel with me." Clare knelt and Lucia copied her. "Now put your hands over your chest like this." Clare crossed Lucia's two arms over her chest and patted them. "Now you hold them there." Then Clare crossed her own arms on her own chest, closed her eyes, and began to speak softly. "Our Father, who art in heaven."

Who was she speaking to? Her father in some city called heaven?

"Amen." Smiling Clare took a broken roll, a fig, and a slab of cheese from a ledge.

Lucia gazed, wide-eyed, at the food Clare placed in her hands. "All for me, Lady Clare?"

"Yes, Lucia. We call each other sister here. Can you say Sister Clare?"

Lucia nodded vigorously and took a big bite of roll. Then she remembered that she had not done what Mama had taught her to do. "Grazie, Sister Clare," she said, her mouth full. "Are you going to eat, too?"

"I will, later. We sisters eat only once a day, for supper."

"Do you eat every day?"

"Yes, unless we don't have anything to eat."

Every day. Imagine that! It must be wonderful to be so rich and live in a big house with beds and kitchens and food every day. How long would Lucia be here before Papa came for her? She hoped it would be a little time. Sister Clare was nice like Mama. And the ladies had a cat. And figs. Lucia would like it here, until Papa returned for her.

～ 19 ～

Sister Felicita

Via di San Petrignano, Assisi (Late May, 1216) ～ A huge sack of flour topped with a napkin of yeast bumped rosy-cheeked Sister Felicita's side as she fairly skipped down the steep Via di San Petrignano on the way back to San Damiano. Dark-eyed Sister Giovanna was practically skipping too, a jug of milk in one hand and a jug of oil in the other. The Perugian shepherd and the Assisian candle-maker's daughter were bringing back ingredients to make fresh bread! The alms were an unexpected gift from Lord Paolo di Scipione di Offreduccio, whose young son Bonaventura had emerged, about an hour ago, from a life-threatening fever. The best doctors in Assisi could do nothing for the child, so Lord Paolo had asked his cousin Sister Clare to send some sisters to pray for the boy. Giovanna and Felicita were the only sisters who served outside the monastery, so they had come to anoint Bonaventura—as they anointed lepers, the wounded, and the diseased—with medicinal ointments made by the sisters from herbs and roots grown at San Damiano. Then they had prayed for him as the enclosed sisters were doing back at the monastery. When the fever had broken, an ecstatic Lord Paolo had loaded the sisters with bread ingredients, proclaiming: "No broken loaves tonight! You will have fresh bread with our deepest gratitude."

Fresh bread! Clare always instructed the sisters to praise God whenever they left the monastery, but today their praise was an anthem, rising to the sunlit May sky, dancing across the silvery-leafed olive trees, rivaling bird song. How good was the good God!

As Felicita and Giovanna approached San Damiano, a huge, colorful cortege, so long that they could not see its end, was approaching in the distance.

"That must be some fine lord," Giovanna said.

"Indeed, but we are richer," Felicita sang. "Our fine Lord erases fever and gives us bread."

"Our Lord owns all the world!" Giovanna cried.

The sisters pulled the bell cord, then ascended the staircase when Sister Pacifica let it down. At the door to the dormitory, they unfastened their heavy boots while Felicita winked at thin, dark-eyed Lucia, standing like a puppy next to Pacifica. Cleaning the serving sisters' boots was Lucia's job. Proudly she hoisted a boot and trotted to the stairs that led to the enclosed yard. Outdoors she would use a sturdy twig to scrape mud from the boots. Then she would wipe them with a moist rag and place them in the refectory, ready for the next excursion.

On nimble bare feet, Felicita and Giovanna hurried downstairs to the refectory. Near the door, spreading the makings of a chasuble across a table, stood lean Sister Ortolana, her wide blue eyes smiling at the beaming sisters. About a month earlier, following the wedding of her youngest child Beatrice, Ortolana, Sister Clare's mother, had entered San Damiano. Felicita gave Ortolana a giant hug, then skipped through the refectory where other sisters were busily working with cloth.

"Sisters! God is so good!" Felicita called as she and Giovanna bounded to a side bench where Clare always washed the serving sisters' feet when they returned. Brushing aside rapid-fire questions, Felicita and Giovanna explained the gifts of abated fever and bread ingredients while Clare sloshed a rag in a pail of water to wash their feet.

The bell at the speaking grill rang. Sister Agnes, who was tending the grill today, went to answer the summons.

With a soft rag, Clare dried the sisters' feet, then kissed them as she always did.

"Before we went to Lord Paolo's, we gave the used tunics to the beggars at the Porta del Sementone. How happy they were!" Giovanna exclaimed.

"One of them had terrible facial ulcers. We washed them and anointed them with the salve you made, Sister Clare. She was so grateful," Felicita chimed.

Clare pushed to her feet and picked up the bucket of dirty water by its rope handle to toss its contents outdoors. "God has blessed so many people through you sisters. God be praised!"

"His Holiness Lord Pope is at the grill!" Agnes's frantic cry startled Felicita. Her heart leaped. The Pope? Here?

"Does he want to come in?" Clare asked peacefully.

"He wants to speak to you at length, see San Damiano, share our meal, and then proceed to Assisi. I think it is about your request to own nothing."

"Very well." Clare placed the pail of water on the floor near the bench and, along with Agnes, walked toward the speaking grill.

Dumbfounded, Felicita stared after Clare.

"How can she be so calm?" Sister Benedetta said, hoisting the pail and heading toward the doorway to empty the water.

"The Pope! Here!" Benvenuta exclaimed.

"What are we going to feed him?" Cecilia asked.

Felicita and Giovanna stared at each other. "Bread," Felicita whispered almost reverently. "God has given us fresh bread for the Pope."

~ 20 ~

Pope Innocent III

Church of San Damiano (Late May, 1216) ~ Pope Innocent III stood near the speaking grill at San Damiano, an involuntary grin spreading across his beardless cheeks. Baptized Lothario Conti, Innocent III was descended on his father's side from one of the four oldest and noblest families in the Roman peninsula. Fifty-five years of age, he had been Pope for eighteen years, having made decisions regarding emperors and crusades, heresies and schisms, plagues and poverty. His influence was felt throughout the world, which is undoubtedly why the lady at the grill had been so flustered when she heard that the Pope was here.

Innocent doubted that he would fluster Lady Clare, a woman he already liked, because her name was a variation of his mother's name, Clarissa. A woman who would ask to possess nothing should take everything, including an unannounced papal visit, in stride. Could enclosed women live in the poverty Clare had requested? Today he would discern the answer.

Clare's almost laughable request reminded him of the one made by Brother Francis of this same city, who had come in 1209 with eleven companions to ask his permission to live as evangelizing paupers, obedient to the Holy See and to Christ. Innocent had dismissed the small, shabby fanatic, but later had a dream in which the massive Lateran Basilica, the seat of the Church, tottered to the point of collapse until Francis propped it up by heaving his shoulder against it. Innocent interpreted the dream to mean that Francis would save the Church, so he had approved Francis's Form of Life.

The curtain at the speaking grill rustled, lifted.

"Most Holy Father, I am Sister Clare." The open, fresh face behind the grill was smiling pleasantly, the deep blue eyes intent on Innocent's face. The stately woman bowed. Innocent bowed in return.

"I would like to see the monastery, then speak with you over a small meal, if I may."

"Certainly, Most Holy Father." The woman bowed again. "If you will exit the church, we will lower the staircase into the enclosure. Please bring the fewest attendants possible, as men do not enter our living quarters."

Innocent scanned the servants, cardinals, and attendants who filled the church. For propriety's sake, at least one ought to accompany him.

A sturdy, gray-bearded cardinal to his left stepped forward. "My uncle, these women and their way of life intrigue me."

Innocent smiled at his grandnephew, who was over a decade older than Innocent but who had the stamina of a much younger man. Cardinal Hugolino dei Conti dei Segni, cardinal bishop of Ostia, former legate to Germany. Innocent nodded. "The others remain here," he said.

Innocent inspected every part of the monastery—the dormitory, infirmary, refectory, choir, parlor, gardens, yard, well, hermitages, enclosing walls and hedges. Furnishings were few and scratched. He exchanged pleasantries with young ladies weeding an ample herb garden. He spoke to others stitching in the refectory. He chatted with ladies shaping a great many loaves of bread in the kitchen. He told a child named Lucia how the golden filigree on his flowing red cape was made.

Then he asked to speak privately to the friars who begged for the women. Innocent and Hugolino met the friars in their poor, simple house that abutted the church. The starkness of the plain-walled dwelling struck Innocent with its rare, unappreciated beauty.

In contrast to the friars who had come to see Innocent with Brother Francis, these friars were elderly.

"Father Francis sent only old men who did not want to come," a bald friar explained. "He feels that it is safer to have old, weak men serving beautiful young ladies."

Innocent nodded. It was safer, but the friars soon made him realize the burden of old, weak bodies begging enough food for a growing community of women.

Smelling the baking bread, Innocent remarked, "It appears that the women have sufficient to eat."

"They have had little at times," the bald friar said, "but something always."

A bell rang for Vespers. Innocent and Hugolino joined the ladies in the choir while the friars and the Pope's entourage chanted the Office in the church.

Upon completing the Office, Innocent and Hugolino returned with the ladies to the refectory for the single daily meal, eaten in silence, as was customary for all religious. The women sat on benches around long, bare wooden tables, while Clare beckoned Innocent to join her at the table closest to the kitchen entrance. An older woman handed Clare a washbowl, a pitcher of water, and a long towel. Setting the bowl on the table, Clare poured water over Innocent's hands, then offered him the towel. She did the same with Hugolino.

Innocent was incredulous. Lowly pages washed the hands of lords and their most honored guests, while others had to use a common washbowl. Innocent had expected to have his hands washed, but not by the abbess. Then Clare did a more amazing thing. She proceeded to wash the hands of each sister, then washed her own hands before carrying the pitcher, washbowl, and towel back into the kitchen.

Within moments she emerged with a tray of small cheese wedges and slices of peeled orange. On Innocent's and Hugolino's napkins she placed a cheese wedge and two orange slices, then proceeded to serve the same to the seated sisters. When she returned to her own seat, she placed the final orange slice on her napkin, then disappeared into the kitchen.

This time she emerged with two bowls of steaming greens, one of which she placed on the table before Innocent and Hugolino. Impulsively, Innocent gently took the other bowl from Clare and brought it to one of the other tables. When he returned, he and Hugolino took from Clare two more bowls and brought them to the other two tables. Then Innocent, Hugolino, and Clare passed small, finely shaped loaves to the women until each had a loaf. The novelty of serving pleased Innocent as few things did.

"Lady Clare," Innocent requested softly, "may we allow speaking at this meal?"

"As you wish, Most Holy Father," Clare bowed.

Innocent turned toward the women. "Ladies, you have a most peaceful place here. And oranges, my favorite food."

"A merchant brought them yesterday from the south," Clare explained.

"So, the good God sent them ahead of me. And you have baked this fresh bread, most tasty with oranges."

The ladies were smiling at him, nodding.

"Ladies," Innocent asked spontaneously "what is the secret of your joy?"

Apparently startled at being questioned, the women looked from one to the other.

"Jesus."

"Our Lord and His cross."

"Living with others who love as we do."

"I just like it here," Lucia said, smiling.

"I do, too," Innocent chuckled. "And, Lady Clare, what is your secret?"

"Contempt of the world always brings joy," Clare answered peacefully. "In the poor, despised Christ, we are made rich."

Innocent nodded. "Your humility humbles me." He raised his distinctively arched eyebrows to emphasize his words. "The sanctity of this place is as a sweet odor reaching throughout the world."

Clare's cheeks reddened. "God be praised for any good you hear of us, my lord."

"My ladies," Innocent said, gazing from one table to another, "I was concerned when you asked to own nothing, but God richly provides. Since He blesses you, I shall also bless you. I grant your request to own nothing."

Huge smiles spread across the women's faces. "Grazie. Mille grazie," redounded in the room.

"God be praised!" Clare bowed deeply.

Innocent grinned. "Now, my lady, shall we eat?"

Clare smiled back. "Certainly. Most Holy Father, would you kindly bless these loaves?"

"Very faithful Lady Clare, I would rather that you bless them. I have heard how well you use the sign of the cross."

Clare gasped. "I would deserve to be severely blamed if I, a vile little woman, should presume to give such a blessing in the presence of the vicar of Christ."

"So that no one may attribute this blessing to presumption, I ask you to earn merit by obedience. Thus I command you under holy obedience to make the sign of the cross over these loaves and to bless them in the name of our Lord Jesus Christ."

Obediently Clare faced the tables, her eyes downcast. Raising her hand, she made a large sign of the cross over the loaves, pronouncing an inaudible blessing.

"Thank you, Lady Clare," Innocent said, reaching for his loaf. How clever! The loaf was marked with a small cross cut into the crust. He glanced at the tables. All loaves were so marked. Strange that he had not noticed the crosses until now.

"Dear ladies," Innocent remarked, "we must tell our household about your custom of carving crosses into the loaves before baking. These symbols recall the Bread of Life who died upon a cross for us."

Murmurs rippled throughout the room.

"Most Holy Father," Clare said, "we always make undecorated loaves here."

Undecorated? Innocent picked up his loaf and turned it over. It was an ordinary, small loaf of bread with a neatly carved cross baked into its upper crust. If the ladies had not carved the cross, then who had?

Astonished, Innocent bowed his head. "Let us thank God," he called in a tremulous voice, "for granting miraculous signs to strengthen our weak faith."

～ 21 ～

Sister Filippa di Leonardo di Gislerio

Hermitage, San Damiano (SUMMER, 1216) ～ Sister Filippa di Leonardo di Gislerio knelt on the ground, bathed in light streaming through the open doorway of this cramped reed and mud hermitage. Instead of fastening shut the thick reed mat that served as a door, Filippa had lifted it off its pegs because the day was warm. The hut was one of several that the sisters had built along the far wall surrounding San Damiano. Sisters could come to these huts any time to pray, but they also took turns staying here for several days in solitude, with a large jug of water and a loaf of bread to sustain them.

Filippa had not intended to come to the hermitages today. With the other sisters, she had been picking raspberries along the enclosure's upper wall when, as sometimes happened without warning, she had been thrown back in time. Suddenly she was no longer a twenty-three-year-old woman, but a fragile child huddled in Mother's skirt while baby brother Teodimo wailed in his nurse's arms and older brothers Oddo and Monaldo scrambled for their swords. She heard warlike shouts, saw flaming arrows streak through nursery windows, felt the awful pumping of thin, short legs as she ran through smoke, past tumbling walls, down tottering stairs into the flame-bright darkness where leering men surrounded her, grabbed her, jeered at her terror.

She was screaming when the sisters had shaken her into sensibility. Unsteady, she had watched them carefully pull the thorny canes from her skirt—she had somehow tangled herself in the thicket. Clare had taken her by the hand and had led her here to pray, then knelt silently beside her, saying only, "May God heal you of these memories, dear sister." Clare was beside her now, bowed deep in prayer.

Filippa had entered the community a month ago because Clare had constantly preached to her about Christ's passion. Her father Lord Leonardo di Gislerio was delighted. Now that Mother was dead, Teodimo a squire, and Monaldo married, Filippa's joining the Poor Ladies freed him to join the Lesser Brothers.

103

Teodimo had no memories of Sasso Rosso's destruction. Monaldo did not let his memories bother him, despite having fought in the Perugian/Assisian war and seeing their brother Oddo and their Uncle Lord Girardo killed. Father must have buried his memories; six years ago, he, along with Uncle Lord Fortebraccio and many others, had returned to Assisi from Perugia and signed the peace pact drawn up under Emperor Otto IV. The pact officially ended Assisi's ten-year civil war by having nobles and common people pledge to work together for the commune's good. For Father and Monaldo, the past was past. Why was it still so present to Filippa?

On the way here, she and Clare had talked about sufferings.

The question was not would we suffer but when, for sufferings were part of this fallen world as surely as slender gray cat snakes were part of these environs, startling when encountered yet hardly unexpected.

Or suffering was like the juice of nightshade berries whose slender vines clambered over the undergrowth and twisted upward toward the sun. As one drop of nightshade juice could poison a goblet of water, so did Adam and Eve's disobedience poison creation, causing sufferings that no one deserved.

Or suffering was the result of demons who could attack body, mind, or spirit.

Or it was the result of human choice for evil.

Or suffering was sent by God to bring about a greater good, as when Filippa's father used to punish her for leaning out of the windows of Sasso Rosso. He didn't spank to be mean but to keep her from tumbling out.

Or suffering could make us turn to God when nothing else would.

It was one thing to philosophize about suffering. It was another to experience it.

Filippa opened her eyes and gazed at a large slab of wood leaning against the hut's back wall. Sister Giovanna had used a red-hot nail to burn a finely detailed outline of Christ crucified into the wood. Today one of the lines appeared too light and thick. Filippa smiled in recognition. A fat yellowish green-striped caterpillar was inching across the belly of Christ. Was Filippa like that caterpillar, touching Christ yet unchanged?

What did Clare say about Christ? "Our Lord was so much more beautiful than any man. Yet, He chose to appear despised, needy, and poor. For our salvation, Christ became the lowest of all, hated, struck, scourged unmercifully, finally put to death on the cross so that we, so poor and needy, might become rich by possessing heaven."

Christ chose suffering to change—not Himself, but us. To do this, He gave up every glory and good of heaven. He gave His all so that we might possess all.

Filippa watched the caterpillar inch toward Christ's shoulder. An idea was forming. To possess the All, one had to relinquish all. "You want everything, don't You?" she whispered to the etching. "Even our sufferings, our memories, our regrets, our plans. What will You do with them, Lord? What will you do with my pain and my sin if I give them to You?"

Filippa cocked her head toward the caterpillar creeping along the upper edge of the slab. That was the wrong question, wasn't it? No one would ever suspect that a caterpillar would turn into a butterfly. If the ugly caterpillar of pain and suffering were given to God, He could do what He wished with it.

She gazed at the Crucified, sensing something new. "You know, don't You?" Jesus had experienced the hurts of humanity. Poverty. Betrayal. Abandonment. Homelessness. Exile. Death of loved ones. Torture. Fear. Assault. Degradation. Misunderstanding. Ridicule. Hatred. Murder.

What did Clare say? "If you suffer with Him, you will reign with Him. If you weep with Him, you will rejoice with Him. If you die with Him on the cross of tribulation, you shall possess heavenly mansions in the splendor of the saints."

Filippa gazed at the Crucified, no longer obstructed by a fat, moving creature. The question was not why had she suffered or why did anyone suffer, but what was she to do with her sufferings?

Her bitter memories were like a big striped caterpillar clinging to her spirit. In her mind, she plucked the caterpillar out of herself and handed it to God. God enclosed the creature in His palm, then opened His hand—a large, yellow-and-black swallowtail butterfly darted out. It flew directly into Filippa's soul and gave it wings.

✎ 22 ✎

Bellezza

San Damiano, Assisi (LATE AFTERNOON, AUGUST 2, 1216) ∼ Bellezza leaned against the outer wall of the Church of San Damiano. She was so tired. Maybe she was pregnant. She had been so tired when she was pregnant with Mattiolo.

Where was Mattiolo? Oh, there, scratching in the dirt with a stick. Maybe if her dark-complexioned husband Scuro could watch their lithe, black-haired three-year-old, Bellezza could rest.

Kissing Bellezza quickly on the cheek, Scuro agreed. Bellezza sat against the wall of the church and closed her eyes.

Bellezza's little family were peasants employed by Lord Gualtieri Cacciaguerra of Spoleto. They were here in Assisi because a year ago Lord Gualtieri's daughter Lady Cecilia had become an enclosed recluse at this monastery. She had written to her family about a special indulgence that could be received today at a small stone church, the Porziuncola, a few miles from here. Lord Gualtieri had brought his family and household—excepting those needed to tend his livestock—to receive the indulgence. Having received it, the lord and his lady were visiting their daughter in this monastery, then the Cacciaguerra household would return to Spoleto.

This morning, at the lord's encampment in the forest, Bellezza had plaited her auburn hair, wrapping it in two spirals on either side of her chubby face. She had donned the russet tunic and perky cap she had made for this special day. With the other peasants, she had stood near the back of an immense crowd surrounding a platform erected near the Porziuncola. She had heard seven bishops—from Assisi, Perugia, Todi, Norcera, Gubbio, Foligno, and Spoleto—speak of the indulgence.

A month ago, Brother Francis, who had also addressed the crowd, had been deep in prayer at the Porziuncola. In a vision, Jesus and His Mother had invited him to request whatever he thought best for the salvation of souls. "Could all repentant persons who enter the Porziuncola, confess their sins, and obtain absolution from a priest, obtain complete remission of all penalty for all sins ever committed?" he had asked.

Jesus had consented to the indulgence if the Pope agreed. So Francis described his vision to the new Pope, Honorius III, who was still in Perugia after his swift election following the death of Innocent III in July. Pope Honorius had granted the indulgence, but not year 'round as Francis requested. "It is the same indulgence granted to crusaders," the cardinals noted. "The Church will never regain the Holy Land from the infidels if the indulgence can be obtained merely by visiting a church." So the Pope had limited the indulgence to August 2. The indulgence could be obtained from Vespers last night until Vespers tonight, provided that one confessed his sins, did appropriate penance, and said required prayers for certain required intentions.

Bellezza had fulfilled the requirements. Now, if only she would never sin again, she would go straight to heaven if she died.

Bellezza felt her exhausted body relax against the wall. Was it possible not to sin? All her sins, it seemed, involved Mattiolo. Scuro had named him Mattiolo, after Scuro's father, but sometimes he so exasperated Bellezza that she wondered if he really was a "gift from God."

Today when the bishop of this commune had been speaking about purgatory, Mattiolo had been scampering through people's legs, pelting a dog with pebbles, throwing rocks at birds, and shredding ferns with a stick. When Bellezza had picked him up, he had pulled her hat from her head and put it on his own, then wanted Scuro to hold him and put the hat on Scuro. Maintaining patience while parenting Mattiolo was the real "gift from God"! If only Bellezza could have that gift!

What had the bishop said? "Only the perfect can enter paradise. Imperfect souls are perfected in purgatory. In purgatory, souls learn to always say 'yes' to God, to give Him the glory, thanksgiving, service, and praise that are His due. The soul is then at peace and enters heaven."

Bellezza was feeling a bit peaceful right now. She seemed to have that peace only when Mattiolo was asleep or in someone else's care.

A terrifying shriek rent the air. Mattiolo! Leaping to her feet, Bellezza bolted toward Mattiolo, who was thrashing and grabbing at his grimy face. Scuro swept Mattiolo into his arms while Bellezza pushed aside the boy's flailing limbs and swiftly examined him. He was dirty but not cut.

Maybe he swallowed a pebble! Bellezza shoved her finger into Mattiolo's mouth, but she could feel no foreign object.

Squatting, Scuro threw Mattiolo over his knee, the child's face downward. With two sharp slaps, he struck his son between the shoulder blades, but nothing dislodged from Mattiolo's throat. Mattiolo coughed and cried louder.

Swiftly a crowd gathered. Questions. Advice.

"I don't know what's wrong!" Bellezza screamed.

A gray-haired friar tried to place his hand on Mattiolo's thrashing head, but Mattiolo flung it off.

"Take him to Lady Clare," the friar ordered.

Mattiolo was kicking and screaming in Scuro's arms as he carried him into the church to the speaking grill, where the friar frantically pulled the cord that rang a bell. To the sound of a door sliding open, the friar barked, "Get Lady Clare!"

Scrambling behind the wall. Mattiolo thrashing. Shrieking.

The black curtain shot up. Behind the grill, a gray-robed woman, her face anxious, beckoned. "Bring the child to the grill."

Bellezza tried to stroke the kicking child. He kicked her away.

The woman put her hand between the iron bars and tried to caress Mattiolo's head. Violently, he shook off her touch.

"What's his name?"

"Mattiolo, my lady." Bellezza's voice quavered.

"Mattiolo, shh. Shh, Bambino." The woman reached again for Mattiolo's tossing head. This time he allowed her to stroke it. "Shh, Bambino. Mattiolo, shh." Mattiolo's sobbing cracked and broke into a whimper. He stopped flailing. How dirty and disheveled he looked!

"Shh, Bambino. I am Sister Clare. I like you, Mattiolo. You are a good boy."

Whimpering, Mattiolo blinked at the woman. "You are a good bambino, Mattiolo." The voice was soothing, gentle. "We're going to ask our good Jesus to bless you." The woman placed her left hand under Mattiolo's chin and tipped his face upward toward her own. At the touch, Mattiolo quieted. With her right hand, Clare traced the sign of the cross over him. "In the name of the Father, and of the Son, and of the Holy Spirit. Amen."

Mattiolo wriggled.

"Oh!" the lady said suddenly. She slipped her hand away from Mattiolo's chin and closed her fist. With her right hand, she stroked Mattiolo's cheek. "You are a good bambino, good Mattiolo."

Mattiolo sighed. His head drooped in Scuro's arms. Just that swiftly, he fell asleep.

Clare held her left hand toward Scuro and Bellezza and opened her palm. In it lay a wet, pinkish pebble.

"It fell out of his nose," Clare said simply.

His nose? Bellezza had never thought to check Mattiolo's nose.

"My lady, grazie," Scuro said thickly.

"Grazie," Bellezza said. The phrase was so inadequate.

"Thank the good Jesus," Lady Clare said. "He has released the pebble."

"But you are the one who prayed," Scuro said.

The lady's smiling eyes were bright. "And so must you pray. Parents must pray a great deal." Clare placed her left hand on Mattiolo's head. "Take Mattiolo before the crucifix," she said, pointing to the one above the altar, "and dedicate him to our Lord, who was once a little boy. With your prayers, your love, and God's grace, may Mattiolo grow to be a fine man."

Clare raised her right hand in blessing. "May the Lord give you faith in His Son and in yours. May you know the gift of your child. May God bless you. In the name of the Father, and of the Son, and of the Holy Spirit. Amen."

As Bellezza blessed herself, an idea came to her. Could raising Mattiolo be a purgatory? Might he teach Bellezza patience? Impatience, not Mattiolo, was Bellezza's barrier to peace. Maybe Mattiolo really was a "gift from God."

PART SIX

A Celebrated and
Holy Manner of Life

~ 23 ~

Lord Ugolino de Pietro Girardone

Church of San Damiano, Assisi (EARLY FALL, 1217) ~ Dismounting, Lord Ugolino de Pietro Girardone left his gray mount in the shade with his squire and entered the Church of San Damiano. His shoulder-length black hair was windblown beneath the fitted linen coif tied under his chin and the tight-fitting green cap above it. Today was windy, just as it had been three days ago when he had overseen the last of his wheat harvest and returned to his palatial home on the Piazza del San Rufino to find two friars from San Damiano waiting for him. Lady Clare, they said, had an urgent, personal message for him. Today had been the earliest he had been able to ride down to the church to receive it.

Ugolino strode through the church and pulled the cord at the speaking grill. His former neighbor, Lady Clare, still looked beautiful after five years behind these walls. He hoped she would be quick, because harvest season was the busiest time of year. Plowing and replanting fallow wheat fields. Picking and drying apples and pears. Gathering chestnuts. Plucking grapes and making wine. Grinding flour. Plus the constant chore of hunting meat for the household.

"Lord Ugolino, I will be brief," Clare said. "I've had a vision. You must receive your wife Lady Guiduzia back immediately and the two of you must have a son who will give you great joy and consolation." The lady's voice was kind but firm. "Ask Jesus to give you the grace to do what He asks. We sisters here shall be praying for you."

What should he say? "Yes, my lady," he grunted.

The curtain dropped back over the grill. The door slid into place. Ugolino stood dumbly, staring at it.

What did God mean, instructing him to take back his wife? Twenty-two years ago he had sent her away, refusing to take her back despite her pleas and those of others. That long-ago day his raven-haired new bride had made him look foolish to his friends when she had refused to sing for them at a banquet, claiming hoarseness from

112

a cold. Ugolino had heard her sing well with a cold, so why the refusal? "Ah, she probably sounds like a frog!" his guests jeered. "Perhaps we need to call her Lord Guiduzia and you Lady Ugolino!"

The painful memory brought Ugolino to his senses. Why was he stupidly staring at a curtained grill? Today he didn't feel like praying before the gold-rimmed crucifix, so he tromped past it, toward the exit of the church.

It wasn't only Guiduzia's refusal to sing. She was willful. She made her gowns in her favorite colors, not Ugolino's. Sometime she refused his advances of love, claiming to be tired. Without consulting her husband, she frequently visited her ill mother, leaving the chief butler in charge of the household. Refusing to beat his wife into submission, as many men would have done, Ugolino sent her home.

On the top step leading out of the church, Ugolino paused. He always prayed in front of that crucifix. Disgruntled, he turned on his heels, approached the crucifix, and knelt. *There. I came back.*

The figure on the cross answered not a word.

How would You like to live with somebody who's willful?

I live with willful people all the time.

The thought caught Ugolino short. Was he being willful by not following Lady Clare's request? Had *he* been willful by not giving his bride a chance?

A line from the Our Father nudged Ugolino's mind. "Forgive us our sins as we forgive those who sin against us." If Ugolino wanted God to forgive him, did he have to forgive Lady Guiduzia? Even more, did he have to ask Guiduzia to forgive him for sending her away?

Ugolino looked intently at the crucifix. Christ's arms were widely spread as if to embrace with loving forgiveness all who approached Him. "Your sins are forgiven you." Christ's words to the repentant woman, to the paralyzed man. To Ugolino. To the world.

Ugolino knew the scriptures. Mother had used them to teach him to read, and now, as part of his nightly routine, Ugolino read Mother's precious, worn bible so that he could fall asleep. Forgiveness was a big theme in the Bible.

Forgive, Ugolino.

But how, Lord, when I do not wish to?

Forgive.

The words rolled over on themselves, like a revolving water-wheel. Yes. He was supposed to visit his mill today. Ugolino said a quick Our Father. There. He had prayed.

Accompanied by his squire, Ugolino guided his horse away from San Damiano. Under bright sun they rode north, past laden olive groves and plowed fields ready for next year's wheat. Tilled lands yielded to the wild Tescio River Valley, where maples and aspens bore faint hints of autumn yellow and red.

Like the leaves, Ugolino was still young and fresh, yet the occasional, slight lapses of stamina, the barely perceptible sagging of his cheeks, the faint wrinkles in his forehead were unmistakable signs. The autumn of his life had begun. Someday his body, like the leaves, would rest in the dark, insensitive earth. Where would his soul be then?

FORGIVE, UGOLINO.

How, Lord?

While still a good distance from the mill, Ugolino heard the faint yet persistent rumble of the upper millstone grinding grain against the bottom stone. At the mill, where the noise was deafening, the waterwheel turned as the Tescio flowed beneath it, striking its paddles. Inside, flour dusted every cog, peg, and board and danced in sunbeams streaming through the doorway and through the chinks in the walls. On a platform above the millstones stood the floury miller, pouring wheat berries into a funnel-shaped bin that led into a hole in the center of the revolving upper stone.

The upper millstone was turning, grinding. From the hole in the stone's center, the wheat berries slid between the upper and lower stones where the rotation pulverized them. The lower stone was sloped downward and outward so that the flour worked its way to the outer edge of the stone and spilled out a chute into an empty sack.

Grain was crushed into flour, flour baked into bread, bread eaten to give life.

More verses from Mother's bible leaped to Ugolino's mind.

"He was crushed for our sins."

"I am the Bread of Life."

Ugolino thrust his hand into an open sack of wheat berries leaning against a nearby wall. Tiny beige grains slipped through his fingers. Ugolino had planted the wheat because he had intended to crush it into flour. Christ had become man to be crushed for our sins and, thus, forgive them.

FORGIVE AS I HAVE FORGIVEN YOU.

Ugolino opened his fingers and the wheat berries trickled between them into the sack.

Teach me how to forgive, Lord.

God did not teach him how to forgive. God taught him how to love. Within days, he began to long for Guiduzia. He yearned to fondle her luscious black hair, to hear her lilting laughter, to sway to her ballads, to smell her pungent perfume, to share his soul with her. He came to realize that even though he was still angry with Lady Guiduzia, he missed her—he loved her. Once he loved, he forgave, for love forgives all. He repented the harsh way he had treated her.

Ugolino sent for Lady Guiduzia.

She had aged. Little wrinkles lined her eyes and age freckles spattered her face. Her thick hair had thinned and was beginning to gray. Her round face had hollowed, making her look her age— close to forty. But her laughter, her song, and the soothing way she listened when he opened his heart were the same. When he asked her forgiveness for sending her away, her wordless kiss gave him his answer.

With time, he noticed other changes. Lady Guiduzia was not so willful anymore. Or perhaps he was more willing to compromise. Perhaps they both had mellowed as they entered the autumn of their lives.

One year later, Lady Guiduzia bore him a son. With awe, Ugolino kissed Guiduzia tenderly, then took the swaddled newborn from her as she lay in bed after the marvelous birth.

Ugolino could not take his eyes from the red-skinned boy, so small in his father's massive hands. "We shall name him Pietro," Ugolino declared, "after my father and after San Pietro the apostle whom Christ so graciously forgave." He smiled at his wide-eyed son. "I will take you to see Lady Clare," Ugolino whispered. "We will bring her woolen cloth to make new habits for the sisters. What do you think, Pietruccio?" Ugolino bounced the boy lightly in his arms. "Will she open the curtain and give you her blessing? Will she, Bambino?"

With dark, unfocused eyes, forgiveness born of love gazed at Ugolino and gurgled in laughter.

∽ 24 ∼

Cardinal Hugolino dei Conti dei Segni

Outside the Church of San Damiano (Holy Week, 1220) ∼ Standing beside Friar Cappellano near the facade of the Church of San Damiano, Cardinal Hugolino dei Conti dei Segni looked above to the second-floor door. He had come to consult Lady Clare, who was too weak to descend the stairs to the parlor. So he would climb up to her.

The door swung open. Sister Balvina di Martino di Ugolino di Offreduccio, a woman as large as her name, appeared in the opening. As deftly as if the staircase were a slipper, Balvina lowered the stairs. The thick chain that held the staircase to the monastery swayed as Hugolino began the ascent. Cappellano followed him.

Hugolino's oval face, always pinched and thin, had grown hollow-cheeked with age and fasting. His trimmed gray beard was still fairly full, as was the ring of thick silver hair that fringed his scalp. Having left his silk shoes and rich cape in the convento, he seemed, not the wealthy cardinal of Ostia and Velletri, but a simple, barefoot man. Hugo.

Hugo had been born the Count of Anagni in the Patrimony of Saint Peter. More titles followed. Priest of the church of Anagni. Papal chaplain to his great uncle Pope Innocent III. Cardinal-deacon of Saint Eustachius. Chief counselor of Pope Honorius III. One of the Pope's many legates. Yet, to him, the most meaningful title was his unofficial one of spiritual father to Brother Francis's and Lady Clare's followers.

In 1216 in Perugia, Hugo had first met Francis. Like Pope Honorius, Hugo had been drawn to Francis's message of peace. In 1217, Hugo joyously accepted Francis's dual request to become the friars' advocate and Francis's spiritual director. Through Francis, Hugo met Clare.

Hugo was immediately impressed with Clare, so much younger than he, yet of the same class. Hugo was the son of a count, Clare the granddaughter of one. He knew what he had relinquished to embrace religious life, but she had surrendered more. Hugo still had fine clothes, good food, servants, and steeds, but Clare had nothing but God. Hugo could reveal his soul to her—she seemed able to read his heart.

He had come to San Damiano this Holy Week because, upon Pope Honorius's directive, he was visiting all communities of women in this part of the empire—to approve, regulate, correct, or even dismiss them. Last year, Hugo had written a Form of Life for the Damianites, parts of which disturbed Lady Clare. Hugo wanted to discuss those sections.

Clare was propped up on her raised bed at the dormitory's opposite end. Sitting on one of the half dozen stools surrounding the bed, Hugo took Clare's thin right hand from the alb she was stitching and kissed it.

"Are you in pain?" he asked as he heard the staircase clunk against the wall and the monastery door swing shut.

"Only when I walk."

"Does not my Form of Life state that ill sisters should be in the infirmary?"

Clare nodded gaily. "Lord Cardinal, as abbess, I must be with my sisters in the dormitory. If you wish to make a healthy sister abbess, I will gladly recover in the infirmary."

Hugo patted Clare's hand. "Stay in the dormitory, Lady Abbess." He lay her hand in her lap. He glanced at Friar Cappellano and Sister Balvina who were standing nearby. "May we speak privately?"

Friar Cappellano picked up two stools and carried them to the opposite end of the dormitory. Offering one to Balvina, he sat on the other, facing Hugo and Clare.

Hugo lowered his voice. "Your letter stated that some portions of the Form of Life I gave you last year displease you. I have given that Form of Life to several convents. It contains regulations demanded of enclosed women, but I also attempted to have it reflect how I observed your living."

"Lord Cardinal," Clare spoke softly, "see the lace on this alb?" Clare pointed to a row of fine lace embroidered with stags and birds. "It resembles a forest glade. Yet it is not a glade. Even so, your Form of Life is quite beautiful, but it does not fully capture how we live."

Hugo felt for the relic he carried in his silk purse. Some time ago Bishop Jacques de Vitry of Belgium had given Hugo a relic of Marie d'Oignies, a holy, austere recluse favored with mystical gifts.

Jacques, Marie's confessor until her death seven years earlier, had advised Hugo, who frequently lost his patience even to the point of swearing, to seek patience through Marie's intercession. Hugo fingered the relic and kept his voice down. "What is wrong with my Form of Life?"

"My lord, we fast daily. Yet you have asked that we also abstain from fruit, vegetables, and wine on Wednesdays and Fridays outside of Lent and that we fast on bread and water four days a week during Lent and three days during the Lent of Saint Martin. My lord, you have mercifully dispensed the young, old, and weak sisters from fasting but have overlooked those who serve outside the monastery. They expend a great deal of energy walking and have been growing faint on such a severe diet, so I have dispensed them as well."

Hugo could see her point. "Very wise, Lady Clare. Continue to dispense the serving sisters."

"Grazie, my lord. Now regarding silence. Here, my lord, we have always spoken of spiritual things. But your Form of Life allows speaking only out of duty. It does not permit encouraging the ill sisters nor talking about God's graces. The serving sisters may not speak, except out of duty, to those they meet in the world. What are we permitted to say to those who approach our grills? Some sisters were forgetting how to talk! We can teach each other much about our Lord. Therefore, I have permitted the sisters to speak, in quiet tones, of the things of God and of whatever is necessary or helpful to one another."

Hugo rubbed the relic. "I trust your experience, Lady Clare."

"And one other matter, my lord. Enclosure is not a prison. It is a gift. It enables us to commune with our Lord in solitude so that we may share His graces with the needy. While the parlor is a place of privacy sealed by a curtain, we raise the curtain in the choir when God's Word is preached. We also raise the curtain at the speaking grill if we wish to bless someone. We have continued these practices even though they are not mentioned in your Form of Life."

"Perhaps I did not observe your practices well enough," Hugo admitted. "Have you anything else?" His lack of irritation surprised him.

"No, Lord Cardinal. God has been good to us."

Hugo released the relic. "My lady, many things are troubling me. May I share them?"

"Of course." Clare's gaze focused on him, encouraging him to speak.

Hugo knew every important person in the Church. Last year he had inspired the crusaders by his eloquent preaching. He had memorized the Bible and was zealous for the faith. But since January, when five followers of Francis had died for their faith in Morocco, Hugo had no spiritual peace. The martyrs' blood had seared his soul. Perhaps Francis felt called to martyrdom, because he had sailed last June for Acre and Damietta—both cities scenes of fighting in the Crusade—and was now on his way to the Holy Land. Clare herself had wished to be martyred. When she remained determined to go to the Holy Land, despite her sisters' pleading, the sisters had prayed, and Clare had fallen ill. Bedfast now, she could go nowhere. Hugo also desired martyrdom. He asked Clare about it. She momentarily closed her eyes in silent prayer.

"My lord, I believe that you are to remain alive and that your martyrdom is to do God's will. You are doing His will now. Time will reveal more."

"My lady, I have been consecrated to God for decades. Yet the life of the friars appeals to me. Ought I become a Poor Brother?"

"God knows the answer to that, not I."

"My soul is disquieted."

"My lord, look." Clare plucked from the floor a wooden frame holding a length of bleached linen, deftly embroidered with a recurring, unfinished pattern of block-shaped crosses. "Your disquiet may be a cross that is preparing you for another cross. Crosses, you know, conform us to Christ."

"How have you created these?" Hugo asked admiringly.

"Like this." Clare drew out a threaded needle thrust into the pattern and plunged the needle through the cloth, bringing it up to create a tiny, perfect stitch.

"Thus, you embroider the stitches," Clare explained. "To create the tiny spaces around the designs and to make lace, you pull out the width-wise threads." With the tip of the needle, Clare deftly drew a width-wise thread away from the fabric. Picking a minuscule blade from the floor, she nimbly cut the thread where it joined two of the crosses. With the tip of the needle, she pulled out the cut thread so that tiny open spaces appeared where the cut thread had been, one space between each cross-wise thread.

"Clever," Hugo said. "If only we could pluck out our bad qualities as swiftly as you plucked out that thread."

Clare smiled. "God is good at drawing threads if we ask."

"Sometimes He draws them very slowly."

Clare laughed. "True, my lord. And look." Clare pointed at the slender, cross-wise threads with the tip of the needle. "When all the width-wise threads are pulled out and only the cross-wise ones remain, you gather a few cross-wise threads together with a tiny stitch here and there, and it looks like lace. Do you think Father Francis will like this deacon's alb? Every stitch has been a prayer for him."

"He will greatly appreciate it, I am sure. Have you a few prayers for me?"

"We pray for you daily, Lord Cardinal," Clare said.

Hugo nodded. "Grazie. I fear my office may endanger my soul."

"God has used your office to bless us and many others. A few days from now, you will give us the Body of Christ on Easter!"

Ugolino nodded, recalled Clare kneeling on the simple wooden kneeler at the window in the choir grill behind San Damiano's altar, tears streaming, her face aglow, as she received on her tongue the Body of Christ. Like Clare, Francis, too, wept and trembled upon receiving the Lord.

"As God uses simple bread to come to us bodily, so He uses you to come to us bodily. We are most blessed in you, Lord Cardinal."

Clare turned the crosses toward Hugo. "Your cross, my lord, is to accept God's way. In time may you see His wisdom."

Hugo gazed at the cloth and Clare's hands resting so peacefully on it. He took one of her hands and kissed it. "Lady Clare, I am a wretched man," Hugo whispered. "I entrust my soul to you. You are close to God while I am burdened with sin. I am unworthy of heaven unless your prayers and tears obtain pardon for me. On Judgment Day you will answer for me if you have not been concerned with my salvation, because I am certain that the most high Judge will grant you whatever you request. Therefore, promise that you will pray fervently for my salvation."

Clare placed her hand over Hugo's. "My lord," her voice quivered, "I am a sinner, too. But of course I will pray for you. Do you pray for me."

Holy Week, Easter passed. From Viterbo, Hugo wrote a letter to Clare, reminding her of her promise. Time passed. Hugo prayed about becoming a friar, but God gave no answer. Francis returned from the Holy Land and met Hugo in Bologna.

In the Holy Land, Friar Stephen had sought Francis to tell him disturbing news of papal privileges and changes in his order. Uneducated, simple Francis, often weak and ill, wished to write a rule for his brothers and another rule for lay people. Yet he felt incapable of governing his order and of challenging directives from those who did not understand it. "The order needs a Cardinal Protector who values our Form of Life," he confided to Hugo. "Please beg Lord Pope to appoint you our Cardinal Protector."

Hugo's heart sank. To be Cardinal Protector, he would have to remain a cardinal, not become a friar. While he prayed about Francis's request, Clare's words came to mind. "Your cross, my lord, is to accept God's way. In time may you see His wisdom."

Was God using Hugo to give Francis's order the guidance it needed to survive? Upon Hugo's request, Pope Honorius made him Cardinal Protector of the Poor Brothers.

❧ 25 ❧

Brother Stephen the Simple

Porziuncola, Assisi (NOVEMBER 1220) ∾ Brother Stephen screamed in his sleep because Brother Leo's dream was coming true in his own dream. A few nights ago, at Francis's bedside, Leo had recounted his dream of many friars crossing a great, flooded river. Those bearing heavy loads drowned, while those carrying nothing crossed safely. Father Francis had explained that the river was the world and the heavy loads carnal goods and desires. Only friars free of worldly attachment cross the river to eternity safely.

In Stephen's dream, he was drowning in a raging, flooded river, pulled down by a heavy keg on his back. He awoke screaming, choking for air. He slept no more that night.

Over the weeks, Stephen's chubby, innocent face grew hollow and tense with worry. Leo's dream, his own, Francis's interpretation became an obsession, for Stephen knew his sins.

Stephen had been defiant. He had sneaked away from the convento to find Francis in the Holy Land and to tell him that the two vicars he had appointed to take his place had changed the Rule.

He was guilty of presumption. He had left Assisi without Francis's permission, then begged Francis's forgiveness when he found him.

He had stolen the new, stricter regulations and given them to Francis as proof that Francis must return home.

He had been disobedient to the new rule. When Stephen found Father Francis and Peter Catani on an abstinence day after the new regulations were in effect, Francis had asked Peter, an expert in canon law, for advice. Peter said that Francis, as head of the order, could decide what to do. Francis had said that they would obey the holy Gospels and eat what was set before them. Meat had been set before them, and all three had eaten it.

He was slothful. Since he couldn't remember all his prayers, he sometimes didn't say them.

He was untrustworthy. Whenever he shared food that he had begged, he always managed to forget someone.

He was stupid because he frequently forgot to do errands.

He should have been named Brother Stephen the Sinful instead of the Simple.

How could God accept him? Stephen's sins oppressed him. Previously happy and carefree, he became despondent, withdrawn. He was going to hell.

Brother Peter Catani, whom Francis had appointed minister in Francis's place, could not lighten his fears. Father Francis, so gaunt, wan, feverish, his red-rimmed eyes watery with an inexplicable disease contracted in Egypt, could not cure him. The doctor's medicines did no good. Stephen's depression deepened until he could no longer eat or work. Nor did he care if he died. He was going to hell.

Francis said that Stephen must see Lady Clare. The friars half carried, half dragged him to San Damiano. He was so totally exhausted when they arrived that he crumpled into a whimpering heap at the speaking grill. Too drained to look into Clare's face, he felt her hand firmly pressing his head, his shoulder. As he heard her speak the words of the sign of the cross, exhaustion overcame him. His heavy eyes closed. He felt his body drowning in sleep.

The dream came again. The river, Stephen crossing it. This time he was bearing on his back a white dove that lifted him in its talons and carried him across the flood to the opposite bank, where he floated above a plain of colorful, fragrant flowers that filled him with joy.

Muddled, Stephen awoke. He pushed himself erect. How had he gotten here, to the speaking grill in San Damiano?

"Brother, are you all right?"

Stephen smiled shyly at the woman behind the grill. "Of course, Lady Clare. Why would I not be?"

"God be praised!" Clare gasped, reaching through the grill to clasp Stephen's hand.

Why did she do that? Had he been sick? He did not remember. He was terribly thirsty, however. Sheepishly, he looked at Clare. "Lady Clare, could you bring me a cup of water please? And…" Dare he ask? "And perhaps a little bread unless I am to be fasting."

"Brother," Clare said, her voice a bit breathless, "no one whom our Lord has just healed is to be fasting."

∽ 26 ∽

Brontolone

Via San Petrignano, Assisi (CHRISTMAS EVE, 1220) ∽ Brontolone hobbled down the steep hill of San Petrignano toward San Damiano. A chill December wind lashed his torn mantle and the ripped sleeves of his tunic. Stupid, ruffian children! They'd pounded him yesterday because he'd not share the fowl some noble had tossed at him. Despite his age and skinny limbs, he'd fought them off, but the scuffle had ripped his garments and injured his back. The Poor Brothers who saw the fight told him that the Poor Ladies would mend his garments and that Lady Clare would pray over his back. They'd better mend them. She'd better pray.

Finally. The church. Brontolone hobbled down five steps leading into the nave, his cloth-wrapped feet slipping on the third step. Dang step!

In the apse on the left side of the altar was that speaking grill the friars told him about. He pulled the bell cord. He pulled again. Again. Again.

Sliding. Unbolting. Through the grill's black curtain, a harried voice. "Pace e bene. May I help you?"

"Friars said ya'd mend my tunic and mantle."

"Put them on the turn, please."

Near the grill was a barrel, its rounded end facing Brontolone. "The turn ain't turned."

The barrel swiveled. It was cut in half lengthwise. Brontolone whipped off his mantle and slipped out of his torn tunic. Throwing the tunic on the floor of the barrel, he snuggled in his mantle. Brr!

The turn swiveled inward. "Where is your mantle?"

"I'd be here in my breeches if I give it to ya'."

"I'll send out my mantle. Put yours on the turn."

The turn swiveled again. Brontolone tossed his torn, threadbare mantle on the turn and wrapped himself in the newer, warmer one.

The turn swiveled inward. "Please wait."

Bolting. Sliding. Why'd they lock everything? Brontolone pressed his face against the grill and shouted, "Hurry up! It's freezin'."

Brr. He stomped his feet to keep warm. Ow! Daggers of pain shot up his back. Dang, stupid kids!

Unbolting. Sliding. So soon?

"My good man, we have a better tunic for you and a fur cape."

The turn swiveled. If these was Poor Ladies, how'd they have fur capes? Brontolone dressed himself in the garments, throwing the fur cape over the mantle he'd been given before.

"What about my blessin'?"

The curtain over the speaking grill drew upward. Brontolone jutted his pointy chin at the tall penitent who was dressed in a poor gray tunic and black veil. She wasn't much to see, rubbing her upper arms vigorously as if trying to warm up.

The lady raised her right hand. "May God bless you." The woman's teeth were chattering. If she was so cold, why'd she not put on one of them fur capes? "May He give you more than you can imagine. In the name of the Father and of the Son and of the Holy Spirit. Amen."

"Nothin' about my sore back?"

"May Christ heal your sore back. Amen."

Brontolone arched his shoulders. Ow! "Didn't do no good. You that holy nun?"

The penitent was rubbing her upper arms again. "You mean Sister Clare?"

"Yeah. You her?"

"Do you want Sister Clare to pray for you?"

"Well, sure. Don't ya' know nothin'?"

"I'll call her."

The curtain dropped. Women. Only a dog was dumber.

Within a few moments the curtain rose. Sister Clare, with her oval face and full lips, was a bit more attractive. She was wearing a patched gray lazzo tunic and a black veil. The taller, shivering penitent stood behind her, now wrapped in a shabby mantle.

"Yer prayers better than hers?"

"Would you let me touch you?"

Brontolone pushed against the grill. Sister Clare placed her hands firmly on Brontolone's shoulders. She closed her eyes and began to whisper.

"Can't hear ya'."

"Shh. Listen to God speak within you."

"Never talks to me."

"Shh."

Why'd she not pray louder? He wanted to know what was said. Moments later, she released her grip. "In the name of the Father and of the Son and of the Holy Spirit," she said. Awkwardly, he signed himself.

Brontolone wriggled his back. Ow! "Still's sore."

"We will pray for you daily," the woman said.

"Little good that'll do." Pulling the fur cape about himself, Brontolone hobbled out of the church. He had to climb all the way to Assisi with his sore back.

Friars. Holy ladies. Rubbish.

Saint Clare
in Art
and
Iconography

〜∂§〜

Elvio Marchionni / FSP, Italy

S: Paupertas

S: Castitas

S: Obedientia

Saint Clare

St. Amata.

St. Beatrix.

St. Agnes.

St. Catherine.

Simone Martini. Chiesa Interiore San Francesco—Assisi / FSP, Italy

❦ 27 ❧

Sister Benvenuta di Peroscia

San Damiano (CHRISTMAS, 1220) ❧ Drawing Clare's mantle around her, Sister Benvenuta di Peroscia closed the refectory door and stepped into the courtyard. The first of the two meals allowed on Christmas and on Sundays had been eaten. With the dishes washed and the refectory tidied, the sisters were laughing and chatting. When the friars arrived, they would gather in the parlor, the friars on the church side and the sisters on the monastery side, to talk about the infant Christ. Since coming here eight years ago Benvenuta had loved this Christmas gathering, but today she was somber.

Benvenuta walked across the courtyard matted with dried weeds and grass. She passed the vegetable garden with its green but wilted parsley. Despite the raw air, she wanted to be alone at the hermitages, to ask what she must now do.

In the leafless forest, Benvenuta followed the path quickly, dried leaves crackling under her bare feet. At the first hut, she pushed aside the leather flap that served as a door and entered, bumping into someone who was kneeling inside. Sister Clare.

Benvenuta sputtered an apology. She would use another hermitage.

"Wait, Sister," Clare said, turning to her with a gentle smile. "You seemed distracted yesterday and today. Is something troubling you?"

"You." The word burst out. "Not you. A vision. Remember when you prayed for that old beggar yesterday? The one whose tunic and mantle were so rotted that we gave him a fur cape and new tunic? After you left, the whole alcove by the speaking grill seemed to be on fire with the fire of God."

"The beggar must have brought it," Clare mused.

"Him? The fire came because of you."

"Me? You prayed there, too."

"There wasn't any fire when I prayed."

"There wasn't any fire when I prayed, either. You saw it after I left."

"That's true. But it had to be because you prayed there. You even gave me your mantle when the beggar took mine."

. "You gave the beggar your mantle first."

"Only to borrow," Benvenuta pointed out. "I didn't think he'd keep it."

"You're only borrowing mine," Clare said, "until the friars can beg wool to make you a new one. And I am warm in this scrap of wool." Clare hugged the ragged piece about her.

The whole conversation was totally confusing.

Benvenuta dropped to her knees and sat on her heels. "I wish I were like you."

"Whatever for?"

"You are holy."

Clare's rich laughter echoed through the little hut. "Oh, Sister, if I am holy, then you are a saint."

"I can't do what you do. I can't pray all night, wear hairshirts, or live on a bit of bread. Or even wash the mattresses of the sick sisters without feeling sick myself. Today at Mass you were weeping to receive our Lord in the Eucharist."

"I always cry. I cannot help it."

"It is the gift of tears. I do not have that gift."

"Oh, Sister, you have other, more useful gifts." Clare sat back on her heels and patted Benvenuta's hand. "Dear Sister Benvenuta, you must imitate Jesus, not me. Poverty and enclosure have value if we are poor in spirit and enclosed in the will of God. This does not happen when we imitate others, because then we may be doing God's will for them instead of God's will for us." Spontaneously Clare threw her arms around Benvenuta and gave her a quick, hearty hug. "Oh, Sister, do not look so sad at my little scolding. I, too, have mistakenly tried to be like someone else. First, Mother. Then Sister Pacifica. Then Father Francis. But we must be like Jesus."

Clare took Benvenuta's hand again. "Do you remember the parable of the wineskins?"

"New wine, new skins," Benvenuta said.

"Yes, because new skins are flexible. They expand as the new wine ripens. Our lives must be like new wineskins, not rigid old ones that cannot expand to hold what God is fermenting in us. Our Rule is like new skins, Sister, confining yet flexible. Within our Rule's constraints, God calls one sister to greater mortification, another to greater prayer, a third to greater service. One sister can read hearts; another, heal; a third listens with the heart." Clare smiled. "God gives the gifts and the call. At times God may change the call or the gift. True poverty is relinquishing our own ideas of how we may be sanctified and following God's plan."

Benvenuta hugged Clare's mantle about her. "God's plan. If only I knew it!"

"But you do know it. 'Love one another as I have loved you,' Jesus said." Clare embraced Benvenuta again. "Sister, all you do speaks of love. Your tending the grill, your painstaking embroidery, your willingness to serve, your fervent prayers."

"They are duties, Sister."

"To do one's duty well is an act of love. But you go beyond duty. You give a beggar your mantle when you know you will be cold without it. You come to the hermitage when the others are laughing in the refectory. You listen patiently to my little lecture while you wish to pray instead. You do another's will rather than your own. That is love, Sister. When you act with love, you are in God's will, you are holy, you are imitating Christ. Your soul is full of love."

Benvenuta thought about the fire. It had been at the place where Clare and Benvenuta had prayed, where they had shown love to a disgruntled, rude beggar. Scripture said that God is love and God is a consuming fire. The fire Benvenuta saw must have been God, must have been love. Benvenuta nodded slowly as she understood. "Sister, to become holy, I think we must become Love—the One who was born this day." A grin spread across her face. "Can we share that with the friars and sisters today?"

Clare laughed. "I think that is just what we are about to do."

PART SEVEN

~∾~

Given Up
Their Own Wills

~∾~

～ 28 ～

Brother Francis Bernardone

Parlor, San Damiano (MAY 1221) ～ Brother Francis Bernardone and the newest brother, youthful, eager-eyed Brother James, sat facing the black-curtained grill in the parlor at San Damiano.

"Pace e bene, Father Francis, Brother James." The pleasant voice was Christiana's.

"Pace e bene." Sister Cecilia's deep, throaty tone.

Francis was not feeling very pleasant. "Christiana, we must discuss this privately."

"Yes, Father."

Francis nodded at Brother James, who moved to the far end of the parlor. He heard a gentle shuffling on the other side of the grill, which meant that Sister Cecilia had likewise moved out of earshot.

Francis moved close to the grill and tried to keep his voice calm and low. "Christiana, two days ago I sent you five women to be accepted into the community. Why have you sent me word that you will accept all but Lady Gasdia?"

The firm whisper came through the curtain. "Lady Gasdia will not persist."

Francis took a deep breath. He and Christiana had an eternal, spiritual bond. A pure and holy love existed between them. Each prayed daily for the other. Each understood this way of life as no one else, and each could see and rejoice in the other's faith and efforts for holiness. So firmly was each committed to poverty, chastity, and obedience, so fully did each understand the other, that one seemed to be half of the other's soul. They even lived in much the same way, often praying through the night, fasting severely, and trading their tunics for poorer ones worn by others.

But sometimes, like now, Christiana exasperated him.

"Lady Gasdia di Taccolo di Aregnato is a holy widow," Francis said in a measured tone. "Her son is married and she is free. She wishes to serve God more totally and believes God is calling her to live here. Her family approves."

"Yes. She told me these things."

"Why do you disapprove?"

"Lady Gasdia has a burning desire to follow the poor crucified Christ. She wishes to possess the kingdom of heaven as do the other four women you sent. When I questioned each one privately, Lady Gasdia was most eager to enter here."

Yes, most eager. Lady Gasdia had been cured of a violent fever at the tomb of San Rufinus, and, ever since, had felt that her spiritual life had been lax. She wished to do penance, to grow sanctified, before she died. Several times she had spoken to Francis about giving herself completely to Christ.

"Lady Gasdia is a pious woman," Christiana was affirming, "with a most loving family. She has been following Christ closely for many years. But, as you know, penance and sanctity are quite possible outside a monastery. Our life here is one of holy poverty and destitution. Those the Lord calls to this life will rejoice always in Him, but others will find only bitterness here."

"Do you think she won't persist because she's so eager?"

"As you have experienced with your friars, often those most eager to enter fall away, while those who struggle intensely with the decision persist. Unless I am deceived, she will not persist, even should she stay here three years."

Francis grunted. "Did God tell you to reject her?"

"He told me to discuss it with you and obey your decision."

Francis took a deep breath. "Brother Elias," the new minister general of the friars who took Peter Catani's place upon Peter's death, "agreed with me that you are to accept her."

Christiana's voice was crisp. "So be it. I disagree. But I will do as you say."

❧ 29 ❧

Sister Agnes

Woods at San Damiano (SEPTEMBER 1221) ∼ Sister Agnes was stumbling through the sun-dappled woods behind San Damiano, her soft blue eyes brimming with tears, her slender form a shadow among the tree trunks. After prayer at the hour of Terce, she had obtained Clare's permission to come to the hermitages to plead for courage. But she had been so bursting with emotion that she could not stay on her knees. So on her small bare feet, she had run into the forest to cry out her prayers.

Oh, God! Agnes had been named after martyrs—Catherine of Alexandria, whose tomb Mother had visited on Mount Sinai and who had been tortured on a spiked wheel in the year 310 before being beheaded, and Agnes, a twelve-year-old virgin beheaded in 304. They had not run from their martyrdom, but she was running from hers.

How could she leave San Damiano? Leaving was a martyrdom.

Nine years ago, at the age of fourteen, Agnes had come here. She had prayed to die here. Now she was being sent to Florence. Oh, the bitterness!

With small, delicate fingers, Agnes pulled aside a bramble that snagged her skirt. Love was a bramble, snagging her. She loved too much. San Damiano. Mother. Beatrice. Clare. All her sister Damianites. The valley of Spoleto, sprawled beyond the dormitory windows.

Could she love an unknown group of sisters the way she loved these?

Like mushrooms, monasteries of Poor Sisters were springing up all over. Vallegloria in Spello. Santa Maria della Carita near the fountain of Carpello outside Foligno. Monticello in Florence. Monte Luce in Perugia. Santa Maria in Siena. Santa Mario da Gattailo in Lucca. Santo Spirito in Arezzo. Some of the sisters had traveled to this place and that to establish monasteries. Pious women, in touch with Clare through letters, had founded others.

The sisters in the new monasteries wanted to live like the sisters at San Damiano. So they wrote letters, full of questions, to Clare. But letters couldn't answer everything. Some things had to be experienced. So Francis, with Clare's approval, had sent Sister Benedetta to Siena and Sister Balvina di Martino to Arezzo. And now they were sending Agnes to Florence.

Why not Benvenuta or Pacifica, Cecilia or Filippa, Marsebilia or Cristiana or Balbina? Why Agnes?

How could Agnes leave Clare? After Christ, Clare was Agnes's support. Clare had taught Agnes nearly everything she knew about religious life. How was Agnes to teach the Monticello sisters without Clare? Without Clare, could Agnes's faith maintain any depth?

Clare. Clare. Clare could read Agnes's soul. One night months ago, after praying Matins at midnight with the friars, then helping Clare extinguish the lamps, Agnes and Clare had joined a few other sisters in the oratory to continue in prayer. As always, Agnes prayed gazing at the shadowy nook to the left of the altar in which the Eucharistic Lord rested in a small silver box.

The Lord had drawn Agnes deeply into His being. Her prayer had become a silent, internal song notated with tears.

My Father, how good, how patient You are! We constantly offend You, yet You mercifully continue to love and call us. Oh, compassionate Lord, luring the most stubborn sinners to Your side!

My Jesus, You have left nothing undone. Your hands and feet, pierced with nails, Your side with a lance. Your wounds spurted the blood of love. What agony to have loved so!

Oh, suffering souls in purgatory, what agony must you feel away from God! May God mercifully grant you the grace to give your wills totally to Him so that you may unite totally to Him!

When the intensity had faded, she had returned to the well-lit dormitory, curled up on her bare plank bed, and fallen swiftly asleep.

The next morning, she had just thrust five loaves of bread into the outdoor oven when Clare came by. Smiling curiously, Clare had casually stated, "Last night, after the others had gone to bed, I saw you praying."

Agnes nodded. "I saw you praying as well."

"I saw you rise from the ground," Clare had said.

Agnes had turned from the oven in utter disbelief.

"I saw a vivid brilliance, an angel, develop next to you."

Agnes had stared incredulously at Clare.

"The angel put a crown upon your head. Later a second crown. Then a third."

Unbelievable.

"Did the devil deceive me, Sister, or did the crowns correspond to your prayers?"

Clare be deceived? Impossible. Yet Agnes had seen no angel or crowns. Nor had she any idea that she had been floating. She only knew that she had meditated thrice, on the Father, Son, and suffering souls.

Now, in the woods, Agnes thought of her prayers that night. Had they been mere words? Or did she trust God enough to give Him all her will? In obedience, she had to leave San Damiano.

Agnes reached the monastery as the bell was ringing for Sext.

In the choir, Agnes tried to pray, to praise. But unbidden tears were streaming down her cheeks and she could barely speak. This was the last time that she would pray here, with her sisters.

The prayers ended as the bell rang. Agnes's heart leaped.

Sister Gasdia, who was tending the grill, peeked into the choir. "Sister Giacoma and Sister Forina have arrived from Monticello."

Agnes grit her teeth. "I will get my traveling pouch."

As Gasdia left, Clare rose from prayer. With the slightest tremor in her legs, weakened with a strange, recurring illness, she approached Agnes and caught her hand. "I will go with you, Sister."

Dazed, Agnes plucked the pouch packed with her mantle from the foot of her bed, flinging it over her shoulder. She reached for the hand-sized cross resting on the wooden block that served as her pillow. Every night she fell asleep clasping in prayer those two dark sticks tied together at right angles. She pressed the cross into Clare's hand.

"Pray for me, dear Sister." Agnes's voice cracked.

Clare hobbled to her bed and took from beneath her own pillow the lighter-toned twig cross she had made and slept with. She gave it to Agnes. "And you for me."

Wordlessly the sisters looked at each other, then threw themselves into each others' arms. The hug between them was savage and fierce. It might have to last until heaven.

~ 30 ~

Sister Gasdia di Taccolo di Aregnato

Dormitory, San Damiano (NOVEMBER 1221) ~ Half asleep, Sister Gasdia heard sleet pinging the shutters of the dormitory windows at San Damiano. Curled into a tight ball on her wooden pallet, her tunic pulled over her bare feet, she shivered. Groggily, she tried to pull up her blanket. Had she kicked it off?

She should arise and find her blanket. But she was half dreaming, walking through the small garden behind her palatial Assisi home. She could see herself clearly. Her shoulder-length auburn hair threaded with silver caught up in a lace cripinette at her neck, the red velvet cap on her head fastened snugly beneath her chin with a black velvet strap. In her oval face, her deep brown eyes were bright as she watched two grandchildren darting among red poppies.

Gently a woolen blanket dropped over her shoulders. Sighing, Gasdia pulled it around her neck. Clare had covered her as she did all the sisters who kicked off their wraps, just as Gasdia used to cover her son and now her grandchildren.

Six months ago, Gasdia, hopeful and zealous, had come to San Damiano. For three months she had lived in bliss, relishing the prayers, silence, and love. Then nagging longings surfaced to see those she had counseled, advised, served, and loved. Her son Pietro. Her grandchildren. Servants. Neighbor women.

Yet she loved the sisters, too. She had shared their concerns, offered her insights, helped many.

Still, the pull to leave was strong and had grown stronger. When she spoke to Clare about it, Clare had told her that she must discern.

So she had prayed, and words had come from deep within. YOU CANNOT STAY.

Today she was leaving San Damiano.

Gasdia felt a gentle shaking and heard a soft, cheery ringing— Sister Clare waking the sisters with a small, silver bell. Time for Lauds and Prime, the second and third of the seven daily offices.

Gasdia pushed back her blanket and nodded to Clare, who was smiling brightly at her. Clare smiled often, even during this penitential season of the Lent of Saint Martin.

Gasdia straightened her veil, awry from sleeping in it, and smoothed the skirt of her tunic. Then, wrapping herself in her mantle, she proceeded downstairs to the dimly lit choir.

Several silent minutes later, Clare, bundled in her patched lazzo mantle, unlocked the small doors that covered the grill in the apse of the church. Drawing back the curtain, she took her place among the sisters. In the church, Friar Cappellano began to chant Lauds. "In the name of the Father and of the Son and of the Holy Spirit." As Gasdia blessed herself, she bit her lip to hold back her tears. Barely two months had passed since Sister Agnes had left for Florence. Gasdia's longings had been surfacing even then, but she had not thought that they would come to this.

Back and forth the stanzas alternated, the friars praying one verse and the sisters the next. A friar in the church read the readings, Sister Filippa read today's prayers. The pace was measured, devout.

In the church, Friar Cappellano began today's Mass. The sleet stopped. A raging wind blew up, snaking frosty fingers through cracks in the shutter over the choir window. The light pressing through those cracks was sickly gray. Gasdia began to shiver. Standing beside her, Sister Pacifica took her large mantle and draped one end of it over Gasdia's shoulders, drawing Gasdia close to her side. The gentle gesture was sweet. Gasdia could not restrain her tears.

When Mass ended, Clare drew the curtain over the grill and bolted the doors. Turning, she raised her hand over the women to give them her usual morning blessing. Making the sign of the cross, Clare prayed, "May the Lord bless you and keep you. May He show His face to you and be merciful to you. May He turn His countenance to you and give you peace. May the Lord always be with you, and may you always be with Him."

One by one, the sisters embraced Gasdia before filing out to their day's work.

"We will pray for you, Sister. Do pray for us."

"Your family will be glad for your return."

"We will miss you."

"Come and visit."

The words did little to assuage Gasdia's pain. Unlike these other women, she had failed in this life. Like them, she could fast, pray, mend, live in poverty. Yet she wanted to be home.

She did not want to leave. And yet she did.

Finally Gasdia was alone with Clare. "We had told your brother and your son to meet us at the speaking grill following Mass," Clare softly reminded her. "Shall we see if they are here?"

Lord Andrea and Lord Pietro were, indeed, at the speaking grill, not in the parlor as they had been when Gasdia entered San Damiano. During the Lent of Saint Martin, except in special and needful circumstances, the parlor remained in penitential silence.

"Mother, it will be good to have you home," Pietro said, his voice joyful. "The children have missed you. Bringing them here to visit has only made them miss you more."

"The house has not been the same without you," Andrea confided. "The servants seem more quarrelsome and discourteous. I cannot bring out the best in them as you can."

Gasdia could say nothing to the black-curtained grill but "Have you brought my clothes?"

They had. They sent them in on the turn, a new, plum-colored gown and cap and a deep chestnut mantle. Accompanied by Clare, Gasdia carried the garments to the dormitory, where she removed her religious garb and clothed herself in worldly clothes. Then, like a wooden puppet, she approached the doorway at the dormitory's far end.

"Lady Gasdia," Clare said tenderly, touching her arm. She held out to Gasdia the wooden cross that Gasdia had kept beside her pallet, two sticks bound together with thread.

Gasdia took the simple sacramental. "Pray for me, Sister," she begged, her voice husky.

"And you pray for us. Always remember that God has the right to call us into whatever He wishes. Our duty is to follow His footsteps wherever they lead. God's vision is better than ours."

The two women embraced quickly. Then Gasdia opened the door to the enclosure and saw Pietro and Andrea at the bottom of the staircase, their horses' heads bowed into the whipping wind. Between them stood a third, riderless palfrey, waiting for her.

"Grazie, Sister Clare," Gasdia said. "Mille grazie for everything."

Clare smiled. "You have not failed, Lady Gasdia. You have grown here. Nourish that growth and continue in it."

"Grazie," Gasdia said again. She stepped out into the bitter, driving wind and began the descent. Suddenly she knew that the Gasdia leaving was not the Gasdia who had entered. What she had learned here about prayer, penance, and love, she could take home. It felt right to be going back.

PART EIGHT

What Is Painful
and Bitter

~ 31 ~

Brother Francis Bernardone

Hermitage within Chaplain's House, San Damiano (APRIL 1225) ~ On a chill April night, Brother Francis Bernardone was lying on a straw bed in a little hut inside the chaplain's house at San Damiano. The house abutted the church so that, through its walls, Francis could hear and join in the Office. Matins had concluded, but Francis had not fallen asleep. Mice that bred in the walls of this cell clambered over him like thoughts that troubled his mind. Too weak to flick off mice or thoughts, he thought he would go mad.

Weeks ago, his concerns had grown so intense that he knew he must be alone to pray. The friars would not allow him to stay at the Porziuncola because the March humidity and fog worsened his health. So he had come here, to the friary closest to the beloved center of his order, intending to stay in one of the ladies' hermitages. The friars had refused, constructing for him instead this indoor hermitage, using reed mats that the Poor Ladies had woven.

Days and nights had merged while Francis lay weakly in the dark, praying, exhausted, depressed. Even meditating on Christ's suffering on the cross, tormented physically and mentally, could not bring Francis peace. On Mount La Verna, he had asked God to allow him to feel all the physical and spiritual pain that Christ had suffered. God was answering his prayer.

Were demons spawning the questions that beat his soul more severely than demons ever beat his body? Or did the questions result from his own sinfulness? How could he be sure of God's grace? Had he founded a burgeoning order on mist? Had his willfulness spawned the tensions dividing the friars? What would happen to his order? Did it matter?

Due to illness, carelessness, or ignorance, he had not always kept the Rule exactly nor prayed every hour of the Office. This he had confessed in a recent general letter to the order in which he had urged all his brothers to follow the Rule with perfect humility and obedience, as Francis would do from now on.

His sin was as black as the darkness into which his eye disease had plunged him. He could not bear even the dimmest light, so the brothers had stitched an oversized hood with a woolen and linen band for him. The band could be tightened across his eyes, blocking all light. When the weather warmed, Brother Elias would send for a doctor to treat his vision, but success was not guaranteed. Francis was in anguish at the thought of remaining blind forever.

However, his eye pain was mild compared to the throbbing of his pierced hands and feet and wounded side. Francis had borne these wounds of Christ since September, when he had been keeping a forty-day fast prior to the Feast of Saint Michael the Archangel on September 29. He had been praying and fasting on torturous Monte La Verna, a count's gift to the order, when one night, around the Feast of the Exaltation of the Cross, a flaming seraph affixed to a cross had appeared in the dark sky. Pondering the apparition, Francis had slowly realized that the wounds of the crucified Christ were appearing in his hands, feet, and side.

He had tried to hide the wounds, but they needed cleansing, bandaging. Already weak from intermittent fevers, persistent abdominal cramps, worsening eye pains, and constant headaches reminiscent of Christ's crown of thorns, Francis asked his confessor, the priest Brother Leo, to tend his wounds without telling others. Dear Brother Leo. Tall, sturdy, young, with a large squarish head and a full, gentle face. Frate Pecorella, Francis called Leo. Brother Little Lamb of God.

But the secret came out when Francis had returned from Monte La Verna, riding a donkey because he could not walk on his pierced feet. Then people who heard him preaching throughout Umbria and the Marches began to proclaim him a saint. He had come here to confront the thought of who he really was.

He discovered that a sinner could not govern an order. Nine years ago, the first trouble in the order had begun, as if Satan had attacked as soon as the Pope had granted the Porziuncola indulgence. First, Francis's worsening health. Then the friars' reluctance to beg for the Poor Ladies. Francis's eye illness. The changes made in the order under the two vicars he had appointed while he was in the Holy Land. Dismissing the vicars in 1220, Francis had appointed Peter Catani. When Peter died the following year, Francis had chosen capable, faithful, intelligent Brother Elias of Cortona as vicar.

But Elias was domineering, even frightening. He had allowed Francis's brother Angelo to construct, at the Porziuncola, a sumptuous building to house the friars for their 1221 chapter meeting. Although the dwelling was antithetical to poverty, Francis could not demolish it because it belonged, Angelo said, to the commune of Assisi. The building stirred in the friars a desire for property, houses, and possessions. The squabbling about his Rule, written that same year and then rewritten in 1223, was ongoing.

The only one he felt sure of was Christiana. And now she was ill. He could not go to visit her, though she asked for him, nor could she come to him.

Maybe he had been wrong to visit Christiana so infrequently, despite her begging. He had always been concerned about purity, even refusing to look at women—except for Christiana and Lady Jacoba di Settisoli, the holy penitent. Francis feared the least thought of carnality. How could he manage love? He made excuses not to visit San Damiano. His trips, illnesses, prayer vigils, fasts, and other concerns left him little spare energy. Friars were not to visit nuns without permission of the Apostolic See. Two years ago, with Cardinal Hugolino's approval, he had added such a provision to his Rule.

Yet Christiana seemed unafraid to love him. She made ointments for his wounds. She had asked to mend his tunic and wished to sew new slippers for his feet. Many times he had worn the pale deacon's alb of fine lace, tiny gathers, and delicate embroidery that she had made for him from the cast-off clothing of the nobility.

Oh, Lord, help me. Give me strength.

TELL ME, BROTHER, a voice within his soul said, IF, IN EXCHANGE FOR THESE TROUBLES AND ILLNESSES, YOU WERE GIVEN A TREASURE VASTER THAN THE WORLD, WOULDN'T YOU BE HAPPY?

The inner voice startled him. *Lord, such a treasure would be most lovely.*

THEN REJOICE IN YOUR TROUBLES AND ILLNESSES, BROTHER, AND TRUST IN ME, AS THOUGH YOU WERE ALREADY IN MY KINGDOM.

An indescribable joy swept Francis's soul, thrusting aside his depression. Surely God was blessing him in these trials, preparing him for eternity! Though too feeble to sing with his lips, Francis sensed a hymn bubbling in his soul. Oh, if only he listened, he could catch the words!

∽ 32 ∽

Sister Filippa di Leonardo di Gislerio

Chaplain's House, San Damiano (APRIL 1225) ∽ Sister Filippa followed Sisters Pacifica and Clare into the reed hut where Father Francis lay. By the light of the candle in Brother Leo's hand, Filippa could see that Francis was a living shell. Tears welled in her eyes as she backed against the hut wall so that Clare could draw near to this saint.

Clare touched Francis's thin fingers with her own bony ones. "Pace e bene, Father," she said softly. "Here is your mended tunic and some new buckskin slippers."

Clare had made the slippers and mended the tunic, cutting a piece from her own mantle to patch it.

Francis feebly reached toward the bundle Clare had placed across his chest. "Grazie for these and for coming to me."

"You are so ill." Clare's voice was beginning to quake. "You could not come to me...I was too ill to come to you. Thanks be to God that I can see you now."

A feeble smile crept across Francis's lips. "But I cannot see you." Indeed, he could not. His eyes were tightly bandaged. "Yet I see you in my mind, wavery and indistinct as on that day on the way back from Siena nine years ago."

Filippa remembered. Francis had been wondering if Clare was all right and if Lord Pope would grant her sisters the privilege of owning nothing. He had seen her in the moon's reflection in a well and knew that all was well.

Clare was smiling. "I fear I looked better then than now."

"Christiana, what is your illness?" Francis's voice was fatherly.

"A weakness that comes and goes."

"Are you eating?"

"Every day I eat at least half a roll, as Bishop Guido commanded me five years ago—at your request, Father."

"Do you sleep?"

"Well enough. The discreets wish me to use straw bedding and pillow as allowed the sick."

"Your discreets are wise." Clare had chosen the discreet sisters to help make decisions for the community. "Your prayer vigils?"

Clare had been remaining in prayer from Compline, the day's last prayer, until midnight, when she would rouse the ladies for Matins. After praying the Office of Terce at midmorning, she had been keeping another prayer vigil.

"The vigils are sweetness, Father."

He smiled. "Continue to keep them. One can keep vigil when sick."

"You are sick, too. We brought warm water, new bandages, and ointments to cleanse your wounds."

"Frate Pecorella cleanses my wounds." His crisp words had a sharpness about them. Then, in a softer tone, "But would you wash my face, Christiana?"

"Gladly."

As Clare tenderly bathed his face, tears trickled down her cheeks and splashed against Francis.

"You wished to speak to me?"

"Yes. Father, if the devil has been tormenting you, you must oppose him bravely and pay him no heed."

Francis drew in his breath in a low whistle. "What makes you share this?"

Clare sat back on her heels. "The friars say that doctors believe your eye disease occurred because of your excessive weeping over our Lord's sufferings. I fear the devil may use it to dissuade you from these fruitful meditations."

Francis nodded. "The devil has tried to dissuade me."

Clare dried Francis's face. "I feared so. For he tried to dissuade me. One night shortly after you arrived here, I awoke. By my bed stood a child as black as night. 'You should not cry so much because you will become blind,' the child said. 'Whoever sees God will not be blind,' I told him. And the child disappeared in confusion."

Francis nodded thoughtfully. "So you have seen the devil."

Francis had seen him, too, the friars said.

Clare's voice was shaky. "Later that night, after Matins, I remained as usual to pray and weep over my Lord. Again the child appeared. 'You should not cry so much. Otherwise your brain will dissolve and flow through your nose because you will have a crooked nose.' 'Whoever knows the Lord suffers nothing that is crooked,' I told him. Again, he scampered off and vanished."

"These frightened you." Francis's tone was soothing.

"He returned." Clare's voice grew lower, quieter. "Last week, while still unable to rise from bed, I was praying at None and thinking of the hour in which Christ breathed His last. I could feel His sufferings as if I were below the cross with Saint Mary Magdalene and our Lady. Quite suddenly the devil child appeared and struck me on the cheek so hard that my eye filled with blood and my cheek was badly bruised."

Feebly Francis reached toward Clare. She caught his fingers in hers. "Does it still hurt, Christiana?"

"Not much now." Clare paused. "Bravely oppose the demon's onslaughts, Father, for the subtle Prince of Darkness will attempt to reduce your soul to nothing."

"This is what I needed to hear. Grazie." His voice cracked. He seemed unable to speak. Finally Francis managed to ask, "Anything else?"

"No."

"Do you remember my sermon here last year when I was on my way from Foligno to Monte La Verna to keep the Lent of Saint Michael?"

Under obedience to Brother Elias, Francis preached to the Poor Ladies as Clare had been begging him to do. Wordlessly he had stood before the grill, his arms raised to heaven. Then he had asked his companion friar to bring him ashes from the hearth. Francis had sprinkled ashes about himself in a circle, then flung a few on his head. Kneeling in the circle, he had bowed to the floor and prayerfully chanted the great psalm of repentance and misery, Psalm 51. "Have mercy on me, God, in Your kindness. In Your compassion blot out my offense." Upon completing the psalm, he had left.

"Did you understand the sermon, Christiana?"

"I understood that we are all sinners."

"The sermon had a deeper meaning. In Foligno, a holy, white-haired priest, perhaps San Feliciano, the city's patron saint, appeared to Brother Elias in a vision. The holy priest told Brother Elias that I would live two more years, making twenty the total number of the years since my conversion. Next year will be the twentieth year."

Clare shuddered. "No! You began this order." Her voice was shaking, her tears swift. "You begot us. You are our father. Do not leave us orphans!"

"Christiana, when I die, the friars and ladies will look to you as mother." Strong, forceful words. "You must take care of your health and get well."

"How can we continue without you?" Filippa heard fear in Clare's voice. "I am but your little plant. Who will feed and water me if not you?"

"God has always fed and watered you. You have always been His. He is all you need."

"God is good, trustworthy, powerful, and great. But I am weak."

"No. Your body is weak. You are strong because you love our Lord. Much love makes much strength. When I die, you must always follow the poor Christ as the head of our order."

"You know I will," Clare's voice quaked. "It is all I ever wanted. Pray for me. Wherever you are, pray for me."

"I will pray for you until you reach heaven." Francis's voice was catching. "Continue to pray for me and for the order. For the order, as I do."

"I shall pray for you until you reach heaven and for the order forever." Their fingers still touching were trembling.

"Be brave, Christiana. God is with you. Now let us bless each other."

⤮ 33 ⤭

Sister Agnese di Oportulo de Bernardo

Oratory, San Damiano (LATE JULY, 1225) ⤳ *Oh, God!* sixteen-year-old Sister Agnese di Oportulo prayed, her lank face bowed to the brick floor of the oratory at San Damiano, her Eucharistic Lord before her. *Papa, do you know what you have done?*

Papa, Lord Oportulo de Bernardo, was podesta of Assisi. Stubborn, strong, intimidating, Oportulo ran the commune like an army, meting unrelenting justice to thieves, bribers, heretics, army deserters, the sacrilegious, and maintaining fierce loyalty to his friends. But he could not embrace Francis's ideal that all people were equal. Thus Oportulo had become entangled in Perugia's bitter civil war.

As had happened in Assisi—in a civil war that had officially ended the year after Agnese was born—the Perugian commoners had ejected the nobility in a bloody struggle to establish a communal government. When the Perugini knights had asked Assisi for help, the knights of both cities had created an alliance that was prolonging the Perugian class struggle. Desiring peace, the Pope had dissolved the alliance, only to have representatives of both cities defiantly meet in Deruta to renew it. When Lord Oportulo swore to observe the agreement, Bishop Guido had excommunicated him. So Brother Leo had told the sisters.

Excommunicated? Slender Agnese could hardly breathe. Papa—cast outside the Church? He could not receive the sacraments nor have public prayers said for him. No indulgences could be applied to his soul nor could he receive Christian burial.

With her high broad forehead wrinkled in misery, Agnese had sent Papa a tearful message via Brother Leo—"Papa, I am praying for you. Repent. Do what the Pope asked."

Suddenly, strong arms embraced her. A face pressed between her bony shoulder blades, radiating strength, sorrow, empathy. The bottom edge of a habit, patched with a zigzag remnant, caught her eye. Clare. In the grip of her spiritual mother, Agnese pleaded for her father. *Oh, God! Oh, God!*

Other sisters entered the oratory, falling to their knees. Agnese heard their whispered pleas, their quiet sobs.

Oh, God!

Agnese had been a skinny, curly-haired, eager-eyed ten-year-old when she had begged Papa to let her join the sisters at San Damiano. After a year of pleading, Papa had relented. Clare had cut her hair around her head and made her a sackcloth tunic and coarse chemise. Pacifica had taught her about the saints and Filippa, stitching. Cecilia had taught her to cook and Giovanna to garden. Agnes had taught her how to pray. Clare had instructed her on care of the sick. Lucia, a dancing-eyed girl three years older than herself, had become her best friend.

A year later, Agnese had been clothed as a sister. She had sold her family inheritance to her family and given the money to the poor. When Papa sent her something, she kept it if she needed it or gave it to another sister or the poor if she didn't. She was happy.

Now ladies closer to her own age were entering—this year, worrywart Sister Angeluccia of Spoleto and, last year, eager Sister Benvenuta of Lady Diambre, whom everyone called Sister Venuta. Since Clare had sent Lucia to Cortona to found a monastery, Angeluccia and Venuta had become Agnese's best friends.

The bell rang for the prayers at Sext. Clare gave Agnese's shoulders a firm, loving squeeze. With a sad smile, Agnese caught Clare's hand in gratitude and held it as they silently descended the stairs to the choir.

The Office was that for the hour of Jesus's death. Clare often wept during this Office. Today Agnese wept as well.

When the Office was completed, Agnese lingered while Clare dropped the curtain over the grill and bolted the shutter. As Clare left the choir, Agnese caught up with her. "Sister, may I wear one of your hairshirts as a penance for my father?"

Clare's finely shaped eyebrows arched as a thin smile traced her full lips. She motioned for Agnese to follow her upstairs.

In the dormitory, Clare lifted her straw-filled pillow. Beneath it lay a horsehair shirt laced with knots.

"Say nothing about wearing it," Clare cautioned, her finger to her lips.

"Grazie, Sister." Stripping off her tunic and chemise, Agnese slipped on the horsehair shirt, tied it to her body, and immediately questioned her idea. Each hair seemed an iron filament. Her clothing worn over the shirt pressed the hairs into Agnese's flesh. *This is penance,* she thought, as she and Clare proceeded to the infirmary to tend the ill sisters.

Agnese struggled through the day, trying not to squirm or scratch. That night, as Clare was washing the feet of the sisters in the refectory, Agnese had an idea. When Agnese's feet had been washed and Clare was about to discard the gray water in the washbasin, Agnese impulsively asked, "Sister, allow me to drink that water as a penance for Papa."

Clare shook her head. "Sister, pray instead."

"Please, Sister. For Papa."

"These penances can become extreme, Sister."

"Please. For Papa. This one time."

Clare glanced from the filthy water to Agnese's pleading face and nodded. "Just this once."

Taking the basin but refusing to look long at it, Agnese swallowed her courage along with a small mouthful of water. The honey sweetness of the water startled and almost gagged her as Clare quickly took the basin away before Agnese could drink more.

"Your sincerity and desire for penance please God," Clare said, "but never again drink anything foul."

Was God pleased? Agnese had wanted to drink the entire basin for Papa's return to the Church, yet she had trouble swallowing a little mouthful. Nevertheless, she still wore the hairshirt. But, oh, it was bothering her.

For three days, Agnese wore the shirt, so distracted by it that she could hardly pray or sleep, until she returned the garment to Clare. How could Clare wear it?

That morning, while Agnese was drawing water at the well, Pacifica approached her. "Sister, are you still wearing the hairshirt?"

Agnese felt her face grow red. "How did you know?"

"Your bed is next to mine. We stand together in choir. You have been itching, squirming."

Agnese hung her head as she picked up her full bucket. "I could not stand it any longer."

"Whose was it?"

Should she tell?

"Whose, my child?" Above her aristocratic Roman nose, Pacifica's dark eyes were gently encouraging.

"Sister Clare's." Agnese's voice was very small.

"Was it the horsehair shirt or the boar's hair one?"

"Horsehair. But it feels like needles."

Pacifica nodded thoughtfully. "The boar's hair shirt is worse. She does not require any of us to wear a hairshirt, yet she, who is often ill, wears one."

"Why do you not take them away from her?" Agnese asked.

"We have been trying to for years. I am going to call the discreets together and discuss this again."

That evening, as the sisters were retiring, Sister Pacifica and the other discreets gathered about Clare's bed. Agnese heard whispers, some quite agitated. When the discreets finally left Clare's bedside, Pacifica was carrying with her Clare's two hairshirts.

Early the next morning, Brother Leo called for Agnese again. "Your father has ordered that no one in the commune may sell anything to the bishop or contract in any way with him or his household. The hatred between the bishop and your father is very great."

Papa! You have not repented nor made peace. You have struck back. Papa! Hatred is not of God. Is it you and the commune against our Lord?

"Brother," Agnese said, her voice quaking, "would you tell Papa that our Lord Jesus Christ begs forgiveness and peace? Ask Papa if he wants to go to hell."

Oh, Agnese had to do more penance for Papa! She began to barely eat. But then she grew so ravenous that she could neither sleep nor pray nor tend the ill sisters. So, she ate again. She wanted to drink the water she used to cleanse the sick women, but Clare had told her never again to drink anything foul. So she thought of cinching her cord, tight, tighter. Clare spotted it and told her to loosen the knot. When she had begged Clare to allow that penance, Clare had told her that joyful obedience and great love in doing daily tasks can win more for God's kingdom than self-chosen penances. Agnese wanted desperately to believe that.

Muggy July slipped onward. The prayers of the sisters continued. One day, very late in the month, Angeluccia, Venuta, and Cristiana de Bernardo da Suppo, who had been Clare's friend since their teens, lay in the infirmary, weak and wan.

"Sisters," Clare said tenderly, kneeling between Venuta and Cristiana's beds, "patiently bear these sufferings because you are following in the footprints of the suffering Christ. These trials bring an eternal reward." Daily she gave similar encouragement to the ill sisters. Then, as usual, Clare traced the sign of the cross over each ill woman.

"I bear suffering so poorly," Angeluccia said, her large eyes brimming with innocence. "Even the little scratchings in my mattress keep my awake."

"Scratchings?" Clare asked abruptly. "Have you heard these scratchings long?"

"They started last night. I should not mind them."

"Yes, you should," Clare said. "There are vermin in your mattress, Sister. But we shall get rid of them."

"I've heard scratchings, too," Venuta said weakly.

"And I, too," Cristiana added.

"Come, Sister Agnese." Clare pointed to fresh mattresses leaning against the opposite wall. She and Agnese dragged the bulky mattresses across the floor and helped the three sisters onto them.

"Oh! The moving made me sick," Angeluccia grunted.

In an instant Agnese had thrust a bowl under Angeluccia's chin while Clare tenderly rubbed her back. When Angeluccia's thin little body sank back onto her fresh mattress, Clare dipped a cloth into a bucket of water and bathed her forehead. Agnese picked up the bowl to dump its contents outdoors.

"When will we get well, Sister Clare?" Venuta asked. "We pray up here when we hear the prayers in the choir, but it's not the same as being with the others."

"It is better," Clare said, "because your prayer is joined with suffering as was Christ's prayer."

Carrying the bowl, Agnese descended the ladder leading to the yard. As she approached scrubby bushes at the edge of the enclosure, she heard a mattress splat on the grass. Turning, she saw a second and then a third mattress tumble out the open doorway. Then Clare started down the ladder.

Agnese chucked the bowl's contents into the bushes as Clare unstuffed the mattresses and tossed the straw into the outdoor oven several feet from the infirmary stairs. Agnese rinsed the bowl and carried it upstairs, then carried a bucket down to fetch cool, fresh water for the ill sisters.

The smell near the well stopped her. Clare was scrubbing the mattress covers. How could they smell so bad wet when they hadn't smelled so bad dry?

Agnese wrinkled her nose as she drew the water to fill the bucket. "Oh, that smell!"

"It is sweet and delectable, isn't it?"

Agnese was dumbfounded. Why did wet mattresses and chamberpots that Clare voluntarily emptied smell sweet to Clare and foul to everyone else? As Clare draped a mattress cover over shrubs to dry, Agnese lugged up the bucket upstairs while offering this duty for Papa.

In the infirmary, Angeluccia was beaded with sweat. Agnese bathed her burning face, struggling to bring down the young woman's temperature. What if Angeluccia died? Now?

As she ran the moist cloth over Angeluccia's bony arms, Agnese bumped into a truth. She could care for the ill sisters and pray for them, but she could not heal them. Nor could they heal themselves. God effected physical healing. Spiritual healing was different. Anyone who wished to be spiritually healthy would be. All one had to do was ask and believe.

But one had to ask for oneself.

Agnese could send Papa a message. She could plead with him, love him, pray, and do penance for him. In answer, God might rain graces on Papa, but God would not force him to repent. Papa would have to decide for himself to return to God, who desperately wanted him back. If Papa repented, God would forgive him, because love could do nothing else.

The hours crept on, shadows lengthened, night came. Agnese was doing all she could for Papa. Papa had to do the rest. Sleep came for Agnese, and with it, peace.

～ 34 ～

Lord Oportulo de Bernardo

Vescovado, Assisi (END OF JULY, 1225) ～ Dressed in armor as the captain of Assisi's army, Lord Oportulo de Bernardo stood straight as a pillar in the enclosed courtyard of Bishop Guido's palace. Although he appeared calm, he was seething within. He had no desire to see, much less speak with, that devious enemy of the commune, the supposed man of God. Oportulo was here to meet the bishop only because Brother Francis, who was suffering unbearable illness at San Damiano, had asked it. Francis's friars were here, standing between the podesta and the bishop, all of them surrounded by a thick crowd that had assembled to watch the confrontation.

From his chair at the foot of the stairs leading into his palace, the aged bishop rose, his long pallium, scrolled with gold, dropping to his feet. Murmuring ceased.

In the silence, stately, good-looking Brother Pacifico, a poet and a ballad singer, called out, "Father Francis has composed 'The Praises of the Lord' to which he asks your full attention." Just that quickly, the friars began to sing a haunting melody.

Oportulo was stunned. He came to hear a song?

> **Most High, all-powerful, good Lord!**
> **Yours are the praises, the glory, the honor, and all**
> **blessing,**
> **To You alone, Most High, do they belong,**
> **and no one is worthy to mention Your name.**

The friars were singing, their eyes raised to heaven, their arms elevated in prayer. Oportulo felt his soul lifting, its coldness melting .

> **Praised be You, my Lord, with all Your creatures,**
> **especially Sir Brother Sun,**
> **Who is the day and through whom You give us light.**

And he is beautiful and radiant with great splendor;
and bears a likeness of You, Most High One.

The words sent shivers along Oportulo's spine. Brother Francis could not bear light, yet he was praising the sun he could not see.

The friars went on singing slowly, plaintively, prayerfully, of all of God's creation. The words and melody were soothing and beautiful, putting all things into perspective.

Sisters Moon and Stars
Brothers Wind and Air
Sister Water
Brother Fire
Sister Mother Earth.

Blind Francis was dying yet he was praising God. Oportulo had much to live for, yet had turned his back on God. He had made no effort to return to the Church, despite the many pleading messages that had come from his dear Agnese. What prayers had she been praying, what sacrifices had she been making—for him? How much suffering had Agnese borne because of his stubbornness?

Praised be You, my Lord, through those who give
pardon for Your love
and bear infirmity and tribulation.
Blessed are those who endure in peace
for by You, Most High, they shall be crowned.

The words that drifted like incense into silence became lances in Oportulo's soul. The friars had sung, "Praised be You...through those who give pardon for Your love."

Tears sprang to Oportulo's eyes as remorse shook his huge frame.

"Truthfully, I tell you all," he called out, "not only do I forgive lord bishop whom I ought to recognize as my master, but I would even pardon my brother's and my own son's murderer!" He knelt at Guido's feet, his head bowed but his voice strong. "For the love of Christ and of Brother Francis, I will make any atonement you wish."

He felt big hands, strong hands, on his shoulders, and looked up into Guido's sagging face. "Rise, my lord."

Oportulo obeyed.

"As bishop, I ought to be humble yet am quick to grow angry. You must forgive me." Guido opened his arms and Oportulo fell into them. The two men embraced, kissing each other on one cheek and then the other.

↶ 35 ↷

Sister Angeluccia

Choir, San Damiano (EARLY AUGUST, 1225) ↷ Sister Angeluccia had been thrust toward the front of the sisters clustered around the choir grill at San Damiano. Thin and weak after her recent illness, she hoped she would not faint. Brother Leo and Brother Pacifico were at the grill.

Leo was speaking. "Dear Ladies, Cardinal Hugolino has obtained the consent of papal court physicians to give Father Francis the best possible treatment for his eye illness."

Angeluccia nodded. He had been treated unsuccessfully in May.

"So within a day or two, Brother Elias will take Father Francis to Rieti." Members of the papal court had been residing in Rieti since June when they had left Rome due to rebellion in the city.

"To bid farewell, Father Francis has composed a song for you, so that you might trust in the Lord always."

Father Francis was going to leave? Angeluccia had not seen him once since he had been here. But still she felt an emptiness to think that he, so near, was going.

Brother Pacifico began to sing a gentle, cadenced melody.

> **Listen, little poor ones called by the Lord,**
> **who have come together from many parts and**
> **provinces.**
> **Live always in truth,**
> **that you may die in obedience.**
> **Do not look at the life outside,**
> **for that of the Spirit is better.**
> **I beg you through great love**
> **to use with discretion**
> **the alms which the Lord gives you.**

Those who are weighed down by sickness
and the others who are wearied because of them,
all of you: bear it in peace.
For you will sell this fatigue at a very high price
and each one of you will be crowned queen
in heaven with the Virgin Mary.

As the friars' voices faded into stillness, the words struck Angeluccia. How the sisters had cared for her in her illness! Would they all be crowned queen partly because of that?

"Sing it to us again, Brothers." The trembling voice was Clare's. She appeared almost stricken, her face streaked with tears. "Perhaps..." It seemed as if she could not go on. "Perhaps these are the last words," her speech quaked, "that Father Francis will ever speak to us."

~ 30 ~

Sister Ortolana di Favarone

Church of San Damiano (SUNDAY, OCTOBER 4, 1226) ~ Sister Ortolana di Favarone was sitting at Clare's bedside with several other sisters, chatting softly about Father Francis, when she heard trumpets blaring and countless men singing exultantly. Curious, the sisters rushed to the windows that opened in the direction of Rivo Torto. In the October sun, up the Via San Petrignano, behind two friars carrying huge lighted candles and six friars carrying a simple wooden coffin, paraded a massive cortege of knights, horses, lords, priests, merchants, and friars, the bright banners of Assisi's many guilds waving over the crowd.

"What is it?" Clare asked from her bed.

"A funeral." Ortolana turned from the window, her voice flat. "Father Francis must have died."

"He said we would see him again! He is a saint. He cannot have been wrong."

Ortolana threw her arms around Clare's shaky body. "Even saints can make mistakes, Chiara."

Yesterday on San Damiano's Saturday cleanup day, Ortolana had just finished scrubbing the church with Balvina and Pacifica when Brother Cappellano had arrived from the Porziuncola where he and the other San Damiano friars, along with many men of Assisi, were keeping vigil at Francis's bedside.

Clare took from her bedside a loosely rolled parchment that Cappellano had brought yesterday in response to her persistent fear that either she or Francis, both deathly ill, would die before seeing each other again. From his bed, Francis had dictated this letter as well as letters to several others and a final Testament to his friars.

Almost savagely, Clare unrolled the parchment and, in trembling voice, read: "I, brother Francis, the little one, wish to follow the life and poverty of our most high Lord Jesus Christ and of His most holy Mother and to persevere in this until the end; and I ask and counsel you, my ladies, to live always in this most holy life and poverty." Clare

160

pressed her fingers into her eyes and wiped her tears. "And keep most careful watch that you never depart from this by reason of the teaching or advice of anyone."

Heaving a huge sigh as if to bolster her courage, Clare continued. "And I absolve you, Christiana, for every transgression of the commands of the Son of God or of mine, which you may have been guilty of."

Clare shuddered. "Brother Cappellano said, 'Tell Christiana that she must now put aside all care and tribulation because she cannot get to see me. Tell her that, before she dies, both she and her ladies shall see me and they will have great comfort from it.' He said we would see him." The sisters had not seen Francis since he had left San Damiano over a year ago.

"God," Clare said fiercely, "would not take our father away from us. After God, Father Francis has always been our one consolation and support. If our father has died...."

Clang! Clang! Clang! The bell at the speaking grill.

"Do you think they would bring Father Francis here?" Pacifica asked.

"We must go down." Clare was struggling to push herself out of bed.

Clustering around Clare, the sisters supported her as they descended to the choir. From the church came vibrant song, exalting God, praising Francis. With shaky fingers, Clare unbolted the wooden doors locked across the communion grill and tugged aside the curtain.

Near the grill stood brothers Elias, Leo, Angelo di Tancredi, Giles, Bernardo di Quintavalle, and others, their faces strained, clustered around a simple closed coffin. With her hand resting lightly on the coffin stood Lady Jacoba de Settesoli, beautiful in her pale linen gown, her finely featured face wet with tears. Behind them the church was filled with men of every class, singing, carrying candles, waving olive branches and silken flags.

"Pace e bene, ladies." Tall, dark-bearded Brother Elias's voice was oddly husky. "Father Francis died at dusk as a flock of singing larks flew heavenward over the Porziuncola."

Larks? Francis's favorite birds sang at dawn, not dusk. Did larks singing at dusk mean that Francis was in glory?

"He promised to come to you," Elias said quietly as the friars placed the coffin on the floor and lifted the lid. They slipped from

Francis's face a white silk veil with the word "Love" embroidered across it in gold silk thread. Francis's body was clothed in a new tunic.

Tenderly the friars lifted the body, leaving behind the veil and a small, red silk pillow—embroidered with the eagles and lions of the Frangipani house, the house of Lady Jacoba's family—which had cradled Francis's head. Six pairs of arms supported the gaunt, limp form, the floppy arms and legs, the sagging, hollow-cheeked head. Francis's skin was pale, his beard trimmed. Across his face, from each ear to each eye, was a nasty red scar. Ortolana shuddered. In Rieti, doctors had cauterized Francis's eyes, searing the skin with a red-hot iron, creating, no doubt, those ugly scars. Miraculously, Francis had felt no pain from the burning nor, perhaps, even from the piercing of his ears, a later effort to restore his sight. Neither treatment had worked. Francis had died blind.

Shaking, Clare opened the little window through which the sisters received the Eucharist. Taking Francis's left hand in hers, she drew his hand through the window and kissed its wound. "Brother Elias, could I have just a fingernail of Father Francis?"

Elias stammered. "Lady Clare, we don't want to desecrate his body by taking relics from it."

Clare nodded, her face pained.

"Lady Clare," Leo offered, "with Brother Elias's permission, I will write some memories of Father Francis and some of his prayers, to console you."

Elias agreed. "Good, Brother Leo."

"Grazie," Clare said weakly. Kissing the wound again, she silently turned to Ortolana who took Francis's chill hand in her own. Years ago she had clung to her dead husband's hand, wondering how she would go on—yet, for the sake of her daughters, she had been strong.

Reverently Ortolana kissed the nail of iron-black hardened flesh, then offered the hand to Benvenuta, who stroked the palm tenderly, pressed it to her cheek, and kissed it. Then Ortolana, Benvenuta, and Clare backed away so that the other sisters could venerate Francis's remains.

"My ladies," Angelo said, his deep voice faltering, "Father Francis asked, before he died, that we again sing for you the 'Praises of the Lord,' along with the final verse that he composed at the Porziuncola just a few days ago."

The friars began, their voices weak.

> **Most High, all-powerful, good Lord**
> **Yours are the praises, the glory, the honor, and all**
> **blessing...**

The voices strengthened and swelled.

> **Blessed are those who endure in peace**
> **for by You, Most High, they shall be crowned.**
> **Praised be You, my Lord, through our Sister Bodily**
> **Death,**
> **from whom no one living can escape.**

The new verse:

> **Woe to those who die in mortal sin.**
> **Blessed are those whom death will find in Your**
> **most holy will,**
> **for the second death shall do them no harm.**
> **Praise and bless my Lord and give Him thanks**
> **and serve Him with great humility.**

As the friars' song faded, the cries of the sisters rose, begging Francis's help, wondering how they would continue without him.

Finally Clare, supported by Benvenuta and Ortolana, was at the window again. The friars lifted Francis's head toward the opening and Clare, weeping, lightly kissed his forehead. "Pace e bene, Father. Grazie for everything. I will pray for you until you reach heaven. Pray for me as you promised."

Gently the friars eased Francis's body into the coffin. Lady Jacoba slipped the funeral veil over his face, then extended her hand to Clare, who clasped it firmly. Jacoba, whom Francis had known for ten years, was a young, auburn-haired widow who was living as a penitent, following a rule for lay people written, at Francis's request, by Cardinal Hugolino. A member of one of Rome's highest ranking families, Jacoba had married into the wealthy Frangipani clan yet, with her two sons, had exchanged her expensive lifestyle for one of simplicity, prayer, and charity.

"They are burying him at the Church of San Giorgio," Jacoba said. "Once my household is in order, I will return to Assisi to live near him." Jacoba smiled weakly. "God has given me a great grace, dear Sisters. A few days ago in Rome, the Holy Spirit spoke to me at prayer. 'Father Francis is dying at the Porziuncola. Take candles and incense for a funeral plus cloth for a new tunic and those almond sweets that he likes. Leave now or you will not see him alive.' Friday, as I arrived with servants carrying these and all else needed for a funeral, a friar was leaving with a letter Father Francis had dictated to me, asking for those very things."

The sisters murmured in joy. "Father Francis allowed me to come into the friary, Sisters, calling me Brother Jacoba." Jacoba was smiling despite her tears. "I made the almond candies, the mortaroli, and he ate a bit of it. The tunic I sewed he wears now. And he blessed me before he died."

Elias's rough, grief-stricken voice broke into the conversation. "We must go."

Only when the coffin had left the church did Clare close the window. Then she turned to face her sisters, her face streaked with tears. "We are filled with grief because our father is gone. Yet let us thank God for our vocation which He, through Father Francis, has given us. Unworthy as we are, Father Francis gave us our lofty profession and his many words, examples, and commands, so that we would in no way turn from a life of holy poverty." Clare's voice strengthened as she spoke. "As he never departed from following the Son of God, so we must bind ourselves again and again to most holy poverty." Taking Ortolana's hand for support, she knelt. "Many have been frail and have abandoned the way Father Francis laid out. So let us bend our knee to the Father of our Lord Jesus Christ. Let us pray to observe the most holy poverty that we have promised to the Lord and our holy Father Francis." Her words were quavering but intense. "May the Lord Himself, who has given a good beginning, also give us the increase and final perseverance. Amen."

Kneeling, the sisters echoed their agreement. So be it. "Amen."

PART NINE

To Progress in Serving God
More Perfectly

❦ 37 ❦

Sister Egidia

Refectory, San Damiano (Holy Thursday Evening, 1228) ❧ In the soft glow of two hanging oil lamps, young, pallid Sister Egidia sat facing the refectory center. Second in a long line of seated sisters, Egidia watched her ill abbess, supported by sturdy Sister Benvenuta, emerge from the kitchen. Alongside her, Sister Pacifica lugged a pail of water and Sister Filippa carried towels.

Like Egidia's, Clare's face looked hollow and gray. For the first time in the two weeks since Egidia had entered San Damiano, Clare had come downstairs. Now she knelt by Agnese, first in line, and began to wash her feet. Every Holy Thursday night after Mass, so the other sisters said, Clare washed the sisters' feet as Christ had washed his disciples' feet.

The room began to whirl.

God, don't let me faint.

In this unrelenting famine, which Father Francis had predicted shortly before his death. Egidia was dying of hunger. She had been a strong enough peasant to survive the fever that had claimed her mother and siblings, but when she had begun to give nearly all her food to Papa, who had died nevertheless, she had weakened. Then, giving her life to God, she had come to San Damiano. Here she continued to eat little so that weaker sisters could have more.

After kissing Agnese's feet, Clare began to cleanse Egidia's, washing, wiping, drying. Clare lifted Egidia's left foot toward her lips. A noblewoman kiss her foot! Unthinkable!

Egidia pulled her foot back. Clumsy in her weakness, Egidia saw, felt, her foot kick Clare's mouth. Startled but smiling tenderly, Clare bent again to kiss each foot, the upper then lower side, then wordlessly moved down the row to Angeluccia.

Stunned, Egidia watched Clare wash and kiss Angeluccia's feet. Cristiana's. Venuta's. Then dizziness slapped her. She crumpled against Angeluccia as everything went black.

Egidia woke to rain lashing the monastery. She was lying in the infirmary next to Sister Giovanna, oil lamps gently brightening the night. Kneeling between the two sisters, Clare was bathing Egidia's face with a moist cloth.

"God be praised!" Clare exclaimed. "This is the first you've opened your eyes in five days! You're burning with fever, Sister."

Five days? Egidia felt so feeble that a dog could have dragged her anywhere.

"Sister Clare," Egidia said weakly, "care for others who may get well. I do not think I will." Clare dipped the cloth into a washbasin and wrung out the water. "You are stronger than on Easter when Brother Cappellano anointed you and recited the prayers for the dying."

Smiling kindly, Clare turned to Sister Giovanna and began to bathe her face.

"We're all going to die!" The anguished words came from once sturdy Sister Illuminata, now wan and thin-faced, who was standing near Clare, holding an open jar that emitted a pungent medicinal scent. "In Pisa we always had food. Here we starve!"

"Hush, Sister." Impulsively Clare threw herself at Illuminata's feet and embraced them. "God will care for us."

"God has forgotten us!" Illuminata cried.

"No, God is trying us."

"You have told us to follow in the footprints of Jesus. Where is He taking us?"

"It is raining," a thin voice said from the mattress to Egidia's right. Pacifica. When had she fallen ill? "Perhaps the famine is over."

Giovanna spoke softly. "At least we have these." With a shaky hand, she lifted a plate of shriveled turnips and held it, wobbling, toward Egidia. "Sister, eat something."

The turnips were jiggling in Giovanna's unsteady grip. The sick sisters always received the choicest foods, so what did the other sisters have? Nothing?

Egidia's stomach somersaulted. "I have no taste for food."

"Surely you would like something," Clare cajoled, turning from Illuminata to Egidia. "We shall ask the friars to beg it for you."

Egidia wanted nothing. Nothing except.... It was Easter. If not for this famine, the people of Norcera, sixteen miles distant, would be eating.... "If only I had a bit of Easter bread baked on a hearth in Norcera and some fish from the Topino River, baked and tender."

"We will pray for them." Clasping Egidia's hands, Clare bent her head. As Egidia closed her eyes, she realized that she, who had always served others, was now being cared for by others. The situation was uncomfortable.

IT IS A SERVICE TO BE SERVED.

The thought startled her.

OTHERS SERVED ME.

You, Lord? Always You served others.

NO, EGIDIA. THINK.

Yes, He was correct. Hadn't Simon helped Jesus carry the cross? Didn't women try to console Him on the trek to Calvary? Didn't a bystander offer Him a drink on the cross?

Does following Christ sometimes mean allowing others to serve us?

Egidia heard an urgent, distant knocking.

"The church door," Pacifica offered.

"Why don't the friars answer?" Illuminata asked, moving out to answer the knocking.

"Maybe it is the friars," Egidia suggested.

Clare shook her head. "The friars know that we bolt the doors at night."

Illuminata returned quickly. "A young man at the door said to give this to you." She handed a plump towel to Clare.

Kneeling backwards, Clare placed the towel on her lap and untied its ends. On the towel lay two small loaves of crusty bread dotted with dried fruits and a large fish, baked and tender.

Egidia stared. "That is Norcera bread, Sister, and Topino River fish."

"God be praised!" Clare said. "The Lord has done this." She placed the loaves and fish on the platter next to the shriveled turnips, then handed the napkin to Illuminata. "Return this to the young man with our deepest thanks. Ask the friars if he might stay the night with them. The weather sounds harsh."

Illuminata hurried out.

"Will you have a bit of this?" Clare asked, breaking off a section of Norcera bread.

Egidia looked about the half-full infirmary. "If we all have some."

Clare smiled. "We will all have some."

Egidia was nibbling the delicious bread when Illuminata reentered. "Sister, the young man did not wish to stay with the friars. He took the towel and left."

"In this storm?" Pacifica asked.

"Maybe he was an angel," Giovanna breathed.

Illuminata nodded thoughtfully. "Maybe. He had the kindest, gentlest eyes I have ever seen."

❧ 38 ❧

All the Sisters

Dormitory, San Damiano (EARLY JULY, 1228) ᛋ "I have had a dream," Clare said to the sisters clustered about her bed. "It holds a message for us all, I believe."

The sisters nodded at Clare, who was more mother than abbess. Deeply prayerful, Clare must have had many visions and dreams, although she rarely shared them. Now, in this light-flooded airy room, the sisters felt buoyed by joy and expectation. Dreams were windows into the soul, and Clare was opening that window.

Clare's blue eyes flashed. "In my dream, I was caring for our holy Father Francis. I was bringing him a bowl of hot water and a towel for washing and drying his hands. He was high above me, so I was climbing a very high stairway to reach him, but I was going very quickly as if on level ground. When I reached Father Francis, he opened his tunic, bared his breast, and said, 'Come, take, and drink.' I drank fully without surprise. Again he asked me to drink and I did. What I tasted was so sweet and delightful that I cannot describe it."

"Certainly you have drunk in Father Francis's sweet counsels," Benvenuta offered.

All the sisters murmured their assent.

"Indeed, I have, Sister," Clare smiled. "The second time, the nipple, through which the milk came, remained between my lips. I plucked the nipple from my mouth, and it seemed to be gold so clear and bright that I could see everything in it as if in a mirror. And then I awoke."

What a strange vision!

"My sisters, our holy Father Francis is far above us in his faith, knowledge, and love, but when he was ill here, we were permitted to care for him as a mother would. Yet he was our mother who nourished us, his daughters in Christ."

The sisters nodded, knowing this was true.

"In my dream, Father Francis said, 'Come, take, and drink.'"

"Christ's words at the Last Supper," Ortolana offered. "'Take and drink. This is my Blood.'"

"Christ gave His life to feed us," Pacifica said. "In a different way, so did Father Francis."

"Your dream reminds me of the prophet Isaiah writing about nursing from the breast of the holy city," Cecilia said thoughtfully. "'Oh, that you may suck fully of the milk of her comfort, that you may nurse with delight at her abundant breasts! ...As nurslings, you shall be carried in her arms and fondled in her lap; as a mother comforts her son, so will I comfort you.'"

Illuminata looked intently at Cecilia. "Jerusalem is the city of God, the heavenly city, the Book of Revelation tells us. To nurse from the city is to nurse from heaven."

"Our holy Father Francis is high up, already in the heavenly city," Angeluccia noted. It was true. On the ninth Sunday after Pentecost, less than two weeks away, Lord Pope was going to canonize Francis.

"And you went up to him as easily as an angel floating up and down the ladder that Jacob saw going up to God," Venuta chuckled.

Clare smiled, her blue eyes bright. "When we love intensely, we ascend quickly and easily to Christ. As he draws us in love, we swiftly run to Him. Father Francis was a living image of Christ. When he nourished us, Christ nourished us. In my dream, Father Francis was, I believe, both himself and Christ."

Giovanna's voice quivered. "Death pulled us too soon from Father Francis. But a mother brings again to her breast a nursling who has pulled away. So God brought us back to Father Francis in your dream."

Clare nodded. "So we must continue to suck of Father Francis's faith and strength, which came from Christ, to suckle Christ's hidden sweetness that God has reserved for those who love Him."

"Our Lord Jesus Christ wishes us to always experience His sweet nurture," Filippa mused.

"And this is why our holy Father Saint Francis left us the golden nipple of Christ's poor and humble way of life," Clare reasoned, "the way that blessed Francis taught by words and example, the way in which we walk."

Clare smiled at her sisters. "An infant is totally poor because it is totally dependent on its nurse. Just so Christ became totally poor for us. Imitating Him, we make ourselves poor and dependent on God, who nourishes us. Poverty looks dark as a nipple to those in the world. But it is gold."

Clare paused as if to let the thought settle.

"Voluntary poverty promises eternal glory to those who possess it. Like a clear mirror, it reflects Christ's poverty and is the gold given us by Father Francis, which nourishes us still."

"Brother Elias needs reminders about poverty, not you," Benvenuta said a bit harshly.

Agreement rippled through the sisters, for they had often discussed the friars' mitigation regarding holy poverty. At Lord Pope's request, Elias had drawn up plans for a massive basilica to be built in Francis's honor. The site was on Hell Hill, a jagged, rocky promontory on the northwest side of Assisi, which, on March 29, had been renamed Paradise Hill. One month later, the Pope had granted a forty-day indulgence to all contributors to the building fund. Brother Elias had set a huge marble vase on the site to collect alms. Brother Leo, sharing Francis's aversion to money, had smashed the vase.

"Sister Clare, do you think God is trying to tell us something by giving you this dream?" Agnese asked.

"Perhaps," Clare offered. "If so, He will let us know."

❧ 39 ❧

Pope Gregory IX

San Damiano (JULY 13, 1228) ∾ With Pope Gregory IX at its head, a pompous entourage wended its way up the steep road from Spoleto toward San Damiano. The July day was pleasant, a good day for travel.

Before becoming Pope in March of the previous year, the silver-haired vicar of Christ had been Cardinal Hugolino dei Conti dei Segni, Cardinal Protector of Francis Bernardone's followers. Having seen how the papacy had consumed his uncle Lord Pope Innocent III, he had resisted his own election. But the other cardinals would not let him refuse, and God had interiorly told him to submit. Yet he thought of himself as he always had: Hugo, servant of God's servants.

Now, like peevish dogs, innumerable concerns, petty disagreements, endless arbitrations, and impossible requests snapped at Hugo. The most dangerous involved the scarlet-haired, scarlet-sinned Emperor Frederick II, whom Hugo had excommunicated last year for yet again reneging on his promise to retake the Holy Land from the Turks. Unapologetic, unrepentant, Frederick claimed he was too ill to begin the crusade.

Frederick's Holy Roman Empire covered much of the continent and extended down the peninsula through Lombardy and Tuscany to the papal states. He also ruled the Kingdom of Sicily, which included the island of Sicily as well as the lower portion of the peninsula including Naples. Squeezed between these two halves of Frederick's kingdom were the Pope's narrow territories—the March of Ancona, the Duchy of Spoleto, and the Patrimony of Saint Peter—with Rome as its key city. Wanting the Pope's lands, Frederick had made Rome so unsafe that Hugo had fled in April.

In May, Frederick's second wife Lady Yolanda had died. A month later, with a force too small to fight a crusade, Frederick had sailed for pagan-held Palestine where Lady Yolanda's father, John of Brienne, was king of Jerusalem. Frederick couldn't have been grieving; he was considering courting a new wife, Princess Agnes of Prague.

Hugo reined his steed to a standstill and, with the help of an aide, dismounted. At San Damiano, he could momentarily forget his office and be poor and humble. Handing his soft shoes and blue silk cape to an attendant, Hugo beckoned his brother Count Philip's son to join him. This nephew was young, dark-eyed, virile Cardinal Raynaldo dei Conti dei Segni, now Cardinal Protector of the Poor Brothers and the Damianites.

Barefoot Hugo and silken-dressed Raynaldo knocked at the weathered door of a little house thrust against the right side of the church of San Damiano. After the friars' initial surprise and acts of obeisance, Hugo got down to business. He wanted to know how the friars fared in caring for the Poor Ladies. He had not expected Friar Capellano's complaints.

"Lord Pope, the number of ladies is growing and we must provide food for them. And only poor food. If someone gives us whole loaves, Lady Clare scolds us. 'Who gave you these?' she asks. She wants broken loaves, the trenchers people use under their foods."

"It would be difficult to reject generosity," Hugo conceded.

Cappellano arched his thick eyebrows. "The ladies like to hear sermons daily, but we are simple men. If I could preach, which I cannot do well, I would preach to the unconverted, not to holy ladies. Moreover, the ladies wish to confess monthly, sometimes more frequently, and receive the Eucharist on all solemnities. They wish us to say Mass within the enclosure for the ill ladies, visit the ill often, and give individual spiritual direction." Cappellano shrugged. "Father Francis wanted this, but it is time consuming. Friars at other Damianite monasteries feel the same."

Last year, Hugo had committed the care of the Damianites to the minister general of the Poor Brothers. At least four friars were assigned to each of the nearly forty Damianite monasteries. The ladies were delighted to have friars as their visitators and supporters. Hugo would ask Raynaldo to check with the friars at other monasteries to see if Cappellano's assessment was accurate.

When he had completed his interview with the friars, Hugo, accompanied by Raynaldo, approached the speaking grill in the church and asked to visit Lady Clare. "Don't tell her who is visiting," Hugo admonished the lady who answered his bell. "I want to surprise her." In his Rule for the Damianites, Hugo had allowed the Pope and Cardinal visitator within the enclosure, if necessity required.

Thus, Hugo and Raynaldo ascended the staircase to the dormitory where Clare lay bedridden.

With her back toward Hugo, Clare was propped in a high bed, rolls of cloth behind her back, above her head a four-pronged tree branch thrust into a narrow wooden post affixed securely to a sturdy wooden base. Bound together with twine, the tips of the branches formed a cone around which was loosely tied a pale, golden cloud of flax. As Hugo stepped into the dormitory, Clare swiftly rolled a spindle against her thigh and let it fall to the floor, twirling rapidly. As the spindle spun downward, Clare quickly moistened her fingers at her lips and rolled them upwards along a thin line of flaxen fibers that led from the distaff down through a notched post at Clare's side, and to the spindle. The fibers twisted together tightly, making a fine, sturdy thread. Seated around Clare on stools were three other sisters, stitching, hemming, or embroidering. Hugo recognized Lady Ortolana but not the two younger ones.

"Always busy!" Hugo said in honest appreciation.

"Lord Pope!" Clare turned her head, delight in her voice. "Lord Cardinal! How are we privileged to have you visit?" Clare grabbed the twirling spindle and, quickly wrapping it with the length of thread she had just spun, placed it in her lap, then bowed low. "Let me kiss the feet of my Lord."

Obligingly, Hugo raised one foot and then the other to Clare, who kissed each, right above the instep. To the other three bowing women, he offered his hand to kiss.

Hugo tapped the spindle in Clare's lap. "Exquisitely fine thread, Lady Clare."

Clare smiled. "Grazie. The fewer the fibers, the faster the spin, the finer the thread."

"What do you make with this wondrous thread?"

"Corporals, Holy Father. Sister Angeluccia is hemming one now."

One of the young sisters held up a small square of unbleached linen. The consecrated bread and wine would rest on it during Mass.

"You must receive fine alms for such fine work," Hugo reasoned.

"Oh, no. We take no alms for anything," Clare said. "The corporals are gifts for the churches."

"Your Holiness," Raynaldo broke in, "your dinner meeting with the bishop?"

"Yes, yes." Hugo pulled up one of the empty stools and sat on it. He glanced at Raynaldo and patted a stool next to him. Raynaldo shrugged and sat.

"We heard that the sisters fared ill during the famine."

"God sustained us, and now it is over, Holy Father."

"True, but we have heard that the Damianites are frequently sick, here and elsewhere. You are ill yourself."

"Illness is a fact of life. Through it, we unite ourselves more closely to the suffering Christ."

"Perhaps your severe life contributes to these illnesses," Raynaldo offered. His strong, highly featured face and direct, pointed gaze commanded respect.

"We are not afraid of illness or austerity," Clare noted.

"Lady Clare, suppose famine returns. Or hostile armies invade Umbria. How will you eat? The friars may beg and work for food, or they may leave an area as I and my court had to leave Rome. But you are here as in a prison. I wish to permit you to own property on which you may grow crops to use and sell. Then you will not be at the mercy of others."

Clare's eyes were wider than Hugo had ever seen them. Her voice came with a deep firmness. "Lord Pope Innocent granted us the privilege of owning nothing."

"This was fine while Saint Francis was alive," Raynaldo offered. Raynaldo was calling Francis "saint" although he was still three days from being canonized. "His charm may fade and you may be forgotten. You must grow more secure, my lady."

Clare looked from Raynaldo to Hugo, lifting her solid chin as she spoke. "Before he died, Father—Saint—Francis instructed his brothers to lovingly care for us always."

"Brother John Parenti is minister general of the Poor Brothers now," Hugo pointed out. "He will determine how they serve you. God does not want you to starve. Therefore, I permit you to own whatever property and possessions you need to grant you a measure of security."

Clare's gaze pierced him. "My Lord, we have taken a vow of poverty here."

"The Damianites in Spoleto and Perugia have accepted the Lord Pope's offer of maintaining some useful possessions," Raynaldo said. "It is the safer choice."

"The other Damianite monasteries may do as they wish," Clare said evenly. "They are not bound to follow our life here."

"On the contrary," Hugo said. "They are following the very Rule that I gave you."

"This is Assisi, Lord Pope. Here we live in poverty."

"If you fear for your vow, I can absolve you from it."

"Absolve me from my sins, Holy Father," Clare said sweetly but firmly, "but never from following in the footprints of my Lord Jesus Christ."

"Christ would ask you to be obedient to His vicar on earth," Raynaldo said.

"I will be obedient," Clare answered, bowing low, "but I will ask the Lord Pope a question. Did God speak falsehood when He told us neither to sow nor reap nor gather into barns but to trust Him as do the birds? Did He not promise to take care of us if we put our faith in Him?"

Hugo felt cornered by the very argument that Francis had always used whenever Hugo tried to force possessions on the friars. Hugo could not counter the argument without denying the Gospel.

"All right," Hugo conceded. "As you wish. But merely ask and I will rescind the privilege of poverty."

"Holy Father, I ask you to reinstate for us, in writing, the privilege of poverty."

The request surprised Hugo. He glanced at Raynaldo, who appeared equally startled.

Hugo struggled to put his feelings into words. "Lady Clare, I am afflicted by innumerable, bitter, and endless trials. We are surrounded by many dangers and are so human and frail that we cannot possibly conquer these without God's help. Yet, we have but a single hope—to bring glory to the Lord and salvation to ourselves and those entrusted to us." Reverently he took Clare's thin hand in his own. "Your faith consoles me, Lady Clare. You are one spirit with Christ. Pray that God will strengthen us and enable us to worthily fulfill the duties He has given us."

Bringing Hugo's hand to her lips, Clare kissed it tenderly. "The Pope and the Church are always in our prayers."

"Then we shall be strengthened," Hugo said hopefully. "You shall receive your privilege of poverty. In writing. And may God grant you the grace to live it."

~ 40 ~

Friar Cappellano

Chaplain's House, San Damiano (EARLY OCTOBER, 1230) ~ Friar Cappellano sat at the small, rustic table in the chaplain's house, staring at the parchments before him. He had read this bull from Pope Gregory IX three times. What should he make of it?

Since Saint Francis's death four years ago, Cappellano had seen the friars go from grief to discord to disobedience. In May, fearful that relic hunters or Perugians might steal Francis's body on the way to its entombment in the new basilica, Brother Elias, with the cooperation of the Podesta and council of Assisi, had secretly carted the corpse from the Church of San Giorgio to the basilica three days early. Somewhere within that huge edifice, Elias had buried the body without informing either the other friars or the papal legates who were to attend the scheduled celebration on May 25.

When the celebration was held without the body, the angry Pope Gregory IX placed the basilica under interdict and deprived it of all privileges. The friars could live neither there nor nearby, nor could they hold chapter meetings there until everyone involved appeared before the Pope, offered explanations, and requested forgiveness—and they had fifteen days in which to do it. In the meantime, Elias's supporters had insisted that all friars, not only those in authority, attend the chapter meeting at the Porziuncola, as they had when Father Francis was alive. The group had forced its way into the meeting and had proclaimed Elias the new minister general while duly-elected John Parenti had, in a dramatic display of destitution, torn off his tunic before everyone. Then golden-tongued Friar Anthony, whose preaching around Padua was converting thousands, had attempted to make peace. Yet even Anthony, young yet pale and bloated with illness, failed to bring the opposing factions together. Finally, the tearful entreaties of five novices, all former knights, had moved the friars to bitter harmony.

Then Elias and his supporters had obediently gone to Rome, so the Pope had lifted the ban on the basilica. Elias had been banished to Cortona to do penance, and the other friar troublemakers had likewise been dispersed. Nevertheless, the remaining brothers in positions of authority could not agree on the interpretation of Francis's Testament and Rule. So they had sent a delegation of friars—Anthony, John Parenti, the eloquent Englishman Haymo of Faversham, and four learned others—to consult with Gregory IX about the documents. The Pope's decision was in the bull that Cappellano now held. Copies were circulating throughout the provinces. The guardian of each convento was to read the bull, implement its decisions, then send the bull to the next closest convento.

The bull stated that Francis's Testament, with its paragraph on absolute poverty and non-ownership of property, could not bind the friars, because Francis had written it without consulting others when he no longer held authority in the order. The friars were bound to obey only the Gospel texts quoted in Francis's Rule.

Cappellano pursed his lips. He knew Francis's Rule and Testament well. "The brothers shall not acquire anything as their own, neither a house nor a place nor anything at all," Francis had written in the Rule. And, in the Testament, "Let the brothers beware that they by no means receive churches or poor dwellings or anything which is built for them, unless it is in harmony with that holy poverty which we have promised in the Rule, and let them always be guests there as pilgrims and strangers." The bull in Cappellano's hand permitted the friars to use property and buildings if they were owned by others, such as the Pope or Cardinal Protector. The bull said nothing about the poverty of such dwellings nor made mention of the friars' living in them as "pilgrims." The friars might live in comfortable conventos for decades and be in accord with what Pope Gregory IX allowed.

Chapter four of Saint Francis's Rule began: "I firmly command all the brothers that they in no way receive coins or money, either personally or through an intermediary." This bull said that the friars could accept money and have an intermediary hold it for future use.

Francis's Rule allowed the ministers and custodians to "alone take special care to provide for the needs of the sick and the clothing of the other brothers through spiritual friends." For all their other needs, "as pilgrims and strangers in this world who serve the Lord in poverty and humility, let them go begging for alms with full trust." The Pope wrote that, if the friars needed anything, benefactors might purchase it for them. Thus, some communities of friars might do no begging, since benefactors could supply all their needs.

Then there was the section about friars visiting monasteries of nuns. Francis had stated that no friars could enter the monasteries of nuns without permission of the Apostolic See. The friars had always understood that this did not apply to the Poor Ladies, to whom Francis had pledged the support of the brothers. Indeed, the friars regularly entered the enclosure of the Poor Ladies to say Mass, preach to the ill, hear confessions, give spiritual direction, anoint the dying, and bury the dead. This bull stated that Francis's prohibition applied to the Poor Ladies. The friars would need papal permission to enter parts of the monastery forbidden to the laity unless a lady was dying and needed the sacraments. Capellano had been praying that his workload regarding the sisters be lightened. Now the Pope had done it.

Lady Clare needed to know. Clutching the bull, Cappellano strode into the church, rang the bell cord, and sent the parchment into the monastery on the turn.

He spoke into the black-curtained grill. "My lady, ask Lady Clare to read the bull carefully, especially the passage stating that friars must have explicit permission of Rome to enter the monastery. When Lady Clare has finished, ring the bell into the chaplain's house and I'll pick up the parchment."

Cappellano was poring over a passage from the Gospel of Mark when the bell rang. He put down the manuscript and went to fetch the bull.

The parchment was lying on the turn. As Cappellano reached for it, he heard Lady Angeluccia's delicate voice from behind the grill.

"Brother Capellano, Sister Clare thanks you for sharing the bull with us. She thanks you for the many years that you and the other friars have assisted us. She wishes you well and bids all the friars God's blessing as you leave."

Cappellano started at the words. "My lady, the begging friars will continue to beg for you and leave the food at the turn."

"Sister Clare is sending away the begging friars. 'If the Pope wishes to take away our spiritual nourishment,' Sister Clare has said, 'then he may take away our physical nourishment as well. If we cannot hear God's word from the friars, we will not accept man's bread from their hands.'"

Incredulous, Cappellano asked, "How will you live?"

"We will send for alms. God will take care of us. Pace e bene, Brother Cappellano."

"Pace e bene," Cappellano said hesitantly. Taking the bull in his hand, he walked slowly out of the church.

Was this what he had wanted? Was this what the Pope had foreseen?

～ 41 ～

Sister Amata di Martino

Oratory, San Damiano (OCTOBER 1230) ～ With the other well sisters, petite Sister Amata knelt in the oratory, her harsh garments in stark contrast to her delicate young face. A thousand distractions were interrupting her prayer.

To Amata's left knelt Sister Beatrice, Clare's blood sister and Amata's cousin. When childless Beatrice's husband had died last year, Beatrice had entered San Damiano to be with Clare and Ortolana. Beatrice was kneeling, her head to the floor so that she resembled a plump, gray biscuit. Obviously, Beatrice was thinking about only Jesus.

Why couldn't Amata keep her mind fixed on Christ?

Amata concentrated on the little silver box in the wall niche to the altar's left. In that box reposed Christ, truly present in the consecrated Host. Amata pictured Jesus smiling lovingly at her. Then the silver box reminded her of a larger silver box she had left behind at Correggiano, a gift on her twelfth birthday from her father, Lord Martino di Ugolino di Offreduccio....

Poor Father! How Amata had distressed him two years ago by abandoning her wedding plans and coming here to join her cousin Clare and blood sister Balvina! Clare had asked God for a special grace so that Amata would neither be deceived by the world nor remain in it. Her husband-to-be was now courting another lady....

Oh! She was trying to imagine Jesus! Why couldn't Amata pray without distractions!

The silver box. Jesus enclosed there as in the womb of His Mother. How did birth cramps feel? Were they like hunger pains? With the friars gone, the sisters had less food. Amata's flat little stomach was pinched.

What was she thinking of? Yes, the Blessed Mother, pregnant. Amata's mother had died. How long ago was that?

The bell rang in the bell tower, ending the period of silent morning prayer. Amata was grateful to begin work.

182

In the dormitory, Clare was propped in bed, spinning. Near her sat Sister Venuta, her eyes intent on the handheld loom in her lap. The loom was a simple wooden frame with nails at the top and bottom over which was looped the fine linen thread that Clare had spun. Deftly, Venuta was weaving a weft thread of linen, threaded through a needle, over and under the warp threads. After each pass, she used a wire comb to push each weft row compactly against the row beneath it. When the corporal was napkin sized, Venuta would remove it from the loom to hem it on all four sides. The rhythmic, measured swish of the comb and the whir of the spindle were the only sounds in the quiet dormitory.

On a wooden stool near Clare's bed, Amata found the sturdy sheet of heavy paper, about a foot-and-a-half square, and the swath of white silk that she had cut yesterday to fit its outline. With fine, delicate stitches, Amata began to stitch the silk to the paper. When she completed the stitching, she would fold and stitch the paper to make a flat box to hold Venuta's corporal. Before sending the corporals to area churches, the friars used to take them to the Bishop of Assisi to bless. Now the serving sisters would do so.

Ringing broke the silence. Amata went to see who was at the speaking grill.

"We have come from Perugia," an agitated female voice said. "Our son has a film over his eye. We have heard that Lady Clare sometimes cures the ill. Could she pray over our boy?"

Touched by the pleading, Amata slipped back the curtain. The wide-eyed, dark-skinned mother was neat and clean, dressed in lazzo, the cloth of the poor. The black-haired child playing with her toes could have been two or three years old. When the child cocked his head toward the grill, Amata was startled at the pale sheath covering his left eye.

"I shall see if Sister Clare can come downstairs," Amata said to the woman.

But Clare's legs had been weak and wobbly for years. She asked a serving sister to bring the child to her. So Giovanna did. Clare blessed the child and touched his eyes, and signed him with the sign of the cross. Smiling, the child took from his mouth a half-eaten chestnut and offered it to Clare. "For you. Eat it."

"Grazie!" Clare took the piece and lay it beside her. "Chestnuts are very tasty."

Amata smiled at the smiling child, his eye still clouded.

"Ask my mother to pray over him," Clare instructed Giovanna. "Mother's prayers are powerful."

Ortolana would be sewing in the refectory. Giovanna carried the boy out as Amata resumed stitching, Clare returned to spinning, and Venuta removed the corporal from the loom. Long minutes later, Giovanna returned breathless, with the child.

"Look, Sisters! Sister Ortolana blessed the boy, but nothing happened. But on my way back here...look!"

The child's eyes were both perfectly clear.

"Mother's prayers have done this!" Clare proclaimed.

"When I saw the miracle, I hurried to show Sister Ortolana. She said your prayers healed him."

"God be praised in either case!" Clare sang.

With a dull thud, the half-eaten chestnut dropped from Clare's bed and bumped the floor. As the boy struggled in Giovanna's arms, she let him down. He popped the chestnut into his mouth as the sisters burst into laughter.

"Come, time to return to your mother," Giovanna beckoned. Carrying the child, Giovanna approached the monastery door and the staircase leading to the world outside. Quite spontaneously, Giovanna waved to someone outside. Amata could hear a deep male voice. Brother Cappellano?

Grinning widely, Giovanna turned toward the sisters. "The friars have returned! When Lord Pope heard how you sent the friars away, he changed his mind and told the minister general to have the friars serve us as they had been doing."

"God has answered our prayers!" Clare breathed.

Amata's insides were tingling at the dual miracles of the child's healing and the friars' return. Both the little boy and the Pope had suffered from clouded vision, but prayers had healed both. God could heal Amata's clouded spiritual vision, too, if she...

A thought pushed into Amata's consciousness. YOU MUST BECOME LIKE LITTLE CHILDREN. Amata's distractions were as unsavory as half-eaten chestnuts, but maybe if she offered them to God with the candor of a child, God would accept them, because right now, they were all she had to give.

PART TEN

Visited by
Divine Consolation

∾ 42 ∽

Sister Agnese di Oportulo de Bernardo

Choir, San Damiano (SUNDAY, APRIL 25, 1232) ∾ On the far left of the stark choir behind the altar at San Damiano, Sister Agnese sat between Sisters Angeluccia and Francesca, her dark eyes closed, her thin face lowered. *Who are You, Lord? And who am I?*

"We are called to be spouses and mothers and sisters of our Lord Jesus Christ," Clare often told the sisters. Until midway through Lent, the words had flown by Agnese. Then a nagging question had emerged. If she was supposed to be spouse, mother, and sister to Christ, she needed to know who He was. She didn't doubt His divinity. She knew His virtues. But did she know *Him?*

During the Easter celebration, she had spoken to Clare about her dilemma. "When our holy Father Saint Francis was still in the world," Clare advised from her sick bed, "he used to pray before the crucifix here. 'Who are You, Lord?' he used to pray. 'And who am I?'" Clare had patted Agnese's hand. "Pray those questions, and God will answer."

Who are You, Lord? And who am I? She had received no answer. Would it come today, on this Good Shepherd Sunday, the Second Sunday after Easter? The church would be full because Assisi's own son, Brother Philip di Lungo, was preaching.

Philip's natural poetic eloquence rivaled that of the famous poet Brother Pacifico, now dead, who had been visitor of the Poor Enclosed Sisters until resigning four years previously. Cardinal Raynaldo had appointed Philip to take his place. It was his second appointment, because when Francis had been in the Holy Land, Philip had asked Pope Honorius III to be appointed visitor when the Cistercian visitor Ambrose had died. That appointment, plus Philip's obtaining certain privileges for the sisters, had angered Francis who then appointed another friar to take Philip's place.

Out in the church, the friars' voices rose. Within the choir, the sisters stood and sang with them. "I saw water flowing from the right side of the temple, alleluia; and all to whom that water came were saved..."

Through the curtain-covered communion grill, Agnese could see nothing. But she could imagine Brother Philip dipping a laurel branch into a deep vessel of water, then sprinkling, like a rain of grace, the altar, himself, his Mass assistants, the people in the church, the choir grill, and, by extension, the sisters behind it.

"Praise God, all nations, extol Him, all you peoples.... Glory to the Father and to the Son and to the Holy Spirit..."

Last Sunday after Compline, Sister Clare had kept the sisters in the choir. She had asked Friar Cappellano to give her, through the communion grill, a small vessel of the holy water used in the sprinkling. Tenderly she had said, "My sisters and daughters, you must always remember this most blessed water that flowed from the right side of our Lord Jesus Christ as He hung upon the cross." Reverently she had blessed herself with the water, then had passed it to the other sisters to do the same.

Agnese had blessed herself and had felt a little shiver of joy. But today she felt herself standing beneath the cross on Calvary, gazing at her crucified Lord, seeing the blood and water from His side covering the world with grace.

Who are You, Lord?

THE SAVIOR. THE LIVING WATER.

Who am I?

THE REDEEMED. THE ONE WHO LIVES BECAUSE OF THE LIVING WATER.

Singing voices edged into her meditation. "I am the Good Shepherd of the sheep. I am the Way, the Truth, the Life. I am the Good Shepherd and I know My sheep, and they know Me. Alleluia."

Shepherd. Way. Truth. Life. *How do the images mesh, Lord?*

Philip's sturdy, clear voice interrupted her musing. She could see the back of his tonsured head through the communion grill. When had Sister Clare moved back the curtain? When had the Gospel been read? When had Agnese sat on the wooden plank that formed her choir seat?

"Who is the Good Shepherd?" Philip asked. "None other but our Lord. 'Come,' He invites His sheep. 'Follow me.'" His words rang out, sparking faith.

What was that indescribable sweetness? The blended scent of flowers, baking bread, spice and incense. A flash drew her gaze down the row of seated sisters. Around Clare gleamed a scintillating light in which stood a sandy-haired boy, perhaps three years old. His simple tunic aglow, His head rested on Clare's knee. Clare's right arm encircled the Child, her hand gently patted His shoulder. The Child's eyes were focused on Philip, His attitude attentive.

Oh, God, do not let me be deceived, Agnese prayed.

I AM IN THEIR MIDST.

Who are You, Lord?

I AM MADE PRESENT WHEN A PREACHER'S WORDS UNITE WITH A LISTENER'S SOUL.

"I am the Good Shepherd," Philip was saying of Christ. "I bandage the wounded, heal the sick, feed the hungry, carry the weak."

Agnese's mind was swirling with images. Christ the Good Shepherd. The Child. The Crucified. The Living Water.

As the sermon ended, the Child turned and gazed at Agnese, then disappeared.

Agnese felt a nudge. She glanced at Angeluccia, who silently mouthed the words: "I know you have seen something."

Agnese nodded and, unable to speak of it, bowed her head.

The Mass continued through the consecration of bread and wine into the Body and Blood of Christ.

I AM THE BREAD OF LIFE. I AM THE WINE OF THE NEW COVENANT. YOU ARE THE HUNGRY, THIRSTY SOUL.

Suddenly the choir was filled with a fiery brilliance that coalesced in flame on Clare's bowed head.

THE HOLY SPIRIT WILL COME UPON YOU. The words of the archangel Gabriel to Mary, the Mother of Christ.

I AM THE VOICE FROM THE BURNING BUSH. THE UNQUENCHABLE FIRE. TRUE LIGHT. HOLY SPIRIT. I AM YOUR SPOUSE. AND YOU ARE MY BRIDE.

The flame over Clare remained throughout the Communion rite before fading.

Mass ended. The hubbub in the church died as worshipers dispersed. In the church, the friar cantor began to pray the hour of Terce. The sisters joined in. The prayers continued, ended.

Who are You, Lord?

CRUCIFIED ONE. GOOD SHEPHERD. HOLY CHILD. LIVING WATER. BREAD OF LIFE. TRUE LIGHT. FLAME OF LOVE.

Who am I?

ONE WHO TRIES TO UNDERSTAND.

How could she understand? There were too many images and now more came. I AM THE TRUE VINE. THE BEGINNING AND THE END. THE ETERNAL HIGH PRIEST. GOD.

Could He not give one simple answer that would sum up all the others?

I AM THE CREATOR. ALL THINGS SPEAK OF ME.

Agnese was sitting quietly, her head bowed, her eyes closed. She could see only darkness. I AM LIGHT IN DARKNESS.

At the thought, her eyes sprang open and her glance fell on her clasped hands. I AM MOLDER OF ALL. ALL RESTS IN MY HANDS.

Her hands were folded on her gray, woolen tunic. I CLOTHE MY PEOPLE WITH RIGHTEOUSNESS.

Agnese had no time to reflect on her racing thoughts. Her glance caught the zigzagging pink bricks on the choir floor. I AM THE SURE FOUNDATION. I AM THE ROCK. Across the floor stabbed a sunbeam from the single choir window behind her. I AM THE LIGHT THAT ENLIGHTENS EVERY PERSON. In the sunbeam, flecks of dust cavorted. I AM THE SPIRIT DANCING IN THE SOUL.

I AM THE CREATOR. ALL THINGS SPEAK OF ME.

There were no simple answers to who God is. There were simply answers. They were all around her. She need only look.

↬ 43 ↫

Sister Aneska

Speaking Grill of the Damianite Convent, Prague, Bohemia (EARLY SUMMER, 1235) ↬ At the grill of the Damianite convent in Prague, Bohemia, thirty-year-old abbess Sister Aneska was deep in prayer. Above her straight and perfectly shaped nose, Aneska's delicately arched eyebrows pursed together with intense concentration.

Lord, what shall I do?

Aneska had been Princess Agnes of Prague, betrothed at the age of three to Boleslaus, young son of Prince Henry the Bearded from Silesia and his holy wife Hedwig. In preparation, she had been educated in the monastery at Trzebnicy, where God had drawn her to himself. Boleslaus had died when Aneska was six, so she had returned to Bohemia to be educated at the monastery in Doksan, where her faith had grown stronger. At age nine, Aneska had been betrothed to Emperor Frederick II's son Henry. After she had fasted, prayed, and done bodily penance to escape this marriage, Henry had jilted her to marry Margaret, daughter of Duke Leopold of Austria. This had so angered Aneska's father, the now deceased Premysl Ottokar, that he would have destroyed Austria had Aneska not begged his mercy. Three years ago, Aneska had received two more marriage proposals, one from King Henry III of England, the other from recently widowed Emperor Frederick II. If anyone could convert the deceitful, licentious, superstitious, excommunicated emperor, Aneska could! Her brother King Wenceslaus I of Bohemia had urged her to accept Frederick's offer, citing Boleslaus's mother Hedwig and their cousin Queen Elizabeth of Hungary as holy married women.

But, hearing from friars about Clare and the holy ladies of Assisi, Aneska longed to live as they did. Again, to avoid marriage, Aneska prayed and did penance. Under her jeweled robes, she wore a hairshirt and girdle studded with iron points. Before dawn, dressed in rough, rude clothes, she had walked barefoot to the churches in Prague to beg God's intervention, then returned to the palace to bandage her bleeding feet and begin a day at court. When the emperor's ambassador arrived to escort Aneska to Germany for the royal wedding, she had sent her own ambassador to the Pope to beg his mediation. His legate returned with the message that Aneska did not have to marry.

But Frederick and the Pope were at war. So Wenceslaus had allowed the emperor to make a decision. Miraculously he had responded, "How can I take offense if she prefers the King of Heaven to myself?"

Thus, with Aneska vowing to pray for Frederick until she died, she had become a Damianite. With Wenceslaus's cooperation, she had built a grand hospice for the poor and then this massive monastery for herself and dozens of other noblewomen who wished to become Damianites. When she requested some sisters to instruct the women in living a consecrated life, Clare had sent five Damianites from Trent, whose Germanic language was fairly common in Prague. Then, in a grand, public celebration on Pentecost last year, Aneska had left everything to embrace the religious life.

For Aneska, that meant living in poverty. So she had asked the Pope to separate the hospice—so generously endowed by her mother Queen Constance—from the monastery, so that the sisters might live without hospital revenue. Many days ago she had received the Pope's letter, which had denied her request, while allowing the hospice to support the monastery. Ever since, she been praying.

Oh, Lord, what shall I do?

At the ringing of the bell at the speaking grill, Aneska's dark, almond-shaped eyes shot open. Through the curtain, she spoke Saint Francis's traditional greeting. "Pokoj a pozehnani."

"Pax et bonum," a male voice responded. Only someone who was not Czech would use the Latin for "Peace and blessings." The next words came in Latin, too. "We are two friars sent by Lady Clare of Assisi."

Aneska's heart fluttered. "Lady Clare has sent a letter to the Princess Agnes and a few items that she used at San Damiano."

Aneska's soul swelled. "Put the goods on the turn," she replied in Latin. "Please return tomorrow, because the princess will wish to send a letter to Lady Clare." A letter asking what to do about the papal decree.

When Clare had written to Aneska last year upon her entrance into religious life, Aneska had written back, requesting some small tokens to link the two monasteries. These gifts had to be the tokens. A rough wooden cross. An earthenware bowl. A string of wooden prayer beads. A black veil, clean but used. Aneska kissed each as she plucked it from the turn. Poor relics used by a saintly woman.

Then, giddy with joy and reverence, Aneska broke the wax seal on the parchment letter.

Her eyes devoured Clare's fine, gracefully penned words. "To the daughter of the King of kings...you have despised the splendor of an earthly kingdom...one thing is necessary...that you always be mindful of your resolution like another Rachel always seeing your beginning."

Rachel was Jacob's wife whom the Church Fathers saw as a symbol of the contemplative life of prayer and penance. Saint Jerome had said that "Rachel" meant "seeing the beginning." Was Clare telling Aneska to recall the poverty she had vowed at the beginning of her religious life?

Aneska read more slowly. "What you hold, may you always hold. What you do may you always do and never abandon."

Yes, Lord.

"But with swift pace, light step, unswerving feet, so that even your steps stir up no dust, may you go forward securely, joyfully, and swiftly, on the path of prudent happiness, not believing anything, not agreeing with anything that would dissuade you from this resolution or that would place a stumbling block for you on the way..."

The papal decree? Stumbling block?

"...so that you may offer your vows to the Most High in the pursuit of that perfection to which the Spirit of the Lord has called you."

She read on as Clare told her to follow the counsel of Minister General Elias. Having been sent in 1230 to do penance, Elias had been reinstated into the order's and the Church's good graces. Elected minister general in 1232, Elias was in Assisi, feverishly completing the upper level of Saint Francis's basilica. Elias, in his contacts with the Pope, could have learned about the papal decree and discussed it with Clare.

"If anyone would tell you something else or suggest something that would hinder your perfection, or seem contrary to your divine vocation, even though you must respect him, do not follow his counsel. But as a poor virgin, embrace the poor Christ."

Perhaps Clare suspected that the Pope would attempt to grant the Bohemian monastery possessions and income as he had granted them to Clare's own monastery and others. Poor, misguided Holy Father! If only he trusted God's providence as the sisters did!

Aneska pressed the letter to her chest. Oh, how her sisters would rejoice as she read Clare's words to them! Unlike many others who would scrape ink off expensive parchment and reply on the same sheet, Aneska would save this letter as she had saved Clare's letter written upon her entry into religious life. The words of that letter came to mind.

> O blessed poverty, who bestows eternal riches on
> those who love and embrace her! O holy poverty,
> God promises the kingdom of heaven and, in fact,
> offers eternal glory and a blessed life to those who
> possess and desire you! O God-centered poverty,
> whom the Lord Jesus Christ... condescended to
> embrace before all else! ...the Kingdom of heaven is
> promised and given by the Lord only to the poor, for
> she who loves temporal things loses the fruit of love.

God had answered Aneska's prayers. Begging God for the proper words, she would write to the Holy Father, telling him that she could not accept his kind offer of stability and again pleading with him to separate the monastery from the hospice so that the sisters could possess nothing but God.

↝ 44 ↜

Lord Giovanni di Maestro Giovanni

Via San Petrignano, Assisi (LATE JUNE, 1238) ↝ Lord Giovanni di Maestro Giovanni walked beside the litter, carried by two pages, on which lay his motionless, hollow-cheeked son. In the five-year-old's skeletal face, red and burning with fever, huge brown eyes gazed blankly at the sky. On the left side of the child's throat swelled a grotesque scrofula, the size of a small, unripe melon. The best doctors and medicines could not cure this son. Only prayer remained.

How fiercely Giovanni loved this child, born in his wife's death agony, the last gift of her long life! Giovanni's other children were adults; this boy, the joy of his father's old age. He could not die.

The steep road sloped toward San Damiano. As procurator for the Poor Enclosed Ladies, Giovanni had often made this trek on horseback. Just three weeks ago he had executed a legal parchment, signed by all fifty ladies, which granted the power of attorney to Lady Agnese's father Lord Oportulo di Bernardo, so that he could sell to the cathedral of Assisi a piece of property belonging to San Damiano.

God, you must let her heal him.

"Her" was Lady Clare who came to the curtained parlor grill when summoned. Extending her hand through the grate, she touched the still child's shoulder. Giovanni heard no words: Clare prayed in silence.

God, please, You have to cure him!

Word of Clare's cures had circulated through Piacenza, Rome, Milan, Padua, Prague, Rheims. Wherever Clare houses were. She had to cure him.

HAVE TO?

The gentle, internal rebuke caught Giovanni off guard.

He is my life, God!

THEN, GIOVANNI, WHO AM I?

A verse came to mind. "He who loves father, mother, husband, wife, daughter, son, more than Me is not worthy of Me."

Giovanni, do you trust me?

Giovanni lay his hand on the lad's burning forehead. What if the child died? Would he be happier in God's kingdom than in Giovanni's household? Did God know what was best?

Within Giovanni's soul, a struggle arose. Didn't the child belong to God more fully than he belonged to Giovanni? As Giovanni curled the boy's thin fingers in his own, silent words cried in the anguish of his soul. *God, heal him, if it be Your will.*

Within moments the boy's fingers felt excruciatingly hot. A tremor shook his body as the child shrieked in sudden agony. As the litter began to quiver, Giovanni threw himself against it to steady it. Clare's hand was making the sign of the cross over the child.

"Papa?"

Giovanni gasped. He pressed the boy's head, temples, cheeks. They were cool. He felt the child's neck. The scrofula had disappeared. "Praised be God! He is cured! Grazie, Lady Clare! Grazie! Grazie!"

ᴄ 45 ᴄ

Sister Balvina di Martino

Infirmary, San Damiano (Mɪᴅ-Dᴇᴄᴇᴍʙᴇʀ, 1239) ᴄ Sister Balvina di Martino had been in the refectory pinning together two pieces of fine purple satin to make a priest's stole when Sister Bonaventura had called all the sisters to the infirmary because Sister Clare wanted to speak to the entire community at the same time. Now Balvina sat on the infirmary floor, her bare feet tucked under her ample gown, her dark eyes bright above her very plump cheeks.

Having left her bed in the dormitory, Clare was seated on a small bench, her usually vivacious face oddly grim. "Sisters, let us begin with prayer." Her voice was quiet, almost flat.

Balvina bowed her head.

"Dear Lord, may we know that You wish us to freely love and serve You. May we accept what we do not understand. May we serve You though all the world..." Clare's voice trembled, halted. "...though all the world go astray. Amen."

Balvina raised her head, her soul troubled at the anguish in the prayer.

Clare puckered her lips. "Sisters, this is difficult news." She hesitated, sighed. "Friar Cappellano has just told me that Friar Elias has joined the emperor and has been excommunicated."

A wave of shocked disbelief swept over the sisters. Balvina sat stupefied. Friar Elias! She could picture him preaching: bushy black beard, deep-set, dark eyes, almost imperceptible swagger, his expressive voice bellowing.

Elias was brilliant, authoritative. Saint Francis had first made him provincial of Syria, then vicar of the order. After caring for Francis in his final illness, Elias had written a touching letter to the friars and sisters upon Francis's death. Elias had designed the massive, marvelous Basilica of Saint Francis. He had been elected minister general from 1232 until Pentecost of this year, even though he had asked the friars to select someone else since his health problems made it difficult for him to live the Rule. The friars told him that he could make exceptions as he saw fit, yet when he rode on horseback, kept servants, and ate the choicest foods, the friars complained. They complained, too, that he tried to govern the order completely on his own, that he hand-picked provincials and custodians who agreed with his policies, and that he had not called a single meeting of the friars since his election. But he had been busy and ill. Besides, he probably trusted the friars he had placed in charge of the many extra provinces he had created. The complaining friars were too hard on Elias, Balvina had often thought. Perhaps they were jealous.

Because Elias had not called a general chapter meeting, Pope Gregory IX did. At this year's Pentecost chapter, Elias had been replaced as minister general by Friar Albert of Pisa, provincial of England, whom Francis had received into the order. On his last visit to San Damiano, Elias had explained that he was going to Cortona to be with friends.

"Friar Elias has been visiting the Damianites in their monasteries in Cortona and Arezzo," Clare was explaining. This was permitted when he was minister general, but now he needed papal permission. "When the Holy Father told Friar Elias to stop his visits, Friar Elias grew angry and joined forces with the emperor."

The superficial reason confounded Balvina. For years, Elias had tried to make peace between Frederick II and the Pope. He knew that joining the emperor meant automatic excommunication. Why did he do it?

"So, my sisters, we must pray for Friar Elias's soul." Clare's voice was forcefully controlled. "And we must pray for the friars and the Church, because this is a great and irreparable scandal." Clare's words trembled. "May no souls be lost through this bad example. May we not lose faith." Clare, who prized Friar Elias's advice, blinked fiercely to quell her welling tears. "Let us fix our gaze on Christ, betrayed by Judas. Though friends disappoint and those we trust fail, yet God is still in charge."

"But why did he do it?" Balvina blurted out.

"Because God gave Friar Elias, like all of us," Clare said softly, "the freedom to choose."

Balvina pressed her face into her hands. Some choices were not good ones. *Dear God, save Friar Elias's soul.*

PART ELEVEN

The Father of Mercies

✎ 46 ✎

Sister Cecilia di Gualtieri Cacciaguerra

Refectory, San Damiano (SEPTEMBER 1240) ✎ Standing in the refectory of San Damiano, Sister Cecilia stared, befuddled, at the stale half loaf of bread before her. At Clare's request, she had taken the other half to the friars who served the monastery. Clare had told her to cut this half into fifty slices so that each sister might have one. "It would take the miracle of the loaves and the fishes to make fifty slices out of that!" Cecilia had blurted out.

"Go and do as I have told you," Clare had calmly replied.

There was no other food in the monastery.

Cecilia could hear the sisters filing into the refectory. Better get started. Her thin eyebrows wrinkled and her full lips pursed as she took up the knife. She was so hungry that she could have eaten the entire piece herself.

How could life change so much in two weeks?

Two weeks ago, Cecilia was coughing so violently that she could not swallow without fear of suffocating. That Friday almost two weeks ago, when the sisters had been fasting on bread and water, Clare had led Cecilia into the kitchen where she had given her a small cake to eat. Cecilia had nibbled the sweet morsel out of obedience. Wondrously, the cake had cured her. She had not coughed since.

Two weeks ago, Assisi had been at peace. Now the emperor's Saracen soldiers had arrived. Followers of Muhammad, Saracens were fierce, warlike people from Morocco and the eastern areas around the Holy Land. Fifteen years ago, Emperor Frederick II had relocated the Saracens from their centuries-old settlement in Sicily to Lucera on the mainland and employed them as personal servants, dancing girls, and soldiers. Having discontinued his attack on Rome in February, the twice-excommunicated emperor was on the march north through the papal states. Now he was here in Umbria, in the papally held Duchy of Spoleto.

Two weeks ago, folks brought alms to San Damiano and the friars begged food in Assisi. Now Saracen troops were killing papal sympathizers. No one came to San Damiano any more. No friars begged. The sisters and friars had eaten all the garden vegetables and used up all the flour. Only this stale loaf remained.

How ironic! Clare's bones and body were badly weakened because she fasted too severely when she was younger. Now, older and wiser, she ate something daily and forbid the sisters to fast as she had done. But there was no food. If this continued, other sisters might end up like Clare.

Taking a deep breath, Cecilia blessed herself. How thin could she cut without the bread crumbling? She cut one slice. My goodness, it was rather plump. She thought she had cut it almost parchment thin. Well, she could cut that plump slice into eight parts.

She made another slice. What was wrong with her? This slice was thick, too. Now she had two slices to cut into eighths.

Cecilia held the loaf under her hand and spread her fingers across it to hold it steady. How odd! She had two ample slices of bread on the table and the half loaf was very small. Yet, her fingers still spread as widely as they had before she made the first cut. Puzzled, she cut again, very, very carefully. And this slice was plump, too.

Cecilia put the knife down. Was it the blade or her cutting? She now had three fat slices of bread. Forty-seven more to go. She could cut each of the three slices into eighths to make twenty-four parts. Then she would have to cut twenty-six thin slices from the loaf. How could she get twenty-six slices from that?

Taking a slow, deep breath, Cecilia held the loaf firmly and began to cut again. The piece was as plump as the other three. And the loaf was no smaller.

Would it happen again? Quickly she cut a fifth thin—no, it was coming out plump—piece. A sixth. Like a mad woman, she began to slice. Seven. Eight. Nine. Slice. Slice. Her mind was reeling, singing. Her hands began to tingle. She began to lose count. She was trembling at what was happening. The slices piling up were already more than she had begun with. What does one do when experiencing a miracle? One keeps on going. Slice. Slice. Slice. Until the loaf was done.

Cecilia's heart was dancing as she lay down the knife and flexed her cramped fingers. The bread was heaped up every which way before her. Could there be...? She began to count the slices as she placed them on two large wooden platters. One, two, three...twenty, twenty-one...thirty-eight, thirty-nine...fifty. Cecilia gasped. What was she supposed to do?

SERVE THE BREAD, an inner voice said.

Yes, Lord. Serve the bread.

She did, one slice for each sister. When Cecilia bit into her portion, the bread was sweeter than the cake that had cured her cough.

~ 47 ~

Sister Illuminata

Dormitory, San Damiano (9:00 A.M., SEPTEMBER 1240) ~ Sister Illuminata stood at one of the dormitory windows of San Damiano, gazing out at the Via Cupo di San Petrignano. She could not be seeing what she was seeing. The shouting that had drawn Illuminata to the window had materialized into a hoard of Saracen soldiers passing by the monastery. All of Assisi had feared the coming of these troops.

In Pisa, Illuminata had been a saddle maker's daughter. She had admired the strong knights who patronized her father's business, secretly believing that, like them, she would not flinch in the face of danger. Now her statuesque body was frozen with fear. She wanted to run, but there was nowhere to go.

Suddenly a horrific bashing shook the dormitory. Again.

"Mother!" The shriek came from Sister Angeluccia who had just raced up the stairs into the dormitory and who had thrown herself at Clare's bedside. "The Saracens are battering the door of the church!"

"Quick, daughters!" Clare commanded from her sickbed. "Gather the sisters and bolt every door and window. Pull up the infirmary stairs! Have Sister Prassede bring the Body of the Lord! May God protect us!"

Angeluccia darted out of the dormitory and down the stairs, leaving Illuminata to bolt the dormitory windows. Into the dormitory hurried Francesca, Benvenuta, Lucia. Quickly the women shuttered the windows. One. Another. Another. As Illuminata bolted the last window, she saw Saracen soldiers swarming over the wall and dropping like vicious ants into the enclosure.

Oh, God, no!

Around Clare's bed, sisters were clustering in anguished terror, hysterical weeping, and stoic heroism.

"Everything is bolted, Mother!"

"Mother, save us!"

"God will protect us. Won't He?"

"Mother, save us!"

Into the dormitory rushed Sister Prassede, bearing in her hands the little ivory-bound silver casket from the oratory. In that casket resided the Eucharistic Lord. Prassede's heavily lidded eyes were wide with terror, her usually doleful expression horrified.

The dormitory shook again with another loud crash. A shocked hush fell.

Cecilia's voice quivered, "The refectory door."

"Sister Prassede," Clare said, her words shaking, "go before me. Sisters Francesca and Illuminata, help me. We will take the Lord to the refectory door where He will have to protect us."

As the women began to protest, Clare raised her hand. "My sisters, do not fear. If the Lord is with us, the enemy cannot harm us. Have confidence in our Lord Jesus Christ." She had told them this several times when the women had voiced their fears about the Saracens possibly invading Umbria.

"I have told you that if the soldiers came here, you were to place me before them. Now we shall go. The remainder of you pray in the oratory or with the sisters in the infirmary. Sisters Illuminata and Francesca, help me, please."

Living this nightmare, Illuminata grasped Clare beneath one arm while Francesca took her by the other one. As they helped her rise, they heard another unearthly crash from the refectory.

"Quickly!" Clare said.

They were hurrying, supporting Clare, almost lifting and carrying her, following Prassede and the Eucharistic Lord. When they reached the refectory, Prassede stopped and looked at Clare as another crash shook the door.

"Right in front of the door, Sister."

Quickly Prassede blessed herself and hurried to the door as a man on the other side of the door began to call out strong, commanding words. Facing the door, Prassede knelt, trembling, holding the Eucharist directly in front of the entrance.

Illuminata and Francesca brought Clare to the entrance, where all three knelt as the door shuddered with another ramming. Immediately Clare prostrated herself, while Illuminata and Francesca drew closer as if to protect her.

Clare's prayers were strong, almost demanding. "Lord, we are here trusting in You. You, Lord, are our spouse. Defend us and save us from these evil men."

The door was bashed again.

"Look upon these servants of Yours," Clare cried, "because I cannot protect them." In a brief hush, a voice, incredibly sweet and calm, filled the silence. I WILL ALWAYS DEFEND YOU.

Illuminata gasped as the door was rammed yet again. "Lord, there are so many good people in the city," Clare pleaded. "So many who trust in and serve You. My dear God, please defend the city as well."

The voice came again, gentle, firm. THE CITY WILL ENDURE MANY DANGERS, BUT IT WILL BE DEFENDED.

Clare raised her head. "Do not be afraid, sisters, because I am a hostage for you so that you will not suffer any harm now nor any other time as long as you wish to obey God's commandments." Then Clare turned toward the ivory box and pressed her face to the floor before it.

Again the door shuddered under an unearthly ramming.

∿ 48 ∾

Saracen Troop Petty Officer

Enclosure, San Damiano (9:30 A.M., SEPTEMBER 1240) ∿ Under a brilliant blue sky, the swarthy, middle-aged Saracen officer laughed as his men rammed a thick tree trunk into the old wooden door. Behind that door, so he had heard, fifty or more consecrated women lived. Only one or two more rammings to collapse the door. He intended to be the first inside.

Emperor Frederick's troops, including this one, had spread through the March of Ancona and the Duchy of Spoleto, pillaging, murdering, raping, attempting to take the cities loyal to the papacy. Now they were headed north, to quell rebellion in the Romagna and to lay siege to Ravenna, Faenza, Venezia, and Bologna. But first they would have fun with these women!

The young soldiers had initially attempted to gain entrance by battering the church door, but the officer had stopped them, for women in these places would not be in the church. Seizing a grappling hook from one of the men, the officer had tossed it high against the pink enclosing wall. When it held fast in a crevice, he had scaled the wall, his troops following him. Having trampled the garden, the men were now swarming and whooping about this door.

"Are you women yourselves!" the officer taunted the battering crew. "Move farther back! Put more force behind you. The wood is rotting. It will shatter soon!"

The bevy of soldiers backed up, carrying the trunk.

From the other side of the door came a woman's voice, strong, unafraid. And then the soldiers ran forward, ramming the door again.

The woman's voice came again from behind the door. Why didn't the woman run?

The men rammed the door again. It did not budge.

The door was old, the hinges weak and rusted, the wood dry. At the bottom and the right side the planks were rotted. The door should have given way.

The woman's voice came again. Deep. Fearless. If they broke in, she would be immediately assaulted. Why was she there?

Thick fear rose inside the officer's innards. Muslims who called upon Allah faced danger as fearlessly as this woman did. The woman had to be calling upon her god.

Allah brought victory in war and vengeance on enemies. He backed the armies that served him. But he was not bringing down a rotting door. Was the woman's god more powerful? Or was her courage stronger than his?

Suddenly fearing to desecrate this place, the officer thrust his fist skyward. "Come!" he cried. "Other troops must be almost in the city! This place has nothing of value. The city has treasure and more women!"

Motioning to the men, he raced to the wall, threw the grappling hook against it, and called the men over.

On sturdy legs the troops pushed up the long hill, falling in with their fellows before the high city walls and strong gates of Assisi.

⤳ 49 ⤶

Sister Cristiana de Bernardo da Suppo

San Damiano (Dusk, June 20, 1241) ⤳ The bell was ringing so wildly at the speaking grill of San Damiano that Sister Cristiana forgot the customary greeting. The breathless, red-faced messenger thrust a tightly rolled parchment through the grill. "My master, Lord Iacopo di Stefano di Presbitero..." he puffed, "...bid me run here with this urgent message...." The youth caught his breath. "Have Lady Clare read it and then return it to me," he panted. "Be quick."

Her doe eyes wide with curiosity and concern, Cristiana raced upstairs with the parchment. Around Clare's bed, the sisters were folding up altar cloths and vestments they had been stitching. Clare was winding the final length of flaxen thread that she had spun to-day on the drop spindle. Swiftly breaking the thread between the spindle and the distaff, she snagged it in a notch on the spindle's end. As Cristiana handed her the parchment, Clare lay the spindle in a small basket on the floor between the legs of the free-standing distaff. Tomorrow she would reconnect the threads and spin again.

Breaking the wax seal, Clare angled the parchment to catch the light. Her face stiffened. Rolling up the parchment, she handed it to Cristiana. "Return this to the servant. Then call all the sisters to me."

A shiver of fear lanced Cristiana's heart as she hurried down-stairs. The youth grabbed the parchment and bolted out of the church. He would want to get home before dark, before robbers patrolled the roads.

Cristiana gathered the sisters—those locking the church for the night, those clearing the refectory tables of the day's stitching, those readying supper, those tending the infirm. In minutes, all the sisters except the infirm ones were at Clare's side.

Clare's expression was grim. "Sisters, I have received correspon-dence from a knight of Assisi. The emperor is sending his armies to Assisi under Vitale d'Aversa."

A gasp of dismay rushed over the sisters.

Her blue eyes gazing intently at the women, Clare went on. "The knights are readying for battle, but they fear that their forces cannot withstand the emperor's. The knights say the city must be handed over. Vitale d'Aversa has sworn that he will not leave until Assisi is taken."

Oh, my Lord, no! A scene of unbelievable carnage flashed across Cristiana's mind.

Sister Gregoria fell to her knees. Sisters Mattia and Lea, then the others, followed Gregoria's example.

"The lord has asked us to pray that this be avoided." Clare paused. Her voice trembled, her eyes brimmed with tears. "We have received many benefits from the city. We should pray that God will protect it."

The sisters nodded.

"Let us remember this intention in Vespers and Compline and pray through the night."

When the Saracens had left San Damiano's enclosure not a year ago, they had marched on Assisi but had not attacked it. However, during the past months, Emperor Frederick II, despite a few defeats, had taken city after city loyal to the Pope.

He had recaptured Ravenna.

The papally held cities of Tuscany peacefully allowed Frederick's troops entrance.

After an eight-month seige, Faenza had fallen.

The papal enclave at Benevento had been obliterated.

Frederick had even prevented the Pope from calling a council in Rome—its aim had been to depose Frederick as emperor. Learning that the Church's prelates from the northern parts of the empire were assembling at Genoa to sail to Rome, Frederick gathered a massive fleet that ambushed the papal vessels, sinking three ships and capturing twenty-two others. Just over a month ago, more than four thousand men—lay men, lesser clergy, priests, abbots, cardinals, bishops, and archbishops—had been imprisoned in Pisa. The sisters had been besieging heaven for their release even as Frederick boasted that God had smitten the Church. Now his forces were marching south to Rome, where Pope Gregory IX lay deathly ill. In the line of march, Assisi was the one city loyal to the Pope.

Other than praying the Office in the choir, Cristiana and nearly all the other sisters spent the night in the oratory, begging God's protection on Assisi, home of their benefactors and relatives. With nearly all the monastery crowded before the Eucharist, the little oratory felt stifling in the still June night. The hours slipped on. Cristiana began fighting sleep. Finally, as other sisters had already done, she plodded up the stairs to the dormitory.

There, in the glow of oil lamps, scattered sisters slept on straw mattresses. Someone had moved Clare's bed to face the unshuttered windows that overlooked Assisi. Clare, who could no longer walk, was propped up, her hands joined, her cheeks shiny with tears, her gaze on a wide, distant ring of flickering lights. Campfires. The emperor's army had surrounded the commune.

Cristiana fell to her knees by Clare's cot, hands groping for hands, eyes seeking eyes. Clare grasped Cristiana's fingers. Clare mouthed the words "Pray. Pray."

Day dawned clear, harmonious, filled with birdsong. How could peace prevail here when Assisi was on the verge of battle?

Clare called the sisters to her. Someone had brought her ashes from the hearth. Silently, Clare removed her veil and sprinkled ashes on the crown of her close-cropped head.

"Remove your veils, sisters," Clare softly instructed. The bare-headed sisters knelt as Clare placed ashes on each head. "Today we shall fast on bread and water. May God reward those who eat nothing as a penance for Assisi. Go to the chapel, sisters, and beg God to free the city."

Cristiana and the other sisters knelt in the oratory, their eyes on their Eucharistic Lord. All day they prayed—kneeling, prostrate, seated. Through the open windows came distant shouts, shrieks. The pounding of hooves. Battle sounds. During the night, Cristiana, weak from lack of sleep and food, fell asleep while praying. The next day the praying and the fasting continued.

Sometime after the Office of Sext, the sisters heard a wild pounding on the church doors, barred against attack. Unmitigated terror seized Cristiana. She flung herself face down on the oratory floor and begged for the mercy and protection of God. Almost simultaneously, there was a sharp ringing at the speaking grill. Three rings in a row. The friars' signal.

Cristiana was answering the bell this week. Her legs weak, she started downstairs to find Pacifica and Beatrice following her. At the grill, Beatrice clutched Cristiana's hand. "We lived together in the same household, Sister. We shall die together." Swiftly the three women embraced, then Cristiana unbolted the little door and squeaked out, "Pace e bene."

"Sister, that knocking was a band of knights from the city." Friar Cappellano's voice was jubilant. "They thank you for your prayers. The knights have defeated Vitale d'Aversa. Today at dawn, the enemy left the commune."

PART TWELVE

To Return to the Lord an Increase of his Talents

❦ 50 ❦

Sister Angeluccia de Angelico

Via San Petrignano, Assisi (Sunday Evening, June 30, 1247) ❦ Sister Angeluccia's delicately white skin was warm in the rays of the descending sun. Today she and Sister Cristi had come to pray at the bedside of the dying Lord Lambertini and to comfort his widow. As on every trip into the city, they'd met beggars who needed bandages, medications, salves, splints, and cleansing agents—not to mention prayers. Tomorrow the women would bring the supplies; tonight they would pray for the intentions.

Angeluccia's aging mind was befuddled by too many things to remember. Sister Cristi, daughter of Messer Cristiano de Parisse, a consul of the commune, was young and, although deaf in one ear, heard most things. She'd remember what needed remembering. Recently a Damianite, Cristi's actual name was Cristiana, shortened to distinguish her from the other Cristianas at San Damiano. With her naturally long stride, Cristi found it difficult to keep pace with arthritic Angeluccia. She did better if they prayed while they walked.

"Let's pray for the emperor again," Angeluccia suggested. Praying for the emperor was Angeluccia's personal ministry, begun in earnest six years ago when Vitale d'Aversa, slain a while ago, had attacked Assisi. Assisi retained its loyalty to the Pope while Frederick and his sons, also kings, still warred against him. The current Pope was not Gregory IX, who had died two months after d'Aversa's attack, but Innocent IV, elected to the pontificate in 1243. Three years ago, for his own safety, Pope Innocent, with his papal court, had fled Rome to lodge in the independent city of Lyons. Innocent IV had deposed Frederick; Henry Raspe, Landgrave of Thuringia, had been elected to replace him. But Raspe had died in February, and negotiations were ongoing to choose his successor.

Despite his deposition, Frederick still reigned as emperor. His support, while growing stronger in some quarters, was waning in others. The Pope had declared that all those who had sworn fidelity to Frederick were absolved from the pledge. Anyone who continued to recognize Frederick as emperor or king was excommunicated. Many people were irate that Frederick had revealed, in one of his many letters, his loathing of the clergy. The Poor Brothers and the Preaching Friars, whom the Pope had commissioned to preach against Frederick, were arousing opposition to him. Cities loyal to Frederick were rebelling. Nobles Frederick had trusted had tried unsuccessfully to take his life.

Angeluccia's feelings were mixed toward the man whom some deemed the antichrist. While abhorring his deceit, faithlessness, and cruelty, she pitied him, too. So many of his wives and children had died. His tormented, power-hungry soul must cause him great suffering. Orphaned at the age of four and placed under the guardianship of Pope Innocent III, Frederick had turned against the Church that had protected him. Yet, should he repent, God's mercy would be his. All the rest of the way down the hill, up the ladder, and into the dormitory, Angeluccia and Cristi prayed Our Father's for Frederick's repentance.

Out of the corner of her eye, Angeluccia saw the accident. Clare, who had grown strong enough to tend the door, pushing the heavy door closed. The door wobbling on its hinges, breaking loose, collapsing inward, falling on Clare. Only Clare's toes showed under the door.

Angeluccia and Cristi both shrieked. Together they grabbed the door, trying to lift it. It would not budge.

"Sister Clare!"

No answer.

"Sisters! Sisters!" Angeluccia screamed.

Cecilia came running. Balvina of Porzano.

The four women pulled and tugged, but the door would not budge. Cristi ran to get the friars.

Cecilia, Balvina, and Angeluccia tried again and again to lift the door. Impossible.

Into the dormitory through the doorless doorway scrambled Friar Cappellano, brothers Marco and Gino. Ordering the women back, they grabbed the door, strained, heaved the door off Clare, and eased it to the monastery floor.

The sisters ran to Clare's frail, crumpled body.

"Sister! Sister!" they called.

As if being roused from deep slumber, Clare pushed herself to a sitting position and shook her head. "I'm all right," she said, wondrously. "It was as if a mantle had been thrown over me."

Cappellano helped Clare to her feet. "My lady, that door is rotted. We will replace it tomorrow."

"The night is warm," Gino noted. "Leave the door where it is. Pull up the ladder when we leave and you will be safe."

"We will do as you say," Clare agreed.

As the friars descended the ladder, Angeluccia's heart began to race as if her fear had been suppressed until the danger had passed.

Clare smiled at the sisters. "Let us go and thank the good God for His blessings."

Together they walked to the oratory to do just that.

～⤳ 51 ⤳～

Lord Scherno

Great Hall of a Great House, Pisa (MARCH 1249) ⤳ Seated on a broad bench, muscular Lord Scherno stretched his chilled feet toward the fire snapping in the fireplace of the great hall in a great house in Pisa. Upon his father's death three years ago, Scherno had inherited this house.

Today's hunt had been unbelievably successful. Sixteen deer and eight boar. Enough to feed his entire household for two weeks.

He heard someone enter the room, but he was too cozy to turn to see who it was.

"My lord."

Ah, Mother.

"I heard that you had a most successful hunt."

He grunted. What was she getting at?

"You now have time to take Lady Pia to the holy nuns. They say the prayers of Lady Clare are most effective…."

Scherno swung around. "Mother, give up! Lady Pia is a hopeless case. If God wanted to heal her, He could do it here."

"Can't you do this for your sister? Please?"

He sprang to his feet, his toes still icy. "Religion destroyed Lady Pia's mind. You expect religion to restore it?" This pious sister of his had prayed long hours in the chapel, lingered after Mass, modestly avoided open windows, and had considered becoming a nun. That was before the demons had destroyed her mind.

"Please. I beg you."

Scherno slapped one huge fist into the other. "I will write. That's all."

His mother, much shorter than he, trembled before him. "Grazie. I will send a servant in with parchment."

"Not tonight, Mother."

"Tonight." The voice was firm.

All right. Tonight.

He took the parchment and reed pen offered him and scrawled: "To Lady Clare. My mother asks you to pray for my demon-possessed sister Lady Pia. Cure her, if you can. As if God cares." He thrust the parchment at the servant and turned back to the fire.

Before Scherno had to hunt again, the answer arrived. He was in his counting room, reviewing accounts with the bailiff, when Mother brought him the parchment. She would not leave until he read it to her.

"It says that Lady Clare and her sisters are praying for Lady Pia," he said, swiftly skimming the finely penned prose. The letter had been written on the parchment he had used—beneath Clare's words, traces of scraped-off ink revealed his own note.

Mother smiled widely. "Thanks be to God."

Scherno spat. "The prayers have done no good." Lady Pia was the same. Her bedroom door was still tightly shut. Servants continued to leave her food at the door because she flung it at them if they entered. He often heard eerie moanings coming from the bedroom and, three days ago, a wild thrashing. Last night, Lady Pia had passed him in the hall, a thin wraith in a white chemise coming from the direction of the chapel, her auburn hair wild as a witch's, a vacant stare on her face, her pale hands folded to unspeaking lips.

Mother reached for the letter and pressed it to her chest. "Grazie." Silently she left the room.

Scherno returned to his accounts, a bit unsettled. Lady Clare had severely admonished him for his lack of faith, had pleaded with him to repent, and had written that she and the sisters were praying with tears for him.

Lent arrived. Easter. Spring crops were planted. Still Pia's bedroom door remained closed, the tray delivered in the hall. The shrieks and thrashing increased. Pia grew worse.

On the Feast of Pentecost, Scherno was surveying the great hall, set for a sumptuous banquet. The long head table for the men, the side table for the women. The guests would arrive within the hour. Satisfied, he turned to leave and met Lady Pia entering.

She was clothed in a saffron gown, her hair caught up in a crispinette of net at her neck, a maroon velvet hat fastened under her chin with a wide band. She seemed as peaceful as she had been before the demons consumed her. Smiling, she placed her thin, pale hand on Scherno's arm.

"My brother, you must write a letter to Lady Clare. Her prayers have driven out the demons. There were five of them."

Scherno looked skeptically into his sister's tranquil gray eyes. "Five?" She was still possessed to think that she knew the number of demons!

"They told me their names as they were leaving."

Scherno laughed disdainfully.

Pia patted Scherno's arm. "Scruple. Shame. Self-hatred. Mistrust of God's Mercy. Refusal to Accept God's Forgiveness."

"What kind of names are those?" Scherno roared.

"They told me the names of your demons," Pia said calmly. "Unbelief. Scorn. Arrogance. Pride. Trust in One's Self. Everyone knew that demons possessed me. You do not know that they possess you."

Scherno stiffened.

"The demons said that Lady Clare's prayers were burning them, because the fire of faith is more consuming than the fire of hell. May the fire of faith cast out your demons, my brother."

❧ 52 ❧

Sister Cristi
(Sister Cristiana de Cristiano de Parisse)

Dormitory, San Damiano (SEPTEMBER 8, 1252) ❧ On a bench next to Clare's raised bed, Sister Cristi's long, lean body felt awkwardly tense. For the hundredth time, she tried to hem the seam in the altar cloth in her lap. But her gentle gray eyes kept glancing from the cloth to Clare, who was barely clinging to life.

In this week's chapter meeting, Sister Pacifica had assigned Cristi the task of tending Clare. In her naturally tender way, Cristi had been bathing Clare's warm forehead, coaxing her to sip a bit of watery broth, turning her body so that she could rest more comfortably.

Beneath the idle distaff, loosely twisted with flaxen fibers, Clare dozed. Clare had spun enough thread to make over fifty sets of corporals and their cases. Would Clare ever spin again?

Clare had experienced her first grave health crisis last autumn, when the Pope and the Curia were still in Lyons. The Damianite sisters had sent word to their fellow religious in area convents, monasteries, and hermitages to pray for Clare. A comforting but perplexing message had arrived from the Benedictine convent of San Paolo delle Abbadesse in Bastia, where Clare had lived for a time after being tonsured by Saint Francis. While deep in prayer for Clare, one of the San Paolo sisters had experienced a haunting vision. The sister had felt as if she and the other San Paolo sisters were attending the ill Clare as she lay on a queenly bed of gold, studded with precious gems. As the sisters had wept, a majestic, strikingly beautiful woman had appeared at the foot of the bed. "Daughters, do not weep over one who is about to be victorious," she consoled. "Sister Clare cannot die until the Lord comes with His disciples."

Shortly after the vision, in early November, Innocent IV and his court had arrived in Perugia, safe now that Frederick II had died in December 1250. Cardinal Raynaldo, protector of the order, had hurried to visit gravely ill Clare. She had begged him to urge the Pope to ratify the Form of Life she had written and to confirm the privilege of poverty for San Damiano. Raynaldo had visited Clare a few times since then. Always she asked the same favor. It had not yet been granted.

An almost imperceptible cough jerked Cristi's attention back to Clare. Before Cristi could elevate Clare's head to help her inhale more deeply, Clare had resumed an easy, shallow breathing pattern.

How ironic that Cristi could hear Clare's faint choking while just months ago she sometimes could not make out her abbess's words! Early in the summer, Clare had felt a bit stronger. She had resumed her spinning and, one summer day, she and Clare fell to talking about Cristi's deaf ear. Clare had asked Cristi to kneel and had prayed silently over her. Then Clare had made the sign of the cross and touched her deaf ear, which had popped inside. Instantly Cristi could hear with it.

Now Clare was too weak even to bless herself.

Oh, God! Cristi prayed—as she had prayed every day since Clare had grown so ill—*can't You let Lord Pope approve her Form of Life before she dies? It is all she wants for herself, Lord.*

Five years ago, Lord Pope Innocent IV had given all the Damianites a Rule. Innocent's Rule had stated that monasteries must hold goods in common and that they were permitted to hold property. Dismayed at the mitigation of their vowed poverty, many of the monasteries, including San Damiano, had asked the Pope to rescind his order; two years ago, he had. Clare then began to write her own Form of Life, putting the sisters solidly under the friars, incorporating sections of Innocent's Rule and Cardinal Hugolino's, and firmly adhering to poverty. Clare had sent her Form of Life to the Pope. Why was he taking so long to approve it?

Yes, Lord Pope had other things on his mind. He was struggling against Frederick's sons for control of parts of the empire. The Holy Land was largely in pagan hands, King Louis IX's crusade in Egypt having failed two years ago. The cruel Tartars threatened eastern lands, even though missionaries were beginning to convert some of the pagans. Heresy persisted despite measures to eradicate it. All these seemed more pressing than approving a lady's Form of Life.

The rustle of woolen habits and the bare feet running on the stairs startled Cristi.

"Cardinal Raynaldo has come to visit Sister Clare!" Venuta's eager whisper was flung Cristi's way as Venuta, along with Balvina, hurried toward the door that opened to the courtyard below. Balvina, still strong despite her age, heaved open the door. Together she and Venuta lowered the staircase. Cristi could hear the stairs creaking under the weight of the ascending cardinal.

Protector of the Order of Saint Damian, Cardinal Raynaldo dei Conti dei Segni was elderly and large, even fat, although next to Balvina his bulk seemed less striking. The cardinal's thin legs and small feet, shoved into his riding boots, seemed disproportionate to the rest of his scarlet-clothed bulk. The sisters said he had been thinner when young, but equally handsome.

As the cardinal and Friar Cappellano approached Clare's bed, Cristi stood to relinquish her seat, but Cardinal Raynaldo waved his big hand, motioning for her to sit, while he and Capellano each took a spare bench from along the wall and placed it next to Clare's bed. At once the cardinal beckoned the other sisters to Clare's bedside. Then he deftly straddled his bench, took a good look at Clare, and bowed his head in prayer.

When he opened his eyes, Clare had opened hers as well. "Lord Cardinal, how good of you to come," Clare said weakly.

The Church official patted Clare's thin hand. "So you are ill again, Lady Clare. As soon as I heard of your illness, I determined to visit you. I have had Friar Cappellano bring with him the Body of the Lord. Would you like to receive Him?"

A radiant smile broke over Clare's pinched face.

Raising his right hand, the cardinal blessed the ill woman and uttered the customary prayers before removing the consecrated Host from the little silver box in Cappellano's hands. With great reverence and with tears streaming down her cheeks, Clare delicately consumed the Eucharistic Body of the Lord while Cristi bowed her head and prayed for Clare's welfare.

In such peaceful, prayerful recollection, the minutes slipped by until Clare broke the silence. "Grazie, Lord Cardinal, for the gift of my Lord. You are so good to me and to my sisters. You are a saint to us."

The distinguished man reddened. "Lady Clare, if you wish to speak of saints, let us speak, not of me, a sinner, but of Stanislaus, bishop of Cracow. Have you perhaps heard of this most holy man?"

No one had, so Raynaldo began to tell them of the holy man, martyred two hundred years ago, whom the Pope would most likely canonize the following year. He then began a long, obviously extemporaneous homily on the virtues of faith, truth, and martyrdom, exhorting the sisters to hold fast to those values. As always, his words were lofty, his sentences complex—so unlike the simple sermons the friars preached.

"Therefore, dear women in Christ, although you may be lodged in this enclosure, your good example must penetrate as a light to the darkened world beyond these walls. May final perseverance and a most happy end be given to you all," the cardinal beamed, raised his hand in benediction, and blessed them with the sign of the cross. "Now, dear ladies, the press of duties calls. I shall bid you farewell with hopes of returning again as my schedule permits."

"Lord Cardinal, before you go, I must ask a favor."

The lord smiled indulgently. "Of course, Lady Clare. What do you wish?"

"Only this, my lord." Down Clare's hollow cheeks ran little streams of tears. "My sisters believe that I am dying. You are the protector of our order. Watch over my soul with your prayers and supplications, and over the souls of my sisters as well."

The tears were coming faster as Raynaldo reached for Clare's hand.

"And I implore you, my lord, to beg Lord Pope and all the cardinals to quickly confirm the Form of Life that I have sent and to grant us, inviolably and for all time, the privilege of poverty."

Raynaldo patted Clare's bony hands. "Lady Clare, I have been doing all within my power to see that your request is granted. I solemnly promise that I will make an extra effort to have the Holy Father act soon. May you and your ladies continue to support my efforts with your constant prayers."

"Lord Cardinal," Clare said with trembling voice, "we pray for nothing more ardently than that the Holy Father allow us for all time to conform ourselves totally to the poor and humble Christ."

↶ 33 ↷

Sister Gatta

Oratory, San Damiano (December 24, 1252) ↷ Sister Gatta was the current cat in a long string of cats that kept San Damiano free of mice. Years ago, following the death of a previous Sister Gatta, a lord had given the sisters this Gatta, then a gray, orange, and white kitten, now old and arthritic.

Right now Gatta was plodding through the oratory without even nibbling a heel or arching her bony head under any elbow. Long ago Gatta had learned that the sisters who tickled her chin, rubbed her tummy, or cuddled her in other rooms ignored her in this one. So she bounded up the stairs into the dormitory and pounced into the lap of the one sister who would caress her. Clare.

Tucked under a gray blanket, Clare was, as always nowadays, lying in bed. On workdays, she would be spinning or embroidering; on prayer days like today she would lie awake, her eyes closed. Gatta curled up in Clare's lap, purring as Clare's thin hand stroked her gray fur. Gatta closed her yellow eyes and snoozed.

Sometime later Gatta awoke, her old body stiff. On achy legs, she pushed erect and stretched. Then she jumped off the bed to walk the pains away. Folded near one of the sisters' mats was a small white towel used to bathe Clare's face. Gatta caught the towel in her claws and began to stretch the kinks out of her toes.

"Sister Gatta!" Clare ordered. "Bring that here!" Clare had taught Gatta the command "Bring." When Gatta obeyed, Clare tickled Gatta's chin. Mouthing the cloth, Gatta began to drag it across the floor.

"Oh, you naughty little thing!" Clare scolded. "You don't know how to bring it. Why are you dragging it along the ground like that?"

Gatta cocked her head. What was wrong? She clawed the cloth into a loose roll and picked it up in her mouth as she would a kitten, carrying it, her head high, to Clare.

"Good, Sister Gatta!" Clare took the cloth from Gatta's mouth and tickled her chin. Then she folded the towel and placed it in a basket in which lay a reed pen and parchment.

"Sister Cristi brought our supper while you were asleep." Clare reached over her bed and plucked a quarter slice of dark brown bread from the dormitory floor. Not very hungry, Gatta sniffed the bread, then sat on her haunches.

Clare laughed lightly. "So you know that Christmas Eve is a fast day! How smart you are!"

Gatta yawned at the unintelligible praise, then leaped into the basket and curled up on the towel.

"No!" Clare picked up Gatta with one hand, and with the other, the basket.

"You can't sleep on my letter to Lord Pope. What will he think if I send him a crushed letter asking him to approve our Rule?" Clare placed the basket by her left side and put Gatta into her lap.

With Clare smoothing the fur along Gatta's spine, Gatta fell asleep. When she awakened, she padded through the dormitory, now filled with sleeping sisters, and used the flat tub of sand placed in one corner just for her. Then she curled up next to Lucia's face. Lucia's measured breathing warmed Gatta's back.

Lucia's kiss to Gatta's head roused the cat from slumber. Stretching, she opened her eyes and saw the dormitory emptying. Every morning the sisters walked down to that room where they sat on benches and said soft words in unison. Clare never went there any more.

Gatta pounced into Clare's lap and felt thin fingers scratching her head as Clare spoke softly to two crossed twigs, tied with twine, which she held in her other hand.

"Well, Lord God, it is Christmas, and I have been left here alone with You."

Immediately Gatta heard beautiful music. She pricked her ears to hear better.

"You hear it, too? An organ."

Clare gasped. She was gazing toward the center of the dormitory. Gatta looked, too. Where had those rows of friars come from?

Music swelled. Friars sang. When the song ended, a deep male voice chanted, "Lord, open my lips." The others responded in uni-

son, "And my mouth will declare Your praise." They were the words
the sisters would be saying now, downstairs.

The chanting went on, reading, more chanting. Gatta grew tired
and yawned. The friars blessed themselves and disappeared.

Puzzled, Gatta nestled under Clare's arm and mewed.

Clare's cheeks were dripping with tears. "My God, I thank You.
To have let me see and hear the brothers in the Church of Saint
Francis praying the Offices of Matins and Lauds for Christmas! Oh,
my God, how have You done such a thing?"

❧ 54 ❧

Sister Andrea da Ferrara

Infirmary, San Damiano (Late Spring, 1253) ∼ On a straw mattress in the infirmary of San Damiano, old, infirm Sister Andrea lay awake, as rigid as a dry stick. Her mind was racing. Would she have another attack? When? How severe would it be? What if she couldn't breathe? Twenty years ago, middle-aged, limber Andrea had come to San Damiano from Ferrara, a city on the plain around the Po River. With her deep brown eyes dancing in her round face, Andrea had been eager for work and prayer. As she aged, she had maintained her vigor and joy until several months ago, when this insidious illness had struck.

Now when she felt winded after climbing the stairs from the choir, she experienced increased difficulty with breathing. Her throat was constricted with swellings that sometimes blocked her breath. No one's prayers had helped her.

Suddenly a piercing yowl shattered the still night. Old Sister Gatta, sleeping next to Andrea, torn by yet another convulsion! Before Andrea could soothe the epileptic cat, the spasm passed. Gatta sighed, arched, curled again into a ball. Andrea was left with a racing heart.

Sister Gatta's first convulsion had been weeks before. Now the spasms came often. As Andrea stroked Gatta's bony gray head, the animal purred.

Without warning, Andrea's throat tightened. She could not breathe. *Oh, God, no!* Impulsively, she clutched her blocked throat and squeezed. Either she would burst these boils, bring them up through her mouth, or choke herself to death. Death or cure.

"Sister, what are you doing?" The sharp rebuke was followed by Sister Filippa grabbing her hands and pulling them away from her throat. Andrea felt light-headed. She shook her head, opened her eyes.

Sister Filippa, her pretty face wrinkled with age and worry, was kneeling beside her. "Stop choking yourself," Filippa ordered.

"I wasn't choking...." Andrea's mouth was moving but no words came out. With horror, Andrea realized that she had damaged her voice box.

"Drink this." Filippa held out an egg whose shell had been slightly cut away on the upright end.

"I can't," Andrea mouthed. She might choke.

"Lady Clare told me to boil an egg, bring it to you, and wait until your voice returned. Here." Filippa handed the egg to Andrea.

Incredulous, Andrea began to suck out the egg's warmed, thickened contents. The mass slid easily down her throat.

"Can you speak?" Filippa asked.

"No," Andrea said, her voice startling her. "Yes," she whispered, awed.

Filippa stood. "Then let us go to Sister Clare."

Clare? What reproach awaited her? Reluctantly, Andrea followed Filippa into the dormitory.

Clare was lying on her side, her back to the wall. She beckoned Andrea closer. "What was the matter, Sister?" she asked quietly, the light from the oil lamps throwing her aged face into bold relief. Clare took Andrea's pale, heavily veined hand in her own. "Sister, confess your thoughts to the Lord, for He has told me what you have done. The Lord Jesus will cure this illness, but you must change your life for the better. You are soon to suffer another illness, and you will not rise from that one."

The totally unexpected words knifed Andrea. Like a dry twig, her sanity snapped. She jerked out of Clare's grasp and bolted for the door. Swiftly she kissed the oratory floor before her Eucharistic Lord, then felt her way down the dark stairs to the burial plot. When her bare feet touched the packed earth at the foot of the stairs, Andrea fell to her knees, her hands pressed against the hard, cold soil. Here were buried Illuminata. Egidia. Marsebilia. Giovanna. And here she, too, would be soon.

Something soft brushed Andrea's thigh. Sister Gatta. In the blackness, Sister Gatta arched her head under Andrea's palm as Andrea settled onto her heels and drew the cat into her lap.

As she stroked the calm, purring animal, Andrea's mind cleared. Who would expect such crazy behavior from someone her age? Clare must be praying for her right now. She could almost feel the prayers reaching downward like tender arms.

Christ would cure her. But then she would die of another illness. Terror rose in Andrea's soul. When would the illness strike? How long would it last? How painful would it be?

Gatta stiffened, shrieked. Another spasm. Andrea embraced the rigid animal and felt the tremor pass, the body relax. Gatta began to purr.

The purring wove through Andrea's mind. "Learrrrn. Learrrrn," it crooned.

"Learn what?" Andrea whispered, rubbing Gatta's shoulders. "Here you are, purring as if nothing happened."

Her words caught her. Whenever convulsions struck Gatta, she rode them out and forgot them. She did not worry about them striking again. Gatta lived in the present. She accepted everything as it came. She was at peace.

What mattered was not why oneIÉuffered but that one accepted it, learned from it, and lived at peace in the now. God had promised to give His people strength to bear whatever came.

Andrea was tired. And she needed to apologize to Clare. Gathering Gatta in her arms, Andrea felt her way upstairs. Clare was lying on the floor, her face downward in prayer or sleep. Andrea would apologize tomorrow.

Quietly Andrea returned to the well-lit infirmary. Cuddling Gatta under her blanket, Andrea lay on her mattress and closed her eyes. *Live...this...moment*, she thought, as she drifted off to sleep.

PART THIRTEEN

The Increase and
Final Perseverance

~ 55 ~

Sister Francesca de Capitaneo da Col de Mezzo

Infirmary, San Damiano (EARLY AUGUST, 1253) ~ On her straw mattress in the infirmary of San Damiano, Sister Francesca was in anguish from the painful throbbing in her head.

From the time Francesca, then Lady Massariola, had entered San Damiano twenty-one years ago, until five years ago when these headaches began, Francesca had been ill only two days. Of average height yet incredibly strong, Francesca had been as robust as the lords in her family—her father, Lord Capitaneo of the castle of Col de Mezzo, her brother Lord Pietro, her uncles Ugolino, Guido, and Bonifazio, Lord Bishop of Todi. None of them, however, ever had headaches like this. The headache might last for hours or days before disappearing. Then it would return. Right now she was biting her lower lip to keep from crying out and waking her ill, sleeping sisters.

The headaches had begun just after the vicious wars around Turin had caused the Poor Enclosed Sisters there to leave their monastery and be dispersed among other Damianites. Even now wars raged. Yes, Frederick II had died three years ago, clad as a penitent in a white Cistercian habit and receiving absolution and the last sacraments from Archbishop Berard of Palermo—in answer to the many prayers offered for the emperor's final repentance. Yes, two years ago Pope Innocent IV had returned to the papal lands, settling in Perugia instead of in unsafe Rome. But Frederick's excommunicated son and heir King Conrad still battled the Pope for power. Assisi could yet be drawn into the fray. Every day the sisters prayed for peace. Francesca offered every headache for that intention.

The pain in Francesca's head swelled. How could she endure it? Maybe if Clare prayed for her.... Clare's prayers had cured Amata of fever, coughing, pain, and dropsy so severe that her little belly had been horribly swollen. They had cured Balvina of a continuous fever and hideous abscess on her breast and of a throbbing pain in her thigh. They had restored Sister Benvenuta's voice when she had been unable to speak above a whisper for more than two years. Clare's prayers had cured Cecilia of a persistent cough, Cristi of deafness in one ear, Venuta of a fistula so large you could put five fingers into the pus-filled abscess. They had cured Andrea of the swellings in her throat.

It was the middle of the night! Yet Clare had told the sisters that they could come to her at any time. Francesca pulled her mantle about her, her head pounding worse for having moved. In agony, she made her way out of the infirmary, through the corridor to the oratory, and up the stairs to the dormitory.

On her raised bed in the corner, Clare lay perfectly still, her eyes closed. Francesca silently knelt at the bedside to wait until Clare awakened. If she awakened. Clare was dying. She had been unable to eat anything for days. Clare's strength was ebbing away.

Francesca felt a gentle, weak touch on her head. Looking up, she saw Clare's blue eyes gazing at her from a hollow, gaunt face, felt Clare's bony hand resting lightly on her scalp.

"What is wrong, Sister?" Clare whispered.

"This headache. Every day I would offer God five hidden deeds of love if I were rid of it."

"Such a beautiful gift!" With trembling hand, Clare made the sign of the cross over Francesca. Her lips moved slightly as her head bowed in prayer. Francesca felt as peaceful as she had during the festival of Calendemaggio. Then she had seen a great brilliance about Clare's head while an incredibly beautiful young boy, sitting on Clare's lap, had leaned against her breast. Surely He was the Christ Child. Francesca had told no one of the vision, nor had she spoken of a second vision she experienced around the Feast of Saint Martin three years ago. Then Friar Cappellano had come to the dormitory to give the dying Clare the Holy Eucharist. Francesca again saw the brilliance about Clare's head as she received the Lord's Body, which seemed to be that same beautiful Christ Child. After meditating, Clare had whispered to her sisters, "God has given me such a gift today that heaven and earth could not equal it." Then Clare's life had been restored.

Francesca shook her head. It no longer hurt. Her headaches never disappeared instantly like this. She was cured.

"Grazie, my mother."

Clare patted Francesca's hand.

"What will we do if you die?" Francesca asked softly.

Smiling weakly, Clare pointed to a basket on the floor near the head of her bed, "There you will find my final testament. It will tell you what you must do when I am gone. You may read it."

With eyes smarting with unbidden tears, Francesca plucked the several parchment pages.

"In the name of the Lord! Amen." So began the document.

The document was beautifully written in Clare's fine hand. She thanked God for their vocation and Francis for his example and support. She spoke of the beginnings of her community and exhorted the sisters always to embrace holy poverty, never turning aside from their promises. She spoke of the simplicity of their dwellings and the humility of their lives, while reminding the sisters that they must love all with the love of Christ.

Francesca's tears flowed as she read Clare's exhortation to the abbess. The abbess must be more virtuous than the others and must lead more by love than by authority. She must be a discerning, gentle mother to her daughters, caring for each and being available to all at any time.

"Let us be very careful, therefore, that, if we have set out on the path of the Lord, we do not at any time turn away from it through our own fault or negligence or ignorance, nor that we offend so great a Lord and His Virgin Mother, and our blessed Father Francis, the Church Triumphant and even the Church Militant. For it is written: 'Those who turn away from your commands are cursed.'

"For this reason I bend my knee to the Father of our Lord Jesus Christ that, through the supporting merits of the glorious and holy Virgin Mary, His Mother, and of our most blessed Father Francis and all the saints, the Lord Himself, who has given us a good beginning, will also give the increase and final perseverance. Amen.

"So that it may be better observed, I leave you this writing, my very dear and beloved sisters, those present and those to come, as a sign of the blessing of the Lord and of our most blessed Father Francis and of my blessing, your mother and servant."

Francesca was trembling as she replaced the parchment in the basket. "Oh, mother, how will we go on without you?"

Clare opened her arms and Francesca embraced her tightly. "When I die, you will continue to follow in the footprints of our Lord Jesus Christ, for He will never die."

⇝ 56 ⇜

Sister Aneska

Kitchen, Damianite Convent, Prague, Bohemia (August 1253) ⇝
In the kitchen of the Damianite monastery in Prague, Sister Aneska
plunged a wretched, tattered tunic into a deep basin of hot water
and strong soap. On her thin hands, red sores, created by the bleach
and soap, stung as she dunked the filthy, foul-smelling garment.
Above her dark, almond-shaped eyes, Aneska's beautifully arched
eyebrows lifted as she scanned the leper's garb. She would wash it
carefully, dry it in the sun, and mend it before sending it back to its
owner—along with a loaf of bread baked especially for the poor in
the massive outdoor oven outside the refectory.

When the portress called Aneska to the speaking grill, the garment was drying. Friars had brought a letter from Lady Clare and
the news that Clare was dying without receiving approval from the
Pope for her Form of Life.

With promises to pray for Clare and her sisters, Aneska took the
letter and made her way to her small, private oratory. Closing the
door, she fell to her knees before the wall crucifix, crying aloud,
"She is dying, my God!"

Aneska had experienced death before. Her father. Her mother.
Two nephews, one brutally murdered. Her dear cousin Saint Elizabeth of Hungary. Their deaths were not as shattering to her as this
one. Aneska shared her lineage with her relatives, but she shared
her soul with Clare. Clare had encouraged Aneska in her vocation
and in her struggle to maintain poverty for the Prague monastery.
She had supported Aneska's successful bid to separate the Prague
monastery from the hospice's support. She had scolded Aneska for
fasting too severely and had advised her to remember that her body
was made of flesh. Clare had agreed with Aneska that certain parts
of the Rule might be mitigated due to Bohemia's harsh climate, and
the Pope had consented.

"Oh, my God! What will I do without her?" Though Aneska had never met Clare, she knew Clare's spirit through the letters they exchanged. The women prayed daily for each other. They would pray for each other until each was in heaven.

Taking a deep, quavering breath, Aneska found a square of linen tucked into the tight sleeve of her undertunic and dabbed her eyes. With shaky hands and a rush of love in her heart, she broke the wax seal on the parchment.

"To that illustrious queen, Agnes, spouse of the Lamb, the eternal King, the half of my soul, and, among all others, my most dear mother and favorite daughter as well, I, Clare, unworthy servant and useless handmaid of the handmaids living in the monastery of San Damiano in Assisi, send greetings along with the wish that Agnes, together with the rest of the most holy virgins before the throne of God, may sing a new song and follow the Lamb wheresoever He goes."

Aneska continued to read. Clare apologized for not writing more often because of "the lack of messengers and the obvious dangers along the roads." Wars had made the roads dangerous—the emperor's and those between Aneksa's brother Wenceslaus and his son Ottokar. Largely through Aneska's prayers and efforts, father and son had agreed to peace. They had made their pact within this monastery, in the monastery's Church of Saint Francis that Aneska had built.

Clare's love for Aneska was evident throughout the letter. Clare called Agnes to surrender to Christ, writing of Him as one would a lover. She exhorted Agnes to look at Christ as if to a mirror, to see reflected there the holy virtues of poverty, humility, and love, and to adorn herself in those virtues.

Aneska devoured the words. The beautiful, intense prose glowed with ardor as Clare, like the bride in the biblical Song of Songs, sang to her Lord, "Draw me after You, let us run in the fragrance of Your anointing oils, O heavenly Spouse."

Aneska's heart was in a turmoil of elation and sorrow. "I have inscribed your happy memory beyond erasure on the tablets of my heart, holding you dearer than all others."

Oh, God! Clare was telling her good-bye.

"What more to say? Let the tongue of the flesh be silent when it comes to speaking of my love for you, and let the tongue of the spirit speak instead."

Oh, my God, let her feel my love for her. Let her know that I am lifting her to Your throne. Oh, my God, if I write to her, will she receive my letter?

SHE WILL BE WITH ME WHEN YOUR LETTER ARRIVES.

My Lord, let her know how much I love her.

THIS SHE ALREADY KNOWS, ANESKA.

Will You be with her, Lord, when she dies? Will You comfort and encourage her? Do not let her die alone! Preserve her from the demon in her final hours.

I WILL BE WITH HER. SHE WILL RECEIVE A SPECIAL GRACE.

Aneska's pounding heart slowed. God would be with Clare. She would know that she was loved. With an aching heart, Aneska found her place in the letter and read it to the end.

"Good-bye, then, dearest daughter, and farewell to your daughters there until we meet at the throne of glory of our great God. And do pray for us. I commend to your charity as warmly as I can, our most dear Brother Amato, beloved of God and of men, and Brother Bonagura, the bearers of this letter to you. Amen."

Aneska smiled thinly. So like Clare, asking the sisters to pray for the brothers who brought the letter. Clare would die as she had lived, concerned for others and loving her God.

Sister Venuta (Benvenuta) de Lady Diambre

Dormitory, San Damiano (Friday Evening, August 8, 1253) ⌐
Leaning against the back wall of the dormitory of San Damiano,
Sister Benvenuta de Lady Diambre struggled against wakefulness.
She had been mulling over the events of yesterday—the aristocratic,
stooped Pope Innocent IV had heard Clare's confession and the
minister provincial had administered the Eucharist to her. They had
been part of a steady stream of cardinals, priests, and friars who had
visited the dying woman. After the Pope's departure, Clare had spoken joyously to her sisters. "My daughters, praise God because
heaven and earth are not enough for such a benefit I have received
from God. Today I have received Him in the Blessed Sacrament and
I have also seen His vicar."

Ow! Benvenuta, whom everyone called Venuta, pushed her aching shoulders against the wall. How long had she been dozing? Here
around Clare's bed were the other Poor Sisters, some lying in tired
heaps, others sitting bleary eyed and half awake, a few sobbing. Many
sisters were too ill with grief to taste food. No one seemed able to do
any decent work. Only prayer went on as usual, broken by sobs and
by voices that cracked with sorrow.

Clare had asked for three things.

First that Sister Benedetta, Clare's childhood friend Lady Ginevra, would return to San Damiano to become abbess. Even before
Venuta had entered San Damiano thirty years ago, Benedetta had
been traveling back and forth from San Damiano to found other
monasteries.

Then Clare had requested that her blood sister Agnes be summoned from Florence so that she could be with Clare when she died.

Finally, Clare had prayed that, before she died, she would receive in her hands her Form of Life approved by the Pope.

Benedetta had arrived and Clare made her abbess. Agnes, accompanied by a few of her extern sisters, had returned to share precious moments with Clare and Beatrice. Yesterday, Lord Pope had left, promising again to look at the Form of Life.

Now that Venuta was fully awake, she was reminded of her age by sharp aches and pains that shot through her back, shoulders, and thighs. She pushed her once stately body erect and stretched to ease the cramps away.

But nothing could eliminate Venuta's crushing grief. She'd felt varying degrees of mournful exhaustion whenever one of the sisters died—Ortolana, Andrea, Egidia, Giovanna, Illuminata, Felicita, others. She had wept when her parents had died—Papa a few years after she'd entered San Damiano and Mama not very long ago. She'd felt overwhelming anguish when, a few years after Papa's death, her brother Pietro's home had been burnt with him in it because he would not sell his inheritance of Papa's estate to Lord Rainuccio di Paolo. Rainuccio had been heavily fined by the commune. The family's large house had never been rebuilt. The property had reverted to the commune, and a sign listing Rainuccio's name and crime had been erected on the property, to remain forever.

Worse than any of these tragedies was Clare's impending death, for Clare's faith and compassion had carried Venuta through her other losses. Who would carry Venuta through this?

"Oh, most Holy Trinity, may You be blessed," Clare was whispering. Her words trailed off even as her lips continued to move. How did she have strength to speak, having eaten nothing for the past two weeks?

Filippa was swabbing Clare's forehead with a damp cloth. "You have a good memory," Filippa said, looking at Pacifica who was sitting on the floor, resting her head on Clare's raised pallet. "Remember well what the Lady says."

"You will only remember these things I now say as long as He who made me say them permits you," Clare noted softly. "Remember, instead, the passion of our Lord. This is Friday on which we are bound to contemplate such mysteries. My Lord, was there any suffering like Yours?" Clare's voice faded. Her blue eyes closed. Her breathing grew shallow.

"Sister!" Agnes, seated next to Pacifica, threw herself over Clare's chest, weeping. Beatrice lightly kissed her hollow cheek.

"Oh, my sister, do not abandon us!" Agnes sobbed. "How can I go on without you?"

Clare's eyes opened. "My dearest sister, it is God's will that I go. Now stop weeping, because you too will come to the Lord shortly after me, and the Lord will comfort you greatly before I leave you."

Venuta forced back a fresh volley of tears. Agnes, too, would shortly die?

Clare's eyes closed. Her whispered, unintelligible words faded.

Benedetta, who was kneeling directly across from Pacifica, lifted Clare's hand and tapped it lightly. No response. Benedetta shook the hand more vigorously. Nothing.

"Sister Clare!"

Benedetta looked from one sister to the next.

"She is insensible."

Venuta shuddered. Insensibility often came shortly before death.

"Let us pray, sisters, and keep vigil," Benedetta said, placing Clare's hand on her hollow chest.

The evening wore on. Clare continued immovable. Someone rang the bell for Compline. Amata remained with Clare while the others filed downstairs to pray.

When the sisters returned, they found Amata wide-eyed. "You had been gone but a few moments," Amata said excitedly, "when she opened her eyes and looked straight past me up there," Amata pointed to the upper corner of the dormitory. "She smiled and asked, 'Do you see the King of Glory?' I saw nothing. She asked me a few more times, 'Do you see the King of Glory?' Then she closed her eyes and became insensible again."

"Go calmly in peace for you will have a good escort..." Clare was speaking, faintly but clearly: "...because He who created you has already provided that you will be made holy. He has infused the Holy Spirit in you and then has always guarded you as a mother does her child who loves her."

Clare's eyes were closed, her dry, cracked lips moving ever so imperceptibly. "O Lord, may You who have created me be blessed."

"Holy Mother," Anastasia asked, taking Clare's thin right hand, "to whom are you speaking?"

"I am speaking to my soul."

Clare's voice faded to silence and she lay as if dead. Then a little breath, a little wheeze, and life continued.

How good and holy Clare was! Venuta dropped to her knees in grateful thanksgiving. God had been so good to bring Venuta here, where Clare had taught her three lessons that were all one ever needed to learn. To love God. To recognize and confess one's own sinfulness. To follow Christ wherever He led.

Venuta's eyes brimmed with love and gratitude.

Light bursting through the door startled Venuta. Who had lowered the staircase for these women, each dressed in white and crowned with gold and jewels? Silently the regal, virginal women slipped in among the sisters, but no one but Venuta seemed aware of them.

The tallest woman who had entered first held back, watching the others. That woman's gown was more radiant, her face more beautiful than any Venuta had ever seen. She wore a larger, more brilliant crown than the others, above which shimmered a golden thurible, such as a priest might use in a great cathedral to burn incense.

The virginal queen now approached Clare, the other women moving aside for her. How tenderly, with the help of the other women, did she drape a narrow length of cloth around Clare's shoulders and across her body! Why, the cloth was a pallium, so fine that Venuta could see Clare through it. How wondrous! As the Pope would embrace an archbishop whom he had just clothed with the pallium as a sign of unity with the Church and the Holy See, so the queen bent over Clare's breast as if to embrace her. The two women seemed to merge, and then queen, virgins, pallium, and light were gone.

Venuta was totally awake. She had been totally awake during the entire vision. The praises in honor of the holy virtues, written by Saint Francis, flooded Venuta's mind. *Hail to Queen Wisdom, to her sisters Simplicity, Poverty, Humility, Charity, Obedience, all the Holy Virtues. Hail to Our Lady, Mary, holy Mother of God.*

The virtues, and the Mother of Him through whom all virtues come, had clothed Clare as one solidly in union with Christ and His Church. How could Venuta speak of such a vision!

~ 58 ~

Pope Innocent IV

Convento at the Basilica of Saint Francis, Assisi (EARLY MORNING, SATURDAY, AUGUST 9, 1253) ~ Pope Innocent IV sat bolt upright in the plush, curtain-surrounded bed in his private quarters at the convento at the Basilica of Saint Francis in Assisi. In a faint glow seeping through open windows, he saw his white overshirt and slipped into it.

An internal pressure had awakened him. APPROVE THE FORM OF LIFE. Couldn't it wait until dawn?

The pressure was insistent. APPROVE IT.

Innocent didn't operate that way, listening to inner promptings. Yes, Cardinal Raynaldo had approved the Form of Life last year. But Innocent wasn't comfortable with it. A year ago or longer, while he was in Perugia, a friar had brought him the document. He hadn't had the time to ponder it.

Pope Gregory IX had died in 1241. His successor, old, ill Cardinal Geoffrey Castiglione, Bishop of Sabina, who had taken the name Celestine IV, had died seventeen days after being elected. Intrigues of Frederick II and dissension among the cardinals had delayed the next papal election until 1243 when Innocent, the former Sinibaldo Fieshci, son of Count Hugh of Lavagna, had been chosen. Generous and magnanimous, always wishing to believe the best of everyone, Innocent nevertheless experienced Frederick's treacheries. Eventually Innocent had excommunicated the emperor, had warred against him, and had fled from him to Lyons. Frederick's death in 1250 had brought no respite. The ruler's twenty-five-year-old excommunicated son, King Conrad, had subdued every city in the lower peninsula except Naples, which was currently under siege. Innocent's attempt to offer this kingdom of Apulia, Sicily, and Calabria to Richard, the Earl of Cornwall and brother of England's King Henry III, had been refused. So he was now attempting to make the same offer to Charles of Anjou, the youngest brother of the saintly French King Louis IX.

Besides these matters, Innocent was enmeshed in additional worldly concerns—battling heresy, converting the Tartars, raising money, forging alliances, providing for relatives, and sending ambassadors to various potentates—some of whom were Frederick II's other crafty, power-hungry sons. In every matter, Innocent based his decisions on logic and strategy—backed up, of course, by prayer. Yet two days ago he had visited Clare—whose decisions were based on prayerful, intuitive following of the Spirit's promptings. He couldn't rule on intuitions and inner proddings, could he? Or should he?

Where was that candlestick? Ow! He'd knocked it over. The golden candlestand bumped along the floor.

"My lord, is something wrong?"

"What is it, Holy Father?"

The racket had awakened two aides who slept, keeping guard, on the floor near his bed.

"I need a light," Innocent said, a bit too gruffly.

"Yes, Holy Father."

In the blackness, the men scuffled. The door opened, and light from the lamp-lit corridor flooded in. An aide scooted into the hall with the candlestick and quickly returned with a lit taper.

"Put the candle on my desk," Innocent directed, easing into the desk chair.

Candlelight flooded the desk as Innocent planted his bare feet on the floor. "Grazie. Go back to sleep. I have work to complete."

The men lay down on their straw mats. Even before Innocent found the Form of Life among the parchments piled into baskets near his desk, the two men were snoring softly.

Innocent unrolled the sheets of parchment and began to read the fine, exact handwriting.

"The Form of Life of the Order of the Poor Sisters that Blessed Francis established is this: to observe the Holy Gospel of our Lord Jesus Christ, by living in obedience, without anything of one's own, and in chastity."

He read on. Clare promised, for herself and all her sisters forever, "obedience and reverence to the Lord Pope Innocent and his canonically elected successors, and to the Roman Church."

Absentmindedly, Innocent stroked his thick white beard, cleft in the center. His gaze moved down the first parchment. All the sisters were to consent to admitting newcomers, who, if they agreed with the Form of Life, were to sell their goods if possible, and distribute the money to the poor, then enter the monastery, tonsured and with but three tunics and a mantle, there to remain for a year's formation—after which they would "be received into obedience, promising to observe perpetually our life and form of poverty."

Poverty. That was the problem. Innocent ran his hand across his bald scalp and down to the halo of thick white hair that ringed his head. Poverty of goods, possessions, spirit. In early May, just a few weeks after moving to Assisi to prepare for the dedication of the Upper Basilica of Saint Francis, Innocent had visited Clare. She had been weak, but eating. Two days ago, he'd visited her again, blessing her and her sisters but noting that she'd been unable to eat for two weeks. The end must be near.

Completely at peace, Clare had kissed Innocent's hand when he offered it and then asked to kiss his foot as well. He had removed his right riding boot and she had kissed, with lips that felt like parchment, first the upper part of his foot and then his sole. With radiant but tired blue eyes, she had gazed at him in gratitude. Embarrassed, Innocent had realized that she was honoring Christ in his person.

That was poverty. Poverty of spirit that died to one's own will by living in God's will. Every moment was either a doing of one's own will or a dying to it, Innocent thought.

Clare had asked Innocent to absolve her of her sins. Startled by her humility, he had blurted out, "Would that I had as much need of forgiveness as you!" Then, dismissing the sisters clustered like chicks around her bed, he had heard Clare's confession. Such sorrow for such slight faults! How deeply Clare loved God and how fully she sensed His holiness! With appointments to keep, Innocent had asked the minister provincial, who had accompanied him, to give Clare the Eucharist.

Before leaving, Clare had asked Innocent, as she had asked him in May, to approve her Form of Life and the privilege of poverty. What a request! No Pope had ever approved a Form of Life written by a woman! Innocent's approval would mean the Church's—Christ's—approval. He paged through the parchments, looking for troubling passages.

No heavy debt may be incurred except with the
common consent of the sisters and by reason of
manifest necessity, and let this be done through a
procurator. Let the Abbess and her sisters, however,
be careful that nothing is deposited in the monastery
for safekeeping...

...by not receiving or having possession or
ownership either of themselves or through an intermediary, or even anything that might reasonably be
called property, except as much land as necessity
requires for the integrity and proper seclusion of the
monastery...

Let the sisters not appropriate anything, neither a
house nor a place nor anything at all; instead, as
pilgrims and strangers in this world who serve the
Lord in poverty and humility, let them confidently
send for alms...

Innocent had dealt with popes beginning with Honorius III, who
had summoned him to Rome to be in his service. Then, in 1227,
Pope Gregory IX had made the then-Sinibaldo cardinal-priest of
Saint Lawrence in Lucina. Innocent knew Gregory's concerns about
poverty in the orders of Francis and Clare. While Saint Francis's order was mitigating some of its founder's dictates, Clare was holding
to her original ideals. How could Innocent approve her Form of
Life? Poverty for enclosed women was illogical. Yet one of the sisters
had hinted that Clare had begged God not to let her die until after
she had received such approval.

I can't keep someone from dying, Innocent mentally reminded God.
BUT I CAN. APPROVE THE FORM OF LIFE, INNOCENT.
Innocent fingered the parchment. *I disagree with it!*
"YOU NEED NOT AGREE. YOU NEED ONLY OBEY."
This is not logical!
"DOESN'T MY LOGIC SUPERSEDE YOURS?"
The question startled him. Quickly he made the sign of the cross.
Swiftly an image came to mind. Jesus, smiling indulgently at him.
All right. He would read it again, try to agree with it. Here. Clare
was discussing the election of an abbess.

Let her strive to preside as well over the others more by her virtues and holy behavior than by her office, so that, moved by her example, the sisters may obey her more out of love than out of fear….

Let her console those who are afflicted. Let her also be the last refuge for those who are troubled….

He kept reading. About weekly chapter meeting, where the sisters would confess their faults and consult together on the running of the monastery. Recitation of the Divine Office, continual fast except for Christmas and Sundays. Confession twelve times yearly. Silence from the hour of Compline until Terce. Care of the grill and parlor. Work inside the monastery. Serving sisters. Care of the sick. Who may enter the monastery. Correction of and penances for sisters who sin. Custody of the monastery door. Regulations regarding the visitator, chaplain, cardinal protector, and those who must do work inside the monastery. Then, Clare's final words, just above Raynaldo's approval: "May we always observe the poverty and humility of our Lord Jesus Christ and of His most holy Mother and the holy Gospel we have firmly promised. Amen."

If I approve this and they starve…

THEY SHALL NOT STARVE.

They will have nothing.

"EXCEPT ME."

Innocent sank back in his chair.

I don't like doing things this way.

WHOSE WILL SHALL BE DONE, INNOCENT? MINE? OR YOURS?

His. It had to be His will.

From the bell tower in the basilica came a sharp tolling. Time for the Office of Lauds already? Indeed, dawn was pinking the sky. Quickly, Innocent summoned his aides, dressed, and hurried to the choir to pray the first Office of the day with the friars. When he returned, he sent for his secretary, asking him to bring a large, fresh parchment.

"Write small," Innocent told the clerk, a young priest himself. "I am going to issue a bull that will precede all of this." Innocent flipped through Clare's parchments so the clerk could estimate the length of the text. "You must put the bull and all this text on a single parchment."

Nodding, the clerk sat at Innocent's desk and took up a reed pen. Incredulous at what he was doing, Innocent began to dictate. "Innocent, Bishop, Servant of the servants of God, to his beloved daughters in Christ, Clare, Abbess, and the other sisters of the monastery of San Damiano in Assisi: health and apostolic blessing." He continued to dictate at a measured pace. "We confirm by our Apostolic authority the Form of Life that Blessed Francis gave you and which you have freely accepted." He dictated a few more lines, then handed the young man the Form of Life, which was prefaced and concluded with Raynaldo's approval.

IT MUST ALL BE COPIED TODAY.

Inside, Innocent moaned. "It must be done today."

"Holy Father, it would take at least two days to write all this well."

"Today. All of it."

"But I cannot write neatly if I write that quickly."

"It is more important that it be finished than that it be neat."

"Yes, Holy Father."

"Take this to your quarters and begin at once. As soon as you complete it, beckon me, even if it's the middle of the night."

And it was almost the middle of the night when an aide awakened Innocent and beckoned him to the scribe's room. The clerk was sitting, hunched and bleary-eyed, at his desk. Innocent glanced over the parchment, written straight across in neat rows that grew more smudged with ink blots toward the bottom.

"It is messy, Holy Father. I was growing so tired."

Innocent patted the young man's back. "It is fine. Would you write just a bit more at the very bottom, please?" He began to dictate. The young man stretched his fingers and began to write.

"Therefore, no one is permitted to destroy this document of our confirmation or oppose it recklessly. If anyone shall presume to attempt this, let him know he will incur the wrath of Almighty God and His holy Apostles Peter and Paul. Given at Assisi, the ninth day of August, in the eleventh year of our Pontificate." He smiled. "That is all," Innocent said. "You have done well. Go and have something to eat. Then you may go to bed."

With a grateful bow, the clerk left. In the stillness, Innocent began to reflect on what he had done. Had he really issued the bull? How would people respond to his approving a Form of Life written by a woman? And such a Form of Life, with its insistence on highest poverty! He had not yet affixed his papal seal. Without it, the documents were invalid. But even with his seal, some would question his decision.

Your decision, Innocent mentally told his God.

He could counter questions before they arose. Taking the reed pen, Innocent began to write, in his small, cramped style, in the left-hand corner of the upper margin. "So be it! S." The S was the initial of his name, Sinibaldo. And then, as an afterthought, he added below it, "For reasons known to me and the protector of the monastery, so be it!"

Taking a deep breath, Innocent looked at what he had written. He could burn this Form of Life. Or he could affix the papal seal to it and send the document to San Damiano.

Can't I have a day to think about it?

He sensed Jesus smiling at him. YOU CAN HAVE TONIGHT.

Of course. It was already dark. No one was going anywhere tonight. He could still change his mind. Tomorrow.

~ 59 ~

Sister Beatrice di Favarone di Offreduccio

Dormitory, San Damiano (Sunday, August 10, 1253) ~ Sister Beatrice di Favarone sat on the floor next to Clare's pallet, her head pillowed on her wide hands, Clare's shallow breathing purring in Beatrice's ear. Beatrice was half asleep, her stocky body tired with waiting and grief. She had seen Papa die, gored by that boar. Mama die, felled by a stroke that left her unable to speak or move. Friends, relatives, monastery benefactors—so many dead. She knew more people, she thought, who had died than who were still alive. Now Clare.

Clare had eaten nothing for sixteen days. She had been unconscious for nearly twenty-four hours until emerging from it yesterday. Today she seemed stronger, but, often just before the end, the body rallied in a frantic, futile effort to live. Death had to be near.

And Clare had prophesied that their blood sister Agnes would die soon, too. Then Beatrice would die, the last of her immediate family, and the Favarone line of the Offreduccio clan would be gone.

"Pace e bene."

"Pace e bene."

The male voices startled her. When had the friars arrived? Could Beatrice be going deaf? Or had she been so sound asleep that she hadn't heard the ringing of the bell to announce the friars' arrival?

Beatrice shook the dullness out of her head and smiled at the four men, seated on Clare's left across from Beatrice. How time had flown!

Here was pale Brother Angelo of Rieti, one of Saint Francis's constant escorts during the last years of his life. Lithe Angelo's body had grown so frail that it seemed poised to drift into the hereafter.

Dear, meek Brother Leo, still the pure, unpretentious priest. Strong and sturdy as he had accompanied Francis even to his death, Leo was now nearly bald, his big broad head hanging forward like that of an exhausted ox.

Small, lively, round-faced Brother Juniper, whom Francis praised for his simple humility, his blue eyes still bright but paler, the laugh lines under his eyes deepened with age.

Young, compassionate Reginald, who had never known Saint Francis, his thick reddish beard streaked vertically and horizontally with auburn in the shape of a faint cross, his dark eyes sparkling like a fox's.

How old they all had grown! How long had it been since Clare had left home to join Francis? She counted backwards. Forty-three years. Longer than many people live. So many of those who were amazed by Clare's bold move were clustered about her now. She and her sister Agnes, then called Catherine. Balvina and Amata di Martino. Benedetta, named Ginevra forty-three years ago. Benvenuta of Perugia. Filippa. Pacifica. Crisitana de Bernardo da Suppo. How could any one of them—how could Clare—have foreseen what would be? One hundred and forty-seven monasteries of the Poor Enclosed Sisters throughout the world. How many monasteries were to come? How long would the Poor Enclosed Sisters exist? Perhaps, Beatrice shivered with delight, until the end of time? All because of Clare's "yes" to God.

"Yes" to the living that brought them together and sustained them daily. "Yes" to the dying that would separate them for a time. "Yes" to eternity, where they would be together to praise the God of "yes."

Reginald's words broke into Beatrice's musing. "Dear Lady Clare, how difficult this prolonged torture must be for you! You must try to be patient during this serious illness, because God will grant you reward because of it."

Clare laughed weakly. "My dearest brother, ever since the Lord's servant Francis told me of the grace of my Lord Jesus Christ, and I came to understand its power, I have never found any pain, illness, or penance that could afflict me."

"How right you are!" Juniper agreed. "You have learned what I did when I determined not to speak."

Beatrice smiled to herself. *Here comes that story,* she thought. Poor, good-natured Brother Juniper! He'd grown so absentminded that he repeated himself over and over. The sisters humored him, listening politely as if they were hearing the story for the first time. Juniper went on to tell how he had determined to keep silent, years ago, for his tongue was his greatest occasion of sin. But how to do it?

"I determined that the first day I would keep silent for love of the heavenly Father. And the second day for the love of Jesus."

Juniper looked from one sister to the other as he spoke. "The next day for love of the Holy Spirit. And then for the love of the Virgin Mother. And then for love of holy Saint Francis, and so on. There are a great many saints," Juniper noted, nodding wisely, "so I found no difficulty in keeping silent for a different one each day. But one day someone said something—I can't recall now what it was—but, oh, did it anger me! I tried and tried to be quiet," Juniper explained, squeezing shut his eyes and crinkling his nose, "but it was so difficult. I was putting so much effort into saying nothing that I thought my tongue would jump out of my mouth! Then something popped in my chest and I felt this big rush of blood in my mouth. I was so angry that I spat it out and marched right into the church before the crucifix."

Juniper put his hands on his hips. "I looked up at our crucified Lord and I said, 'See, my Lord, what I am bearing for love of You.' And then," Juniper's voice grew soft with wonder, "the Crucified Christ raised His arm from the wood of the cross—although His hand was nailed there, He raised His arm from the nail—and He laid His hand on the wound in His side and He said, very quietly, 'And I, what am I bearing for you?'"

Juniper hip-hopped from one foot to the other. "My ladies, I was another man after that. Indeed, not making light of your sufferings, Lady Clare, but all we bear in no way compares with the sufferings of our Lord."

"Ah, you are so right," Clare said with a weak smile. "Your stories always warm our spirits. What else can you share today about the Lord?"

"His Passion, my lady. Did you not call us to recite His Passion to you and passages of Scripture?"

"Oh, how I wish to hear those!"

From a deep pocket in his tunic, Leo pulled a small, worn volume. Carefully paging through it, he began to read. "When the hour came, Jesus took his place at the table with the apostles. He said to them, 'I have wanted so much to eat this Passover meal with you before I suffer!'" In his rich, gentle voice, Leo slowly read the entire Passion, ending with the burial and resurrection of the Lord.

As Leo closed the book, Angelo turned to Clare, his large, deep-set eyes glistening with tears. "When good Saint Francis was dying,"

Angelo recalled, his thin voice tremulous, "he asked us to sing 'The Praises of the Lord.' That strengthened him. Would you like us to sing it for you?"

"Oh, yes!"

Leo and Angelo glanced at each other. As if as one, they began to sing:

> **Most High, all-powerful, good Lord, Yours are the praises, the glory, the honor, and all blessing. To You alone, Most High, do they belong, and no one is worthy to mention Your name...**

The friars sang on, their voices a bit shaky, until they came to the end:

> **Blessed are those whom death will find in Your most holy will, for the second death shall do them no harm. Praise and bless my Lord and give Him thanks and serve Him with great humility.**

By the end of the song, Beatrice could see little through her tears. She could only make out Leo kissing the litter on which Clare lay and Agnes embracing Clare and sobbing.

"Praise God, my sisters and brothers," Clare advised, her words surprisingly strong. "God will bless us always through a holy death. Waste no time in grief, but strive instead to observe the highest poverty." Then she beckoned to Sister Benedetta. "Whose feast is today, Sister?"

"San Lorenzo's, the patron of Perugia," Benedetta answered.

"Let us ask San Lorenzo to intercede for us before the throne of Christ, that the Holy Father might approve our Form of Life." Every day, Clare asked that day's saint for the same intention. At every Office of Compline, the sisters entreated the day's saint for just such a favor.

The bell rang at the speaking grill. Sister Anna went to answer.

"We must hold to poverty, sisters." How often during this illness had Clare told them this! "The glorious Virgin of virgins carried our Lord Jesus Christ bodily. Likewise, you too carry Him in your chaste and virginal body by determinedly following her footsteps of humility and poverty."

Clare looked from face to face. "As poor virgins, embrace the poor Christ."

"Pace e bene," a strange friar said, drawing close to Clare's bed, Sister Anna beside him. "Lord Pope Innocent has sent me to you with this."

The friar handed Clare a rolled parchment, sealed with the wax seal of the Pope.

Clare's trembling hands fumbled with the seal. "I cannot break this." The words quaked. "Sister Benedetta..."

With strong, steady hands, Benedetta broke the seal. She unrolled the document and held it so that Clare might read it. Beatrice could see Clare's eyes widening, filling with tears, a radiance spreading across her face. With feeble hands, Clare reached for the parchment and Benedetta released it into her grasp. The paper rolled itself into a scroll. With great effort, Clare brought the roll to her lips and kissed it.

"It is a papal bull," Clare whispered in awe. "Lord Pope has approved our Form of Life and the privilege of highest poverty. Go into the oratory, my sisters and brothers, and fall on your faces before the Lord to thank Him for this wondrous grace. Thank as well all the saints to whom we have prayed. And beseech God's favor upon Lord Pope who has granted our request."

❦ 60 ❧

Sister Agnese di Oportulo de Bernardo

Dormitory, San Damiano (MONDAY, AUGUST 11, 1253) ～ Sister Agnese di Oportulo de Bernardo was growing accustomed to sleeping sitting up. She had awakened next to Clare's bed, her lank body more rested than it had been for days. Today in Assisi would be merrymaking, dancing, and music, processions and prayers—especially in the church of its patron saint, San Rufino. Perhaps San Rufino would cure someone, as he often did on his feast. Clare, perhaps?

Sister Pacifica was kneeling by Clare's head, pressing a moist cloth to Clare's parched lips.

"My sisters, are you here?" Clare asked weakly, the parchment still clutched in her hands.

"Yes, Sister."

"Is Brother Leo here?"

"Yes, my lady," Leo answered. "Brother Angelo is with me." Keeping vigil.

Clare's eyes were closed, her voice faint. "My sisters, my brothers, I wish to confess to you all my sins and faults."

A tremor of holy awe passed over Agnese. The sisters always confessed when they sensed that the end was near.

"Brother Leo, please hear my confession. Sisters, would you help me to bless myself?"

Beatrice took Clare's right hand in hers and guided it through the sign of the cross while Clare prayed. "I wish to confess all the sins of my past life, Brother Leo. I confess any harshness in the correction of my sisters. All misunderstanding. Times I overworked the sisters. Insensitivity to their pain. To their weakness. Any judgmental attitudes."

Agnese was awed by Clare's long list of possible offenses, including those that she may have committed as a child or as a young woman. The list was thorough, yet Agnese could see very few of the failings in Clare.

"So for all of these, and for all those I have forgotten, I am sorry. May God forgive me, and may you, my sisters and brothers, forgive me as well."

Leo pronounced absolution over Clare and gave her a few prayers to say. She prayed them quietly, reverently. He blessed her again, then administered the sacrament of the dying.

"Pray for me, my sisters and brothers," Clare said softly. "Praise the Lord always. Remember His Passion." She paused. "My sisters," Clare's voice was faint, her words spoken slowly, "I bless you during my life and after my death, as I am able, out of all the blessings with which the Father of mercies has and does bless His sons and daughters in heaven and on earth...and a spiritual father and mother have blessed and bless their sons and daughters. Amen."

"Amen," the sisters softly echoed.

"Always be lovers of your souls...and those of all your sisters," Clare whispered. "And may you always be eager to observe...what you have promised the Lord.... May the Lord...always be with you." The words seemed to be struggling to emerge from Clare's parched lips: "and may...you always...be...with Him.... Amen."

"Amen," the sisters prayed.

The blessing seemed to have sapped Clare's strength. She lay still, her breaths shallow and intermittent.

PRAY THE PRAYER OF THE FIVE WOUNDS.

It took only the simplest interior prompting to have Agnese pray one of her favorite prayers. She began to pray softly.

LOUDER.

Agnese raised her voice so that Clare could hear the prayer that Clare loved and that she frequently, perhaps daily, prayed.

"O Lord Jesus Christ, praise and glory to You for the most sacred wound in Your right hand."

The sisters joined in. Angelo. Leo. Many sobbed out the words. "Because of this sacred wound, grant me the pardon of all the sins I have committed by thought, word, deed, and omission. Give me the grace to venerate Your most precious death and these Your sacred wounds worthily, and grant that, by your help, I may mortify my body and be able to thank You for this great gift, You who live and reign forever. Amen."

Together they all recited the Our Father and the Hail Mary, then began the prayer of the wound of the left hand. They proceeded to the two wounds in the feet and to that in Christ's side. While they prayed, Clare softly repeated some of the Passion and, every so often, breathed out "Jesus, Lord Jesus," as if riding out a spasm of pain.

"Five wounds of God," Agnese said.

"Be my medicine," the sisters responded.

"By Your five wounds," Agnese intoned.

"Free me, Christ, from my falls."

"Give me peace, O Christ."

"By Your five wounds."

"Let us pray. All-powerful, eternal God, You who redeemed the human race in the five wounds of Your Son, our Lord Jesus Christ, allow those who venerate those wounds each day to escape a sudden and eternal death because of His precious blood. Through the same Christ the Lord."

"Amen," Clare whispered. "Precious...in the sight of the Lord...is the death...of His holy ones."

Agnese began again to say the Prayer of the Five Wounds. She had reached the wound in the side of Christ when she felt a hand resting lightly on her arm. Benedetta, reaching across Clare's chest.

"Your prayers have given her comfort, Sister." Benedetta glanced at Clare. "She is peacefully gone."

PART FOURTEEN

In the Name of the Lord!

∼ 61 ∼

Iacobello

Bridge outside Narni, Italy (EARLY AUTUMN, 1253) ∼ The light came slowly, as if the moon were rising. The misty light widened. Iacobello saw leaves drifting. Red. Brown. Yellow. Green. He was dreaming. For the past twelve years, the only time that blind Iacobello could see was in his dreams.

A shadow appeared, became a figure approaching him through the falling leaves.

A beggarwoman, her step firm, her carriage straight. He could see her finely patched, rough gray tunic, cinched at her waist with a three-knotted rope that bumped her skirt as she walked soundlessly through the dry leaves. A breeze billowed her thin black veil away from her face, revealing the veil's white lining. The woman's oval face was ageless. She could have been twenty-five years old, like Iacobello. She could have been sixty. The woman's face and tunic were immaculately clean, so unlike a beggar.

Iacobello could see the faint smile on the woman's face, her blue eyes bright with love. Many years ago, Iacobello had seen that look of love on the faces of young noblewomen who came into his master's candlestick shop. The women would ask his master questions about his silver. They would lightly finger the wares, telling of their beloved lords for whom they wanted to purchase precious silver gifts.

This beggarwoman could have no money. Yet, she was noble, regal, serene.

"Who are you?" he called out in his dream.

The woman smiled more widely, the smile spreading up to the high cheekbones that emphasized her deep blue eyes. The woman was so close that Iacobello could smell on her garments the sweet, heavy incense of churches on holy days.

Bending toward Iacobello, the woman gently invited, "Iacobello, why don't you come to me in Assisi and be cured?"

Iacobello awoke with a start. His blind eyes strained into the blackness. Off to his right a river gurgled and splashed. A dry leaf fell against his brow. Near his feet wheezed the measured breathing of the boy Pasquale, who led Iacobello about. A short distance away, two other beggars snorted in their slumber.

Come to Assisi and be cured? Iacobello thought of his arm and his head. Just a few weeks ago, Pasquale, leaving Iacobello at the gates, had entered Terni to beg. That night the boy did not return. The next morning, when the gates opened, Iacobello had felt his way into Terni, seeking the lad.

Suddenly, swiftly, Iacobello had tripped, bashing his forehead against a rock and breaking his arm. A kind knight had paid a doctor to set his arm and bandage his head, and had sent a servant to search for Pasquale, who had become confused by the city and been locked in.

Iacobello's splinted arm now hurt very little. In two weeks, the doctor said, he could remove the splint. The wound on his forehead was nearly healed. Iacobello had removed the bandage a week ago. The beggarwoman could not mean that she would cure his arm and his head. They were already practically cured.

Could she mean his blindness?

Iacobello began to tremble. He had given up hope of seeing again. Now he hungered for sight. He wanted to see the river, the leaves, the moon and stars in the black sky. He wanted to shape candlesticks again, to marry, and to bring home his meager pay to a wife as he had brought it to his mother, dead these two years. His mother, who had persistently prayed that the slowly advancing blindness would be cured.

Why had he become blind? Because he had sinned? He remembered some harsh words, some laziness, a few lies, the stealing of two coins he'd secretly repaid. Would God blind him for those sins?

"Iacobello, why don't you come to me in Assisi and be cured?" What did the woman mean by that?

At dawn, when he heard the other beggars stirring awake, Iacobello told them of the noble beggar.

The beggars began to talk excitedly together.

"Assisi."

"Must be that nun. Lady...Lady..."

"Clare."

"That's it. She died. In August. A saint, they say."

"The Pope wants to canonize her."

"Her tomb is honored by the Lord."

"A madman from France was cured there."

"A boy with a demon cured, too. And a cripple."

"Iacobello, you lucky fool. God wants to heal you at the tomb of the holy nun."

Iacobello's mind was reeling. A holy nun, a saint, had appeared to him. God wanted to heal him. Grappling for Pasquale, Iacobello shook the thin, lithe body awake.

"Pasquale! A holy nun wants to heal me! We must go to Assisi!"

All day they traveled and, as night fell, they were near Spoleto. Outside the city walls, they curled up for the night.

The vision came again.

"Iacobello, why don't you come to me in Assisi and be cured?"

The next day, Iacobello urged Pasquale to hurry so they might arrive in Assisi before dusk. Upon their arrival, they inquired where Lady Clare was buried and were directed to the Church of San Giorgio. Such a crowd pressed around the doors that Iacobello and Pasquale could not get in before the church doors were locked for the night, so they sat at the threshold to spend the night.

Iacobello felt a hard lump under his hip. A stone—it would do for a pillow. His heart was pounding. He must get in! Around him he heard snoring and wheezing, but Iacobello was wide awake. He must get in.

Sounds faded. Haze appeared in his darkness. Iacobello saw huge carved doors that slowly opened into a church, into light where the noble beggar stood, smiling.

"The Lord will bless you, Iacobllo, if you enter."

Iacobello awoke with a start. He heard a key in a lock. A creaking. The doors of the church were opening.

Iacobello jumped to his feet. The crowd began to surge forward, squeezing him backward. His anguish burst forth.

"Let me in," he shouted like a madman. "The holy nun promised to heal me if I can get in. For the love of God, let me in." His voice cracked into a sob. His face was wet with tears. "I want to see. Dear God, please let me in."

He felt the crowd shifting, felt himself being prodded and pushed. He felt for Pasquale's hand and found other hands, pulling him along, pushing him. Suddenly he was stumbling down a narrow flight of steps, bumping against bodies on the way.

"For the love of God, let me through," he kept pleading. "The nun said she would heal me." The tears were coming faster. The hands were pushing, leading.

"Thank you. Let me in. She promised to heal me."

The pushing stopped. Iacobello was thrust up against a wall. Someone grabbed his hand and stretched it forward. He felt rough, cold stone. He ran his hands along the slab and found a corner. Sides, bottom. A stone casket suspended on an iron grate.

The tomb.

His anguish escaped his lungs in a great sigh. A warmth engulfed him. His clothes seemed aflame. He was melting. He pulled off his mantle. His tunic. His shoes. His stockings. The coolness of the church swept over him, tingling.

Here he was, a sinner, at the tomb of this holy woman. The enormity of his sins swept over him. How could he have thought that little sins were permissible? Little blemishes marred a candlestick as little sins marred his soul. Noblewomen wanted perfection in silver wares; God desired perfection in souls. The holy nun had eradicated every sin from her life. Otherwise people would not be calling her a saint.

How could he show her, show God, show these people that he was a sinner and that he was sorry?

The laces that had tied his stockings to his legs! Iacobello felt for them, found one. With deep repentance, he tied it about his neck as if it were a noose. A little murmur shivered through the crowd at this common sign of penitence. Iacobello was kneeling, weeping. Seeing with his eyes did not seem so important now that he could see with his soul.

"I am sorry, Lord. I am sorry," he whispered over and over.

All those years, his mother had prayed for him. She must be praying still. The holy nun had the heart of a mother to answer his mother's prayers.

His mind felt so stretched, so weary. He felt a deep, inexplicable peace. He bent to the floor and felt himself drifting to sleep.

He saw a great light and in it the holy nun, her face bright with love as she looked toward the Lord Christ. The lady's gaze was drawing Iacobello's attention to Jesus.

Jesus bore a bloody gash in His forehead. Iacobello remembered. Christ carried His cross. He fell beneath its weight. Several times. He fell, not because He could not see but because others were blind. Others like Iacobello.

Iacobello had heard some friars preaching in Spoleto. They said that sins hurt Christ. Iacobello's sins. Yet, Christ's gaze was gentle and compassionate, not angry. Like a beggar, Christ extended His hands toward Iacobello, who could see the bloody nail wounds in them.

Suddenly Iacobello knew. His blindness was no punishment for sin. It was to bring him to this moment of interior sight when he could clearly see both his own sins and Christ's mercy. Despite Iacobello's unlovableness, God still loved him. Iacobello touched the wounded palm, putting into it the only alms he had. Himself.

"Get up. Get up, because you have been freed!"

It was the voice of the holy nun.

Iacobello looked from Christ to her. She had disappeared. Then Christ, too, vanished.

Tears were dropping from Iacobello's cheeks to his thighs, running down his legs, etching little rivulets of clean pale skin against the gray grime. God, his breeches were filthy. His mother never let them get that bad.

Iacobello gasped. He could see his breeches, his thighs, his tears rolling down his legs. The moment seemed suspended in time, as if he could touch it.

He lifted his head. Just in front of him hung a gray casket, suspended on hooks and resting atop an iron grate. On either side, masses of candles blazed. On the right lay a pile of ragged clothes. His clothes. At his left, a shaggy-haired, grimy boy was staring at him.

"Pasquale?"

The boy squealed.

Iacobello threw his arms around the boy. "Pasquale, I can see!"

God was too good. Iacobello wanted to know God, to know Lady Clare, to go to confession. He had to find a priest.

Gathering up his clothes and shoes, Iacobello wedged them between his mending right arm and his body. Then he pushed himself erect and turned to the packed crowd, every face radiant in the candlelight. Taking Pasquale's hand in his own left hand, he began to push through the people. "I can see! Praise God and Lady Clare, I can see!"

∿ 62 ∾

Sister Agnese di Oportulo de Bernardo

Dormitory, San Damiano (MID-OCTOBER, 1260) ∿ With pains shooting through her shoulders, Sister Agnese stooped to her bed of straw and felt beneath her straw pillow for a simple wooden cross. A bit over fifty years old, Agnese felt herself weakening. Two years ago, Sister Pacifica had died at the age of ninety. Agnese would never reach that age.

Ah, here was the cross. In Agnese's bony, heavily veined hands, the simple cross sang with memories.

How long ago had she made this? Long ago when she and Lucia were children, before Father Francis died. All these years she had fallen asleep praying and clutching the cross.

"Sister, are you ready?"

Young, vibrant Sister Giuseppina was offering Agnese her left hand. Agnese grasped Giuseppina's arm and stood.

Next to Giuseppina stood rosy-cheeked Sister Sofia with Sister Gatta, orange and white, nestled in her arms. Today the sisters were leaving San Damiano, never to return.

The three women moved toward the stairs that led out of the dormitory. "The cross means a lot to you, doesn't it?" Giuseppina asked in her sweetly musical voice.

"Oh, yes."

How could Agnese explain? She had wept over this cross when Papa had been excommunicated. She had tried to do penance by wearing Clare's hairshirt, drinking foul water, and cinching her cord tightly until Clare had forbidden her. One Good Shepherd Sunday, when Agnese had seen the Christ Child at Clare's side, she had finally understood the profoundness of the cross.

The sisters walked through the oratory. None bent to kiss the floor, because the Body of Christ had been taken to the Monastery of Saint Clare in Assisi.

Saint Clare, yes. Immediately after Clare's death, Pope Innocent IV had begun an inquiry into Clare's sanctity. Upon Innocent's death, Cardinal Raynaldo had become Pope, taking the name Alexander IV. He had canonized Clare in 1255.

The sisters had always known that Clare was a saint. They had secretly kept her hair, blond at first then turning silver gray, cut during their periodic tonsurings. They'd also saved Clare's tunic, mantle, and hairshirt. These relics, and the deacon's alb that Clare had embroidered for Francis and Francis's breviary—gifts from Brothers Leo and Angelo—were being transferred to the Monastery of Saint Clare.

"Behave, Sister Gatta!" Sofia scolded, scratching the squirming cat's chin.

"What number Sister Gatta is she?" Giuseppina asked Agnese, helping her down the narrow stairs that led to the choir.

Agnese had to think. The Sister Gatta when Agnese had entered San Damiano was gray. So was the second. The third, black with white paws, had mysteriously disappeared. Sister Gatta number four had died about the same time as Clare. "This is Sister Gatta Five," Agnese figured.

"Be still, Sister Gatta!" Sofia scolded. "When we get to the Monastery of Saint Clare, you will have a much larger place to explore."

So Agnese had heard. Clare's body had been laid to rest at San Giorgio in the same place that Francis's body had lain while the Church of Saint Francis was being built. At the same time, some San Damiano sisters had moved to a temporary monastery at San Giorgio because Abbess Benedetta intended to build a permanent monastery there for the sisters along with a huge church dedicated to Clare.

Working through the bishop and the Chapter of San Rufino, Benedetta had exchanged the San Damiano complex for the Church of San Giorgio, its adjacent Hospital of San Rufino, and a small amount of land. Then, stubbornly persistent, she had overcome tremendous opposition to build a magnificent edifice to house Clare's body on the site. The disputes over property, rights, and cleric's ideas would have discouraged a lesser person, but Benedetta, a knight's true daughter, had gotten her way.

First the Monastery of Saint Clare had been built around the Church of San Giorgio. To build the Church of Saint Clare, Benedetta had obtained as architect the highly esteemed friar

Filippo da Campello, designer of the Church of Saint Francis. As agreed, the outbuildings of San Damiano had been demolished and the stones used to build the Church of Saint Clare. Benedetta had commissioned a painted crucifix, reportedly quite beautiful, to hang in the new church. On October 3, Clare's body had been transferred from the Church of San Giorgio to the Church of Saint Clare. The ceremony, Agnese had heard, had been magnificent, with a joyous, reverent crowd of prelates, abbots, friars, and laity. Benedetta, gravely ill at the Monastery of Saint Clare, must have been thrilled.

Sofia opened the door to the silent, empty choir, guiding Agnese through. To the right lay the empty burial plots: the bodies of the sisters had already been moved to the Monastery of Saint Clare.

Of all the sisters at San Damiano, only Benedetta and Agnese had known Clare in the early days. All the others had died. Now Benedetta was dying and Agnese, too.

Into the parlor Agnese shuffled, through the doorway, around the grate, out into the visitors' area into the shadowy church. Above the altar was the empty space where the crucifix that had spoken to Saint Francis had hung. With the sisters, that relic was moving today to the Monastery of Saint Clare. The dove above the altar, where the Body of Christ had been kept, was empty.

The other sisters waited near the doors of the church. One by one, they ascended the steps to the outer courtyard, Giuseppina helping Agnese while Sophia carried the snoozing Gatta.

In the blinding sunlight, a male voice questioned, "Are you the last?"

"Yes, my lord," Agnese smiled at the mounted knight, one of many sent by the commune to accompany the sisters. In a cart rested the San Damiano crucifix, assorted kitchen vessels, and the relics.

Two young sisters closed the door of the church. Led by the cart and surrounded by plodding horses, the group started slowly up the hill.

Agnese had not been up this road for forty years.

Good-bye, San Damiano, her soul whispered.

"Tell us, Sister Agnese, what was it like when you first came here?" Giuseppina asked.

"Yes, Sister, tell us," the other sisters begged.

What was it like? Agnese had been a curly-haired eleven-year-old who, for months, had begged her papa to live at San Damiano. Oh, the joy, the freshness, the poverty of that beginning, when she, Lucia, Angeluccia, and Venuta were all giddy girls! How all four of them had admired and loved Clare, who had become their Mama! She had guided all of them through the trials, struggles, and opposition of those early days.

But these young sisters, some of whom had not known Clare, had experienced only the glory of the recent years. Now people thought that the Poor Enclosed Sisters were heroic and angelic. Their order's founder a saint. Their new dwelling, the Monastery of Saint Clare and its adjacent church, magnificent substitutes for humble San Damiano. Knowing only praise, would these sisters hold to the poverty, humility, and spark of the beginning?

Agnese's gaze shifted to the simple wooden cross. "The beginning was like this," she said, showing the sisters the cross. "Sister Clare used to say, 'Look upon Him who became contemptible for you, and follow Him, making yourself contemptible in this world for Him. Gaze upon Him, consider Him, contemplate Him, as you desire to imitate Him. Then you shall share everlasting treasures in place of those that perish, and you shall live forever.'"

The talking and the walking, Agnese knew, would soon exhaust her. What could she say that would explain everything?

"We were faithful at the beginning," Agnese reflected. "Faithful to poverty. Joy. Humility. To the cross and to Him who suffered on it. If we are faithful to the end, we will be His forever."

CHAPTER NOTES

The following notes will help the reader separate fact from fiction in this biography. References are expanded in the bibliography.

All historical details in this book are accurate. But conversations, except where noted, are conjectural.

All descriptions of Assisi (its buildings, monasteries, convents, architecture, streets, outlying districts) are accurate unless otherwise noted. All other towns named existed and their history is portrayed accurately.

The names, backgrounds, occupations, relationships, and social standings of all characters are accurate unless otherwise noted. However, the physical descriptions are conjectural unless stated otherwise. The ages of the characters, with the exceptions of Clare, Francis, and Clare's sister Catherine, are approximations based on available information.

The physical descriptions of Clare and Francis are taken from the primary sources (see bibliography), paintings of the period, and detailed studies of their skeletal remains. An anatomically accurate model of Clare's body, which holds her remains, can be seen in the Basilica of Saint Clare in Assisi. Clare's habit is described in her Form of Life and in artwork by her contemporaries. Her mantle is on display in the Basilica of Saint Clare.

Details regarding life in the commune of Assisi reflect Fortini's research, the primary sources, and the way that various social classes lived in twelfth and thirteenth century Italy. Whether these individuals lived in precisely the way presented is pure speculation, but the general outlines of their lives is factual.

Except where noted, this book follows Omer Englebert's chronology for Saint Francis as printed in his 1965 biography, *Saint Francis of Assisi: A Biography.* Other historians dispute some of these dates.

NOTE: Unless otherwise specified, all references to Armstrong refer to Regis Armstrong, *Clare of Assisi: Early Documents.* All references to Fortini refer to *Nova Vita di San Francesco (4 vols).*

PART ONE

To Set Out on the Path of the Lord

1. Lady Ortolana di Favarone, Bedroom, Offreduccio House, Assisi, Italy *(Late January, 1200)*

The history regarding the merchants' uprising and the destruction of Sasso Rosso is accurate. The Offreduccios and Gislerios may well have been friends. Ortolana's fiery dream is my invention; she heard the words "Your child will be a light to all the world" while she was praying before a crucifix. The sources do not tell where this crucifix was nor what it looked like. Some historians believe it was at the shrine of Saint Michael in Monte Gargano, while others place it at the Cathedral del San Rufino. The postulated description of the San Rufino crucifix is likely for the time.

The wealthy Offreduccios owned all the lands attributed to them in this book. Their house, quite large for their time (15 to 20 meters or 16 to 22 feet long), was located next to the Cathedral del San Rufino. The layout of the Offreduccio house and the way the family lived there is imagined from what was typical for the period. At some point, Count Offreduccio died and Favarone inherited the house. Clare's family was wealthy and generous.

Most likely Ortolana was in her teens and Favarone in his twenties at the time of their marriage. Most modern historians agree that Clare was the eldest child. Ortolana was a pious, generous woman who went on the pilgrimages noted in this chapter, possibly all prior to Clare's birth. The pilgrimage to the Holy Land must have taken place in 1192 because of unrest in the area prior to that year.

Without saying when he began his employment, Ioanni stated in the *Process* that he was the Offreduccio house watchman when Clare was a young girl.

Without giving any other information about her, Fortini mentions an Assisi woman named Domina Savia who was insane.

A group of pious, unnamed women relatives used to meet in Ortolana's house. Presumably, Bona and Pacifica were among them. Alguisa, a relative and neighbor, could have been part of this group. Her two children Emilia and Paolo seem to have been older than Clare.

Ladies-in-waiting were women of slightly lower noble rank who were companions to higher ranking ladies. In the *Process,* Bona and Pacifica say they "stayed" with Ortolana. Pacifica accompanied Ortolana on her pilgrimages and Bona accompanied Clare on her meetings with Francis. Pacifica said that she was "always" with Clare. Without being titled "ladies-in-waiting," Bona and Pacifica seem to have filled that role.

Pacifica was known publicly as a penitent. In the *Process,* Pacifica said that she did not know Favarone and had never seen him. Perhaps Favarone was away from home a great deal, hunting and visiting his properties. Men and women had separate rooms in noble houses and this prevented mingling of the sexes. It's unlikely that Favarone was an invalid. He could not have been dead, because he fathered three daughters. Clare's canonization proceedings imply that Favarone was still alive when Clare was in her late teens. Could Pacifica have never seen Favarone because she had secretly embraced a penitential, reclusive life and purposely attempted not to see Favarone or any other man? Public and private recluses were common in Umbria, the area of Italy where the city of Assisi is located.

In the *Process,* Pacifica and Bona are listed as daughters of Guelfuccio, not as wives of this or that lord. This may indicate that they never married.

The Cathedral del San Rufino was being enlarged in 1193, the usually accepted year of Clare's birth. In *St. Clare of Assisi* Nesta de Robeck lists Clare's traditional birthdate as July 16, but the date is not provable.

Mothers usually taught their daughters, so Ortolana probably educated her daughters. Women made their families' clothes, and Clare learned fine stitching from someone, most likely from her mother. It seems plausible that Ortolana made Clare's baptismal gown, whatever that gown looked like.

Priests were instructed to condemn the common practice of having servants care for the children of the nobility. Ortolana, being a pious woman, would likely follow this instruction and breastfeed and care for her own children.

2. Lord Favarone di Offreduccio, Piazza della Minerva, Assisi
(Late January, 1200)

Favarone is barely mentioned in the primary sources, yet he must have been a religious man because he permitted Ortolana's pious practices and seems to have given more generous alms than were expected.

The details of Assisi's violent climate and civil war are taken from *Nova Vita.* In 1182, about the beginning of a fifteen-year famine, a stranger went about the streets calling "Peace and all good." Yet civil war, not peace, came to Assisi. Sometime between 1198 and 1202, at the beginning of Assisi's civil war, Monaldo took up residence in Perugia. Clare's family followed him. Most likely the other Offreduccios did the same.

This chapter postulates that Monaldo made his move after the lords of Sasso Rosso switched their allegiance to Perugia, beginning with Lord Girardo di Gislerio's request for Perugian citizenship on January 18, 1200. On January 23, Girardo's brother Lord Fortebraccio and nephew Lord Oddo became Perugian citizens. Soon after, the other Gislerio family members followed suit.

The Offreduccio family owned the lands and buildings mentioned. Medieval lords visited their properties, stayed overnight with the managers of their lands, accepted tolls, tributes, and taxes from those who used their property, and saw that justice was done for their serfs and landlords. The fictional incident involving the thief illustrates how the nobility would have handled such a crime.

Sometime during this period, a simple-minded man of Assisi began to treat Francis Bernardone in the fashion mentioned in this chapter. His words are taken directly from the primary sources. Francis was five feet, two inches tall, as evident from his skeletal remains in the Basilica of Saint Francis.

Clare counted her prayers on pebbles, as monks did, and was known as a prayerful, holy child who sent some of her own food to the poor and who did penance. The primary sources give no other details about her childhood.

3. Lady Benvenuta di Peroscia, Children's Play Room, Benvenuta's House, Perugia, Italy *(Early Autumn, 1205)*

Clare's family lived with Benvenuta's family in Perugia. In *Clare: Her Light and Her Song,* Sister Mary Seraphim records Benvenuta's family name as Peroscial. The primary sources do not mention Balvina's or Ginevra's families as relocating to Perugia, although they probably did. Filippa did relocate with her family. History records no details of Clare's stay in Perugia.

Fortini speculates that Oddo and Girardo di Gislerio were killed in the war with Assisi, because their names disappear from the archives at that time. But this could be a false supposition, as historian David Flood pointed out to me. Using Assisi archives, Fortini gives 1205 as the year when Clare's family returned to Perugia. Other historians give other years.

Deruta, a town in the outlying districts of Perugia, is still recognized for its fine ceramics. Whether these ceramics were sold in Perugia and not in Assisi is unknown.

The Life of Saint Clare Virgin stated that Clare, in religious life, wore a cord with thirteen knots, representing Christ's thirteen wounds, underneath her habit. No one knows when Clare adopted this penitential cord.

The primary sources mention that Clare prayed while prostrate and frequently cried profusely while praying. Apparently, Clare had what medieval people called "the gift of tears," an ability to release intense emotions through spontaneous weeping.

Marionettes were popular children's toys. Canons (clerics) in several medieval churches, possibly including San Pietro, used marionettes and puppets to teach bible stories. Using puppets to dramatize non-religious tales came later.

4. Lady Pica, Bernardone House, Assisi *(Early Autumn, 1205)*

The civil war between the nobles and the common people established Assisi as a commune, that is, a city-state ruled by citizens elected by the people, not by the lords. Upon their return to Assisi, Monaldo and Favarone absolved Assisi from making restitution to them, as did the other nobles mentioned in this chapter. Favarone and Monaldo's homes were damaged.

The history regarding the war with Perugia, the treaties, and the jockeying of Philip, Otto, and the Pope is accurate. At the time the papacy was a political as well as a religious institution. It held cities and lands.

Francis's birth, activities, illnesses, and visions follow the primary sources. He had at least one brother named Angelo. *The Legend of Perugia* states that Francis spread extra bread on the table for the poor when his father was not home, and Pietro seems to have been away a good deal. If the San Rufino beggars begged from Francis, he would have fed them.

Pietro could certainly have instructed Pica to welcome the nobles back to Assisi, because he was always looking for ways to please his customers and increase business. It is possible that Clare visited the Bernardone shop.

Thomas of Celano's *Second Life* mentions a bride in the vision of the enchanted, armor-filled castle. No mention is made of a woman in Francis' ecstasy in the street, although at this time he told his friends that he was thinking of taking the most beautiful, noble bride in all the world. Biographers believe that he had in mind the woman of the first vision, whom historians consistently identify as Lady Poverty. Could Lady Poverty have resembled Clare? Noble Clare lived in a large palatial house filled with the armor of knights. She eventually relinquished this to embrace Gospel-inspired poverty, to become Lady Poverty in the flesh. Francis consistently hesitated to become involved with women, yet the histories insist that he wanted to meet Clare. God gave Francis a vision about noblewomen living at San Damiano. How did Francis know which noblewoman to entrust with this vision? Did God use Francis's visions to pave the way for his acceptance of Clare? Together Francis and Clare begot many spiritual children. These followers turned to Clare as "mother" when their "father" Francis died.

5. Lady Balvina di Martino, Offreduccio House, Assisi
(Late January, 1206)

Clare seems to have kept in touch with her friends in Perugia. The year 1206 was known for its heavy snows.

Fortini's research indicates that Balvina and Amata were Clare's cousins, daughters of her cousin Martino. Possibly Amata was born at Correggiano and her mother churched at San Rufino.

Englebert gives January 1206 as the date of Francis's disrobing. Other historians list the month as February or April, or the year as 1207. The activities of Francis, his parents' reactions, the unfolding of the trial, and the bishop's response are in the primary sources. No account mentions snow.

Prior to reaching marriageable age, children were given complete freedom to play in the streets. When girls attained marriageable age, they were then kept indoors, out of danger and away from prying eyes. As a child, Clare could have witnessed Francis's disrobing. If she did not, she certainly heard of it because it became the talk of the town.

Francis's action had an immediate, profound effect on Clare, who stated that shortly after Francis's conversion, she herself began to do penance. She did not detail what she meant.

Francis's disrobing broke no moral or civil laws, because people were not prudish about nudity. Men and women slept nude, except for hats that they wore to bed. Maids assisted lords and ladies at their baths, often taken together. Within the home, people often saw each other without clothing. Clothing was not worn for modesty; it was worn to indicate social class. Only those who had nothing to wear appeared unclothed in public. To appear naked in public was a disgrace because it indicated the depth of the individual's poverty and his or her exclusion from a clothed society.

PART TWO

~⁊⁊~

The Lord Gave the Light of His Grace

6. Lord Ranieri di Bernardo, Piazza del San Rufino, Assisi
(May 1210)

Intermarriage among distant family members maintained social standing and property within the family. Clare's parents wanted her to marry magnificently. Clare rejected all her suitors, including Lord Ranieri di Bernardo, a distant cousin, who remembered Clare's beauty even in his old age. Ranieri testified in the *Process* that he had many times asked Clare to marry him, but she always refused and even preached to him about leaving the world. He did not state how or when he courted Clare, but any courtship would have taken place in a group setting such as a riding party.

Most people who initially thought that Francis was crazy eventually became supportive. Ranieri may have been one of these people. Francis most likely had volunteer work crews helping him rebuild abandoned churches.

At this time, Francis was also tending lepers at the leper hospital of San Lazzaro. Sometimes Clare sent food, either with Bona or with the family almoner, to the poor and possibly to lepers.

In the *Process,* several witnesses describe Clare's penitential practices at this stage of her life. Clare's sister Beatrice states that after Francis heard of Clare's holiness, which was common knowledge in Assisi, he went often to preach to her. Yet Lady Bona states in the same *Process* that Clare secretly and frequently went to speak to Francis.

What San Damiano looked like before Francis renovated it, how many times Francis worked on San Damiano and when, and what renovations he made are all speculative. Father Marino Bigaroni believes that San Damiano originally looked as this chapter describes it. Bigaroni believes that Francis renovated it twice, once prior to the incident in this chapter and then again, more extensively, a few years later. San Damiano's cross and its location in the church are accurately described.

In the *Process,* Cristiana, daughter of Lord Bernardo da Suppo, implies that she lived with Clare for a time. She does not state the years or the reasons.

In the *Process,* Lord Ugolino de Pietro Girardone states that he sent away his wife, Lady Guiduzia, but he gives no year or reason.

Prior to his conversion, Francis was friendly with many young men of Assisi, possibly including Rufino and Giles. In "The Life and Sayings of Brother Giles" in *The Little Flowers of Saint Francis,* translated by Raphael Brown (1958), Giles stated that life in the world was boring.

At the time of this story, all the friars mentioned had joined Francis. Their backgrounds are accurate.

The descriptions of all places, objects, and activities associated with Francis are correct. The chapels San Pietro della Spina and the Porziuncola, both of which Francis rebuilt, are listed as chapels for rural people in a footnote in chap. 6 in Helen Moak's English translation of Fortini's biography of Saint Francis.

From the primary sources and from their skeletal remains in the Basilica of Saint Francis in Assisi, we know that Angelo di Tancredi was tall and robust and Rufino shorter and presumably delicate looking.

Francis rebuilt the churches mentioned and was working on the Porziuncola at the time of this story. In her Testament, Clare relates Francis's prophecy about San Damiano.

7. Lady Bona di Guelfuccio, Offreduccio House, Assisi
(Late Autumn, 1210)

Bona stated in the *Process* that before Clare was tonsured, she sent Bona on the pilgrimage to Saint James in Compostela, Spain. The year 1210 was a jubilee year for the shrine with special indulgences for pilgrims. Perhaps Clare sent Bona to Saint James in 1210.

Celano's *Second Life,* section 155, records Barbaro's abusive attack on a fellow friar and his subsequent penance. Any friar who got angry followed the prescription of prostrating himself and begging the offended party to put his foot on the bad-tempered one's mouth. Barbaro went beyond this by impulsively chewing ass's dung to curb his temper. Fortini speculates that this incident occurred at Limigiano and that Rufino was the nobleman who witnessed it.

Rufino di Scipione, Clare's first cousin, joined Francis and his friars sometime in 1210. The Offreduccio family's reaction to this is unknown.

The *Fioretti* tells how Francis sent timid Rufino to preach in his breeches. The account does not name the church nor does it state that Rufino's family saw him preaching. Those who did see him jeered until Francis, clad in his own breeches, preached as well. Then the congregation's attitude changed.

The description of the friars' tunics is accurate.

Clare did send votive offerings and alms to the friars working on the Porziuncola.

8. Brother Philip di Lungo, Porziuncola, Assisi
(Late Autumn, 1210)

Philip di Lungo's origin and the date he joined Francis is controversial. This text follows Fortini's research, with which Englebert agrees.

Possibly through the intermediary Brother Rufino, Clare and Francis somehow arranged to meet. The primary sources make it clear that Francis wanted to snare Clare for his order and that he preached to her about leaving the world. She equally wished to speak to him about her vocation, because she had determined to remain a virgin. Possibly she had even considered entering a convent. These secret meetings took place for over a year, with Bona accompanying Clare, and Philip accompanying Francis. We do not know where or how these meetings took place.

Francis's words about obedience, poverty, and contempt of the world are taken from his "Letter to All the Faithful," as translated in *Francis and Clare: The Complete Works.*

9. Lady Beatrice di Favarone, Piazza del San Rufino, Assisi
(January 1212)

Favarone disappears from the histories about this time, although Fortini, in "New Information about Saint Clare of Assisi," lists a 1229 document that mentions a Favarone without giving an ancestral name. Favarone di Offreduccio was not the only Favarone in Assisi, as evident from a 1233 document that mentions Favarone di Cannara. About this time, Monaldo and the other relatives assume authority involving Clare and her sister Catherine. If Favarone were alive, they could only have assumed this authority if Favarone had been incapable of making decisions. This is possible but not likely. If Favarone had opposed Clare's vocation as Pietro opposed Francis's, biographers would have certainly emphasized it because it would make Clare's story parallel Francis's. The fact that Favarone is not mentioned and that other relatives had authority to act in his place suggests that Favarone must have died.

I believe that Favarone died sometime between Clare's first meeting with Francis and her total embracing of religious life. This is based on the information stated above as well as on Lady Bona's testimony in the *Process,* in which Bona says that Clare went secretly to visit Francis so as not to be seen by her parents.

PART THREE

On Bended Knee to the Father

10. Bishop Guido, Sasso del Maloloco, Commune of Assisi
(Early March, 1212)

The Carceri or caves of Saint Francis are located in a rocky, mountainous area known then as Sasso del Maloloco.

According to Fortini, Bishop Guido was the most powerful lord of the commune of Assisi. He owned half the commune's property, including the monasteries and convents mentioned in this chapter. In his article "The Church of San Giorgio in Assisi and the first Expansion of the Medieval City Walls," Father Mario Bigaroni states that Guido physically beat and wounded the nuns of the community of San Donato di Flebulle. In this chapter, Guido's spiritual life is postulated from what we know of him and his admiration for Francis.

Guido appears to have been Francis's friend, probably knowing Francis quite well during his merchant days. Quite likely many of Pietro Bernardone's fine cloths graced the bishop's household.

In his Testament, Francis stated: "When God gave me some friars, there was no one to tell me what I should do." Yet Francis subjected himself totally to Church authority so as not to be branded a heretic or a madman. Thus, he certainly seems to have sought Guido's permission for his lifestyle.

No historical source tells of a meeting such as the one portrayed in this chapter. Yet it seems that such a meeting would have taken place. Francis would probably have not taken responsibility for Clare without the bishop's knowledge and at least his tacit permission.

How did Clare leave Assisi at night when the gates should have been locked and guarded? Did she bribe the guards to let her out? Was the city gate in the vicinity of the Porta Moiano left open because of renovations on the luxurious baths and fountains there? Father Rene Charles Dhont includes a footnote on page 7 of his book *Clare among Her Sisters* that reads: "Clare profited from the plan to open the gates of the city which, in the Middle Ages, were closed and guarded during the night." Were the gates left open on Palm Sunday so that those celebrating with their families could return to their homes in the villages after dark? Or was Bishop Guido part of the plan to let Clare escape? When Clare's relatives attempted to make her renounce her vocation, the Church did not support their efforts. Does this mean that Guido, as the Church's representative, had taken Clare under his protection?

The order of penance was an approved, ecclesiastical form of life that people could embrace on their own. Because Clare's tonsure took place during a penitential season and at the hands of the friars (not the bishop), it was not a juridical act of consecration of a virgin. The tonsure signified Clare's entry into a life of penance and could have been administered by anyone, even by Clare herself.

In his article "San Damiano—Assisi: The First Church of Saint Francis," Father Mario Bigaroni states he believes that San Damiano, which was under Bishop Guido's control, had previously been a monastic foundation, probably set up as a satellite monastery to a larger abbey where monks could pray and work. History does not record when Francis and Clare first conceived the idea to send Clare to San Damiano or when they first asked the bishop for use of the complex. The renovations Francis suggests in this chapter were later made by him.

11. Brother Francis Bernardone, Offreduccio House, Assisi
(Palm Sunday Night, March 18, 1212)

The primary sources record that Clare sold her inheritance and gave all the money to the poor, although historians dispute if she did this before or after entering religious life. Clare's actions angered her family.

The primary sources also state that Bishop Guido presented an olive branch (or, in some translations, a palm) to Clare on Palm Sunday. Was this the bishop's signal to Clare and the friars that he approved their plans?

The Life of Saint Clare Virgin states that Clare was accompanied to the Porziuncola "by a virtuous companion." This could have been a friar or someone other than Lady Pacifica, but for good reasons many Clare scholars identify this companion as Lady Pacifica. For Clare to have gone off with a man would have scandalized her family and cast suspicion on the friars at a time when sexual misconduct among the clergy was common. Bona had always accompanied Clare on her visits to Francis, but Bona was on pilgrimage to Rome, according to her testimony in the *Process*. For propriety's sake, Francis always sent his friars out in pairs and he most likely would have wanted Clare to have a female companion whenever she came to see him.

The hypothetical idea that Pacifica accompanied Clare as her lady-in-waiting accounts for the facts as Pacifica herself stated them. In the *Process*, Pacifica said that she "always" served Clare and entered the order "at the same time" as Clare. However, most historians believe that Clare alone was tonsured at the Porziuncola on Palm Sunday night 1212 (or 1211 as some scholars believe) and that Clare's sister Catherine, not Pacifica, was the first one to embrace Clare's form of religious life. Pacifica's attendance on Clare as a lady-in-waiting would be historically possible and would be consistent with this commonly accepted information.

The primary sources give conflicting information about just who tonsured Clare—Francis or the brothers. The names of the friars who were at the Porziuncola that night are not listed. The friars named in this chapter belonged to the order at the time. Quite likely Philip accompanied Francis and Clare to San Paolo delle Abbadesse, since he had accompanied Francis to all his meetings with Clare.

The sources tell us that Clare put aside her fine clothing once her hair was cut. Perhaps she acquired her own penitential tunic or perhaps the friars gave her one. What happened to Clare's discarded clothing? Possibly Francis returned it to her family, just as he had returned his clothing to his father, or gave it to the poor.

12. Lord Monaldo di Offreduccio, Offreduccio House, Assisi
(Monday of Holy Week, March 19, 1212)

Clare escaped through the "door of the dead," having removed by herself the rubble blocking it.

How did Clare fit in with the San Paolo community? Was she considered a postulant (person discerning a vocation to religious life) sent there by the bishop? Were the nuns willing to accept her as a member of their community although she had no dowry? Did she become one of the monastery servants? Did she live as a hermitess or a penitent? History gives no answers.

Although we do not know how Monaldo learned of Clare's disappearance, he and other unnamed family members rode to San Paolo to confront Clare. The Holy Week struggle in this chapter is based solidly on the primary sources.

In the *Process*, Lord Ranieri di Bernardo states that he married one of Clare's relatives, but he does not mention the year.

13. Lady Catherine di Favarone, Strada di San Martino, Assisi
(April 4, 1212)

The Life of Saint Clare Virgin states that Catherine initially had her mind set on "carnal marriage." After becoming a penitent, Clare began to pray that Catherine would join her. Sixteen days after Clare's consecration, Catherine came to Clare. The *Life* does not say if she came alone or with a companion. By this time, Clare was at Sant'Angelo in Panzo, where Francis had moved her a few days after the confrontation by her relatives.

In *Without Turning Back: Life of Saint Agnes of Assisi,* Sister Chiara Lucia Garzonio states that Catherine made three visits to Clare before the Holy Spirit inspired her to join. Other writers imply that Catherine came to Clare only once.

For many years, historians believed that Sant'Angelo was a Benedictine monastery for nuns, similar to other Benedictine foundations around Assisi. Modern historians such as Marco Bartoli *(Clare of Assisi,* p. 55), Jon Francois Godet-Calogeras *(Out of the Shadows,* pp. 106–107), and others believe that Sant'Angelo was more likely a community of female penitential recluses in the model of the Beguines. The Beguines were groups of pious women in the area of Belgium who supported themselves through their cloth trade and who lived together without a common rule.

History records no details of the Sant'Angelo community. In this book, the Sant'Angelo women are imagined as living as penitential hermits and as generally following a lifestyle that would be described in the Rule of 1221, which Saint Francis and Cardinal Hugolino composed for the Brothers and Sisters of Penance (translated in Habig's *Omnibus).*

The violent confrontation of the Offreduccio family and Catherine's miraculous deliverance is accurately portrayed. In the histories, Monaldo is named as the leader of the twelve knights (not all are named) who came to retrieve Catherine.

The legal age for entrance into religious life was twelve. At some time shortly after this chapter's savage episode, Francis tonsured fourteen-year-old Catherine and renamed her "Agnes."

PART FOUR

✌⁓

To Dwell in the Church of San Damiano

14. Lady Pacifica di Guelfuccio, Sant'Angelo d'Panzo, Panzo, Italy *(May 1212)*

Clare scholars disagree on the date Clare went to San Damiano, giving dates anywhere from May through October 1212 (or 1211 depending on the historian's choice of year for her tonsure).

Pacifica seems to have joined Clare in the religious life about the time she went to San Damiano or shortly thereafter. The reasons for Pacifica's decision are not known.

15. Giovanna, San Damiano, Assisi *(Late Fall, 1212)*

A document that names all the sisters in San Damiano in 1238 mentions three Giovannas. We know nothing of these women.

The Giovanna in this chapter typifies women of the lower social classes whom Clare accepted and even invited into her community at a time when convents were strictly for noblewomen. This chapter also attempts to explore how women were received into the community, following guidelines in Clare's Form of Life.

The black curtain-covered grills were part of the traditional enclosure for anchorites. Clare's Form of Life tells us that the curtain could be lifted at the speaking grill when talking to someone but that it was never to be removed in the parlor. I conjecture that this may be because the speaking grill most likely opened into the very public church, while the parlor was probably a separate room for lengthier, private conversations. Always keeping the parlor grill covered with a curtain would preserve the good reputations of those speaking in the parlor.

16. Lady Ginevra di Giorgio di Ugone, Bedroom, House of Lord Giorgio di Ugone, Assisi *(Late Summer, 1214)*

In 1214, Ginevra changed her name to Benedetta (sometimes written Benedicta) and joined Clare and the other sisters named in this chapter. No other details are available. Nothing indicates that the miracle of the oil jar, which occurred in 1214 prior to Ginevra's entrance, figured in her conversion.

No dates are preserved regarding the marriages of Emilia and Paolo and the births of their children.

The miracles at the tomb of San Rufinus, as stated in this chapter, are on record in the Cathedral del San Rufino and are recorded in Fortini.

Since medieval people thought that light frightened away demons, they kept their sleeping quarters well lit. The Benedictine Rule, which Clare was later made to adopt, stipulates that the dormitory must be lit by candles. Yet a cat, which Clare at some point obtained, can leap up on a ledge and knock over a candle. Later rules for the Clares, including Isabella's Rule of 1259 and Urban's Rule of 1263, stipulate that a lamp (not a candle) must be kept burning all night in the dormitory. Was this done at San Damiano? Most likely, yes.

The Damianites used cast-off clothing to make priestly vestments and altar linens which they gave away, just as the friars gave away sacred vessels and irons for making altar breads.

Francis intentionally chose elderly, reluctant friars to serve the sisters. The begging friars at San Damiano were certainly Franciscans, but the chaplains may have been Franciscans or Cistercians. The first visitator to the San Damiano community was a Cistercian.

The incident of the filled oil jar follows that given in the primary sources. *The Life of Saint Clare Virgin* mentions that there was no oil even for certain unnamed ill sisters. As a medicinal, olive oil was taken by mouth and also gently rubbed into wounds and sores.

The *Process* states that the wall on which Clare left the jar was "near the entrance of the house." For years, Clare monasteries have used the turn to exchange goods between the inside and the outside of the monastery. The "wall near the entrance to the house" may have been the turn. Brother Bentevenga went to get the oil jar and found it filled.

Some sisters at San Damiano served outside the monastery. When they began to do this is not known nor are the names of the serving sisters recorded. Two Felicitas appear on the 1238 document that lists all the San Damiano sisters, but we know nothing about them.

17. Brother Francis Bernardone, Church of San Damiano
(December 1215)

At this time, through Masseo, Francis consulted Clare and Silvestro about his living a hermetical life of prayer. Both told him to preach. The primary sources for the life of Saint Francis tell us that Masseo was tall, robust, and handsome.

Francis made the journeys mentioned in this chapter. God's revelation at Compostela is in the *Fioretti.*

A meeting such as the one described here must surely have taken place between Francis and Clare, probably sometime fairly soon after Francis returned from the Fourth Lateran Council, which had opened November 11, 1215, in Rome. If Francis did visit Clare, he would have taken along another friar as a companion. According to Clare's Form of Life, any sister who spoke in the parlor had to have two other sisters with her. By never meeting alone with anyone, the friars and sisters insured their own virtue and good reputation. This was especially important because some other religious groups were being accused of scandalous behavior.

Francis states some of the decisions of the Fourth Lateran Council in this chapter. Francis probably adopted the Tau as the symbol of the Lesser Brothers following Innocent's praise of it at the council. There is no evidence that Masseo ever carved a Tau or that Francis ever gave one to Clare.

Apparently both Francis and Clare realized how the council's decisions threatened the existence of the Order of Poor Ladies who, at the time, were following a Form of Life that Francis had written for them. Most likely this Form of Life closely paralleled the friars' Form of Life. When Clare wrote her own Form of Life, she included Francis's in it.

Because of the council's decisions, Clare was forced to choose a rule approved by the Church in order to become canonically established. The *Process* says that in 1215, probably in the wake of the Council, Francis had to practically force Clare to accept the Benedictine title of abbess. This would imply that she accepted the Benedictine Rule—at least officially. Also about this time, Clare exchanged her bed of vine twigs and stone pillow for a plank. Francis, who used to perform a forty-day fast during certain penitential seasons, confronted Clare on different occasions about her own rigorous fasting. The fasting regulations that Francis gave to Clare are detailed in Clare's *Third Letter to Agnes of Prague.*

Tradition tells us that Clare thought of petitioning the Pope for the privilege of poverty. The current debate about whether the privilege can be found appears in various references listed in the bibliography. Historian David Flood (interview with author, 1997) believes that Clare went in person to obtain the privilege—if she did attempt to receive it—but this cannot be proven.

PART FIVE

~☙~

The Abundant Kindness of God

18. Lucia, Via San Petrignano, Assisi *(Late Winter, 1216)*

Little is known of Sister Lucia of Rome, the eighth witness who testified in the *Process* and whom Clare, during the early years at San Damiano, accepted into the monastery "because of the love of God when she was very little." Lucia founded the monastery of Cortona in 1225 and died in 1253, according to a footnote in Armstrong.

How, in the earliest years, did someone from Rome hear of San Damiano in Assisi? Did Francis tell Lucia's family when he was in Rome in 1215 for the Lateran Council? If Lucia belonged to a wealthy family, why would they place her in San Damiano, the poorest of monasteries? If Lucia had been of noble stock, why is she listed in the *Process* as being of Rome without mentioning her family background? This chapter is one fictitious possibility that attempts to answer these questions while adhering to the few facts we have.

At this time, a Sister Balbina was in the San Damiano community. She could be the Sister Balbina (also spelled Balvina) who, according to Fortini, came from the castle of Porziano. The uncertainty arises because Fortini does not say which year Sister Balbina of Porziano entered San Damiano

19. Sister Felicita, Via di San Petrignano, Assisi *(Late May, 1216)*

"The sisters who serve outside the monastery," as Clare calls them in her Form of Life, were allowed to wear shoes when they left the enclosure. Presumably, these were not the soft-soled, cloth shoes of noblewomen, but heavy boots used by peasants who traveled the roads. Clare admonished the serving sisters to praise God for His creation and to speak only of heavenly things. Clare does not describe the duties of the serving sisters. Historians assume that they served in the manner described in this chapter. The serving sisters may have also begged alms, although the friars assigned to San Damiano had the duty of begging for the sisters. Perhaps, since Clare called them serving sisters and not questing sisters, their main role was service.

Clare used to wash the feet of the serving sisters. We have no details on how she did this.

Lord Paolo and Brother Rufino were both sons of Clare's uncle, Lord Scipione di Offreduccio. Paolo's son was Lord Bonaventura. The incident involving Bonaventura's fever and an alms of bread ingredients is fictional.

The year that Ortolana entered San Damiano is unknown. Whether Beatrice had ever been married is likewise unclear.

20. Pope Innocent III, Church of San Damiano *(Late May, 1216)*

Some historians say that the incident of Clare making the sign of the cross over the loaves and a cross appearing on each, as told in the *Fioretti*, never happened. The story does not give the year or the Pope. The *Fioretti* story states that Agnes and Ortolana were in the monastery at the time and that Francis sent people to them and to Clare for prayers and cures.

The relationships between Innocent III and Cardinal Hugolino are accurate. Their physical descriptions are taken from paintings.

It was customary at the time for all religious to eat only a single daily meal. Clare's Form of Life stated that silence was to be maintained in the refectory during meals. The *Process* states that Clare washed the sisters' hands at table and served them herself. Today, visitors to San Damiano are shown Clare's seat near the entrance to the kitchen.

Currently some scholars are questioning whether the privilege of poverty was actually granted to Clare in 1216 or at all. A summary of both sides of the debate can be found in the footnotes of Leslie Knox's dissertation, "The True Daughters of Francis and Clare."

21. Sister Filippa di Leonardo di Gislerio, Hermitage, San Damiano *(Summer, 1216)*

In the *Process,* Lady Filippa stated: "Four years after Saint Clare entered Religion," she entered because Clare "described how our Lord Jesus Christ suffered passion and death on the cross for the salvation of the human race."

Filippa called herself "the third sister of Lady Clare." She was not the third to join Clare in religious life nor was she a blood sister. However, if Filippa, Balvina, Ginevra, Benvenuta, and Clare had the sisterly relationship in Perugia that was portrayed in Part 3, then Filippa was indeed the third of those sisters to enter San Damiano, having been preceded by Benvenuta and Ginevra.

Fortini details the burning of Sasso Rosso and postulates the probable deaths of Lord Oddo and Lord Girardo during the Assisi-Perugia War. These events may have had a traumatic effect on Filippa, who experienced them as a child.

Fortini names Teodimo and Monaldo as sons of Lord Leonardo. I have postulated the probable ages of Filippa's brothers from other information Fortini records of them. Filippa and her family returned to Assisi in 1210. On November 10, 1210, Lords Leonardo and Fortebraccio di Gislerio signed the peace pact in Assisi. About the time that Filippa joined Clare, Lord Leonardo became a follower of Francis. We have no information on Filippa's mother.

Most likely, the sisters had hermitages, little cells in the woods, for solitary prayer. Sister Giovanna's icon is imaginary.

Built on six acres of ground, part or perhaps all of San Damiano was walled-in so that the sisters could work and walk outdoors within the walls. Clare's Form of Life states that the land within this enclosure should remain uncultivated except for a garden.

The climbing nightshade, European cat snake, and swallowtail butterfly are found throughout this part of Italy and were even more common in Clare's time.

Clare's words, remembered by Filippa, are based on parts of her First and Second Letters to Agnes of Prague.

22. Bellezza, San Damiano, Assisi *(Late Afternoon, August 2, 1216)*

In the *Process,* Sister Benvenuta mentions that Mattiolo, a three or four-year-old boy from Spoleto, was brought to Clare. He was apparently dangerously injured. When Clare made the sign of the cross over the child, a pebble dropped from his nose. Other sisters witnessed the cure, but Benvenuta did not recall the year.

Lord Gualtieri Cacciaguerra was the father of Lady Cecilia, who joined the San Damiano community in 1215.

The history of the Porziuncola indulgence and the ceremony granting it follow the research of Fortini. The seven bishops mentioned were present. Tradition accepts the Porziuncola indulgence, but some modern historians question whether it was ever granted.

Father Francesco Bartoli, as quoted by Father Leone Bracaloni in "Storia di San Damiano in Assisi" (pp. 69–77), states that the same seven bishops who granted the Porziuncola indulgence also gave one to San Damiano. Father Mario Bigaroni postulates that the indulgence was granted to the oratory, not to the entire church of San Damiano, because the oratory was the presbytery of the original church. In a letter to me (May 22, 1997), Father Bigaroni explained that only public churches and not private oratories could be so indulgenced, and that if the indulgence had actually been granted and was not merely a legend, it would not have happened in the time of Saint Clare. Historian David Flood (correspondence, April 28, 1997) also doubts that there ever was a San Damiano indulgence.

The Porziuncola indulgence may now be gained in any public or semi-public oratory in the world beginning from noon August 1 until midnight August 2. It cannot be gained in a private chapel. The person wishing to gain the indulgence must fulfill the following requirements: intend to gain the indulgence; be detached from all sin; while in the church pray one Our Father, one Apostles' Creed, and one other prayer of the individual's choice; pray for the intentions of the Pope (prayerfully saying an Our Father and a Hail Mary will suffice, although other prayers may be said); and receive the Sacraments of Reconciliation and Eucharist within one week either before or after August 2. The indulgence, if the person gaining it is free from every sin including venial sin, remits all the temporal punishment due to sin and may be applied to the person himself or herself or to a soul in purgatory. If there is any adherence to sin in the person gaining the indulgence, the indulgence becomes partial.

PART SIX

~⁊ᴀᴇ᷍∾

A Celebrated and Holy Manner of Life

23. Lord Ugolino de Pietro Girardone, Church of San Damiano, Assisi *(Early Fall, 1217)*

In the *Process,* Lord Ugolino de Pietro Girardone stated that Clare had a vision in which God had instructed Ugolino to take back his wife Lady Guiduzia, whom he had dismissed twenty-two years earlier for unexplained reasons. Clare promised a son from the union. After being dismayed at first, Ugolino began to desire his wife and so followed Clare's advice. A son was later born who was still alive at the time that Ugolino testified in the *Process.*

Ugolino implies that the vision occurred after Clare entered religious life, but he gives no year. Nor does he mention when his son was born.

Ugolino's family was part of the San Rufino consortium and neighbor to Clare's family. Fortini lists several court cases involving Ugolino and his family. Ugolino's son Pietro was a witness in a court case in 1239. Fortini lists no other children of Ugolino. Assuming that Pietro was the predicted son and that the young man had to be at least fourteen or fifteen years old to be a witness, we can approximate when Pietro may have been born. The arbitrary date of this chapter has been figured from that calculation.

24. Cardinal Hugolino dei Conti dei Segni, Outside the Church of San Damiano *(Holy Week, 1220)*

Papal histories list Cardinal Hugolino's birth as anywhere from the mid-1140s to 1170. Many sources (but not all) say that Cardinal Hugolino was eighty years old when he was elected Pope on March 19, 1227.

In his *First Life of Saint Francis,* chap. 27, Celano calls the bishop of Ostia "Lord Hugo." The primary sources mention Hugolino's habit of visiting the friars barefoot. His physical description is based on paintings. His titles and activities are accurately described. Hugo's bad temper, swearing, and his reliance on Marie d'Oigines's relic is mentioned in a footnote to p. 175 in Englebert's *Saint Francis of Assisi.*

Sister Balvina di Martino di Ugolino di Offreduccio joined the San Damiano community in 1217. In the *Process,* she and Sister Cecilia mention that before Clare became so ill, she desired martyrdom after hearing of the slaughter of five friars in Morocco. In Marco Bartoli's biography of Saint Clare he assumes that Clare did not go to Morocco precisely because she became ill. We do not know Hugo's response to the friars' martyrdom.

During her illnesses, Clare seems to have stayed in the dormitory, not the infirmary. Visitors were not permitted in the dormitory, but an exception would have been made for a papal legate or friar.

Clare's Form of Life, approved in 1253, and Hugolino's of 1219 differ from each other in the ways described in this chapter. In addition, Clare's Form of Life states that the sisters were to continually keep silence in the dormitory. Yet the *Process* gives several instances where Clare spoke from her sickbed. It seems that the continual dormitory silence would apply not to Clare but to the other sisters who wanted to talk among themselves. They were to speak elsewhere. However, those who came to Clare for counsel and who worked about her bed while she sat and stitched or spun could have conversed with her following the section of the Form of Life that permitted speaking "with discernment in the infirmary for the recreation and service of the sick." Moreover, Clare's Form of Life adds that the sisters "may communicate whatever is necessary always and everywhere, briefly and in a low tone of voice."

The Basilica of Saint Clare in Assisi possesses the alb, accurately described in this chapter, that Clare made, at some point, for Francis. No one is sure of Clare's embroidery techniques. According to *The Dictionary of Needlework,* the method described in this chapter was common for the period.

Hugo visited Clare often and exchanged several letters with her. Only two are preserved, one written after celebrating Holy Week (presumably in 1220) and another in 1228. Hugo's conversation with Clare is based on what he wrote in his 1220 letter of her holiness and tears, their discussion of the Body of Christ, and his entrustment of his soul to Clare's prayers. In the *Process,* Sisters Benvenuta and Filippa mention Clare's tearful, trembling reception of the Eucharist.

On August 27, 1218, Pope Honorius III authorized Cardinal Hugolino to investigate and regulate the lifestyles of women religious. In 1219, Hugo gave women's communities "the Rule of Saint Benedict to be observed in all things which are in no way contrary to that same Form of Life that was given to you by us" (Form and Manner of Life Given by Cardinal Hugolino, *Clare of Assisi: Early Documents,* p. 91). Clare's community tried to live the Rule but found it too severe and were thus given permission to live as they had been. In 1220, presumably at Francis's request, Hugo was made Cardinal Protector of the order.

25. Brother Stephen the Simple, Porziuncola, Assisi
(November 1220)

Brother Leo's dream of the drowning friars is recounted in the *Fioretti,* chap. 36. Fortini places this dream in autumn, 1220. Brother Stephen's cure is mentioned in the *Process* and in *The Life of Saint Clare Virgin.* The stories say that Brother Stephen suffered from "madness," without describing the ailment. The stories add that Francis sent Stephen to Clare to make the sign of the cross over him, and that Stephen fell asleep "in the place where Clare usually prayed" (without giving any more details about the place) and awoke cured. A Brother Stephen did travel to Egypt to bring Francis news of the troubles in the order. There he met Francis and Peter as they were about to eat meat, as this chapter describes. It is assumed that this is the same Brother Stephen who was healed through Clare's prayers.

When Francis returned from the Holy Land, he dismissed the rebel vicars and appointed Peter Catani in their place. The generally accepted year is 1220 but dates as early as 1217 and as late as 1221 are also postulated.

26. Brontolone, Via San Petrignano, Assisi *(Christmas Eve, 1220)*

The fictitious character Brontolone represents the poor and needy who the friars referred to San Damiano for counsel and help. He also reminds us that despite Clare's cures of physical and spiritual ailments, not all were healed.

27. Sister Benvenuta di Peroscia, San Damiano *(Christmas, 1220)*

In the *Process,* Benvenuta said that she had seen above Clare's usual place of prayer a great brilliance that she thought were real flames. No one else saw the vision, and it happened before Clare fell ill. There is no further explanation.

According to Clare's Third Letter to Agnes, the sisters had two meals on Christmas and Sundays and only one meal on the other days. It seems reasonable that the friars would make a Christmas visit, but we have no proof.

This chapter is an attempt to show how Clare may have consoled and admonished her sisters. Some of Clare's thoughts expressed in this chapter are in her writings.

PART SEVEN

~⦵~

Given Up Their Own Wills

28. Brother Francis Bernardone, Parlor,
San Damiano *(May 1221)*

Sister Cecilia in the *Process* says that Francis sent five women to Clare to be received. "Lifting herself up" (from praying prostrate? from her bed where she was lying ill?), Clare said she would receive four of them but not Lady Gasdia di Taccolo, because she would not persist should she stay at San Damiano for three years. Only under great pressure from an unnamed source (or sources) did Clare accept Gasdia. According to Sister Cecilia, both she and Sister Agnes witnessed the prophecy, but she gives no specific year.

Fortini mentions a Pietro di Gasdia as being a witness in a legal matter in 1201 (vol. 3, p. 201). Lady Gasdia's brother Lord Andrea was an important personage in Assisi in 1235 (Fortini, vol. 2, p. 417). A Gasdia (no surname) was cured of fever at the tomb of San Rufinus (vol. 1, part 2, p. 9). Lady Gasdia's approximate age is calculated from Fortini's supposition that Pietro was her son, who would have to have been at least fourteen or fifteen to be a witness. Since Pietro was listed as "di Gasdia," his father may have been dead.

Peter Catani died in March 1221. By the chapter meeting held in May 1221, Francis, who had suffered illness and eye disease in the Holy Land, was weak and ill. With Cardinal Hugolino's approval, Francis made Brother Elias of Cortona minister general of the friars.

29. Sister Agnes, Woods at San Damiano *(September 1221)*

This is the traditionally accepted year that Francis sent Agnes to Monticello in Florence, although some scholars place the event in 1219 or 1228–1230. We have no details on Agnes's parting. In *Without Turning Back: Life of Saint Agnes of Assisi,* Sister Chiara Lucia Garzonio mentions that Sister Giacoma from Monticello accompanied Agnes to Florence, along with the brothers. Since the friars traveled in pairs, it seems likely that the sisters did also. I have chosen Sister Forina as Sister Giacoma's traveling companion. According to Sister Chiara Lucia, Fortina was sent in 1222 to found a Damianite monastery in Milan, along with Giacoma and two other sisters.

Clare's visions during Agnes's ecstasy are in biographies of Agnes.

I unsuccessfully attempted to verify the exact years of Balvina and Benedetta's transferals. It seems likely that their transferals could have taken place when the monasteries were founded, both prior to 1221.

Hugolino's Rule allowed each sister two tunics—most likely the outer tunic and inner chemise, which was the style for all women at that time—a mantle, and a scapular that covered and protected a sister's tunic while she worked. Not all communities used the scapular. In her Form of Life, Clare only mentions a small mantle (a short cape), which Poor Clares of the Primitive Observance use today.

30. Sister Gasdia di Taccolo di Aregnato, Dormitory, San Damiano *(November 1221)*

The *Process* states that Lady Gasdia remained at San Damiano for six months. It does not give the reason she left nor any details of her departure.

No sources tell how the friars and sisters at San Damiano prayed the Divine Office, which was either chanted or sung.

The dossal of Saint Clare, which shows scenes from Clare's life, depicts Clare in bed fully clothed. In medieval times, people wore hats to bed so the sisters most likely wore their veils while sleeping. Even though medieval people slept nude, the dossal indicates that Clare's sisters slept clothed.

The primary sources mention Clare covering her sisters at night, calling them to prayer with a hand-held bell, and lighting and extinguishing the lamps. The bell can still be seen at San Damiano.

PART EIGHT

What Is Painful and Bitter

31. Brother Francis Bernardone, Hermitage within Chaplain's House, San Damiano *(April 1225)*

Francis went to San Damiano in March 1225, where his eye disease rapidly worsened. All the details concerning Francis in this chapter and the next are in the primary sources. God's words to him during his depression are in *The Mirror of Perfection* (sec. 100).

Brother Leo's nicknames and care of Francis are also in the primary sources. Leo's physical description is based on an examination of his skeletal remains, venerated in the Basilica of Saint Francis in Assisi (Padre Anacleto Iacovelli, "Le Tombe dei quattro [Cavalieri della Tavola Rotonda] e quella della [Dama Romana])."

In sec. 112 of the *Second Life of Saint Francis,* Celano states that Francis claimed to recognize only two women by sight, presumably Clare and Lady Jacoba. In his *Major Life of Saint Francis* (chap. 5, sec. 5), Bonaventure states that Francis behaved this way because he thought that looking at a woman could enkindle flames of passion or stain purity of heart. Not looking at women was considered a sign of sanctity.

Clare patched Francis's tunic and make him slippers and ointment. Most likely she did this while he was at San Damiano. Some time earlier, she had made him a deacon's alb. The alb and slippers can be seen in the Basilica of Saint Clare in Assisi. The tunic is on display at the Basilica of Saint Francis in Assisi.

At San Damiano, Francis stayed in a hut constructed of reed mats and eventually overrun with mice. *The Legend of Perugia* (sec. 42–43) states that his hut was inside a house, probably the chaplain's, which, due to the sisters' enclosure, would have been someplace outside the walls of San Damiano.

32. Sister Filippa di Leonardo di Gislerio, Chaplain's House, San Damiano *(April 1225)*

Doctors told Francis that excessive weeping caused his eye disease. Modern doctors speculate it was due either to inflammatory glaucoma, tuberculosis of the eyes, conjunctivitis, iritis, cataracts, trachoma, or ophthalmitis. See the article by Father Octavian Schmucki, "The Illnesses of Saint Francis of Assisi before His Stigmatization." Sister Joanne Schatzlein and Father Daniel P. Sulmasy believe that Francis suffered from a borderline or tuberculoid type of leprosy that would affect his eyes ("The Diagnosis of St. Francis: Evidence for Leprosy"). The friars made Francis an oversized hood and blindfold to help block the light.

Many have proposed theories regarding the illness that kept Clare bedridden. Most likely Clare suffered loss of bone mass and other ailments resulting from many years of severe fasting (interview with Linda A. Hughes, Remuda Ranch Center for Anorexia and Bulimia, February 1995). At some point, Francis ordered Clare to sleep on a straw mattress. She continued to keep her two daily prayer vigils.

The sisters' concern for Clare's health is detailed in the *Process,* which also reveals that Clare began to eat at least half a roll daily under Bishop Guido's command. But by that time Clare's health had already been broken.

The vision of Clare in the well is part of *The Little Flowers of Saint Clare.*

In her article "The Refining of the Light," Sister Mary Francis Hone suggests that Clare's spiritual battles, described in this chapter, may have come in the wake of a doctor telling Francis that weeping was causing his blindness.

Celano's *Second Life of Saint Francis* (sec. 207) recounts the "silent ashes" sermon.

Mechtild Flury-Lemburg ("The Cowl of St. Francis of Assisi" in *Textile Conservation and Research)* details in words, diagrams, and photos, how Clare cut a large piece from the back of her mantle to patch Francis's tunic.

Did Clare ever speak to Francis or act as his nurse while he was at San Damiano? After Francis's death, Clare had a vivid dream in which she is bringing a towel and warm water to Francis to tend his wounds. Did she actually do so or just yearn to do it? Would Francis have wanted to speak to Clare about the order before he died? History does not answer these questions.

33. Sister Agnese di Oportulo de Bernardo, Oratory, San Damiano *(Late July, 1225)*

The history of the Perugian civil war and the family history concerning Sister Agnese are accurate. Agnese entered San Damiano as a child. Clare's Form of Life tells how children were received in the monastery.

Sister Lucia was sent to found a monastery in Cortona in 1225, according to a footnote to her testimony in the *Process* in Armstrong. Sister Cristiana de Bernardo da Suppo, who had lived with Clare's family and who discovered the open door of the dead on the night of Clare's departure from the Offreduccio house, entered San Damiano in 1220. Sister Angeluccia entered in 1225 and Sister Benvenuta de Lady Diambre in 1224. Their ages are not recorded. I have given Sister Benvenuta the nickname Venuta.

The incident concerning Lord Oportulo's excommunication and subsequent reconciliation follows the story as told in the *Mirror of Perfection* (sec. 101). The exact date of this reconciliation is debatable, so I have followed the date given by Fortini.

In the *Process,* Agnese tells of her requests to wear Clare's hairshirt and to drink the water that Clare used to wash her feet. The *Process* states that at one unnamed time when Clare was ill, the sisters took away her hairshirts, one of which is on display in the Basilica of Saint Clare in Assisi.

The *Process* tells how Clare cared for the ill sisters. The sisters marveled that rank mattresses smelled sweet to Clare and that she did not mind washing even vermin-infested bedding and chamberpots. We do not know which other sisters also worked in the infirmary.

None of the primary sources give the names of the sisters who were called "discreets," meaning they advised the abbess and vicaress and assisted in making community decisions. Clare's Form of Life designates that her community have such sisters.

34. Lord Oportulo de Bernardo, Vescovado, Assisi
(End of July, 1225)

Most Franciscan scholars agree that Francis wrote the Canticle of the Sun while at San Damiano. The *Mirror of Perfection* (sec. 90) says that he called it "The Praises of the Lord in His Creatures."

The reconciliation between Bishop Guido and Lord Oportulo follows Fortini's account.

35. Sister Angeluccia, Choir, San Damiano *(Early August, 1225)*

In late summer or early autumn 1225, Brother Elias took Francis from San Damiano to Rieti for treatment of his eyes. Presumably papal court physicians, or others in Rieti whom they recommended, offered this treatment.

This chapter's exhortation, which Francis wrote for the sisters, was found in 1976. The translation used is from *Clare of Assisi: Early Documents*.

36. Sister Ortolana di Favarone, Church of San Damiano
(Sunday, October 4, 1226)

Saturdays are cleaning days in many convents, so I have supposed that this was true of San Damiano.

The primary sources for Saint Francis mention that larks, which sing at dawn, were heard singing for a long time over the Porziuncola at dusk at the time of Francis's death.

At the time of Francis's final illness, Clare believed that she was dying and feared that she would not see Francis again. In her Form of Life, Clare records part of the final letter beginning "I, little brother Francis," that Francis sent to the sisters shortly before his death. *The Legend of Perugia* and *Mirror of Perfection* tell of an additional part of this letter that absolved Clare of any guilt in transgressing God's laws or Francis's rules. These two sources also record Francis's oral admonition that Clare was to stop grieving because she would see Francis again before her death. The friar who brought these messages to Clare is not named.

Although the sources state that many friars and men of Assisi were with Francis in his final hours, only Elias, Giles, Leo, Bernardo di Quintavalle, and Angelo (presumably Angelo di Tancredi) are named in the primary sources.

Francis wrote the final stanza of his "Praises of the Lord," also called the "Canticle of the Creatures," in his last days at the Porziuncola.

The primary sources record the incident of Francis's writing to Lady Jacoba to request the items mentioned in this chapter and her arriving with the items before the letter was sent. Since Francis allowed Jacoba to come into the friary, it seems reasonable that she was allowed to join the funeral procession. No stories exist about Jacoba visiting San Damiano. After Francis's death, Jacoba moved to Assisi. She died there sometime before 1300 and is buried near Francis.

Accompanied by a multitude of friars and men of Assisi, Francis's body was joyfully carried to San Damiano before being interred in the Church of San Giorgio. The description of the body matches that in Celano's *First Life of Saint Francis*. The eye treatments Francis received would have left the scars mentioned. By the time Francis's body reached San Damiano, rigor mortis, which stiffens corpses shortly after death, would have reversed itself and the body would have been pliable. Rosalind Brooke, in *Early Franciscan Government* (p. 142), states that Clare requested a fingernail. There is no evidence that she received it. The Damianites bewailed Francis's passing as this book suggests, according to Celano in *The First Life of Saint Francis*.

After Francis's death, Clare states in her Testament that she frequently had the community renew its commitment to poverty. The words that Clare uses in this chapter are a close adaptation of those in the Testament.

PART NINE

෴

To Progress in Serving God More Perfectly

37. Sister Egidia, Refectory, San Damiano
(Holy Thursday Evening, 1228)

In the *Process* Sister Agnese states that Clare sometimes threw herself at the feet of her sisters to console them, and she did this for Illuminata of Pisa. We know nothing else about Illuminata or Egidia, whose names appear on a 1238 list of San Damiano sisters.

The *Process* tells of the incident of an unnamed serving sister kicking Clare's mouth on Holy Thursday, but no year is given.

Celano, in the *Second Life of Saint Francis* (Sec. 52–53), describes the famine that followed Francis's death.

The undated incident of an unnamed, infirm serving sister asking Clare for bread from Norcera and fish from the Topino River and receiving it as this chapter describes, is recorded in codex 442 in the library of the Commune of Assisi, according to Father Benvenuto Bughetti, OFM. Some historians accept this story as only a legend.

38. All the Sisters, Dormitory, San Damiano *(Early July, 1228)*

Clare's dream is related in detail by Sister Filippa in the *Process*. The interpretations of it are taken from the writings of various scholars of Clare.

39. Pope Gregory IX, San Damiano *(July 13, 1228)*

Physical descriptions of Raynaldo and Gregory are based on paintings.

The titles Gregory IX held and the political problems he faced are accurately described. From this time on, the friars often tried to relinquish their care of the sisters.

Gregory IX regularly corresponded with Clare and greatly admired her. He seems to have visited her whenever possible. Early in his pontificate, Clare asked him to reinstate the privilege of poverty. It was granted on September 17, 1228.

Clare used to spin very fine thread to make corporals given to area churches. The manner of spinning is that which Heather Minto, an expert on medieval spinning and weaving, showed to me and which she felt was the method Clare probably used.

40. Friar Cappellano, Chaplain's House, San Damiano
(Early October, 1230)

This chapter is based solidly on what actually happened in the Franciscan Order from late May, 1230, when Elias secretly buried Francis's body, to early October of the same year when friaries would have been receiving notice of what Pope Gregory IX determined in his bull *Quo Elongati.*

The Life of Saint Clare Virgin mentions Clare's reaction when Gregory IX said the friars could not enter the monastery without express permission of the Apostolic See. This would certainly be a deprivation for women who, as enclosed recluses, could not leave their monasteries without episcopal or papal permission.

Most scholars believe that Clare sent away the friars in the wake of *Quo Elongati.*

In *The Legend and Writings of Saint Clare of Assisi,* Ignatius Brady says that Clare sent away the friars either following *Quo Elongati* or following *Etsi Omnium,* a 1236 bull of Gregory that told "all the Christian faithful who read these letters" that the Poor Ladies must follow Hugolino's Rule of 1219 regarding permission to enter the enclosure of nuns. Hugolino's Rule of 1219 permitted no entry other than manifest necessity. Outsiders could enter to dig a grave or repair the monastery. A chaplain could enter only to hear confessions and administer the Eucharist to dying nuns and, if the abbess permitted, to conduct prayers at a deceased nun's burial. *Etsi Omnium* excommunicates those who disobey. If directives regarding the chaplain had been settled in 1230, then *Etsi Omnium* would refer to entry by other parties.

41. Sister Amata di Martino, Oratory, San Damiano
(October 1230)

In 1228, Clare persuaded Amata, daughter of Lord Martino di Ugolino di Offreduccio, to enter San Damiano. Amata says she looked on Clare as her mother. Fortini mentions that Amata had been engaged before she joined Clare.

Clare's sister Beatrice entered San Damiano in 1229. We do not know if she had ever married or had children.

The *Process* says that many corporals were made from thread that Clare spun. To weave the corporals, the sisters most likely used a simple hand loom, affordable for the poor, as opposed to a large, free-standing, expensive floor loom. After the sisters had folded the corporals into silk-lined paper boxes, the friars took them to the bishop to be blessed and then to the churches around Assisi.

In the *Process,* Amata tells of the cure of a young Perugian boy with a film over his eye. She said the child was "brought to Saint Clare who touched the eyes of the boy and then made the sign of the cross over him." Clare then said, "Bring him to my mother, Sister Ortolana." Amata does not give the year of this cure nor state where Clare or Ortolana were when the child was brought to them. According to the histories, however, Clare was bedridden.

When Gregory IX heard that Clare had sent away the friars, he immediately rescinded his directive and told the minister general of the friars to have the friars continue to serve the sisters as before.

PART TEN

~~∂6~

Visited by Divine Consolation

42. Sister Agnese di Oportulo de Bernardo, Choir, San Damiano
(Sunday, April 25, 1232)

In the *Process,* Agnese tells of her visions of the Christ Child and the flaming brilliance around Clare while Philip di Lungo was preaching on Good Shepherd Sunday around 1232. Philip's words are not recorded, nor did Agnese disclose what her visions meant to her. Also in the *Process,* Angeluccia tells how once, after Compline, Clare had holy water used in the Easter sprinkling rite brought to her and how she advised the sisters to always keep it in mind.

43. Sister Aneska, Speaking Grill of the Damianite Convent, Prague, Bohemia *(Early Summer, 1235)*

In "The Canonization of the Czechs' Agnes," Petr Pit'ha gives Agnes's Czech name as Aneska. Princess Aneska of Premysl (Agnes of Prague—the Premysl family was the only native dynasty that ruled the Czechs) successfully petitioned Pope Gregory IX to grant her permission to refuse marriage to Emperor Frederick II who was courting her, and then to enter religious life. Frederick's agreement is in the historical record.

Aneska (Agnes) built a Damianite monastery in Prague and entered it as a Poor Enclosed Sister in 1234. The remarkable woman earned widespread admiration.

Some discrepancy exists in various historical sources concerning certain dates in the life of Saint Agnes of Prague. This book follows the chronology given by Regis Armstrong, OFM Cap., in his article "Starting Points."

In response to Agnes's request, at some point Clare sent Agnes the gifts mentioned in this chapter. The five sisters from Trent arrived in Prague prior to Agnes's entry into religious life. Father Celsus O'Brien, OFM, in his booklet "Clare of Assisi in Her Writings," speculates that Clare chose these sisters because Trent was part of the Austrian Tyrol, so the sisters spoke a Germanic language that was fairly widespread in Prague.

Clare's first letter to Agnes was written shortly before Agnes entered religious life, but Agnes may have received it later.

The quotes from Clare's letters are taken from Armstrong's translation. Father Regis speculates that Clare wrote the second letter to respond to the Pope's decree allowing Agnes's monastery to use revenue from the hospice. Gregory wrote to Agnes regarding this on May 18, 1235, and on July 25 issued a bull establishing the connection between the hospice and the monastery.

44. Lord Giovanni di Maestro Giovanni, Via San Petrignano,
Assisi *(Late June, 1238)*

As procurator for the Damianites, Lord Giovanni di Maestro Giovanni acted as their agent in procuring supplies and in conducting their other business.

Fortini discusses the document, dated June 8, 1238, that gave Lord Oportulo the power of attorney to sell a piece of property belonging to San Damiano. Fifty sisters signed the document. Since Lord Giovanni was procurator, he may have helped execute it.

In the *Process,* both Filippa and Francesca mention that Clare, through her prayers, cured Giovanni's unnamed five-year-old son of both fever and scrofula. The testimonies say that the child was "carried" to Clare. At this time, carriages were not invented. People did use carts to carry goods, but these bumped along over the heavily rutted roads and would have been very uncomfortable for an ill child. A litter would have been a smoother way to carry a sick lad to Clare.

The *Process* states that word of Clare's many healings, using the sign of the cross, spread throughout the empire.

45. Sister Balvina di Martino, Infirmary *(Mid-December, 1239)*

None of the primary sources state how Clare and her sisters received news of Friar Elias's defection nor how they responded to it. But they must have been deeply shaken by the news, as were the other early followers of Saint Francis. Having allied with Frederick II, Elias spent Christmas of 1239 with him in Pisa (Brooke, *Early Franciscan Government,* p. 39).

Elias's physical description is taken from a 1236 image of him, reproduced as an engraving and printed as frontispiece to Brooke's book *Early Franciscan Government.*

PART ELEVEN

~~⁊◈~~

The Father of Mercies

46. Sister Cecilia di Gualtieri Cacciaguerra, Refectory,
San Damiano *(September 1240)*

In the *Process,* Sister Cecilia recounts the undated incident of the half loaf that multiplied to fifty slices when Cecilia cut it as Clare had directed. Also in the *Process,* Amata details how Clare cured Cecilia of a violent, long-lasting cough. Cecilia confirms the incident. In September 1240, Saracens invaded Umbria. Most of those in Frederick's employ came from Lucera, having been deported there from Sicily.

47. Sister Illuminata, Dormitory, San Damiano
(9 A.M., September 1240)

In the *Process,* Sister Francesca details how both she and Sister Illuminata of Pisa, who had died before the *Process* inquiry, had supported Clare in her confrontation with the Saracens. Francesca states that both she and Illuminata heard Christ assure Clare that He would protect San Damiano and Assisi.

Paintings often depict Clare holding the Eucharist herself, but Francesca says she had it brought to the refectory door where she prostrated herself before it in prayer. Francesca does not say who brought the Eucharist. From her testimony, it seems as if a sister carried the Eucharist, although some historians believe that it was carried by the chaplain.

Sister Prassede's name appears on the 1238 list of sisters at San Damiano. We know nothing else about her.

48. Saracen Troop Petty Officer, Enclosure, San Damiano
(9:30 A.M., September 1240)

The *Process,* as well as the early histories of Clare, mention Saracen troops scaling the walls of San Damiano and entering the cloister. We do not know why they left without harming the sisters.

49. Sister Cristiana de Bernardo da Suppo, San Damiano
(Dusk, June 20, 1241)

In 1220, Lady Cristiana, daughter of Lord Bernardo da Suppo, entered San Damiano. She had lived with Lady Clare's family in Assisi and had discovered the open door of the dead that Clare used on Palm Sunday night, 1212.

This account of the attack on Assisi by Vitale d'Aversa fleshes out the detailed accounts of Filippa, Francesca, and Cristiana in the *Process.* Filippa and Francesca both state that Clare was told of the impending attack but do not say who told her or how the message was brought. Lord Iacopo di Stefano di Presbitero was a knight of Assisi who so esteemed Clare that he named her, along with his blood brother, as testamentary executrix of his will, according to Fortini (*Francis of Assisi,* p. 364).

In her book *Early Franciscan Government,* Brooke states that Elias, in league with the emperor, promoted an abortive plot to hand Assisi over to Frederick's forces (p. 175). Is this true? If so, was d'Aversa's attack the result of this plot?

Cristiana states that she was the one who, at Clare's command, called the sisters to prayer. Cristiana gives no more details because Filippa and Francesca had previously testified to Clare's admonitions to pray and fast and her placing of ashes on the sisters' heads. We can imagine the sisters' terror at Frederick II's victories, especially over the Church prelates, and the Assisian knights' doubts as to their own ability to withstand Aversa's massive army. Fortini (*Francis of Assisi,* p. 362) declares that on June 22, "The city people attacked the imperial camp at dawn and put the enemy forces to rout." A footnote to Fortini states that for centuries, Assisi celebrated this victory with a colorful festival in gratitude for Clare's prayers.

PART TWELVE

~⋙~

To Return to the Lord an Increase of His Talent

50. Sister Angeluccia de Angelico, Via San Petrignano, Assisi
(Sunday Evening, June 30, 1247)

In their testimony in the *Process,* Sisters Angeluccia, Cecilia, Balvina of Porzano, and Cristiana de Messer Cristiano (whom I have nicknamed Cristi to distinguish her from Sister Cristiana di Bernardo da Suppo) tell of the monastery door falling on Saint Clare. This chapter follows their account. While three unnamed friars had to lift the door from Clare, the sisters do not say why the door fell or how it was repaired.

From their testimony, one learns that this accident happened about seven years previously, on a Sunday evening in July during the octave of Saint Peter, whose feast was celebrated on June 29. Sister Cristiana states that at the time of the *Process* she had not yet been in the monastery seven years. This would place the incident in 1247. The 1997 World Almanac indicates that June 29, 1247 fell on a Saturday. Medieval people considered the new day as beginning at sunset, so the evening of June 30, a Sunday, would be, to Clare's sisters, July 1. This was when the door fell on Clare.

Angeluccia mentions that she was present when the accident occurred, but she does not say why. However, in the *Process,* Angeluccia is the only sister who mentions how Clare admonished the serving sisters to always praise the Lord when they left the monastery. Could this mean that Angeluccia was a serving sister who was returning from some errand outside the monastery on a day that Clare was tending the door?

51. Lord Scherno, Great Hall of a Great House, Pisa
(March 1249)

The *Process* mentions a pious lady from Pisa who came to San Damiano to thank God and Clare. Clare's petitions had cast out five demons from the woman, who said that Clare's prayers were burning them. No other details are given.

Parchment was expensive. It was a common practice to scrape ink from parchment and reuse it. Clare wrote many letters, but only four are extant—the letters to Agnes of Prague, whose wealth precluded her from having to reuse the parchment.

In the *Process,* Sister Benvenuta mentions that Clare would weep over worldly people, reproach them, and exhort them to penance.

52. Sister Cristi (Sister Cristiana de Cristiano de Parisse), Dormitory, San Damiano *(September 8, 1252)*

Clare was the first woman in history to write a Form of Life for an order. Sometime prior to the events detailed in this chapter, she had completed her Form of Life and submitted it to the Holy Father for approval.

The Life of Saint Clare Virgin describes the vision of the nun at San Paolo and Raynaldo's visit, which a footnote dates as September 8, 1252 (Catherine Bolton Magrini, trans., Editrice Minerva—Assisi, p. 70). However, in *Clare of Assisi* (pp. 177–78), Marco Bartoli implies that the visit was much earlier, probably at the end of 1251, shortly after the Pope's arrival in Perugia on November 5, 1251. It seems likely that Raynaldo visited Clare more than once during this time since he greatly admired her. This chapter reflects that probability.

The Life of Saint Clare Virgin indicates that Raynaldo (who, according to Horace Mann [vol. 15, p. 10], was "very fat") exhorted the sisters, gave Clare the Eucharist, and promised, when asked, to be an advocate for the privilege of poverty. Saint Stanislaus's history is found in Butler's *Lives of the Saints.* Raynaldo's final blessing is from his 1228 letter to several Damianite monasteries (Armstrong, p. 106). In 1253, Innocent IV canonized Bishop Stanislaus of Cracow.

We have no records of which sisters cared for the ill Clare. They probably took turns. In the *Process,* Francesca tells of the over fifty corporals made by Clare and sent to the churches of the area. Also in the *Process,* Sister Cristi (Cristiana) mentions how Clare cured Cristi's deafness.

53. Sister Gatta, Oratory, San Damiano *(December 24, 1252)*

Francesca tells in the *Process* about the undated incident of the cat rolling the towel and bringing it to Clare when no one else was around. Filippa, Amata, and Balvina di Martino mention that, on the Christmas Eve before her death, Clare, bedridden and alone, saw and heard the friars in the Church of Saint Francis praying the offices of Matins and Lauds.

54. Sister Andrea da Ferrara, Infirmary, San Damiano *(Late Spring, 1253)*

The *Process* for Clare's canonization was conducted in November 1253 by Lord Bartholomew, Bishop of Spoleto. In the *Process,* Sisters Filippa and Benvenuta detail the undated incident regarding Sister Andrea, whose boils in the throat were most likely lymph nodes swollen with tuberculosis bacteria. Under Sister Cecilia's testimony, Lord Bartholomew implies that Andrea also testified briefly to Clare's healing abilities. The sisters do not say that Clare predicted Andrea's death or that Andrea had died.

Following Clare's canonization in 1255, *The Life of Saint Clare Virgin* was published in 1256. Sec. 59 details the incident regarding Andrea and states that shortly after being cured of the swellings in her throat, Andrea died of a different disease, as Clare predicted.

It seems that Andrea was alive at the time of the *Process* but dead when the legend was written.

PART THIRTEEN

⤺∾

The Increase and Final Perseverance

55. Sister Francesca de Capitaneo da Col de Mezzo, Infirmary, San Damiano *(Early August, 1253)*

Francesca's visions and cure, as well as the other cures mentioned in this chapter, are detailed in the *Process.* Fortini tells of Francesca's background in his chapter on Saint Clare in *Francis of Assisi.* Gilliat-Smith, in his book *Clare of Assisi: Her Life and Legislation* (p. 104), mentions that about 1248 wars caused the Turin sisters to leave their monastery and settle elsewhere.

The quotes from Clare's Testament are taken from Armstrong. Scholars dispute whether Clare wrote her Form of Life prior to her Testament or vice versa. Some scholars question the authenticity of the Testament. A summary of the pros and cons of this debate can be found in Leslie Knox's dissertation, "The True Daughters of Francis and Clare."

Clare's state of health at this time follows the histories.

56. Sister Aneska, Kitchen, Damianite Convent, Prague, Bohemia *(August 1253)*

Biographies of Aneska (Agnes) of Prague tell how she cooked for the monastery and secretly washed clothing from lepers and her ill sisters, chafing her skin with the strong soaps and bleaches used in those days. In the middle of the night, Aneska would rise and secretly mend the garments.

Since Agnes was Princess of Bohemia, she had the funds to build and expand her monastery, adding a private oratory for herself. Her earliest biographer tells how her sisters would hear her speaking to God in the room and would sometimes hear a gentle male voice answering her.

Most historians believe that the two women had an extensive correspondence, although no letters from Agnes to Clare have been identified. In the third of her four extant letters to Agnes, Clare advised her to fast with moderation.

The translation of what is called Clare's Fourth Letter to Agnes was made by Mother Mary Francis, PCC in her booklet "Dance for Exultation: Letters of Saint Clare to Saint Agnes of Prague," and is used with permission. Most historians agree that Clare wrote the letter shortly before her death.

57. Sister Venuta (Benvenuta) de Lady Diambre, Dormitory, San Damiano *(Friday Evening, August 8, 1253)*

This account follows closely that given by various sisters in the *Process* and in *The Life of Saint Clare Virgin*. Francis's words are found in his "The Salutation of the Virtues" and "The Salutation of the Blessed Virgin Mary" as translated in *Francis and Clare: The Complete Works*. Fortini recounts how Venuta's brother Pietro was murdered. Venuta told no one of her vision until asked to testify to Clare's holiness in the *Process*.

58. Pope Innocent IV, Convento at the Basilica of Saint Francis, Assisi *(Early Morning, Saturday, August 9, 1253)*

Innocent, who was lodging with the friars at the Basilica of Saint Francis, visited Clare twice during her final illness, the last time being "a few days before her death." The description of these visits follows the accounts in the *Process* and *The Life of Saint Clare Virgin*. The parchment on which the papal bull was issued is described accurately—all Poor Clare monasteries have received reproductions of the original, now kept in Assisi. Several scholars reason that the smudges and blots on the Form of Life indicate that it was copied hastily. The parchment(s) on which Clare wrote her Form of Life to send to Innocent IV have not been preserved.

The physical description of Innocent IV is taken from historical artwork portraying him. We do not know the mental process by which he approved Clare's Form of Life.

59. Sister Beatrice di Favarone di Offreduccio, Dormitory, San Damiano *(Sunday, August 10, 1253)*

The account of Clare's death follows that in the *Process* and in *The Life of Saint Clare Virgin*. Some of Clare's words are closely adapted from her "Second" and "Third Letters to Agnes of Prague," as translated by Mother Mary Francis, PCC. Her final blessing is a portion of "The Blessing of Clare of Assisi (1253)" as translated by Armstrong (p. 82).

Angelo is generally assumed to be Angelo of Rieti, although he is not so identified in the stories about Clare. No background information exists on Brother Reginald. He may have been an English friar, since some English friars were in Italy at this time.

We are not sure if Clare heard "The Praises of the Lord" on her deathbed.

No record exists of Lady Ortolana's death, although it seems to have occurred before June 8, 1238, since her name is not on a document signed at that time by all the San Damiano sisters.

Brother Juniper's stories are told in *The Little Flowers of Saint Francis*.

The number of Damianite monasteries at Clare's death was 147.

60. Sister Agnese di Oportulo de Bernardo,
Dormitory of San Damiano *(Monday, August 11, 1253)*

No record has been kept of the sins that Clare confessed. Since brothers Leo and Angelo were with her when she was dying, she may have confessed to Leo, who was a priest.

Agnese did pray the Prayer of the Five Wounds according to a footnote to Agnese's testimony in the *Process* in Armstrong. Agnese does not state whether she prayed this silently or aloud.

PART FOURTEEN

In the Name of the Lord!

61. Iacobello, Bridge outside of Narni, Italy
(Early Autumn, 1253)

Clare was buried at San Giorgio in the same place that Saint Francis had been buried, the description of which is accurate. Many miracles took place at her tomb and through her intercession. This chapter mentions Iacobello's cure, details of which are in the historical record, and a few of the other miracles described in *The Life of Saint Clare Virgin.*

62. Sister Agnese di Oportulo de Bernardo, Dormitory,
San Damiano *(Mid-October, 1260)*

After her death, Clare's order continued to grow. I used the names Giuseppina and Sofia for two sisters who entered after Clare's death and had never previously known her.

Despite opposition and obstacles, Benedetta, with the support of the Pope and the Bishop of Assisi, was instrumental in building the Monastery and Church of Saint Clare, now called the Basilica of Saint Clare. The building sequence follows that suggested by Marino Bigaroni in his article "The Church of San Giorgio in Assisi and the First Expansion of the Medieval City Walls." Clare's body was moved to the new church on October 3, 1260.

It seems that immediately after Clare's burial at San Giorgio in 1253, some sisters transferred from San Damiano to San Giorgio to be near Clare's body. They lived there at a temporary monastery built for them.

Historians dispute the year during which the remaining unnamed sisters left San Damiano. Some believe that it was as early as 1257, while others agree with the traditional date, shortly after October 3, 1260 (see Luke Wadding, *The History of the Glorious Virgin Saint Clare,* p. 119). When the last sisters left San Damiano, according to Wadding, they took with them the relics mentioned in this chapter as well as the large, painted crucifix, all of which can today be seen in the Basilica of Saint Clare in Assisi.

Benedetta died in 1260. If Wadding is correct in his details of the move from San Damiano to Assisi, there may be one weak clue as to when Benedetta died. Historians imply that Benedetta had ordered the San Damiano crucifix moved to the Monastery of Saint Clare. Therefore, she may have died after the transferal.

Footnotes to the *Process* as found in Armstrong give the death dates of the sisters mentioned in this chapter with a footnote to Pacifica's testimony noting that she was ninety when she died. *The Collectanea Franciscana Bibliographia Franciscana: 1931–1970* Index gives Pacifica's date of death as about 1258. Agnese died in 1261, according to a footnote to her testimony in the *Process*.

Select Bibliography

This book is the fruit of years of extended study and research on Saint Clare. The full bibliography runs to twenty-two pages. Because this book is intended for the general reader, I am listing only a few of the sources that deal more directly with information about Saint Francis and Saint Clare.

Armstrong, Regis J., OFM Cap. "Starting Points: Images of Women in the Letters of Clare." From "Collectanea Franciscana" (62) 1992: 63–100. *Greyfriars Review* 7.3 (1993): 347–80.

Bargellini, Piero. *The Little Flowers of Saint Clare.* Translated by Edmund O'Gorman, OFM Conv. Ann Arbor, Mich.: Servant, 1972.

Bartoli, Marco. *Clare of Assisi.* Translated by Sister Frances Teresa, OSC. Quincy, Ill.: Franciscan Press of Quincy University, 1993.

Bigaroni, Mario, OFM. "The Church of San Giorgio in Assisi and the First Expansion of the Medieval City Walls." Translated by Lori Pieper, SFO, *Greyfriars Review* 8.1 (1994): 57-101.

Bigaroni, Mario, OFM. "San Damiano—Assisi: The First Church of St. Francis." Translated by Agnes Van Baer, OSC. *Franciscan Studies* 47 (1987): 45-97.

Brady, Ignatius. *The Legend and Writings of Saint Clare of Assisi.* St. Bonaventure, N.Y.: Franciscan Institute, 1953.

Brooke, Rosalind B. *Early Franciscan Government: Elias to Bonaventure.* Cambridge, England: Cambridge University Press, 1959.

Brown, Raphael, trans. *The Little Flowers of St. Francis.* Garden City, NY: Hanover House, 1958.

Brunette, Pierre, OFM. "Clare and Francis: A Saintly Friendship." Translated by Paul Barrett, OFM Cap. *Greyfriars Review* 11 (1997): 185–227

Carney, Margaret, OSF. *The First Franciscan Woman: Clare of Assisi and Her Form of Life.* Quincy, Ill.: Franciscan Press of Quincy University, 1993.

————. "Francis and Clare: A Critical Examination of the Sources." *Laurentianum* 30 (1989): 25–60.

Celano, Fra' Tommaso. *The Life of St. Clare Virgin.* Translated by Catherine Bolton Magrini. Assisi, Italy: Editrice Minerva, 1994.

Clare and Francis of Assisi. *Francis and Clare: The Complete Works.* Translated by Regis J. Armstrong, OFM Cap., and Ignatius C. Brady, OFM. New York: Paulist Press, 1982.

Clare of Assisi: Early Documents. Translated by Regis J. Armstrong, OFM Cap. St. Bonaventure, N.Y.: St. Bonaventure University, 1993.

Cunninghan, Lawrence, ed. *Brother Francis: An Anthology of Writings by and about Saint Francis of Assisi.* New York: Harper & Row, 1972.

De Robeck, Nesta. *St. Clare of Assisi.* Chicago: Franciscan Herald Press, 1951, 1980.

Dhont, Rene-Charles, OFM. *Clare Among Her Sisters.* St. Bonaventure, NY: Franciscan Institute, 1987.

Englebert, Omer. *Saint Francis of Assisi: A Biography.* Translated by Eve Marie Cooper. Ann Arbor, Mich.: Servant, 1965.

The First Rule of Saint Clare and The Constitutions of Saint Coletta. Boston, Mass.: Angel Guardian Press, 1924.

Flury-Lemberg, Mechtild. *Textile Conservation and Research.* Riggisberg, Switzerland: Abbegg-Sfiftung, n.d. "The Cowl of St. Francis of Assisi," pp. 314-317.

Fortini, Arnaldo. *Francis of Assisi.* Translated by Helen Moak. New York: Crossroad, 1981.

————. *Nova Vita di San Francesco.* 4 vols. Santa Maria degli Angeli Edizoni. Assisi, Italy: Tipografia Porziuncola, 1959.

Francis, Mother Mary, PCC. "Clare of Assisi: Mirror of Humanism." Roswell, N.M.: Poor Clare Monastery, 1994

————. "Dance for Exultation: Letters of Saint Clare to Saint Agnes of Prague." Roswell, N.M.: Poor Clare Monastery, 1997.

Frances Teresa, Sister, OSC. *Living the Incarnation: Praying with Francis and Clare of Assisi.* London: Darton, Longman, & Todd, 1993.

————. *This Living Mirror: Reflections of Clare of Assisi.* Maryknoll, N.Y.: Orbis, 1995.

Francis of Assisi. *The Prayers of Saint Francis.* Translated by Ignatius Brady, OFM. Ann Arbor, Mich.: Servant, 1987.

Garzonio, Sister Chiara Lucia, OSC. "Agnes, The Clara's sister and the very first diffusion of her 'charisma.'" *CTC Communion and Communication* 9–10 (April 1990): 8–9.

————. *Without Turning Back: Life of Saint Agnes of Assisi.* Florence, Italy: Libreria Editrice Fiorentina, 1991.

Gilliat-Smith, Ernest. *St. Clare of Assisi: Her Life and Legislation.* New York: E.P. Dutton & Co., 1914.

Godet-Calogeras, Jean Francois, ed. *Out of the Shadows: Clare and Franciscan Women.* Chicago: Haversack, 1994.

Habig, Marion A., ed. *St. Francis of Assisi: Writings and Early Biographies (English Omnibus of the Sources for the Life of St. Francis).* Quincy, IL: Franciscan Press, 1991.

Moorman, John. *A History of the Franciscan Order from Its Origins to the Year 1517.* Oxford, England: Clarendon, 1968.

Nugent, Madeline Pecora, SFO. *Saint Anthony: Words of Fire, Life of Light.* Boston, Mass.: Pauline Books & Media, 1995.

Saint Sing, Susan. *A Pilgrim in Assisi: Searching for Francis Today.* Cincinnati, Ohio: Saint Anthony Messenger Press, 1981.

Seraphim, Sister Mary, PCPA. *Clare: Her Light and Her Song.* Chicago: Franciscan Herald Press, 1984.

Wadding, Luke. *The History of the Glorious Virgin Saint Clare.* Adapted from Luke Wadding's *Annals.* Translated into English from the French of Francis Hendricq by Sister Magdalen Augustine, PC, 1635; set into modern English by Celsus O'Brien, 1992. Galway, Ireland: Connacht Tribune, 1992.

Pauline
BOOKS & MEDIA

The Daughters of St. Paul operate book and media centers at the following addresses. Visit, call or write the one nearest you today, or find us on the World Wide Web, www.pauline.org

CALIFORNIA
3908 Sepulveda Blvd, Culver City, CA 90230 310-397-8676
5945 Balboa Avenue, San Diego, CA 92111 858-565-9181
46 Geary Street, San Francisco, CA 94108 415-781-5180

FLORIDA
145 S.W. 107th Avenue, Miami, FL 33174 305-559-6715

HAWAII
1143 Bishop Street, Honolulu, HI 96813 808-521-2731
Neighbor Islands call: 800-259-8463

ILLINOIS
172 North Michigan Avenue, Chicago, IL 60601 312-346-4228

LOUISIANA
4403 Veterans Memorial Blvd, Metairie, LA 70006 504-887-7631

MASSACHUSETTS
885 Providence Hwy, Dedham, MA 02026 781-326-5385

MISSOURI
9804 Watson Road, St. Louis, MO 63126 314-965-3512

NEW JERSEY
561 U.S. Route 1, Wick Plaza, Edison, NJ 08817 732-572-1200

NEW YORK
150 East 52nd Street, New York, NY 10022 212-754-1110
78 Fort Place, Staten Island, NY 10301 718-447-5071

PENNSYLVANIA
9171-A Roosevelt Blvd, Philadelphia, PA 19114 215-676-9494

SOUTH CAROLINA
243 King Street, Charleston, SC 29401 843-577-0175

TENNESSEE
4811 Poplar Avenue, Memphis, TN 38117 901-761-2987

TEXAS
114 Main Plaza, San Antonio, TX 78205 210-224-8101

VIRGINIA
1025 King Street, Alexandria, VA 22314 703-549-3806

CANADA
3022 Dufferin Street, Toronto, Ontario, Canada M6B 3T5
 416-781-9131
1155 Yonge Street, Toronto, Ontario, Canada M4T 1W2
 416-934-3440

¡También somos su fuente para libros, videos y música en español!